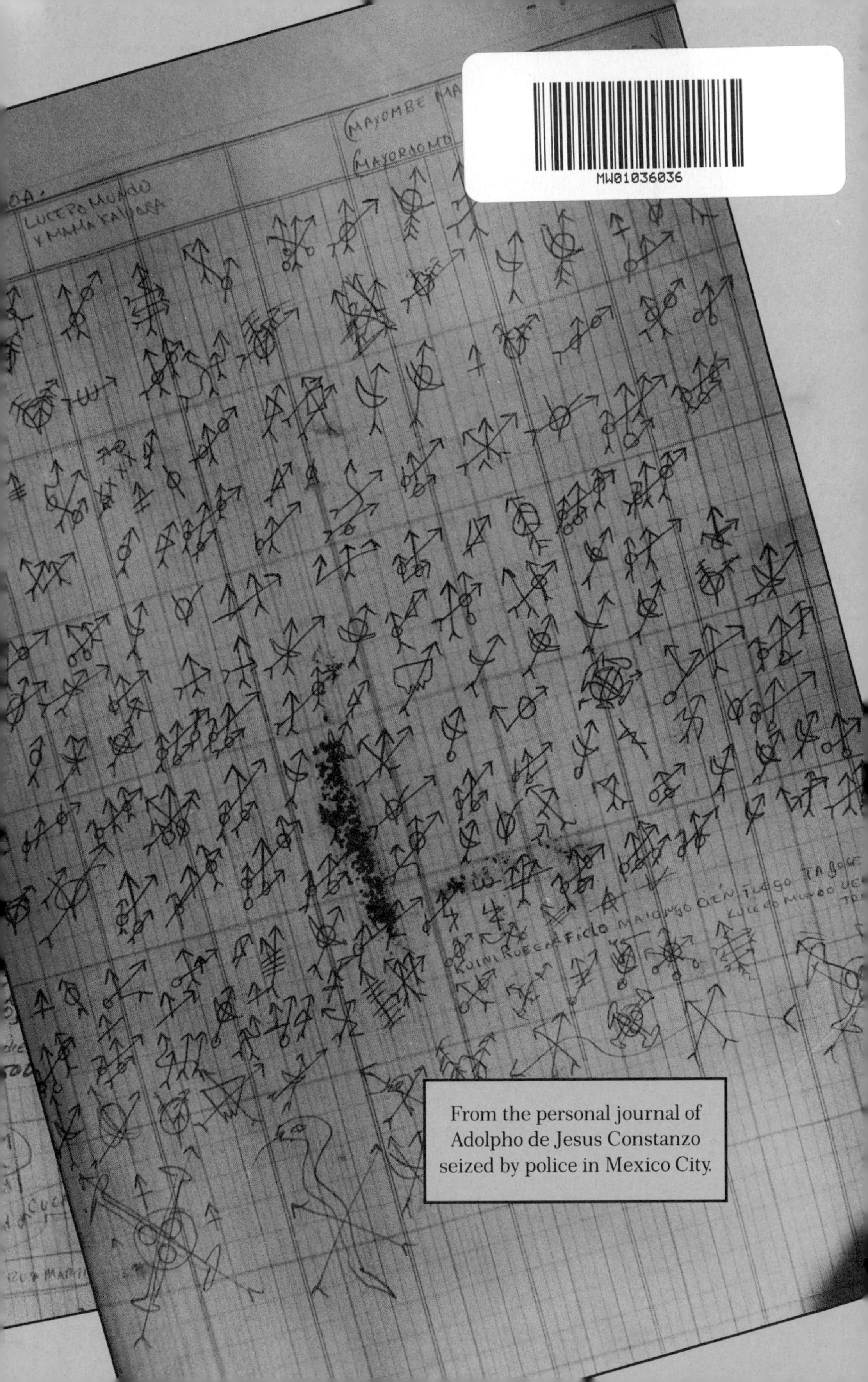

From the personal journal of Adolpho de Jesus Constanzo seized by police in Mexico City.

BURIED SECRETS

EDWARD HUMES

BURIED SECRETS

A True Story of Serial Murder, Black Magic, and Drug-Running on the U.S. Border

A DUTTON BOOK

DUTTON
Published by the Penguin Group
Penguin Books USA Inc., 375 Hudson Street,
New York, New York 10014, U.S.A.
Penguin Books Ltd, 27 Wrights Lane,
London W8 5TZ, England
Penguin Books Australia Ltd, Ringwood,
Victoria, Australia
Penguin Books Canada Ltd, 2801 John Street,
Markham, Ontario, Canada L3R 1B4
Penguin Books (N.Z.) Ltd, 182–190 Wairau Road,
Auckland 10, New Zealand

Penguin Books Ltd, Registered Offices:
Harmondsworth, Middlesex, England

First published by Dutton, an imprint of New American Library, a
division of Penguin Books USA Inc.
Distributed in Canada by McClelland & Stewart Inc.

First printing, February, 1991
10 9 8 7 6 5 4 3 2 1

REGISTERED TRADEMARK—MARCA REGISTRADA

Library of Congress Cataloging-in-Publication Data

Humes, Edward.
Buried secrets / Edward Humes.
p. cm.
1. Murder—Mexico—Matamoros (Tamaulipas)—Case studies. 2. Human sacrifice—Mexico—Matamoros (Tamaulipas)—Case studies. 3. Drug traffic—Mexico—Matamoros (Tamaulipas)—Case studies. 4. Kilroy. Mark James, d. 1989. 5. Murder victims—Texas. I. Title.
HV6535.M43M383 1990
364.1′523′097212—dc20 90-46461
CIP

PRINTED IN THE UNITED STATES OF AMERICA
Set in Primer
Designed by Leonard Telesca

CONTENTS

ACKNOWLEDGMENTS

Works of journalism require not just a teller of tales but the assistance, insight, and knowledge of those who witness events worth telling. The list of people who helped tell this tale is a long one indeed—so long I can only name a few of you here, though all have my heartfelt gratitude.

In particular, I wish to thank Special Agents Armando Ramirez and T. K. Solis of the Drug Enforcement Administration, and John Crews of the U.S. Attorney's Office in Brownsville, who provided firsthand accounts of key events on both sides of the border. Likewise, in Florida, Rafael Martinez and Candice Leek of the Institute of Police Technology and Management in Jacksonville provided invaluable expertise and understanding of the events in Matamoros and ritual crime nationwide, while Bill Gomez and Bob Fiallo of the Metro-Dade Police Department in Miami shared their unique experiences with crime and Afro-Caribbean mysticism.

I must also thank Lisa Baker, of the *San Antonio Light,* for her time and thoughtful insights into the border drug trade and corruption; Federico Ponce and Octavio Campos, of the Federal District Attorney's Office in Mexico City, for the documents, interviews, and unprecedented access that provided much of the meat for *Buried Secrets;* Candice Hughes and her fellow correspondents, of the Associated Press Mexico City bureau, for helping me slip through more than a few government mazes; Lindajoy Fenley and Roxana Avelias, *interpretes extraordinario;* the editors and staff of the *Brownsville Herald* for their hospitality; and the

Plantes and Dentler families, for opening their homes to a stranger and letting him leave a friend.

My editor at Dutton, Laurie Bernstein, provided endless support and intelligence throughout this project; I'll be thanking her for years to come.

Finally, my deepest thanks go to Donna Wares for her support, her wise critiques of the manuscript in its various incarnations, and for putting up with me even when I was a monster.

AUTHOR'S NOTE

Wherever possible, scenes and dialogue in this book are based upon the recollections of those who were present during the events described. This information is drawn from court testimony, sworn declarations, and from interviews conducted by the author.

Firsthand sources were not always available, however, and in some instances, the author has relied upon the recollections of secondary witnesses—followers of Adolfo de Jesus Constanzo who provided information on events Constanzo previously described to them. Such "hearsay" information is used only when confirmed by at least two sources, human or documentary.

A few scenes are, by necessity, speculative—particularly those depicting Constanzo's training and initiation in black magic, for which no witnesses are available. To reconstruct such scenes, the recollections of his followers were combined with scholarly descriptions of similar rituals in an attempt to provide the most likely portrait possible of these important milestones in Constanzo's life.

In all cases, the identity and quality of sources for major events are provided in the form of footnotes. Whenever facts are in dispute, footnotes also indicate the opposing points of view.

Finally, no one can truly know the thoughts and motivations of another. One can only extrapolate these inner secrets from a person's words and deeds. It is up to the reader to decide if the interpretations presented here provide insight into the mind of a killer.

CAST OF CHARACTERS

THE LEADER

Adolfo de Jesus Constanzo, Miami-born priest of Santeria and the black-magic religion of Palo Mayombe.

THE FOLLOWERS

In Mexico City:

Martin Quintana Rodriguez; bodyguard, Constanzo's lover.

Omar Francisco Orea Ochoa; student, Constanzo's lover.

Jorge Montes, "Doctor Hindu," "Carta Brava"; fortune teller/ psychic.

Juan Carlos Fragosa, craftsman.

Damian/Damiana; transvestite nightclub singer.

Francisco, real estate speculator.

Maria del Rocio Cuevas Guerra, "Karla"; fashion model/folk healer.

Dr. Maria de Lourdes Bueno Lopez; physician.

Enrique Calzada; boyfriend of Karla.

Salvador Vidal Garcia Alarcon, "Chava"; group commander for the Mexican Federal Judicial Police *Antinarcoticos*.

Florentino Ventura Gutierrez, former head of Federal Judicial Police, head of Interpol in Mexico.

In Matamoros:

Sara Maria Aldrete Villareal, "La Flaca"; college honor student.

Hernandez family drug-trafficking organization:

Elio Hernandez Rivera; head of the drug operation.
Ovidio Hernandez Rivera; Elio's brother and lieutenant.
Serafin Hernandez Garcia, "Little Serafin," "El Chaparro"; nephew, college student.
Alvaro de Leon Valdez, "El Duby"; gunman.
Sergio Martinez Salinas, "The Butterfly"; drug trafficker.
David Serna Valdez, "The Flirt"; drug trafficker.
Malio Fabio Ponce Torres, "El Gato"; student, drug trafficker.
Aurelio Chavez; foreman at Rancho Santa Elena.
Carlos de la Llata; drug dealer, friend of El Duby.

Other Members of the Hernandez Narcotics Organization (Not Followers of Constanzo):

Brigido Hernandez; father of Elio; owner of Rancho Santa Elena.

Serafin Hernandez Rivera, "Old Serafin"; brother of Elio, father of Serafin Hernandez Garcia, middleman for family drug deals.

Saul Hernandez Rivera; brother of Elio, founder of the family drug business, assassinated in January 1987.

Domingo Reyes Bustamante; caretaker at Rancho Santa Elena.

Crime Partners of Constanzo/Hernandez Family in Matamoros:

Guillermo Perez; federal police comandante, ousted for corruption and drug trafficking, a fugitive in Mexico and the United States.

Juan Garcia Abrego; alleged crime lord of Matamoros, fugitive in Mexico and the United States.

CAST OF CHARACTERS

THE VICTIMS

Bodies found at Rancho Santa Elena:

Mark Kilroy, vacationing University of Texas junior.

Victor Saul Sauceda, ex-policeman, gangster.

Gilberto Sosa, Brownsville, Texas, drug trafficker.

Jose Luis Garcia Luna, fourteen-year-old farm worker—and Elio Hernandez's second cousin.

Ruben Vela Garza, drug smuggler.

Ezequiel Rodriguez Luna, drug smuggler.

Ernesto Rivas Diaz, drug smuggler.

Joaquin Manzo and Miguel Garcia, Mexican federal policemen under Salvador Vidal Garcia and, before becoming victims, followers of Constanzo.

Jorge Valente del Fierro Gomez.

Three unidentified male corpses.

In the orchard near Rancho Santa Elena:

Moises Castillo, farmer.

Hector de la Fuente, drug trafficker.

In Mexico City—bodies found in the Rio Zumpango:

Guillermo Arturo Calzada Sanchez, co-owner of F.M. and Associates, a front for a cocaine trafficking gang.

Rosalia Ibarra de Calzada, Calzada's wife.

Guadalupe Calzada Sanchez, Calzada's mother.

Jose de Jesus Gonzalez Rolon, Calzada's partner.

Federico de la Vega Lostolot, alias El Titi, Calzada's bodyguard.

Gabriela Mondragon Vargas, Calzada's maid.

Celia Campos de Klein, secretary at FM and Associates.

In Mexico City—dismembered corpse on street corner:

Ramon Paz Esquivel, alias La Claudia, transvestite antique dealer and roommate of Constanzo follower Jorge Montes.

In Mexico City—suspected but not proven:

Sixteen ritually murdered children under the age of sixteen.

MEXICAN OFFICIALS

In Matamoros:

Comandante Juan Benitez Ayala; head of the Mexican Federal Judicial Police Antinarcoticos unit.

Agent Miguel Antonio Rodriguez, "El Lobo"; Benitez's second in command.

Agent Raul Morales; led the initial investigation at Rancho Santa Elena stemming from a traffic stop.

In Mexico City:

Federico Ponce Rojas; assistant attorney general for the Federal District of Mexico.

Paquito Blanchette, lead investigator for the Miguel Hidalgo District, Mexico City.

Rodrigo Martinez, "Superman"; chief of police for the Miguel Hidalgo District.

UNITED STATES OFFICIALS

Drug Enforcement Administration:

Armando Ramirez, Resident Agent in Charge, Brownsville.

T. K. Solis, Special Agent, Brownsville.

CAST OF CHARACTERS

U.S. Customs:

Oran Neck, Resident Agent in Charge, Office of Enforcement, Brownsville.

Robert Gracia, Special Agent, Brownsville.

U.S. Attorney:

John Grasty Crews, Assistant U.S. Attorney, Brownsville.

Cameron County Sheriff's Department:

Detective Ernesto Flores.

Lieutenant George Gavito.

Sheriff Alex Perez.

THE CONSULTANTS

Rafael Martinez, anthropologist, Miami.

Candice Leek, instructor, Institute for Police Technology and Management, Jacksonville, Florida.

BURIED SECRETS

PROLOGUE

Matamoros, Mexico, March 13, 1989

Squinting through gray curls of smoke, the priest considered his offering. Would the gods be pleased? The priest did not think so.

Yes, the sacrifice had been made as the ancient laws required: cigar smoke and rum to summon the seven powers, a headless turtle, the head of a goat, blood from a rooster. And, of course, a human life ended now, a man raped, battered, and sliced, his heart torn beating from his chest, his blood still draining into a clay pot.

In the guttering candlelight inside the temple, the priest squatted and listened to the steady dripping. The satisfaction he should have felt at the sound was absent. He stared at the offering, the duct tape still covering the now-lifeless eyes, while the mouth remained free, so the man could scream his pain and terror as he died.

Except he had not screamed.

And that was the problem.

It was important that the offering die in confusion and pain and, most of all, in fear. A soul taken in violence and terror could be captured and used by the priest, turned into a powerful, angry servant that would wreak horrible revenge on the priest's enemies. This was the essence of his witchcraft, the dark heart of his religion, *Palo Mayombe*.

Always before, the offerings had screamed—at the slice of the knife or the hack of the machete; sometimes merely at the thick smell of death that rushed at them when the priest opened the door to his small, dark temple, a vile smell that erased any hope of salvation.

But this time they had chosen a hard man—a drug dealer, a man who practiced his own sort of violence. He had stubbornly refused to lose control; he simply gritted his teeth, his eyes steely. And even after those eyes had filmed over in pain, even after the priest had covered them with tape to bring on the terror of blindness, still the man refused to scream.

In the end, the priest was the one who cried out, shrieking in frustration at the man who died in silence, even after the priest began skinning him alive.

No, the gods would not be pleased with this one. Nor could this soul be bent to the priest's will.

He had lost—for the first time ever, he had lost. Some dark tide had turned, he imagined, and the ground was slipping loose beneath him. He could feel it.

Silence filled the little temple now, marred only by the dripping of blood, slowing, almost stopped. He rose and spat on the corpse. Then the priest took a deep breath, opened the door, and called to his followers to get rid of the body.

Standing there, he sensed the fear in their eyes as they saw him filling the doorway, with flickering candles and death at his back. They shuffled by him, heads bowed, and the priest felt better, as he always did when he saw how others feared his power.

Everything would be fine. There were plenty of other offerings to be made.

Plenty of other screams to be wrenched from men's souls.

"Next time, bring me an American," Adolfo de Jesus Constanzo told his followers. "A young American. A student. Someone blonde and soft."

Yes, Padrino, his followers agreed, eager to please this dark, deadly man, their *padrino,* their godfather. They would do it that night. As soon as they buried this body, they would drive to Matamoros and do it. They would find some drunken college student on his spring break and take him here.

"Bring me someone I can use," Adolfo de Jesus Constanzo told his flock. "Someone who will scream."

PART I

TWELVE DAYS IN APRIL

Whoever fights monsters should see to it that in the process he does not become a monster.

—Friedrich Nietzsche

1

The road to Matamoros is a serpent writhing toward the Gulf of Mexico, its twists and bends mimicking the flow of the Rio Grande and the U.S. border just beyond. Ancient buses and diesel-spewing trucks rumble eastward through a succession of dusty villages, flashes of peeling stucco and neon beer signs quickly swallowed by the next curve.

Between these small towns, fields of sorghum, cotton, and corn quilt the flatlands abutting the road. Small brown women, stooped and clad in black despite the thick heat, walk the road's shoulders by day, carrying shopping bags or ragged bundles of sticks to kindle their cooking fires. Men work bent in the fields, the dust of the ranches cemented to their skin by sweat, enduring the same grueling labors Mexican peasants have weathered for generations.

At night, others travel the road, silently and invisibly, the headlights on their new pickup trucks doused when they reach a certain spot, a certain dirt turnoff to a moon-silvered ranch.

At these hours, the only sounds are the whispering of cornstalks in the evening breeze and the occasional insect crackle of CB radios buzzing in the darkness as the men at the ranch speak to their partners on the other side of the border. If the right words are spoken, there is the sound of gentle splashing, men driving and wading across the low, muddy waters, bearing bundles wrapped in plastic to eager hands on the U.S. side.

This scene is repeated dozens of times a night in dozens of places along the road from Reynosa to Matamoros, the two Mexican cities marking the center and the eastern boundaries of the lower Rio Grande Valley—the hottest drug-trafficking spot on the border.[1] Here, the quickest route from the fields and the poverty is to take that road at night, to assume the time-honored role of *contrabandista*. Smuggler.

The grandfathers did it in the '30s, running good tequila and bad whiskey for the boys from Chicago. In the '60s, the next generation found the token patrol the *gringos* kept on their border easy to elude as they filled a new and insatiable demand for marijuana. Now the drug of choice is the *polvo blanco,* the white powder—cocaine—worth more than its weight in gold, the latest sure ticket to wealth and power.

In the process, the smugglers created something new on the border: a burgeoning Mexican middle class, hungry for washing machines and imported cars and good schools for their children. Their fine new mansions stand shoulder to shoulder with the crumbling adobe boxes most typical of border towns, poverty stacked next to incongruous wealth in a patchwork maze of potholed streets and piebald lawns. With that taste of prosperity, there was no going back. Whole families entered the drug business, blood ties spawning trust, generation following generation on that serpentine road of contraband and wealth.

In the Mexican town of Matamoros, separated from Brownsville, Texas, by a thin, muddy river and a few impotent strands of barbed wire, smuggling has become a way of life.

So it was with the Hernandez family of Matamoros, mid-level drug smugglers, neither big time nor small time—just one of hundreds of gangs with connections to the city's powerful crime and drug barons. The family was unique in one regard, however: It operated with a singular and savage ruthlessness borne of a past pocked by poverty and a desperate desire never to be poor again.

The four Hernandez brothers built their drug business gradually over a decade and they had prospered—until the cleverest brother, Saul, was shot in 1987. Suddenly everything turned sour. For more than a year afterward, the business went downhill.

Then, just when their prospects had hit bottom, El Padrino appeared. With him, their luck and their fortunes changed—like magic. By the spring of 1989, blood and money flowed freely for the Hernandez family and their secret, dark leader.

From their ranch on the highway to Matamoros, they were building an empire.

A long day slowly drew to a close at the thirteen-kilometer checkpoint on the road to Matamoros. Out in the broad, humid flatlands east of the city, out where the smugglers liked to pull off the road and hump drugs across the Rio Grande, Mexican federal drug agents had set up an impromptu roadstop to search passing cars and trucks for narcotics.

April Fool's Day of 1989 had been a wearying day of lifting grimy spare tires from wheel wells, of poking through truck beds piled high with manure, of questioning the *touristas* peering owlishly from behind their sunglasses. The late afternoon was stifling, the roadside grit rasped under the agents' eyelids and between their teeth. But at least there had been no major problems . . . until the shiny red pickup truck blew by.

The truck didn't stop for the orange cones and warning signs. It didn't even slow down. The Mexican agents watched in disbelief, too surprised to raise their automatic weapons. The young, dark-haired man behind the wheel of the new Chevy pickup stared straight ahead—not oblivious, exactly, but simply ignoring the agents. As if they didn't matter.[2]

Squinting into the hazy sunlight, one of the *federales* turned and said he thought he recognized the driver from the bars downtown. He was a loudmouthed punk from a rich contrabandista family—one the comandante had pursued in the past and said to watch out for. His name was Hernandez, the agent said: Little Serafin Hernandez.

"He did what?" Comandante Juan Benitez Ayala asked a few hours later, when the agent called long distance to report what happened. "He ignored you, Raul? Is that what you're calling to tell me?" he asked, almost chuckling.

"That's not all, Comandante," Agent Raul Morales said, uncertainty creeping into his normally resolute police monotone. "We followed him to a ranch. After he left, we looked around. And we found something strange: a statue made of cement. An evil-looking head, pointed at the top, shaped like a pear. Its eyes and mouth and nose were made of little sea shells."

Any sign of amusement left the comandante's voice. He had heard of such things, evil and dark. "It looks like it's frowning, Raul? Like it's angry?"

"Yes, Comandante. Exactly. What is it?"

The hiss of the long-distance phone wires filled the silence before Benitez[3] finally spoke. "It means we've got brujos, my friend," he said slowly, reluctantly.

Brujos. Witches.

Later, after Comandante Benitez had hung up, he brooded over the situation in his motel room. The call had found him hundreds of miles from home, across the border in Arizona for FBI training, part of an exchange program for select Mexican officers. He had been flattered to be picked, but now he cursed the timing of the seminar. He should be back in Matamoros where, predictably, one more thing was going wrong.

The comandante had come to Matamoros only a month before, and he had been beset with problems from the outset. Smuggling was out of control. Corruption was rampant on the Matamoros city police force. Then there was the missing American college student—the Mark Kilroy mess, with all its attendant bad press and official pressure to find the missing student. And now, as if Benitez's plate were not full enough, the notorious Hernandez family was up to something. Something to do with witchcraft.

Just one month he had been commander of the Mexican Federal Judicial Police *Antinarcoticos* office, yet already it felt like ten years' hard labor. Benitez rubbed his eyes and stretched out on the motel bed, considering the past four busy weeks.

The young federale's first assignment had been to arrest his predecessor and all his agents, as well as the two federal prosecutors assigned to Matamoros, all for drug trafficking. The old comandante, Guillermo Perez, and his men had created a cottage industry out of seizing drugs on the highway, then reselling them to the powerful crime bosses who controlled Matamoros and its various police agencies.

Holed up in a seedy motel on the outskirts of town and maintaining strict secrecy, Benitez had assembled a cadre of handpicked agents from other cities, commandeered three squads of army troops, then stormed the Antinarcoticos headquarters early one morning to make the arrests. Only the old war horse Perez had been warned and managed to escape barely in time. He departed so hastily, though, that he left five million dollars in cash and two jewel-encrusted Rolex watches stuffed in a desk drawer. It represented but a fraction of his profits over the past year.

Comandante Benitez, though, was different. Unpredictable. His slim, youthful, deceptively innocent appearance was out of step for a veteran of the crusty, backstabbing ranks of the Mexican federales. His shaggy black hair was parted down the middle, and his smooth poker face was dominated by piercing black eyes, set amid perfect Indian features. He was a study in contradictions: profoundly superstitious yet well educated, savvy without being corrupt. At thirty-five, the boyish Benitez had a fearsome reputation, viewed by his enemies and his peers alike as uniquely dangerous—because he rarely could be bought.

"They all think they're protected, all those asshole smugglers who paid off the old comandante," Benitez had told his U.S. Drug Enforcement Administration (DEA) counterparts in Brownsville. "Well, there are people I can't touch, people who are protected, who I'd need an army to take down. But the list is very short." Benitez had flashed an icy smile then. "The rest—they're mine," Benitez promised. "They'll see. And so will you. Soon."

And he had been true to his word. Within a month of his arrival, there had been more drug seizures by his agents, more arrests, and more cooperative ventures with the DEA than in the previous two years in Matamoros.[4] Cooperation between the DEA and the Mex feds had never led far in the past; Benitez was a welcome aberration. U.S. authorities were so impressed they invited him to the special school in Arizona.

But despite Benitez's efforts, one cooperative investigation had led nowhere. Mark Kilroy's disappearance in Matamoros during a spring-break vacation remained a troubling mystery.

Kilroy had been but one of two hundred and fifty thousand college students who flood the impoverished border for a month each spring, drawn by the white sands and warm waters of South Padre Island, just north of Brownsville, and the wild, freewheeling cantinas of Matamoros, just south. At night, sunburnt and thirsty, the spring breakers drive down from South Padre Island to invade Matamoros, where the beers are cheap and the drinking age negotiable. Seething masses of youths fill the bars and restaurants, spilling out onto the border town's streets in impromptu sidewalk beer gardens. Public drinking is illegal, but no one does anything about it. Spring break is a huge boost to an otherwise stagnant economy, and if it means putting up with drunken, howling gringo teenagers vomiting and passing out on the streets, no one seems to care. The locals greet the students—and their swollen billfolds—with broad smiles and double Margaritas for two dollars. And, by the way, Comandante, if the kids want to buy a joint or a gram or something on the street, well, don't bust their chops, okay? It's bad for business.

Benitez, accustomed to his previous federale duty amid the desolate jungles and Pacific Coast of the Mexican state of Oaxaca, had been more than happy to steer clear of the spring-break morass—until the Kilroy disappearance sucked him in.

A handsome, blonde college junior from the University of Texas at Austin, Kilroy had been out with three friends, partying until the bars closed. At two in the morning on March 14, the four young men were walking, drunk and exhausted, back to the international bridge to Brownsville. Somehow they became separated. Three of them got across. Kilroy did not.

That in itself would have been bad enough, Benitez knew. But it got worse. Mark's Uncle Ken Kilroy was a U.S. Customs supervisor in Los Angeles. That relationship meant this would not be treated as a run-of-the-mill missing-persons case. The unwritten policeman's code had been activated: One of our own has been touched.

Immediately, a police task force was formed in Brownsville to search for Mark, even though U.S. lawmen had no jurisdiction to investigate crimes committed in Mexico. Television crews sprang into action. Newspaper articles on the disappearance started frightening away tourists. The mayor of Matamoros, the governor of the surrounding state of Tamaulipas, and Benitez's commanders in Mexico City, alarmed at the negative publicity and its potential impact on tourism, began to pressure Benitez and other police commanders in the area. The Matamoros economy depended on spring break, and all of Mexico depended on tourism. Mark had to be found.

Typically, the Matamoros city cops tried to claim that Kilroy must have vanished in Brownsville, not Mexico, hoping to shift blame, to preserve the tourist trade. But the boy's friends said otherwise. Only Benitez, the new cop in town, promised to do whatever he could to help—then carried through on his promises. He supplied agents to accompany U.S. investigators anywhere they needed to go in Matamoros, showing a photograph of Kilroy's smiling, blonde face to potential witnesses, questioning informants, running down tips. None of it led anywhere, though. The boy had vanished without a trace—kidnapped, it seemed, for unknown reasons.

The sad fact is, people vanish all the time in Matamoros. The plaza near the bridge and the accompanying strip of souvenir shops and tourist bars are nice enough, but the rest of the city of two hundred thousand is poor and crime-ridden. Gunfire echoes nightly in some of the barrios as rival gangs battle for supremacy. There were sixty open cases of *desaparecedos*—the disappeared—on the books of the Matamoros city police from the first three months of 1989 alone. All but Kilroy were Mexican citizens, though, and therefore none of the others had generated news coverage or investigative task forces. They were just gone.

Life is cheap on the border, even the *mariachis* sing of it. You can hear them on the weekend in the town square, belting out the traditional Mexican ballad, in which the chorus concludes, over and over: "Life is worth nothing." The special treatment for Kilroy was a political reality, a given because the boy was a gringo, because he had connections, because economics and politics dictated that his life was worth more than the other desaparecedos. It left a bad taste in Benitez's mouth.

So in a way, his agents' encounter with the Hernandez family was almost a relief, a welcome departure from the Kilroy case. As he sat in his motel room and pondered what his men had told him, he had no way of knowing that Mark Kilroy's disappearance and Little Serafin Hernandez's flagrant running of a drug checkpoint were intimately related. He only knew he had to learn what the Hernandez family was up to.

Raul Morales, the agent he'd put in charge of the checkpoint, was a good man. He had done just what Benitez would have suggested had he been there: Instead of cranking up the siren, pursuing and arresting the youth, Morales and another agent had climbed into an unmarked Bronco and discreetly followed.

"Let's see where he leads us," Morales had said. Then he laughed. "Look at that guy. What does he think, he's invisible?"

The two agents quickly caught up with Little Serafin's red pickup, then dropped back about a quarter-mile. They probably could have tailgated if they had wanted to—the driver seemed that uncaring.

The sun was low in the sky, glaring into the agents' eyes as they drove westward, squinting with concentration at the pickup ahead. They were quiet, expectant. The only sound was the singing of rubber on asphalt and the occasional wet thump of bugs striking the windshield.

After a few miles the truck reached the *curva de Texas,* a point where the road veers sharply toward the border. Just beyond the curve, the pickup turned right onto a rutted dirt ranch road, then bounced out of sight, trailing clouds of acrid dust. Agent Morales and his assistant drove on a short distance down the highway, made a U-turn, then pulled off to the side of the road to watch.

A half-hour later, they saw the pickup pull back onto the road and drive off, back toward Matamoros. When Serafin was out of sight, they crossed the highway, turned onto the ranch road, and slowly drove into the property, following the path Little Serafin had taken before.

The dust was still settling from Serafin's passage as they negotiated the narrow, half-mile dirt track. Through the brown haze, they soon could see ahead a large, corrugated steel warehouse, several parked trucks and cars, a decaying scrapwood shack to the left of the warehouse, and the usual assortment of crowing, barking, and bleating farm animals.

The late afternoon was still hot, but a cooling breeze moved through the crops, making the tips of the sorghum sway, sweeping the scent of dirt, manure, and charcoal into the agents' Bronco. As they braked to a stop in front of the warehouse, a short, heavyset man in work-stained clothes emerged from the shack and hesitantly approached, wishing the visitors *buenas tardes*.

Pretending to be a lost traveler, Agent Morales asked for directions, then gently plied the man for information.

"Oh no, señor," the man told them, smiling nervously. "I do not own the ranch. I am only the caretaker. I feed the animals. I watch the place."

He said his name was Domingo and that he was not sure who owned the ranch—an obvious lie, the agents thought. Domingo said the spread was called Rancho Santa Elena.

While Morales spoke with the caretaker, the other agent casually poked around. He was drawn to a brand-new blue Chevy Suburban, with the distinctive antenna of a car phone attached to its rear. He peered inside the cab, as if admiring the fine interior, and confirmed that there was, indeed, an expensive cellular telephone installed in the Chevy's console.

Then he spied a patina of green dust in the rear cargo area and on the seats. A veteran of many car searches, the agent knew immediately what it was: traces of marijuana, the fine dust and resin that shakes loose from bales of the drug no matter how carefully wrapped and handled.

Just as he was turning away, something else caught his eye. Lying on the rear floor of the Suburban was a statue of gray cement, the evil head with its eyes and mouth of ivory-colored sea shells, set in a permanent grimace. The agent had never seen anything like it.

By this time, Domingo was getting very nervous, and the agents knew it was time for them to leave if they wanted to allay suspicions. They bid the stout caretaker farewell and drove off.

Morales returned to the office and called his comandante. Benitez, a full-blooded Oaxacan Indian raised in a most traditional culture, was given to his own brand of superstition and ritual. Among other precautions against witchery, he had a Mexican *curandero,* a folk healer, on his staff—a man whose profession was to remove curses, cleanse the soul of evil, and perform other acts of white magic. Benitez knew immediately what his agent had seen in the backseat of that blue Suburban: The figure was Eleggua, the trickster god of the Afro-Caribbean religion of *Santeria.*

Eleggua was master of the roads, opener of the way, a warrior deity particularly favored by drug traffickers and those who wanted to place curses on enemies. Benitez had seen such statues in Oaxaca. Legend held that if the proper offerings were made to Eleggua, he could make you bulletproof—and invisible. You could walk right by a policeman—or drive right by him—and he'd never see you.

The discovery of black magic mixed with drug trafficking was not in itself surprising. More and more, contrabandistas were looking for any edge they could get, turning to witchcraft and ritual to ward off police and to curse rivals. In some locales—Miami, San Antonio, Houston, Mexico City, and Benitez's old stomping grounds in Oaxaca—the mingling of magical practices and drug smuggling had become common, though police generally dismissed it as irrelevant superstitions.

In time, events in Matamoros would change that attitude for good. But in April of 1989, the Mexican investigators had no way of guessing the deadly extremes witchcraft had assumed at Rancho Santa Elena.

What surprised Benitez was not so much finding a statue of Eleggua, but finding one in a Hernandez car. It didn't fit with what he knew of the family.

Although never successfully prosecuted, the Hernandezes for years had been well known to the police on both sides of the border. They were considered moderately successful smugglers who moved ton-loads of pot and the occasional kilo of cocaine. Black magic was not their style. But there were reasons that might have changed: Benitez also knew the family had suffered crippling setbacks during the past two years.

In January 1987, the smartest and second eldest brother, Saul Hernandez Rivera, manager of the family drug business, had been shot to death on a Matamoros street, an unintended victim of a gangland hit. Saul had been the one Hernandez brother with connections to Matamoros' most notorious drug barons. Those connections died with him.

Less than a month later, the eldest Hernandez brother attempted to fill Saul's shoes but it ended in disaster. On the night of February 4, 1987, Serafin Hernandez Rivera—Little Serafin's father—was busted with eight other men while awaiting a marijuana-laden plane at an abandoned airstrip fifty miles north of Houston. The drugs were lost and Old Serafin's brother had to bail the shaken trafficker out of jail.[5]

Then, that summer, Benitez had personally overseen the third and final disaster for the Hernandez clan. Mexican federal drug agents had doused the family's marijuana plantation in rural Oaxaca with gasoline and reduced the rich green crop to ashes. Benitez, then stationed in Oaxaca, had led the squad that burned the 370-acre Hernandez marijuana ranch.

When he transferred to Matamoros, one of his first orders to his men was to watch out for the Hernandez family. All the same, there shouldn't have been much to watch for. In the space of a few months, the family's leader, their supply, and their connections had been taken away, while prison threatened the eldest son. That should have finished them.

Yet here was one of their kids—Little Serafin, a twenty-year-old college-student nobody—driving a brand-new truck with a car phone to the family ranch, where, obviously, the family still smuggled drugs. Benitez had to know more. He instructed Agent Morales to hold off arresting Little Serafin for the time being. Instead, they were to ply the lowlife haunts of Matamoros' shantytowns, dredging up informants who might know what the Hernandez gang was up to these days. Benitez wanted information on the size, the members, and the connections of the Hernandez smuggling organization. Then he would move against the whole gang, not just a gofer like Little Serafin.

Benitez ordered his agents to watch the ranch daily. In the meantime, he would call his friends at the Drug Enforcement Administration's Brownsville office to ask for help with the car phone. They owed the comandante for a host of drug busts he had handed them, not to mention the Kilroy search. Little Serafin's truck had Texas plates, and the car phone had to be from the U.S. side. DEA would know how to get the phone number and the name of its owner, so Benitez could begin listening in.

Someone was paying Little Serafin's phone bills. Maybe that would provide a lead.

Already there were hints. Even by the time Morales called him, Benitez's agents had learned that the Hernandez boys were living in fine homes, driving a fleet of brand-new trucks, and walking the streets like swaggering feudal lords. They did not act like a family down on its luck. Anybody who stopped at one of the tourist bars on Matamoros' main street, just a block from the bridge to Brownsville, could find Little Serafin or one of his young cronies peddling baggies of pot and grams of cocaine to the gringos. The

Hernandez boys walked around like they owned the town, talking about all the protection they had, the cops they had bought, some weird religion that made them invincible—and a priest of black magic who led them: their godfather, Adolfo de Jesus Constanzo. They would say his name with reverence and fear and, most of all, faith.

Utter faith in their strange religion, it turned out, was why Little Serafin had blown through the checkpoint that afternoon. As he explained much later in his confession, he thought he was mystically protected. Police couldn't stop him, or catch him, or shoot him. They couldn't even see him. His padrino had told him so.

He was invisible.

The agents who followed Serafin from the checkpoint had joked about it, but they had been right. This Constanzo had told his young follower he could move unseen past the police, and Little Serafin had believed it, without question, literally.

When Comandante Benitez retells that one a year later, he still smiles. "*Estupido, no?*" he says.

At the time, however, the name of Adolfo de Jesus Constanzo meant nothing to the Mexican police. All that was about to change, though, thanks to Little Serafin's silly April Fool's Day ride. The dark hand of El Padrino had been exposed at last.

2

Sunrise comes hot and clear in the Rio Grande Valley. Heat waves dance and dust devils swirl as the orange light turns gritty white. The sun punishes blacktop until the roads shimmer with an illusion of wetness, and Brownsville turns stark as a photo negative. Water becomes a dazzling mirror inside the coiling *resacas,* cool, palm-tree–lined canals that meander through town like gleaming green snakes. Their lushness is contrasted by the brown, vacant lots that pock downtown, where broken bits of glass glitter in the sun like lost jewels, then crunch and vanish underfoot.

On April 8, 1989, a dark-haired man, sternly handsome, climbed out of his silver Mercedes into that merciless morning light. His expensive shoes clocked a steady beat on the cracked and dusty sidewalks of downtown Brownsville, cruising past boarded-up storefronts and a billboard of a man behind bars with the caption, "Robert Garcia Bail Bonds: The key to set you free."

The man never broke stride, ignoring the long line of cheesy discount fashion shops and wholesale appliance outlets; his shopping tastes ran to Gucci and Ralph Lauren, not Woolworth. He was a familiar figure in Brownsville, yet few knew his name. Heads turned to watch him in silence as he passed.

The heat seemed to have no visible effect on the man. His blindingly white shirt and pants were perfectly pressed and immaculate, unsullied by anything as base as perspiration. Around his neck, four or five chains and amulets—two of gold, the others of beads—rattled like a watchman's keys. Bright morning glare bounced off his dark sunglasses, masking his eyes from view. Above them, his thick brows were knitted into a single, angry vee.

The place he sought was on Washington Street near the corner of 11th: a tiny Brownsville store called La Esmeralda, barely three blocks from the bridge to Matamoros. La Esmeralda was a *yerberia,* an herb store, a small, cramped place where the shelves were lined with dried healing plants, bags of special incense, glass-encased holy candles, and the brightly painted figures of the *santos,* the Catholic saints.

Inside, an ancient electric floor fan stirred a sluggish, musty breeze on hot days. Outside, an exotic mix of strange odors wafted onto the sidewalk through the open door, informing those who know such things that La Esmeralda was a place devoted to faith and magic.

Mexican folk healers—the curanderos—came here to buy the herbs that cure sickness of the soul—to them, the true root of disease and ill fortune. The faithful crossed the border to La Esmeralda to buy incense that promotes good luck, soap that washes away curses, oils that, when rubbed into the flesh, assure wealth and prosperity.

Even as they place their faith in such magic, these same customers consider themselves the most devout of Catholics. It's just that this is a land where magic has always existed, rooted in the distant past when the Coahuiltecan Indians ruled, long before the Europeans claimed this valley by the Rio Grande. Walking to church a thousand years later, the old women in black still give a ritual pat to every passing child they glance at. How else could a mother know her child was being spared the evil eye?

But tucked away on back shelves at La Esmeralda, peeping out from behind the familiar objects of Mexican magic, lie darker things, foreign things—not evil in themselves perhaps, but capable of evil should someone with the power wish it so. They are the tools of brujeria. Witchcraft.

Look more closely, and there on the shelf behind Saint Lazarus is Ochosi, a small, stylized bow and arrow of iron, symbol of one of the deities of the magical Afro-Caribbean religion of Santeria. Ochosi is not native to Mexico, but more and more it is becoming known here. With the proper blood sacrifice of chicken and goat, the hunter god Ochosi wards off police and jail—very useful on the border in certain lines of work.

And there, on the next shelf, is the conical head and evil grimace of Eleggua, god of the roads, the same figure the drug agent spotted in a car at Rancho Santa Elena. This, too, is foreign to Mexico, but some local people perceive his value. Eleggua can tell you when to run a load of dope. Or when not to.

"I need some palo azul," the stern customer in white told the man behind the counter. *Palo azul*—literally, blue stick—is a rare, powerful herb, seldom requested.

The storeowner, Luis Valdes, was of Cuban descent, as was his white-garbed customer that morning. Cuba is home to Eleggua and Ochosi—and palo azul.

Valdez knew the herb was used in the rites of Palo Mayombe, a dark sister religion to Santeria. African slaves brought both religions to the New World, where they merged with Christian folk legends and seemed—on the surface—to be similar. But whereas the santero priest usually seeks luck and life for himself, the palero most often seeks death and revenge for his enemies. A palero's followers call him their godfather, their padrino.

Valdes eyed his customer cautiously. The Cuban had been in the store a few times before in the past year, usually with a tall, thin woman named Sara. The quiet, regal woman was his priestess, Valdes had assumed. There was always a high priestess in Palo Mayombe. This time, though, the dark man in white had come alone.

"I have no blue stick," Valdes told the man in Spanish. "But I can order some. It will take a few days."

"Never mind," the man snapped. He couldn't wait for a special order, he said. Trouble was brewing now, not in a few days. Certain spells had to be cast. He had no time to waste.

He removed his sunglasses and gave the store's shelves a cursory look, his eyes as veiled and emotionless as a lizard's. Then he shifted his gaze to Valdes, staring at him in the same cold, appraising way, as if he were no different from the statues and talismen on the shelves.

Valdes tried, but could not meet that gaze for more than a few heartbeats. The room suddenly felt tight and close despite the fan in the corner. The shopkeeper shuffled nervously behind his counter.

At last the customer concluded his look around the store, then requested several other types of herbs. Valdes gathered the items, wrapped them in old newspaper, and dropped them into a brown paper bag, glad to busy himself with mundane tasks. Without word of thanks or farewell, the man paid, signed a receipt in Valdes' record book, then stalked out, his white clothes dazzling in the sunlight. Valdes could hear the hard click of his shoes move down the sidewalk, then the sound faded into the morning traffic noise.

After a moment, Valdes looked down at the signature in his receipt book, so full of flourishes it was barely readable. Still, he could make it out: Adolfo de Jesus Constanzo.

El Padrino's search for mystical herbs came in response to a disturbing discovery: He had learned the police had been to the ranch. That meant the police were investigating the Hernandez family and the movement of drugs through Rancho Santa Elena.

So far, Constanzo knew, the Antinarcoticos didn't know his identity, nor did they suspect what else went on at the ranch. They only knew of the Hernandez clan, the outer, obvious layer of El Padrino's organization, behind which he could operate safely, hidden from sight. With the right herbs and secret incantations, he aimed to keep it that way.

And if he had to cast off the Hernandez family in the process, well, it was their own fault for getting caught.

With the magical herbs on the new leather seat beside him, Constanzo drove his Mercedes carefully through town, back to the Holiday Inn on the freeway, where preparations were underway for his gang's biggest drug deal in months. As always, he obeyed every traffic sign, maintaining a steady two miles an hour above the speed limit. El Padrino would never be brought down through something so stupid as a traffic violation. He was proud of his perfect driving record.

So he was all the more irked when he learned how the police had been drawn to the ranch: Little Serafin's idiotic drive past the checkpoint. Constanzo had shrieked at the Hernandez nephew, left him cowering and whimpering in a corner. He threatened to take his soul for the spirits. Little Serafin would not be so stupid again. Of that, Constanzo was certain.

Constanzo had come from Mexico City to Matamoros and had chosen the Hernandez drug trafficking family carefully, deliberately.[1] They had been directionless, desperate. Their leader by default, the youngest brother, Elio, was vicious but easily influenced, easily awed. Best of all from Constanzo's standpoint, none of them was very bright. That suited El Padrino's needs well; it let him walk in, work his magic, and take over virtually overnight.

But the sheer stupidity Little Serafin had shown was more than even Constanzo had anticipated. How could he just drive through a police roadblock like that when, that same week, they were planning to move a ton of marijuana across the border? The deal had been more than a month in the making, worth three hundred thousand dollars in cash. Yet, with those valuable drugs stowed at the ranch warehouse, Little Serafin had led the cops right to it. Miraculously, the police hadn't found the stash. El Padrino shook his head as he drove and remembered. To Little Serafin and the others, this near-disaster only provided additional evidence of Constanzo's magical might. He had never thought any of his followers would take his promise of invisibility so literally.

In a way, though, despite the inconvenience it had created, El Padrino had to smile at the blind faith he had instilled in his burgeoning cult. They believed anything he said, did anything he wished. His high priestess, Sara, charged with teaching his followers the practices and taboos of Palo Mayombe, deserved much credit for that. She had done her job well. Perhaps too well, Constanzo thought. They feared her almost as much as they feared him. At some point he might have to do something about the strikingly tall woman waiting for him patiently at the Holiday Inn. Yes, he might at that.

But for now, despite the police interference, matters seemed well in hand, Constanzo decided. A magical shield protected them: The same night as Little Serafin's ride, the gang had offered a sacrifice to counter any threat. An enemy of the cult had been brought to the ranch and his soul had been given to the spirits—a bloody offering in El Padrino's secret temple. The ceremony hadn't been as good as the gringo's—none had ever been that good, before or since—but it had served Constanzo's needs. The trip to

La Esmeralda for more magic was but an extra precaution, an afterthought.

Constanzo remained confident, in part because the police had blundered just as badly as Little Serafin. They had returned to the ranch three days after the checkpoint incident, tipping their hand. While waiting for the car-phone information from the DEA, the Mexican agents had grown impatient and returned to Rancho Santa Elena to renew questioning of the caretaker, Domingo. But this time the agents made the mistake of telling Domingo they were cops.

They had done this to scare him, a standard police tactic, and it worked: Domingo practically babbled. He admitted lying before and that he really did know who owned the ranch: the Hernandez family.

"I haven't been here long, though," the panicked caretaker told the agents. "I was just walking by the place in February. Señores Elio and Ovidio were here. They offered me the job, so I said yes."

Elio Hernandez, though the youngest, seemed to be in charge, Domingo told them. He was quick-tempered and mean, a little Napoleon, raging one moment, making grand gestures of generosity the next. Ovidio was older, bigger, slower, and kinder but he listened to Elio. And the kindly eyes of Ovidio could turn killer-mean in an instant.

"What else?" Agent Morales demanded when Domingo fell silent. "Or do we have to bring you in?"

"No, no," Domingo sputtered, images of horrific Mexican jails spinning before his eyes. "No, everything was fine for a while, but then I realized the bosses here are doing . . . suspicious activities. I don't know what, I swear, but they're doing something."

"What's in the warehouse?" Morales asked.

Domingo shook his head. "Nothing. It's empty."

The agents pressed him for more, nearly reducing him to tears, but Domingo had nothing to add. As afraid as he was, he was still holding back.

The conversation frustrated the Mexican agents. They continued to suspect a drug-running operation at the ranch, but Domingo provided no useful new information, nothing strong enough to warrant a forcible search of the place. The warehouse was securely locked and Domingo had no key. If they broke in and nothing was found inside, then the investigation was ruined; the Hernandezes would know police had been there.

Finally, the agents left, cautioning the caretaker to keep his mouth shut. "If you tell them, things will go badly for you," the agents warned him.

Domingo nodded vigorously. "I'll say nothing."

Predictably, as soon as the agents were gone, Domingo immediately went to the house of the ranch foreman, Aurelio Chavez, and told him about the police visit. Domingo didn't know much but he did know this: People had a habit of showing up at the Rancho Santa Elena and never leaving. Like that blonde kid last month, the one he had failed to mention to the agents. Domingo had no intention of suffering a similar fate by talking too much with the police. No jail could be as bad as what could happen to him at Rancho Santa Elena. So to protect himself, he spilled his guts to Chavez.

Chavez was part of the gang and a follower of Constanzo. He immediately called Elio Hernandez to report what Domingo had said about the agents' inquiries. Elio called the Brownsville Holiday Inn, where El Padrino was staying, and broke the bad news.[2]

"I will perform a ceremony," Constanzo replied. "We will be protected from harm. Like always."

In four days, the gang was supposed to ship the 1,800 pounds of marijuana across the river to buyers on the Texas side. Under the circumstances, the Mexican agents' sudden interest should have caused Constanzo and his henchmen dire concerns for their safety. The danger of exposure was obvious. Yet the only reaction was Constanzo's trip to the yerberia that afternoon, a search for mystical protection, capped by one of his bizarre, awesome ceremonies at the ranch.

Otherwise, it was business as usual. The Hernandez boys continued strutting around town like monied peacocks, certain that El Padrino would protect them all with his magical shield. And on April 8, they went through with their deal, hungry for the money a ton of pot could bring, contemptuous of being caught, as only invincible, invisible men can be. The drugs moved across the river to the buyer's representative, a man they knew only as Chacho, who handed over a valise full of cash. Armed with the knowledge that they were under investigation and that Mexican agents probably were watching the ranch, the gang simply chose a point on the river the agents couldn't see from the Matamoros road.

What they didn't know was that agents of the U.S. Customs Service, in a separate and completely coincidental investigation, had set up a surveillance post on the Texas side of the river, directly across from Rancho Santa Elena. Customs agents in Brownsville—the same ones who had formed a huge, if ineffectual, task force to search for Mark Kilroy—had gotten a tip that a large load of marijuana would move on the night of April 8 at that spot. Though they had no idea who the smugglers were—they were told only the place, not the players—the Customs agents were lying in wait at exactly the spot Elio had chosen for moving the drugs.

Even this didn't stop El Padrino. Just after midnight, after three hours of surveillance, the Customs agents left the mud and mosquitoes along the river, assuming the tip on the drug shipment was wrong. They had been told the deal would take place earlier in the evening, and they simply gave up. Such tips often proved wrong.

The drugs were carried across the river a half-hour later, once members of the Hernandez family, on lookout, gave the all-clear sign. Despite police scrutiny on both sides of the border, the drugs moved effortlessly, as if by magic. The brujo Constanzo took full credit for the seeming miracle.

But their luck was not destined to hold.

While U.S. Customs agents missed a drug shipment, Comandante Benitez had returned from Arizona and was preparing to move against the Hernandez family on his side of the river. By the next morning, Sunday, April 9, the comandante had assigned several agents to watch the ranch and a Hernandez hideout on Avenida Lauro Villar in Matamoros, ready to move.

The DEA agents in Brownsville had come through with Benitez's car-phone information—and not just the one from the blue Suburban, but ten other cellular phones as well, all owned by a company called Hernandez Ranches, Inc. Benitez was astounded at their cockiness. The gang hadn't even used a phony name. With the numbers in hand, Benitez had immediately begun eavesdropping on the gang's phone calls.

Listening raptly that Sunday morning, the first thing he heard was Little Serafin bragging about the huge load of dope moved the night before to Chacho. Benitez knew this information would give him a psychological edge during future interrogations. It was important for the suspects to believe he already knew everything. Then they would talk all night.

Next, Little Serafin said he was going to meet his Uncle Elio at the house on Lauro Villar. Within minutes Benitez had two of his best agents staking out the address.

The last thing Benitez overheard before Little Serafin hung up was something about a man called El Padrino. "Who do you think that is?" Benitez mused. His agents only shrugged.[3]

At about ten that morning, the stakeout paid off. The federales parked near the Lauro Villar house saw two young men get out of a red pickup truck with Texas plates, then enter the front door. One was pale and short, with a droopy mustache too big for his face. The other was dark, taller and slightly effeminate in his prim walk, in the slight cant of his wrist. Dressed in designer jeans and wearing expensive gold wristwatches, they were a couple of spoiled, rich kids come to collect their share of the payoff from the previous night's drug deal, the onlooking agents figured.

A few minutes later, as the pair left the house, the agents braced them at the door and asked who they were. It was Little Serafin and his friend, David Serna, another member of the Constanzo gang.

"This house is my uncle's, Elio Hernandez," Little Serafin told the police, the door still ajar. Before he could pull it shut, Agent Raul Morales stuck out his arm and grabbed the edge of the door.

"You don't mind if we go in, do you?" Morales asked.

Without waiting for an answer, the two Mexican narcotics agents entered the house and began a search. Although no drugs turned up, the police did find numerous tools of the smuggling trade: a .38-caliber revolver, a .30-caliber Browning automatic pistol, a .22-caliber target pistol, and a 30:06 rifle. All were illegal weapons, since in Mexico civilians are barred from owning most firearms.

Outside, Morales spotted a familiar powdery green residue in the bed of Serafin's pickup truck. Sweeping a finger across the metal pickup bed, he studied the dark dust on his hand. "Nice big load last night, was it?" the agent asked.

Little Serafin just smirked.

The agents handcuffed David and Serafin and drove them to Rancho Santa Elena, stopping at their office only long enough to pick up another contingent of agents. The confiscated weapons were left in Benitez's office.

At the ranch, the agents forced Serafin to unlock the big metal warehouse. Inside, they found the remains of the night's pot shipment—three nylon bags of leftover marijuana, a total of twenty-nine kilograms (about sixty-four pounds). Pungent residue suggested to the agents that much more marijuana had been stored there in the recent past.

Next to the pot, they found more weapons: two .22-caliber rifles, a 12-gauge shotgun, and a .45-caliber silenced machine gun. And parked inside the warehouse this time was the same blue Suburban Morales had seen when he followed Little Serafin a week before. Once again, it had pot residue inside, but there no longer was a strange statue in the backseat. The van was covered with dried river mud from the shipment the night before.

The geese and chickens screeched loud protests as the agents stomped about the property, looking for more contraband. They found nothing else—then.

The caretaker, Domingo, was nowhere to be seen. The agents left with Little Serafin and David, carting drugs and weapons back to the federales' headquarters. Benitez's wood-paneled office—a well-appointed leftover from Comandante Perez's corrupt regime—started looking like a dictator's arsenal with all the seized weapons piled on the floor, stacked in front of the artificial fireplace like cordwood.

Meanwhile, other agents kept watching the Lauro Villar house. They were rewarded early in the evening when they snared two more gang members. One was wisecracking Elio Hernandez, stopped as he drove up to the house in the middle of a car-phone conversation. He spoke a few hurried last words, then hung up as the agents approached. With him was another gang member, Sergio Martinez.

As with the others, the police grabbed this pair easily, by surprise and without resistance. It had been so easy—not a single shot fired—and the agents began to congratulate themselves for nailing yet another drug ring. All that remained was a thorough interrogation, and soon the whole gang would be behind bars, they told themselves.

Only one thing bothered them: None of the gang members seemed the least bit concerned. It was the damnedest thing, as if they had been arrested for a traffic ticket. Elio had actually laughed at his interrogators. "You can't keep me here," he had declared with complete conviction. "Soon, I'll be gone."

"They weren't worried at all," Benitez recalled later. "They thought we couldn't hurt them. They thought they were protected."

It took a while to convince them otherwise.

Interrogations of the smugglers began Sunday evening. After three hours of questions, Elio and the others were still laughing, still certain that nothing could happen to them. It unnerved Benitez's men.

The comandante decided to break off questioning. Let the suspects stew overnight in a squalid lockup, he figured, while we round up other gang members. Questioning would begin in earnest Monday morning, when the gang members would either provide some answers or face some ungentle persuasion.

The agents knew their methods of persuasion would most likely be effective. Virtually every criminal defendant in Mexican custody eventually confesses. Of course, virtually every defendant later recants, claiming to have been tortured into admissions of guilt.

"You have to remember, there's a difference in confessing in Mexico and confessing over here," Cameron County Sheriff's Lieutenant George Gavito, one of the U.S. investigators searching for Kilroy, would later explain. "Take it from there."

A favorite Mexican interrogation technique involves soda water laced with a heavy dose of Tabasco. The bottle of reddish liquid is shaken, then shot up an untalkative suspect's nostrils. First comes a hideous sensation of drowning as the foaming liquid floods breathing passages, followed by an indescribable searing pain as the peppery liquid scores sensitive nasal tissue. It leaves no visible scars. The method has proved most effective, especially when combined with more ordinary beatings and deprivation of food and water.[4]

The Mexican police euphemism for this is *presion moral*—moral pressure.

But before the interrogations could resume the following morning, the caretaker, Domingo Reyes Bustamante, was hauled into the Antinarcoticos office. He had shown up for work at the ranch Monday, unaware of the arrests the day before. Waiting agents arrested him immediately and brought him trembling before the comandante. The agents took one look at Domingo and knew not even the threat of torture would be needed with him.

Poor, plump Domingo was no hardened criminal. Nor did he have any belief in witchcraft and magical protection to support him as he winced beneath the angry stares of impatient policemen. Once he saw the Hernandez boys in jail, he realized they were as vulnerable as anyone. His fear of the police became greater than his fear of the drug smugglers.

In short, he started talking his head off.

Yes, the ranch owners smuggle dope, he told Benitez. There was a ton of it, more or less, stored there until just two nights ago.

"Tell me who is involved," Benitez asked. "Who have you seen at the ranch?"

Domingo named everyone in custody and several others—names Benitez had heard mentioned during the tapped phone conversations. "People come and go all the time at the ranch," Domingo said. "Some are friends of the bosses, or workers. But there are others. They are treated very badly."

There had even been an American there once, Domingo volunteered, then trailed off, looking uncertain. Some of the agents in the room who had been quietly talking among themselves suddenly fell silent. All eyes focused on Domingo.

"Tell me about him," Benitez commanded.

With a reluctance that only increased Benitez's suspicions, Domingo recounted a day during the past month when he saw a young gringo tied up in the back of a blue Suburban at the ranch. The youth had been inside it all night.

"I felt sorry for him. I made him something to eat. I brought him some eggs and some water for breakfast. Then the bosses came and took him away.

"It happened about three weeks ago, maybe a month," Domingo added. "That's all I know."

Benitez exchanged a look with his top agent, Miguel Antonio Rodriguez, who was nicknamed *El Lobo*—The Wolf. The comandante felt a sick tug at his insides.

"Describe the gringo," Benitez said.

Domingo shrugged, then, after a moment's thought, brightened. "I remember. He was a *guero*."

Guero. Blonde.

Benitez rummaged through his desk and pulled out a black-and-white glossy photo of Mark Kilroy—handsome, gringo, blonde Mark Kilroy.

He showed the photo to Domingo.

The caretaker didn't hesitate.

"Yes. That's him. The guero."

3

Suddenly, the separate investigations of drugs, gangs, and a missing college student from Texas became facets of the same dark puzzle. A simple drug-smuggling case had turned into something far uglier, something Comandante Benitez had to understand and end—quickly.

The interrogations became unrelenting. It was time for a little "moral pressure."

The comandante felt a peculiar satisfaction when the man who had started the case with his drive through a drug stop, Little Serafin, turned out to be the first suspect to crack. Confronted with the combination of Domingo's startling statements and the peppery bottle of soda water, the young trafficker panicked.

He admitted it was true. They smuggled dope for a living.

And yes, they had killed Mark Kilroy. The ritual taking of a life brought them great magical power and success, he said.

"It was our religion, our voodoo," Little Serafin explained, in a reverent tone that suggested his participation in human sacrifice was no different from a Catholic buying a mass card. "We did it for success. We did it for protection. He told us killing would bring us power. He told us our souls were dead.

"When that happens, you can do anything. To anyone."

Little Serafin smiled.

The interrogation of Little Serafin took five hours. As they listened, the agents sometimes crossed themselves. Some of them had wondered why their superstitious comandante kept strings of garlic, religious candles, amulets, and other charms of good luck in his office. Now they were glad to have them as they listened to young Hernandez's tale unfold.

They had heard of black magic all their lives. Now they were seeing its work:

A man with no soul.

And Little Serafin did seem cold, without feeling, without any idea that what he had done was morally monstrous.

Diffidently, as if contemptuous of the policemen's power over him, Little Serafin told how he, his uncle, and all the others in the gang belonged to a voodoo sect led by El Padrino. The godfather, he said, was Adolfo de Jesus Constanzo, a Cuban-American witch from Miami, now living in Mexico City.

"Adolfo is very powerful, very smart. He runs our business in Matamoros. He has connections all over Mexico. Movie stars go to him. Congressmen."

He was a man to be worshiped, Little Serafin said. He was a man to be feared.

"We did whatever he asked. It is our religion. . . . And if we didn't do as he said, he would kill us. Or worse."

With breathtaking calm, the young Hernandez told how they had kidnapped Kilroy from the streets of Matamoros, luring the drunken youth into a pickup truck with the promise of a ride across the bridge. They blindfolded and bound him with duct tape, then brought him to the ranch, all the while promising he would not be hurt. But the next afternoon, when El Padrino arrived, a dozen or more of Constanzo's followers gathered around the shack they used as a temple. Kilroy was stripped and dragged inside, where Constanzo beat, tortured, sodomized, and mutilated him, then murdered him with a machete blow that laid open his skull.

Little Serafin's eyes gleamed when he described the final act: Constanzo scooped out Kilroy's brain and placed it inside a terrible, magical cauldron he called the *nganga*. This was where their dark gods dwelled, inside the little temple, a nondescript wooden shack tucked behind a corral only three hundred meters from the warehouse at Rancho Santa Elena.[1] This temple of death was so deceptively innocent looking that agents had visited the ranch three times and never noticed it.

A few days after his confession to Benitez, Serafin elaborated on the chilling story of Mark Kilroy's abduction and murder, in English this time, for the videotape camera of DEA Agent T. K. Solis. On it, Little Serafin referred to Kilroy by his first name, Mark, as if they were old friends.

"Adolfo told us we had to go get a white male, a young white male," Serafin told the camera. "Like a spring breaker. He wanted to put his brains in . . . because it was going to give the spirits more power."

Little Serafin recited this tale with little expression on his face, except during moments he considered humorous. Then he'd giggle.

Mark Kilroy's disappearance was no longer a mystery, though the bizarre circumstances of his murder still remained incomprehensible to the agents sitting mesmerized in Benitez's office.

To Little Serafin, though, the matter was simple. Constanzo offered them money, power, success, even better luck with girlfriends, he boasted. That's why he went along with the ceremonies, with the murder of Kilroy.

Most important, El Padrino protected him from enemies, which was why Little Serafin was willing to talk so freely. What Benitez knew didn't matter to him.

"You won't be able to keep us here," Little Serafin said, just as Elio had threatened before. "You'll see."

"Yes," the comandante answered gravely. "I will."

After Benitez heard the confession, he had Serafin repeat it in greater detail, then repeat it again—always with the bottle of soda water and the bottle of Tabasco nearby, a constant reminder of the pain that would reward any deviation or hesitation.

When he had heard it all a third time, though, Benitez no longer had any stomach for it. Elio and the others would also have to be broken, but that could wait. They weren't going anywhere, no matter what Little Serafin thought.

To Benitez, none of it made sense. Sure, the Hernandez boys were career criminals, but they had never been vicious, sick murderers; that didn't fit. In the violent world of drug trafficking, revenge killings and the businesslike termination of rivals and squealers were daily occurrences, a given on the border. But now Benitez faced something far different: murder with a religious fervor, killing for the blessings of some dark god who promised to turn blood into money in return for men's souls. What had made a mad killer out of a nobody like Little Serafin Hernandez? The guy couldn't even earn decent grades at the tiny two-year college in Brownsville he attended, much less cut a bargain with the devil. How had he become a man who could describe the mutilation of a Mark Kilroy and giggle? How had this evil godfather, this Adolfo de Jesus Constanzo, turned simple drug smugglers into men with no souls?

Whether it was the power of black magic or persuasion, one thing seemed clear to Benitez: This El Padrino possessed a potent power of some sort. He was dangerous. He had to be caught.

The comandante and El Lobo decided to take a drive out to Rancho Santa Elena to look around for themselves. His men were out combing Matamoros for the other gang members, but he couldn't wait. He had to see the place.

By the time Benitez and his assistant reached the ranch, it was after nine o'clock Monday night. The two men were edgy, anxious to see if Little Serafin's tale was true, wanting, but unable, to disbelieve it. Could such things really have happened in their midst?

There had been vague rumors for years of some sort of violent Santeria or Satan-worshiping cult in the Matamoros area, sacrificing farm animals and kidnapping children. But the rumors had been dismissed as ghost stories. Perhaps this gang was at the root of those rumors, Benitez mulled. In which case, might there be more killings than Kilroy's to account for?

The ugly possibilities seemed endless.

When Benitez and El Lobo stopped by the dirt road leading to the ranch, stars and moon cast a ghostly light on the swaying tips of the sorghum. The summery heat that had persisted throughout April had finally given way, and the night felt unseasonably cool, temperatures hovering just above the forties. When they opened the Bronco's windows, the wind's cold hand slapped at them.

Outside, nothing moved. There was no sound but the wind in the crops. The road, a silver ribbon in the pale moonlight, was devoid of traffic, a lonely thing, yet infinitely more comforting and familiar than the dark ranch before them. The two men stared at the place, just an ordinary ranch they had passed without a thought many times before. But now, call it intuition or imagination or just plain nerves, this place felt different. It felt palpably evil to the two policemen.

"Let's wait for daylight, boss," El Lobo said. "And more men."

"Yes," the comandante replied. "Let's."

When Cameron County Sheriff's Detective Ernesto Flores arrived at Comandante Benitez's headquarters the next morning, he found fourteen grim Mexican agents pulling on camouflage outfits and loading submachine guns in preparation for what looked like a major assault on well-armed enemies. Even the comandante, who strode silently into his inner office, slamming the door behind him, had a bulletproof vest strapped over his shirt.

Six hours earlier, at one in the morning, Flores had been awakened in his Brownsville home by the fast-talking, deep-throated voice of his lieutenant, George Gavito.

"They might have something big," Gavito had said. "I want you at Benitez's office by seven."

That was all he said. That was all he had to say: Flores felt certain "something big" must concern Mark Kilroy. The detective had been assigned to search for the missing college student for the past three weeks. Every lead had dried up, every tip had been a bust. There was no ransom note, no witnesses, no trace. And like everyone else involved in the search, Flores had come to the grim conclusion that Kilroy almost certainly was dead.

Maybe they finally found the body, he had figured as he dressed and made the drive to the comandante's office. Of course, it could be just another bum lead. That's why he was being sent, Flores told himself ruefully, while his superiors stayed home in bed.

Two sleepy U.S. Customs agents had also trudged into Benitez's headquarters, summoned from bed by a call from their boss, Oran Neck. When Flores asked if they knew what was going on, the agents just shook their heads.

"Maybe this is another false alarm," Flores said, eyeing the Mexican SWAT team, wondering if he had jumped to conclusions about Kilroy. "This looks more like some kind of drug raid."

None of the Mexican agents would talk. Benitez stayed holed up in his office.

Then, at seven o'clock sharp, everyone piled into a half-dozen unmarked Antinarcoticos cars, still offering no explanations to the puzzled Americans. "Just come," one of the Mexican agents instructed. "No questions."

As he was waiting for his ride, Flores noticed a pot-bellied man, barely over five feet tall, getting into Benitez's Bronco with the comandante. His name was Eluterio, a Mexican curandero. Eluterio and Benitez were having an animated discussion about something Flores couldn't hear, though he did catch one word: *exorcismo*. Exorcism.

Next, Flores saw a young man with a droopy mustache being escorted from the building. He was in handcuffs and was being pushed roughly into a car by two unsmiling federales. It was Little Serafin Hernandez. For no particular reason—other than naked hatred—the agents cuffed Serafin on the side of the head as he struggled to get into the car without the use of his hands. Then the agents climbed in after him and pulled the door shut. Flores wondered what it meant.

Weary and cold, his bushy steel-gray hair blown wild in the wind, Flores shrugged and climbed into a patrol car with his Customs colleagues. They'd just have to wait and see what was coming.

The convoy of federales spun out of the unpaved, gravel lot in front of their headquarters and headed through town, turning west on Highway 2, out into the fertile ranchlands along the river. After twenty minutes of near-reckless high-speed driving, they turned off onto the dust and bumps of the Rancho Santa Elena access road. The fleet of federales cars ground to a stop at the warehouse, then continued slowly in single file down a path to its right, little more than two tire ruts with weeds in between. The weeds were matted and greasy from the chassis of passing cars. The Bronco with Little Serafin led the way. He was guiding the convoy.

The ruts skirted the edge of a cornfield for several hundred yards, turning right twice, then finally curving into an open area surrounded by haystacks, abandoned farm machinery, and piles of trash. A few mangy, emaciated cows grazed on the hay. In the clearing was a corral, its fences bleached gray by sun and rain and neglect. The bare dirt inside was lumpy, the color of ash, as hard-packed and lifeless as a lunar sea.

To the side of the corral, the focus of attention, stood a tiny, squarish shack, barely fifteen by twenty feet around, covered in tarpaper, its tin roof sagging and its windows boarded with plywood. There was nothing special about the shack. There were hundreds just like it on other ranches along the road to Matamoros. In all the times the Mexican agents had come to the ranch to question and search, they had never even noticed this lonely shed at the edge of the property.

At one side of the building was a cardboard box half filled with glass-encased votive candles, the kind used in religious ceremonies. The brown carton was open and sagging from exposure to the elements. Near it were a few pieces of scrap wood, an empty rum bottle lying on its side, dust, and nothing else.

Flores looked around, wondering what was supposed to happen. Why all the guns for this? When he asked his driver, the Mexican agent practically spat the answer: "Brujos."

Witches.

The policemen and their lone prisoner emerged from their cars amid a clatter of weapons and the hiss of their whispers. No one spoke in normal tones of voice. They were jumpy, as if they expected an army of the dead to rise up from the dust, ready to consume them.

Then Flores understood. The agents were not keeping their fingers twitching at their weapons' triggers because they were afraid of men. They were afraid of demons, of curses, of evil. They had grown up on the border and believed in black magic. So did Benitez. Flores had seen the garlic and amulets in the comandante's office, the trappings of a true believer.

As Flores watched, the agents gripped their weapons even more tightly and strained to see some evidence of the evil they knew lurked here. But nothing moved. Nobody was home.

A heavy silence settled on the gathering as the agents stood their ground, surveying the scene. In the distance a truck or car was heard starting, then driving away, the sound carried by a breeze. Later, Benitez would learn from agents posted outside the ranch that the truck he had heard belonged to Aurelio Chavez, ranch foreman and cult member, who made his escape from the other end of the ranch, out near the muddy irrigation channel. Chavez had seen the Mexican agents before they could spot him, then eluded them on back roads he knew far better. But for the moment, no one at the corral reacted to the sound. The Mexican agents seemed transfixed.

The weather had remained unusually cold, a sunless morning beneath a gray pot-lid sky. Winds moved through the corn and sorghum like invisible waves breaking on a distant shore, cold and cheerless. The agents were bundled in winter coats, their exhalations visible in the gray morning air. Little Serafin, his fancy black cowboy boots scuffed and dusty, wore only a blue workshirt and jeans. He shuffled from foot to foot, looking uncomfortable but otherwise unmoved.[2]

Then the breeze shifted and several of the agents took a step backward, as if they had been struck. An unmistakable sweet, cloying odor had wafted their way. Flores recognized it immediately.

"Death," he muttered under his breath. "It smells like death."

Benitez looked grim, wearing cammies, a black jacket with the federales insignia on its back, and a machine gun confiscated from Elio's house slung over one shoulder. The gun had words carved into its butt: *Cuerno de Chivo,* Horn of the Goat, common Mexican slang for the Soviet-style AK-47 with its distinctive curving magazine. He waved to an agent who was carrying a Sony video camera. "Come closer," the comandante said. "Get everything."

The entire operation would be thoroughly documented on videotape. To the bemusement of U.S. authorities, the finished tape would come replete with a studio-produced lead-in featuring salsa music, hot and jumpy. Lengthy rolling credits listed all the agents involved, naming Comandante Juan Benitez Ayala as the "producer." Such a flashy prologue to an evidence tape is not unusual in Mexico. It was included for the benefit of official viewers in Mexico City, so there would be no mistake about who should get credit for cracking the case.

The rest of the tape was strictly amateur video, complete with shaking camera, strange angles, poor lighting, and some strange, static-filled pauses that seemed to occur at rather convenient times. Those pauses were deliberate edits, representing the dozen or so occasions when the Mexican agents battered Little Serafin with their hands or clubs to get more information, or to wipe that constant smirk off his face, or simply because they felt like it.[3]

"The guy was kind of hard to take," Flores recalled later. "He had no remorse at all. It was incredible. So every cut in the tape, they beat the hell out of him."

At Benitez's command, several agents began yanking the boards off the shack's windows. Then they broke open the door. Two agents warily peered in, but only for a moment. Then they staggered back, reeling from the stench pouring from the building. It was an invisible wall shoving them away, a slaughterhouse wind none of them had ever imagined and none would ever forget. After a day at that ranch, the odor would get into their clothes, their nostrils, their cars; it would cling for days, defying soap and open windows.

Some agents tried entering using handkerchiefs as masks. They came out gagging. Then Serafin was dragged over.

"Make him go in there," one agent shouted, and they all quickly agreed.

As an agent took off Little Serafin's handcuffs, the prisoner looked longingly at the dirt road leading off the ranch.

"Run, run. Go ahead, run," one of his captors hissed through his teeth. "Please."

When Little Serafin just stood there, unwilling to run and take a bullet in the back, the agent grabbed him by the ear and pulled him into the shack. The agent with the camera cautiously shot over Little Serafin's shoulder, keeping as far away as he could. The video camera still shook with his retching.

Inside the shack, two candles still burned on the floor. Someone had been there to light them that morning. Serafin said he didn't know who had been there.

Next to the candles were four small kettles, one containing the glassy-eyed, severed head of a goat, another holding a dead rooster. In the others lay a rotting turtle, twigs, coins, gold beads, and the grim statue of Eleggua. Scattered on the floor around these pots were dozens of half-smoked La Palma cigars, empty rum and tequila bottles, chile peppers, and pennies for the god of metal, Oggun.

From a roof beam dangled two bloody wires twisted into loops the diameter of human wrists—tools for hanging the dead so their blood could be drained, Little Serafin explained.

Covering everything in that shack were spatters of sticky, black blood. Most of the objects in there were strange to the agents, but if they recognized nothing else from the bizarre rituals practiced in this place, they recognized the blood.

Near the center of the shack squatted a large cauldron crammed with twenty-eight wooden sticks. They were branches cut in arcane ceremonies and used in the rites of Palo Mayombe. The *palos*, or sticks, were plunged into a dark liquid inside the cauldron, mixed in with shells, railroad spikes, bones, peppers, garlic, an Ochosi bow and arrow, scorpions, spiders, a dead black cat, and other objects not readily identifiable: dead things and pieces of dead things.

A black pulpy mass floated in the middle of it all, flecked with fragments of white bone and strands of hair. Recalling Serafin's confession, Benitez realized the black thing was a rotting human brain.

"This is Adolfo's nganga," Little Serafin said. "This is where the spirits live. This is where Mark's brain is."

Much of the stench in the shack emanated from this thing and the rot inside it. An agent barked an order at Serafin and he dragged the nganga to the door, out into the air and the light. The iron pot was heavy and it took several mighty tugs to wrestle the thing out, making Serafin breathe hard. He was retching and gagging when he finally looked up and wiped his hands on his jeans. The agents would not go near that awful pot.

The curandero, Eluterio, gestured to Benitez. The comandante cocked his machine gun and fired a burst into the air, signaling the start of a ceremony to drive away the evil spirits. It was time for an exorcism.

With the grimace of a soldier charging into combat, Eluterio rushed into the shack and began knocking things over. First, he scattered the evil ritual objects around the room while sprinkling holy water from a small bottle. Then he began systematically throwing the dozens of rum bottles as hard as he could to the cement floor of the shack, driving the evil spirits from the place by destroying the vessels that held them in a shower of glass. He tipped over plates and bowls, kicking at them with his white sneakers.

The Mexican police looked on, nodding with approval. They were not interested in preserving evidence, in searching for fingerprints, in photographing the murder scene before it was disturbed—none of the procedures the gringo police treasure above all else. But even if the destruction of such evidence meant letting murderers go free, they would have done nothing differently. There was evil here, and it had to be driven off with rituals more powerful than the black magic Constanzo conjured. To do otherwise would be to court doom. None of the Mexican agents would go in that shack until the black magic had been dispelled.

The Americans were astonished at this display, but dared not object. The Mexican agents seemed on the verge of panic, their fingers still riding the triggers of their rifles. Benitez, his smooth face expressionless and his eyes mere slits, stood impassively, gripping his gun and watching.

Finally, Eluterio emerged, a look of satisfaction on his face. He nodded: It was safe, at least temporarily. The agents relaxed and drew near, peering inside the shack.

Their gaze settled on a stained machete on the floor. Recognizing it as the tool Constanzo used to strike Kilroy down, one of the agents muttered, "That's the goddamn machete."

Serafin actually smiled at this, nodding to confirm the cops' suspicions. "Yes, that's it."

The videotape shows how the agent responded to Serafin's smile. He grabbed the young suspect with one hand and hauled him around the corner of the shack, out of sight of the camera. As he rounded the corner, the agent reached into the nganga and drew out one of the sticks with his free hand. Then the video soundtrack reveals a loud thump, after which the agent came back without the stick, dragging Serafin, whose knees were buckled and whose face was contorted with pain. According to Flores, the agent had teed off on Little Serafin's head like a batter slugging a high fastball.

With the shack's evil disarmed by white magic, it was time to find the body. Then they could all get out. Studying the lumpy soil in the corral, the comandante asked, "Where is Kilroy? Show us the place."

"There's a wire," Serafin answered. "It's easy to find. I'll show you." He led the agents to a patch of dirt just outside the corral. "It's attached to his spine," he added.

The group stopped. There, as Little Serafin had said, was a metal wire, the kind clothes hangers are made from, sticking two to three feet out of the ground. The wire was not a marker, Serafin explained. It was attached to Kilroy's vertebrae so that, once the body was fully decomposed, his spinal column could be pulled free, cleansed of flesh, and ready to be made into a necklace. Adolfo and several other cult members, possibly Sara, wore such necklaces, Serafin said.[4] "I don't have one of my own," he added, almost sorrowfully.

An agent produced a shovel. "Dig," he said.

Serafin hesitated, just for a moment. He looked to his left, where three guns were trained on him. He bent to dig.

The dirt was hard and the digging slow. With each shovelful, the graveyard odor increased. The agents milled around, the sound of digging rising and falling as Serafin labored.

At one point, weary and gagging, Little Serafin asked for a drink of water. The agents were merciless.

"You want water? We'll give you water," one said.

The next moment was edited from the videotape as two of the Mexican agents dragged Little Serafin from his digging and hauled him to a sluggish and polluted irrigation canal north of the corral. They pushed him to his knees and held his head under the foul, muddy water until he was nearly drowned. Then they hauled him back, sputtering and choking.

"You've had your water. Now dig."

When Serafin reached a depth of about four feet, his shovel rang against something hard: bone. Serafin yanked it free of the grave with a pull on the wire. The object on the other end didn't look human, or even real. It was Kilroy's spine and lower back, hacked from his body and buried on top of the other remains.

Benitez couldn't resist a note of macabre humor. "You put a wire up his asshole!" the comandante muttered. He was the only one who laughed at the joke. The sound rang hollow and false in the cold morning air.

The digging continued. Serafin had started at just before eight o'clock and was still at it by ten, his hands torn and bleeding from hacking the month-old grave, when Kilroy's severed legs appeared. They had been cut off just below the knees and again at the ankles.

Someone wanted to know why that was done. Was it part of the ceremony?

"No," Serafin answered. "So he would fit."

Another static-filled pause in the tape. Another beating.

After the legs were pulled out, Serafin had to get down on his knees and dig with his hands, scooping out the brown, loamy under-soil fistful by fistful. The stink must have been unbearable, but Serafin no longer seemed to mind. His face was dreamy, almost peaceful.

Comandante Benitez, meanwhile, was looking at other patches of dirt inside the corral. They were humped high, as if other holes had been dug, then covered over again . . . as if they, too, were graves. The comandante and his men had come out looking for a single body, but at that moment he had a sudden realization.

They had stumbled upon a killing field.

"Others are buried here, too, aren't there?" Benitez asked, his voice a tired monotone.

From his hole, hands and face streaked with dirt, Serafin blandly agreed. "Yes, there are more bodies."

"How many more bodies?" an agent growled.

"*No se,*" Serafin answered. I don't know.

Another edit in the tape.

By this time, Sheriff's Lieutenant Gavito and Brownsville Customs head Oran Neck had arrived, called to the scene by one of the Hernandezes' confiscated car phones, since they had been in charge of the unsuccessful search for Mark Kilroy.

Gavito, a tall, overweight man in a creamy Stetson, towered above the Mexican agents. He immediately began joking and laughing with some of the men assembled at the ranch, trying to relieve their tension. Or his.

Neck, grim and quiet, had the dental charts supplied by Kilroy's parents in a manila folder tucked under his arm. If Kilroy had been buried a month here, he knew the teeth might be the only means of identifying him.

Finally, Serafin emerged from the hole he had dug. Mark Kilroy's body at last was uncovered.

The camera zoomed in for a close-up. Faces grimacing with disgust peered down into the grave. The body had been buried face down. Mark's killers had simply tossed him in and allowed the body to fall however gravity dictated.

The cult's rituals were concerned with killing, not burying, Little

Serafin explained. What came after death was just an inconvenience, like washing the dishes after Christmas dinner.

Someone gingerly reached into the grave and turned Mark Kilroy over to face the cloud-clotted sky. The body was naked, bloated and pale, caked with dirt. Unrecognizable.

The right arm was flung across the chest, as if he had been trying to ward off a blow. Much of his face was still covered with gray duct tape, strangely unsoiled amid this terrible scene. That simple utilitarian tape seemed all the more horrible because it was so completely ordinary.

Neck climbed into the hole with the dental charts, peering at the body, trying to make a match. He was no forensic specialist—the official identification would be made the next day by experts. Nevertheless, at a press conference a few hours later in Brownsville, Neck and Gavito would state that they had found a body, and that it was definitely Mark Kilroy's.

They were, of course, right.

Benitez, meanwhile, radioed his headquarters. He asked for the morgue truck, then he told his dispatcher to send a backhoe.

"There's a lot of digging to be done," he said. "A lot of digging."

When the backhoe had scraped away three or four inches of topsoil from the corral, the outlines of eight more graves stood out in bas-relief, a hellish roadmap guiding the mechanical shovel as it delved deeper.

The rest of the victims were quickly uncovered. One grave alone held three bodies—men who had been tortured, mowed down with a machine gun, then dumped unceremoniously one on top of the other.

All twelve of the dead bodies had been male, not a woman among them. They were buried naked. Most had been mutilated, sodomized, castrated, bludgeoned, and partially decapitated. Brains and hearts had been ripped from the bodies, used in the cult's ritual pursuit of power in ways the lawmen could only guess at.

"All these years a cop," Detective Flores muttered to no one in particular, "and I've never seen anything like this. No one has."

Across the bridge, police descended on the Holiday Inn in Brownsville, ready to arrest the man responsible for the carnage at Rancho

Santa Elena. But they found only an empty room. Adolfo de Jesus Constanzo had been alerted almost immediately of the arrests in Matamoros. He and his closest followers were gone before Little Serafin could confess.

The search for the leader of dead souls had only just begun.

PART II

MAKUTOS AND MASANGOS

(Spells of Protection, Spells of Evil)

An apology for the Devil: It must be remembered that we have only heard one side of the case. God has written all the books.

—SAMUEL BUTLER, "Notebooks"

4

Adolfo de Jesus Constanzo grew up poor, a child of Little Havana's darkest corners, a part of Miami where English is a foreign tongue and black magic is as real as the relentless heat of summer.

His birthplace is a world where brown old men read the future in the hollow rattle of dried kola nuts. Street-corner drug deals conclude just as easily with the crack of gunfire as with the snap of crisp bills. Rock houses dealing crack cocaine may come equipped with altars to the gods of Palo Mayombe, and the local drug smuggler and the local high priest of Santeria might be brother and sister, father and son, or one in the same.

Drugs, worship, and violence have become inextricably linked in the steamy neighborhoods of Miami, where a forty-year tide of immigration has remade the city, making it unlike any place in America, a beautiful and dangerous jewel on the Atlantic. The city pulses now with a vitality and identity never possible when the Miami area was little more than retirees and beachfront. At the same time, though, the atmosphere has been infected by a dark plague of crime and an intense, widespread devotion to magic, primeval and unforgiving.

This mixture grows ever more volatile, fed by an immensely profitable narcotics trade and the ever keener competition it brings among drug smugglers, their rivals, and the police. Always, the smugglers seek an edge—through bribes, extortion, murder. And now, magic.

It came from Africa, ancient beliefs carried by slaves to Cuba and Haiti and now, to the shores of the promised land. Many of Miami's smugglers have roots in rural Cuba or Colombia—lands where magic is deeply ingrained, a part of the culture. It was natural for the smugglers to turn to Santeria and Palo Mayombe. For many, devotion to these religions' darkest teachings came long before they entered the drug trade. Belief was a birthright.

So it was with Adolfo de Jesus Constanzo.

He was born in Miami on November 1, 1962, to a fifteen-year-old refugee from the Cuban revolution, a girl newly arrived in America. Adolfo would be the oldest of four children by three different fathers. He would always be mother's favorite.

When Adolfo was six months old, he was brought before a wealthy palero of Haitian descent, a powerful wizard of Palo Mayombe. This grizzled man held the infant in the crook of his brown arm, blowing thick Cuban cigar smoke around him, then scrutinizing the child through the cottony haze. Little Adolfo remained strangely quiet throughout this examination. He stared up at the old man with wide, dark eyes.

As an adult, Constanzo would tell this story as if he remembered that moment, as if he could still see the old man's dark face looming huge over him.

At last, the Haitian looked away. "The child is a chosen one," he said. "He is destined for greatness, for power."

The palero offered to become Adolfo's teacher, his padrino. Constanzo's mother, already a priestess of Santeria, eagerly accepted this honor.[1]

Many years of study and apprenticeship lay ahead of that baby, but even then, before he could walk or speak or be weaned from his young mother's breast, Constanzo's dark path had been chosen for him.

Squatting before his padrino's blood-caked altar, little Adolfo grew up learning how his spiritual ancestors, the African slaves, brought their beliefs to Cuba. There, the primitive African magic had undergone a fantastic transformation, melding with Christianity into new and strange hybrids.

The Yoruba, a tribe that once ruled what is now southwestern Nigeria, passed on the worship of a pantheon of deities called *orishas,* each with power over a force of nature or an undertaking of man. Eleggua, the trickster, controlled all roads; Olofi was the father of all the orishas; Chango was a warrior, master of lightning, thunder, and fire. There were dozens of other major gods and hundreds of minor deities.

Each god possessed different powers. Each required a different animal to be sacrificed—hen, ram, goat, pheasant, cat—with the animal's blood offered as a sacred gift. The corpses would then be sprinkled with salt or honey and laid before the images of the gods. Whole meals sometimes were prepared and laid out next to the sacrifices for the gods to eat.

By appeasing the right orisha with the correct offering of blood and life, you could gain wealth, love, victory over an adversary, or see the future. Masters of this magic believe they can see events before they occur, stop an enemy before he acts, or cause bullets to pass harmlessly through their bodies. Priests in the religion can use this power to perform *limpias*—cleansings—of the bodies and spirits of believers.

A classic love spell used by many santero priests in Miami requires an appeal to the goddess Oshun, who has power over matters of love, money, and marriage. She is represented by the Christian figure of Our Lady of Charity or a necklace of white and yellow beads. To compel a man to propose marriage, the priest will tell a female client to light a candle to Oshun. Then she must place a photo of her man in a bowl, put five fishhooks over it (each orisha has a number; Oshun's is five), then cover it all with honey—the goddess's favorite food and a symbol for sweet, sticky love. Both candle and bowl must be placed before a statue of Our Lady of Charity, who then will accept the honey as payment and magically use the hooks to ensnare the man's love.

A more extreme and powerful spell requires the lovelorn woman to hollow out the bulbous root of the lily plant, fill it with magical oils, and turn it into a lamp by inserting a cotton wick. The wick first must be soaked in the sperm of her lover, whose will then becomes subject to any person who lights the lamp. He can be compelled to propose marriage—or do anything else—because the sperm represents his very essence. Burning it weakens his willpower.[2]

The most powerful spells in Santeria and Palo Mayombe require bodily fluids, such as sperm or blood, which the believers consider sacred. Even the most benevolent ceremonies and spells require the blood of animals—usually chickens—to be ritually shed and offered to the orishas or the spirits of the dead. This is considered a divine act, not evil—by most.

But a minority of believers worship only the darkest aspect of their religion. For them, the shedding of blood represents a taking of life rather than a freeing of the spirit, a route to evil power. And it need not be relegated to animal blood.

Constanzo's Haitian padrino was such a man. He was not interested in love spells or acts of benevolence, only in spilling blood and taking life. He passed that bloodlust on to his young apprentice, dispensing lessons, beatings, and exposure to the macabre in equal measures until nothing had an effect on him. Adolfo took the beatings as if they were a part of growing up; he met the horror with a child's eagerness.

"This doll is your most hated enemy," his padrino told Adolfo during one lesson. The old Haitian brandished a small rag doll made of black cloth, then doused it in the blood of a freshly killed rooster. "Spill the blood of a chicken on this doll, bury it in a cemetery, then make an offering to Oggun, the god of iron. Your enemy will die in a car accident."

This was knowledge little Adolfo could use, knowledge that would take him places—not like the history and math courses he hated at school. Instead of reading comic books or watching television or playing with other children, Adolfo learned the tales of the orishas: how thunder is the voice of Chango and how Ochosi, the great hunter, accidentally killed his own mother with a cursed arrow intended for a thief. How awful that story was, Constanzo thought. He could never imagine being without his mother. Never.

One true story showed how the Yoruba had fooled their Spanish captors into thinking they had abandoned their native religions. The Spaniards had insisted that their chattel convert to Christianity or die. They were gratified when the slaves immediately seemed to adopt Christ and the Christian saints as their own with almost no objections. And if they wanted to place fruit and dead chickens and other offerings before the crucifix and the figures of the saints, well, it was strange but acceptable, even biblical. Hadn't Abel done much the same, and Abraham?

The Spaniards failed to realize that their slaves had only hidden the old religion behind a mask of Christianity. Deprived of their old totems, the Yoruba and their descendants invested the saints and other Christian images with the same powers as the orishas.

The image of Christ was really Olofi, the creator and the creation, father and son all in one. Chango was Saint Barbara, a cold, golden-haired beauty gripping her fell sword. Eleggua was hidden inside the image of the Christ child; you offered toys and candy to gain his favor.

In time, the religion of the transplanted Yoruba came to be known as Santeria—literally, the path of the saints. The worshipers—in Cuba, then later in America—kept elaborate altars in which figures of Christian saints were draped with beads and arrayed with a host of ritual objects related to each orisha. There would be a bow and arrow for Ochosi, a railroad spike for Oggun, candy for Eleggua.

Because of the bloody religious fervor of the Spanish colonials, these rituals always were cloaked in secrecy. To be found out meant death. Secrecy and distrust of outsiders still pervades these magical religions, as strongly in modern-day Miami as in colonial Cuba.

"Everything must always be done in secret," Adolfo's padrino would tell the wide-eyed boy, punishing the slightest transgression with a beating, then winding up with a moral about the evils of Christians—the nonbelievers. "The fate of the Yoruba slaves must never be forgotten," he'd say, terrifying young Adolfo with images of inquisitors and torture chambers.

At least one hundred thousand active practitioners of Santeria live in Miami today, and several times that nationwide.[3] One estimate puts the number of believers in this secretive merging of Christianity and African magic in the United States at five million and, in all of Latin America, at one hundred million.[4]

A similar, secret melding of religions occurred with the more malevolent beliefs of the Bantu people, in particular those from a region in the African Congo known as Mayombe.[5] They, too, were brought to Cuba by slavers, and they, too, hid their gods inside the saints, using the same names and images as the Yoruba. But the similarities end there.

Although the orishas of Santeria can be capricious and cruel, inflicting terrible punishments and sometimes serving evil ends, they are essentially creatures of light and life—the magic they allow is more often white than black. They form a spiritual link between a believer's ancestors and the forces of nature. Not so the evil gods and spirits of the Congo. The believers of Mayombe sought power over the dead, so they could then wreak death on others. They were interested only in the dark force hidden inside the orishas.

The true power of Congo magic, though, lay in a miniature, magical universe of rot, decay, and death created inside a black cauldron—a feared and secret receptacle called the nganga. Inside this cauldron, the spirit of a dead man could be imprisoned and enslaved. The spirit ruled the little nganga universe, but the magician ruled the spirit. Blood, spices, coins, animal remains, bones, scorpions, spiders, railroad spikes, antlers, and a host of other ingredients make up the nganga universe. Twenty-eight sacred sticks are then thrust into the cauldron, making it resemble some huge and terrible pin cushion. But the single most important ingredient is a human skull and brain, preferably freshly dead, the source of the dead spirit to be entrapped. As more ingredients are added and more spells are cast, the carcasses and blood that feed the spirit begin to rot and stink unbearably—and the nganga becomes all the more powerful.

In time, the religion of the Congolese became known in the Americas as Palo Mayombe. The name derived from the twenty-eight magical sticks used to energize and control the nganga—the Spanish word for stick is *palo*—and the African name for the land where the magic originated.[6]

Like Santeria, Palo Mayombe was exported from Cuba to Miami, then began moving throughout the United States. Once completely separate, in recent years the two religions have become intertwined,[7] as they were in Constanzo's household. Often, believers practice both, keeping an altar of Christian saints dedicated to Santeria in the house for white magic and an nganga outside in the shed or the garage, reserved for black magic.

Most paleros are adamant about keeping the wicked nganga away from living areas. Otherwise, its evil will contaminate the magician's family and homelife, killing everyone in time—much like the slow but deadly effects of exposure to a toxic chemical or radiation. Pregnant women are particularly warned to stay away from the nganga, as if it were some terrible nuclear reactor of evil.

During his training, Adolfo sometimes was allowed into the old shed where his padrino kept his nganga, but he had to wear a blindfold. Only those initiated into the mysteries of Palo Mayombe could look inside the nganga and live, his padrino taught him, another lesson enforced with a beating when Constanzo attempted to peek one day.

"Some day, I'll have my own nganga," eleven-year-old Adolfo declared the first time he breathed deeply of the stench inside that terrible shed.

"You will have the greatest nganga of all," his godfather answered.[8]

There is nothing innately evil about Santeria, or even Palo Mayombe. These religions offer no morality at all—you get out of them what you bring to them.

Most practitioners of these magical religions are law-abiding. They seek success, health, and spiritual well-being, as do the followers of most religions. Many, when sick, will see both a doctor and a santero, doubling in their minds the chances for a cure. And tales of miracle cures abound. They are not religions primarily of the poor and uneducated. Believers come from all classes and backgrounds.

But the amorality of Santeria and Palo Mayombe opens a door to a dark side, in which even the most evil initiate can succeed and be rewarded through the religion. As long as the proper sacrifice is made, any request is permitted. Bad luck, sickness, pain, and death are as easily sought as magical blessings and cures. This is a powerful draw for criminals, for the ancient magic is even better than the expiation of sin Catholicism offers them. In these religions there is no such thing as sin at all.

Adolfo's godfather made a living advising and protecting Miami's drug dealers with his magic.[9] He held ceremonies to stave off arrests, to protect drugs from seizure, and to choose propitious moments to transport a load. There was no stigma in assisting the traffickers, the old man taught his apprentice. "Let the stupid nonbelievers kill themselves with drugs," the palero said. "We will profit from their foolishness."

Believers never use drugs, the old man said. To do so would

mean certain death when the spirits entered your body and found it polluted.

The nonbelievers didn't matter.

Like everything else his padrino taught him, Constanzo took this lesson to heart. Though he would come to buy and sell roomfuls of marijuana and cocaine, he didn't use the drugs himself, nor would he allow his followers to sample the wares.[10]

Thanks to the works of the old Haitian and others like him, courtrooms in Miami must be swept clean almost daily of magical works and spells—*trabajos* as they are called. Bailiffs are continually stumbling on magical powders dusted across the jury seats or small bundles of herbs wrapped around bloody notes containing the names of witnesses, judges, and prosecutors. These are meant to influence the course of trials and testimony. The effect on witnesses who are believers can be devastating. There have been cases in which key witnesses have fled town, changed their stories, or grown ill after learning that a spell had been cast against them. Skeptics call this the power of suggestion at work, or the effects of psychological terrorism.

Believers nod their heads and call it magic.

Headless chickens and other animals, and sometimes human bones and skulls, are found on railroad tracks (a place controlled by Oggun) and at crossroads (for Eleggua). A full-time crew for the Metro-Dade Department of Public Works pulls garbage from the Miami River every day by the ton, much of it related to rituals. In a three-month period in 1989, the crew removed two hundred decapitated (but not plucked) chickens; twenty-two similarly headless ducks; and an assortment of eels, iguanas, pelicans, pigeons, snakes, turtles, cats, and dogs—beheaded or marked in ways consistent with Palo Mayombe and Santeria. One day, a calf's head turned up in a nearby canal with its brain removed.[11] Later, a headless goat was found floating next to a murdered drug trafficker—the santero's way of paying for taking a life by offering another to the orishas.

Cemeteries are a favorite dumping ground as well, fertile ground for curses and talismen. Offerings to the orishas and dolls representing someone's enemy are daily finds. Grave robbing and desecration is a nightly activity in Miami, as paleros dig to obtain the human remains needed for their ngangas. Cemetery operators are loathe to report these deeds because of the negative publicity they generate; people don't want to bury their loved ones in a place frequented by grave robbers.[12]

And when a palero must magically dismantle his nganga, the skull often turns up back at a graveyard, grinning at the lawn cutters and grave diggers who arrive in the morning. The coroner's office in Miami is kept busy trying to determine the origin of such human remains. Were they bought from a medical supply house, a common and legal method used by many paleros? Or were they stolen by grave robbers? Worse still, were they obtained through murder?[13]

Answers come hard, if at all. Often, cases are closed by the coroner without any firm conclusions.

As the War on Drugs began in earnest in Miami in 1979, with bolstered budgets and an influx of narcotics agents, the police began stumbling on strange altars and bizarre objects inside the homes of drug dealers they were busting. Police would arrive to serve an arrest warrant and discover a bristling cauldron with dead animals and a human skull riding on the reeking debris inside, feathers and candles stuck to its yellowing dome. Then the drug investigation became a homicide case, usually unsolvable. Where had the skull come from?

At first, the police had little interest in the religious leanings of drug dealers. Few realized what they were dealing with when they found huge and gaudy displays of Christian saints, Elegguas, Ochosis, and other signs of occult worship at the scenes of drug crimes. And those who noticed didn't really care. What did it have to do with catching crooks?

But a bizarre shooting in 1986 in Miami turned a few cops around. Though department-wide policies have been slow to change, a few individual officers now make it their business to understand the occult.

The shooting occurred during the attempted arrest of a Colombian cocaine smuggler, who also happened to be a devotee of Santeria. DEA agents based in Miami had burst into the man's apartment, guns drawn, shouting, "Police!" They found the suspect sitting unarmed in a chair in the living room, a picture-perfect bust, since all they had to do was slap on the handcuffs. Or so it seemed.

Instead of obeying the armed agents' orders to freeze, the drug dealer leapt up, raced down a hall to a room in the back of his apartment, and slammed the door shut behind him—a fairly unusual reaction for a man staring down the gray metal barrels of six police specials.

As the startled agents took cover at the end of the hallway and ordered the smuggler to surrender, the man suddenly kicked the door open and leapt from the back room. He had donned several beaded necklaces and a golden amulet. The jewelry swayed crazily as he jumped and spun into the hall, a gun in each hand. He came out firing.

One DEA agent was shot through the eye, partially blinding him for life, before anyone reacted to the kamikaze stunt. Then the other agents opened fire and the trafficker died instantly in a hail of bullets.

At first, investigators assumed he had been insane, but later, they pieced together the real story. Some months before, the smuggler had sought protection from a santero priest, who performed a ceremony to make him bulletproof. The priest gave him magical beads and a gold amulet, guaranteeing the protection—so long as his enemies lacked similar immunity. Just as Constanzo had assured the Hernandez boys they were unstoppable, so did this unfortunate trafficker's padrino guarantee his invincibility.

He had seen the agents enter, wearing no protection. They were nonbelievers, vile animals who couldn't pierce his magical shield. The man died thinking he could escape by shooting his way out, certain that his chain of beads had rendered him bulletproof.[14]

Since that shootout, some drug investigators in Miami have made it a point to determine the religious leanings of their targets before rushing in. Metro-Dade Narcotics Officer Bill Gomez goes further still: He wears his own Santeria beads when arresting dealers devoted to that religion or Palo Mayombe.

"It calms them down. They think we're protected, and they don't put up a fight," Gomez explained. "We joked about it; I call it 'Santero Vice,' but it's better than getting shot at."

Of late, the same strange altars and ngangas and human remains grown common in Miami have started turning up amid illegal drugs and dirty money throughout the United States. Police have stumbled on such crime scenes in New York, Houston, Dallas,

San Antonio, Sacramento, Los Angeles, and San Francisco. But Miami is the center, in Little Havana, where the streets teem with such mysteries, where whole stores called *botanicas* deal in nothing but the needs of the city's twenty thousand santero and palero priests. Miami has become America's new Salem, a center for twentieth-century witchcraft, just as it is the nation's center for cocaine.

The witchery was brought by the Cubans who fled Fidel Castro's revolution in the 1950s, Constanzo's mother among them. The magical presence was stoked even further by the infamous Mariel boatlift of 1980, which brought to Miami one hundred thousand earnest Cuban refugees, and another twenty-five thousand devoutly superstitious criminals from Cuba's worst prisons.[15]

Legend among the expatriate Cubans of Little Havana has it that even Castro is a priest of Santeria, as was his predecessor, the U.S.–backed dictator Fulgencio Batista. And all the other Cuban presidents before them.

Some santeros say Castro and Batista fought not only with armies on the battlefield but with magic, dark and hidden. Castro's sorcery was more powerful in the end, but not powerful enough to destroy Batista, who was able to flee to Spain with millions plundered from the Cuban treasury. According to the legend, Castro's soldiers were paralyzed by an invisible force as they stormed the Presidential Palace, giving Batista a chance to escape in a waiting helicopter.[16] He was invisible, protected—a familiar Santeria theme.

It was one of Adolfo Constanzo's favorite stories.

5

If Miami was the ideal breeding ground for a fledgling padrino, Delia Aurora Gonzalez del Valle was the ideal mother.

She showed him the way.

Adolfo Constanzo's earliest childhood memory was not of a favorite toy or a parent's smile, but the gurgling death rattle of a chicken's slit throat, its blood offered up to ancient African gods. He knew a home filled with decay and blood, inuring him to death. His reward for good behavior was the gift of an animal to mutilate and kill.[1]

From infancy, Adolfo found comfort in the smell of death and rotting flesh, not the morning smells of frying bacon and brewing coffee. Those odors were alien to him, strange scents emanating from the neighbors' homes in the quiet Miami suburb of his youth.

"Stay away from them," his mother would say when Adolfo went outside to play. "They do not believe. They are animals."[2]

Blood, death, and belief: Those were the three themes of Adolfo's childhood, drummed into him over and over by his mother and his Haitian padrino.

There was the power that shedding blood brought, the essence of Santeria. Give blood to the gods, and they will answer your prayers.

There was the daily embrace of death and decay inside Delia's filthy and bloodstained home, the basis of Palo Mayombe's magic. Above all, a palero must relish the stench of decomposing flesh, for he must take the evil spirits of the dead inside him, becoming possessed by them.

And finally, there was the firm conviction that nonbelievers were more worthless than the animals sacrificed at Delia's altar. No difference.

This was Constanzo's substitute for a moral code, the path his mother taught him when he came home from school and the truly important studies began. The opposing teachings of schools, church, and law had to be tolerated—they were cover, part of the secret, a gesture toward normalcy—but everything else in young Adolfo's life seemed designed to counter those influences. Even the teachings of mainstream Santeria, which emphasize spiritual peace, balance, and tolerance of others' beliefs, were forsaken by Delia.

At her thick knee, Constanzo learned not to fight children with fists but to curse them, to skulk through the night to leave headless chickens lying on their doorsteps, evil notes tied inside their severed necks—dark appeals to the gods to sicken or destroy.[3]

Neighbors of the Constanzo clan sometimes made such grisly finds, a note of reeking horror lying next to the morning paper, an ugly gift tucked in with the mail. They always suspected Delia and her silent, brooding Adolfo, though they never caught them in the act.

Troublemakers, one neighbor called them. Her son had argued with Delia one day; the next, a headless chicken lay bleeding on their doorstep. Down the street, on another neighbor's doorstep, a headless goose was found, its severed head wrapped in a red handkerchief lying next to it, string tied around its beak. All it took was parking in a space Delia coveted, or perhaps staring too long at the family's litter-strewn yard, or simply attempting to exchange pleasantries with the rotund and unpleasant Delia. Worst of all was insulting her precious Adolfo.

More than once, Adolfo had run to his mother in a rage and she had stormed outside, cursing the children who had dared mock her son. "Do you know who we are?" she would scream, as if they were royalty. Then she would shout obscenities at them, while Adolfo stood shielded by her bulk, smiling.

That night there would be magic in the house, an offering to the saints. A doll to bloody and bury. That was how you got revenge, Constanzo learned. With magic.

And if the magic didn't work, the fear it generated worked just as well, he soon realized. People steered clear. It didn't matter if the magic was real or not. It only mattered what people believed.

From the time Adolfo was one until he was age ten, the family lived in San Juan, Puerto Rico, where his mother worked in advertising and marketing. In 1972, Adolfo and his family returned to Miami for good.

Little is known of Constanzo's years in San Juan, other than his mother's assertion that he was a good, quiet child, chosen as a Catholic altar boy and gifted at tennis.

But a family friend and eventual follower of Constanzo, Maria del Rocio Cuevas Guerra, recalled that little Adolfo's training in the occult also began in Puerto Rico, with side trips to Haiti, where Voodoo, the sister religion of Palo Mayombe, is practiced widely.[4] Delia and Constanzo's younger brother, Fausto, however, deny this vehemently, saying they were good Catholics. The Constanzo family consistently has denied involvement in magical religions, despite overwhelming evidence and testimony to the contrary.[5]

Yet at the same time, Delia and Adolfo's brother often bragged of his mystical abilities. They would say Adolfo began to develop strange powers as a child, just as his Haitian padrino had predicted. They boasted he could travel outside his body and that he displayed extrasensory perception by age thirteen. He could read the thoughts of the living and contact the spirits of the dead, and his touch could heal the sick and troubled, Delia claimed.

When he turned fourteen, Adolfo had a vision of Marilyn Monroe, after which he assured his mother, who was a fan of the late sex symbol, that Monroe had not committed suicide after all. Later, in 1980, Constanzo is said to have correctly predicted President Reagan would be shot but would survive. "He knew things," said Delia.[6]

"What he said came true," brother Fausto Rodriguez said.

Others in Miami tend to view claims of Constanzo's psychic prowess less charitably. "The mother used to brag about how powerful her kid was," said Ernesto Pichardo, a priest of Santeria in

Miami and an unofficial spokesperson for the religion. "You listen to her, you'd think he was another Messiah."

Upon the family's return to Miami, Delia kept sheep and chickens in the eternally fouled and filthy yard of the one home she owned, a dark, Spanish-style house on 94th Court in suburban Coral Park Estates, where Adolfo spent the rest of his childhood.

A neighbor saw a member of the family leave the body of a decapitated goat lying in the street late one night. Complaints to the police led nowhere.

Delia would never answer the door when someone knocked, a lifelong pattern. Letter carriers, police, landlords, visitors of any kind—no one ever got in without breaking in.

Neighbors shunned the family in fear and revulsion. None of the children would play with Adolfo or his brothers and sister. Delia's neighbors in Coral Park Estates rejoiced when the bank foreclosed on her in 1984, forcing her and her brood to begin a long series of moves.

Constanzo's father had fled Delia long before, when Adolfo was only six months old. There was a kindly stepfather for a time, who died of cancer just after the move back from Puerto Rico when Constanzo was ten. There followed a second stepfather and a third, men who arrived in rapid succession, who had little fondness for Adolfo, and who departed quickly through the magic of divorce. They left behind two younger brothers and a sister for Adolfo.

Delia's third husband disliked Adolfo intensely, punishing him and beating him frequently, Constanzo's brother Fausto recalled.

"But my mother didn't want anyone punishing him but her. That's why they got a divorce."[7]

It was Delia alone who occupied the center of Adolfo's universe, his guide through the maze of orishas and magic and blood sacrifice, showing him how to tend his altar of saints, how to ask those ceramic figures with their staring eyes for favor.

Hidden in the back of the house, there was always the nganga, bristling with gnarled sticks. Together, they would stir that magic pot—"playing" with the nganga, paleros call it—conjuring evil spells with a cauldron bubbling, not with witches' brew but with rot and decay.[8] His devotion was cemented by this bizarre upbringing, and it never failed. He was always her precious Adolfo. He always called her Mommy.

Mommy was a habitual criminal, with a dozen aliases, innumerable addresses, and no legitimate source of income.[9] She has been convicted of grand theft, writing hot checks, and child neglect, and she has been arrested for criminal trespass, armed assault, and shoplifting (with her daughter, fifteen years old at the time, as an accomplice). Despite her lengthy record, Delia's plethora of aliases, married names, and changing addresses has so confused the court record that she has been treated repeatedly as a first-time offender, then let loose from jail even though arrest warrants on her were outstanding.[10]

Even Delia's physical descriptions have varied wildly, frustrating police attempts to keep track of her. One arrest report in 1986 describes her as five feet, six inches tall, 155 pounds, with black hair and brown eyes. A year later, another arrest description puts her at five feet, eight inches tall, an obese 180 pounds, with black eyes and a mole on her nose.

Her pattern of crime stretches across more than ten years and thirty separate court cases, showing how she and her children would let the eviction notices and unpaid rent bills pile up, then suddenly and quietly leave with their former homes in shambles. Then they would do it again. And again. They would change the locks and the landlords would come to the door and pound and pound. Delia would never answer, never leave until she was just one step ahead of the handcuffs.

Time after time, landlords happy to be rid of the Constanzo clan would open the door to reclaim their apartments only to find the living quarters transformed into dark and filthy caverns—robbed, vandalized, and filled with spattered blood, animal droppings, and human excrement. They would leave behind destroyed electrical appliances—battered with a club or some other blunt instrument. Bathroom fixtures and faucets would be stolen or twisted into useless pieces of iron. Holes would be pounded into walls, feces and decaying food would be strewn across carpeting, all of it swarming with maggots, roaches, and other crawling insects. Even electrical outlets would be pried loose and stolen.[11]

Invariably, signs of occult worship were found as well, left behind amid the stinking refuse: an altar to Santeria in the house or, in one case, a reeking nganga that police stumbled upon during a search for stolen property. At one of her old houses, stained clothes were found buried in the backyard.

The areas Delia chose to live in were always unkempt, filled with run-down frame houses where the ragged lawns were never trimmed. But they always lived near the mansions of the very prosperous. Despite her noxious life-style, Delia had come to America with visions of an ideal life in the promised land, insisting she would become wealthy and that one day her precious Adolfo would be a star. Though her houses were always tucked behind some industrial plant or shopping center, where the heat boiled off the asphalt parking lots like steam from a cauldron, she could still turn to Adolfo, point at the nearby prosperity, and say, "Someday, you'll be just as rich. Richer."

This is the sort of mother Constanzo had:

In April 1987, police arrived at a supposedly vacant apartment in the tiny city of Sweetwater, just outside Miami's city limits, skirting the dank eastern edge of the Everglades. Delia and her children—minus Adolfo, who had struck out on his own by then—had taken up residence in the vacant apartment without permission from the owner, having skipped out on a previous landlord without paying the rent. Someone in the neighborhood had reported a "foul odor" emanating from the apartment's barred doors and windows a few weeks after Delia began squatting there.

When Officer Maria Elena Pla knocked on the door, Delia stuck to her usual tactic: She didn't answer. When Pla opened the unlocked apartment door, the stench almost knocked her over. It was so bad, Pla thought there might be a dead body inside. She summoned other officers for backup and waited until they arrived. Anything could be in there, she thought.

Once the reinforcements came, they ventured inside. Twenty-seven animals roamed through the dark, filthy house—hens, geese, roosters, goats. Plates of blood lay scattered across the floor, slopping on the rug, congealed and festering. The sickened officers called out "Police," several times. They heard no reply.

As Pla ventured upstairs, she saw dried feces and blood caked on the stairway carpet and walls. At the second-floor landing, piles of newspapers stained with urine and blood greeted her. Then at the sound of the approaching officers, Delia opened her bedroom door, peered out at the police, then slammed the door shut again, locking herself in.

"Open up or I'll break it down," Pla shouted.

Finally, Delia acquiesced. The door creaked open, letting out a rush of foul air.

Inside the bedroom the police found Delia's youngest son, a mentally disabled fourteen-year-old named Alejandro, lying in a bed covered with urine and old feces.

Little Aurora, then eleven and Delia's youngest, was also lying in a filthy bed in another bedroom. She blinked mutely at the stunned officers, cowering like some nocturnal animal spooked by approaching headlights.

All the bedrooms, including Delia's, had garbage, feces, papers, and empty food boxes and cans scattered throughout. Animals milled everywhere.

Amid the refuse, Pla and the other officers were shocked to find a pile of cash, stocks, bonds, and property records showing Delia owned real estate. An inventory of the property seized from the apartment would later show Delia also had a $3,500 white mink jacket, a $2,300 fox-lined suede coat, a $4,000 gray Canadian fox jacket, and a $1,800 blue fox stole. All were in Delia's size, incongruous in Miami's tropical swelter. All had been sent by her loving son, Adolfo.

Along with the furs, police found $450 in cash, $950 in gold jewelry, two cordless phones, and several videotaped movies, including *Animal House* and *Prom Night,* a bloody B-grade slasher film.

"Why would you live like this if you don't have to?" Pla asked, staring at the reeking mess and the children's vacant eyes, then at the pile of furs and jewelry.

Delia just shrugged.

When police arrested and handcuffed her, she screamed obscenities. She was later convicted of child neglect.

She got probation and kept her children. Nothing changed.[12]

Throughout his youth, Adolfo was an obedient, devoted son, always giving his mother presents, always turning to her for advice.

When he finally left home for Mexico—a reluctant parting in

1984—Adolfo continued to send money home, keeping Delia in furs and stereos. She and her other children visited him often, at his expense.

While under her tutelage, little Adolfo embraced everything his mother taught him, except for one strange deviation: He became obsessively neat. Though the rest of the family home might be squalid, his room was always a spotless oasis, his closet and clothes arranged just so.

From the time he was one year old, Adolfo always laid out his robe next to his bed, so he could put it on should he have to rise in the night. His clothes had to be folded neatly and put away, or he couldn't sleep. He washed himself three or four times a day.

In later years, even as a fugitive, he relentlessly ordered his followers to keep their hideouts immaculate: tubs and toilets scrubbed, kitchen cabinets organized, groceries lined up like soldiers at attention. Messes could send him into frothing rages.

Many of his followers would find this obsession strange in a man so dedicated to the rot of decomposition, who found the stench of death so appealing.

In a life programmed for him from infancy, neatness was Constanzo's one pitiful act of rebellion.

6

Even in the stifling gloom of the little shed, the black stain of spilt blood remained visible on the packed dirt floor. Animal blood or human? Adolfo didn't know. Nor did he care.

To the initiate, just twenty-one years old, the puddles of dried blood seemed almost to glow with power, the sacred *menga,* the essence of life. Adolfo stared in fascination, not horror. His padrino had never let him in this place before without a blindfold.

The aluminum shed lay in back of the old Haitian's house, the kind of place other homeowners use to store lawnmowers and dusty boxes of Christmas decorations. Not here.

There were no windows in this place. The door was shut tight. The room was eight feet long, narrow as a coffin. Inside, the air was ovenlike with Miami's summer heat. An odor of rotting carrion assailed Adolfo's nostrils, a graveyard reek mingled with the scent of cigars and rum and, pervading all, the coppery scent of fresh blood.

In the sunlight seeping in at the base of the shed's walls, Adolfo could make out a cauldron filled with sticks. It was the nganga his padrino had taught him about but never before let him see. Adolfo knew, though he could not see it through the gloom, that a human skull, doused in blood, lay at the center of the dread cauldron, the key to the nganga's terrible power.

"It is time," the padrino said.

Adolfo stiffened as the old man reached behind his head and placed the blindfold over his eyes. Adolfo's lips felt dry and cracked, his throat constricted, his body drenched in sweat. But he would not show fear, not to anyone, not even to his padrino. This was the day Adolfo had long awaited, the day he would be *rayado en palo*—"cut" into the cult of Palo Mayombe.

The term was literal. Adolfo could hear his padrino's knife against the wetstone, a grating screech that set his nerves on edge, a sharp blade to carve the mystical symbols of Palo Mayombe into his flesh.

On this day in 1983, Adolfo the apprentice would become Adolfo the master. He, too, would be a padrino.

"I will not fear," he told himself, teeth clenched as the scrape of knife on stone continued. The dark world of the dead would open to him today, Constanzo told himself. He would inherit power over men's souls. He would learn to cast the *makutos* and the *masangos,* magical spells that would protect him from evil and allow him to work evil on others.

Then he would become rich and powerful; he would immerse himself in blood and money. Adolfo felt an almost sexual thrill at the image of it. Today his soul would die. And he would be reborn.

His padrino pulled him from his reverie, asking him the ritual questions.

"Yes," Adolfo answered, he had followed instructions scrupulously. He had slept seven nights under the sacred ceiba tree. He had taken the ritual baths in secret herbs.

"Yes," he had brought his white clothes to a cemetery and buried them in a fresh grave for three weeks, as instructed. And yes, today he had retrieved those clothes and put them on, the cemetery dust thick in his nostrils, a dank smell of death he had inhaled like a rare perfume.

Finally, he answered, "Yes," he had given daily thanks and offerings to *kadiempembe,* Constanzo's personal guiding spirit—Palo Mayombe's version of the devil, devourer of souls.

"Is this what you desire?" the padrino asked, the final question in the ritual. "For after today, there is no going back. Once you accept kadiempembe, once you are rayado, God is no more for you. Your soul will die."

"My soul is dead," Constanzo replied, never hesitating. "I have no God."

Speaking in the ancient, dead language of the Congo, the padrino summoned the spirits of the dead as he brushed his blindfolded apprentice's body with branches of the ceiba tree wrapped with herbs. The branches scratched across Adolfo's sweat-slick skin, an angry tickle.

Then his padrino ran a live chicken up and down Constanzo's trembling body. Adolfo felt the caress of its feathers, heard the chicken's muffled clucking as the animal magically drew everything foreign from his body, making him pure, ready to accept the spirits of the dead inside him. Then came the sound of a strangled death cry as the padrino slit the chicken's throat. A moment later, Adolfo heard its blood dripping into the cauldron, menga to give the spirits power. To give him power.

A sizzling sound and an acrid smell followed—gunpowder burning explosively on the tip of padrino's knife, held over the flame of a candle.

Next he felt a burning pain in his left shoulder, followed by another intense pain in his right. The hot blade was scoring him, moving with surgical skill. He was being marked, *rayado;* he was being given the scars of the palero. The marks would be his personal signature, his *firma,* different from all other paleros, a crosshatch of arrows and bows and exes.

The agony of the cutting brought tears to his eyes, yet it was a pain he treasured. As the blood coursed down his back, a warm trickle of power, the blindfold was suddenly ripped from his eyes. His heart pounded in rhythm with the pulsing pain in his shoulders. He felt giddy, reborn.

Candles burned now, lighting the nightmarish scene before him, a montage of slaughtered animals, human remains, offerings to pitiless gods of evil. Blood covered everything. Fat flies circled lazily in and out of the light, their buzzing filling Constanzo's head.

In one hand the padrino held a bloody knife. In the other he held out a gift to Adolfo, a long, thin object inside a black cloth bag.

Adolfo eagerly opened it and pulled free the *kisengue,* the palero's sceptre. With it, Adolfo would rule the powers of darkness. It was a human tibia, stripped of flesh, polished and smooth and white. Truly, he was now a member of the cult of Palo Mayombe.

Adolfo gripped the bone hard and shook it defiantly, his eyes fixed on the skull at the center of his master's nganga.

"Come," the padrino said after a moment, opening the door to the shed. "We have work to do. It is time you had your own nganga."

Adolfo turned to him, reluctantly tearing his eyes from the cauldron. "Where will I find a skull for my nganga, Godfather?"

The Haitian smiled mirthlessly. In a moment the same smile twitched onto Constanzo's lips. Adolfo realized they would do whatever it took to get a skull, without compunction, compassion, or fear. Desecration, murder, what did it matter?

That was the beauty of having no soul: utter freedom.[1]

Young, darkly handsome, his face an appealing yet emotionless mask, Constanzo was nevertheless an outcast once he gave his soul to kadiempembe. His mother and his godfather had seen to that.

His few bouts with normalcy had failed. Young Adolfo's grade-school performance was lackluster. Later he tried college, enrolling in a community school, but he dropped out after a single semester. Schoolwork was not for him, not because he lacked intelligence but because he simply wasn't interested.

For the same reason he had shown little aptitude for a career; he had lost the few jobs he ever held, all of them menial. He talked of becoming a fashion model, but it was just talk.

In 1981, Adolfo tried shoplifting, a crime at which his mother was most proficient. But even at that, he was a failure, arrested twice, one time for stealing clothes, the other for trying to leave a store with a chainsaw.

His mother had a more lasting impact in another area, though. He remained the dutiful son, never bothering the jealous Delia by bringing home girls. He knew no girl would ever match his mother's standards, his vision of the perfect woman. Instead, Constanzo had roamed Miami's gay bars since his late teens, looking for submissive men he could dominate or, when the mood struck him, humiliate.

In addition to black magic, his padrino had initiated him into homosexuality during their times together in the reeking shed, surrounded by blood and rot. In time, Constanzo found the trappings of death in his godfather's shed increased his pleasure in sex.

Indeed, only in this shed did the young Adolfo seem to succeed at anything. Inside the shed, at the altar of death or when he was seized by the spirits and seemed to know the future, Constanzo became the star Delia always wanted him to be, his followers would later say. Because of this, his path seemed obvious: He, too, would rule such a place. He, too, would bring initiates inside a dark temple and take them down the magical path to power.

He would learn to lead, he vowed. And an outcast he'd no longer be.

Once he was cut into Palo and had learned the curious art of constructing an nganga, Adolfo was ready to conduct his own magic. There was a great deal of money to be made through black-magic trabajos, both in the legitimate role as healer and adviser, and in the dark role as a magical gun for hire to the drug dealers.

Constanzo knew his padrino had made a small fortune protecting the cocaine dealers, striking out at their enemies and the police, leaving the little bundles in courtrooms, digging away in the cemeteries at night. He was ready to do the same.

The old Haitian sometimes went further than most other paleros, not content to deal strictly with skulls rooted from freshly dug graves, Constanzo knew. In his youth in Haiti, the old man said, he had killed for his skulls, had felt the power of the knife as he cut open a man's chest, exposing the beating heart, the ultimate sacrifice. He had told Constanzo of the strength that lay in murder, the overwhelming power it brought.

"You will know such power some day," the old man said vaguely. Such talk terrified young Constanzo, and excited him.

After much discussion with his mother and his padrino, Constanzo decided that his best opportunities lay outside Miami. He needed fertile, new territory, where his black-magic beliefs and his burgeoning psychic powers would be most appreciated. He decided upon Mexico.

Adolfo and his mother had visited Mexico City together several times that year at the old man's suggestion. Constanzo had seen the card readers preying on the tourists and the rich. He had seen the way Mexicans fear and respect the power of magic in ways the gringos did not, and could not. They knew little of Santeria and Palo Mayombe in Mexico, but that could change quickly. Constanzo could see to that.

Yes, it would be perfect. He could start a dual trade there. He could finally find work as a model—a perfect cover and a perfect entree—while building his reputation as a witch. During his visits to Mexico City in 1983, he had met a man with contacts in the modeling industry, and the man, attracted to Constanzo, said he would help get Constanzo's career started, promising him fame and money.

Adolfo certainly was good looking enough for the part—a trim five feet, eleven inches, and 160 pounds, with long black hair and delicate eyelashes that softened his stern, angular face. He had grown from a pouting tattletale of a child into a man who moved with a quiet yet arrogant grace, a seemingly supreme confidence. You could see it in his face, even in photos, a look that dismissed his surroundings but which, when he wished it, could favor a person with an intent, probing stare. Something about that look attracted; more than a few men and women would vie for the chance to be the object of his dark stare. Few could see the outcast within him.

To his family, the move to Mexico and the promise of stardom were prophetic: Delia always had said he would be a star someday. "People were always asking, 'Who's that?'—everybody believing he was somebody and asking if he's a movie star," she once said. "He had cachet."[2]

In mid-1984, Constanzo packed his bags and kissed Delia goodbye, promising to call and write often. He would keep her constantly informed of his inevitable climb to wealth and stardom, he swore.

He would take his time at first, work the simplest magic, card readings, and spiritual cleansings, nothing too risky. He would build toward his goal slowly, making money, finding true believers, constructing the dread nganga, and then . . .

"Then your time will come," the old Haitian whispered. "You'll know when. And the power you have now will grow even greater."[3]

7

When everything is just right, when the phones are working and the electricity is on and the roads haven't washed out and the winds, for once, have scrubbed the chocolate-pudding skies blue, then Mexico City seems a wondrous place, an urban oasis.

So long as this fragile equilibrium remains undisturbed, so long as nothing goes wrong, Mexico is a city of the world, a great metropolis, romantic, cultured, and vibrant.

Imposing European edifices frown down on sprawling plazas, whispering of history and dead kings. Museums and galleries abound.

Massive cathedrals jockey with archaeological digs at their feet, excavations baring ancient Aztec splendors, spirits of two eras forever side by side. Expansive parks, emerald leaves lush and glistening, claim huge swaths of the city, their twisting paths revealing the Mexicans' endless passion for monuments, for lost causes and forgotten heroes.

This is the Mexico City of tourists, a cultured place of expensive restaurants, rude waiters, nighttime trysts, and cappuccino in chic cafes.

But most of all, it is a creature that lives solely in one-week installments, a city found imprinted only on vacationers' color film, filtered through tinted tourist cab windows and reflected in hotels' mirrored lobbies.

It is the Mexico City seen from your 747 window as you settle back and relax, a perfect green gem that shrinks and fades from view while the jetliner climbs safely away, bound for home. It is a mirage.

For those who live out their lives in it, there is another Mexico City—for them, the *real* Mexico City. Theirs is the place where nothing is ever just right.

Scratch that veneer of civilization ever so slightly, pull back the Teflon-thin coating of twentieth century, and the real Mexico City floods forth, a place of squalor and poverty, where the air is certifiably toxic, where corruption is rampant and the water is undrinkable.

This is also a city with many a dark place, full of crime and mystery and black magic, steeped in beliefs that have no place in a modern city, no paragraph in the tourist guide book.

Here, the hotel maid who fled her tiny village's poverty will tell you no, she does not understand what allows the light to be trapped in a light bulb. Is it magic?

Here, the housewives and businessmen frequent the tea-leaf reader and the card reader and the curandero.

There is a witch's market downtown and it thrives, a place where luck can be bought and revenge exacted with a pin and a doll. Walk down the narrow aisles of Mercado Sonora, crammed with black candles and strange powders, and you can feel it. The air vibrates with the hot pulse of the primitive: a thousand invisible drums beating to rhythms our minds have forgotten but our genes still know, embedded memories longing to be wakened.

In Mexico City, they do awaken. The old spirits that dwell in the Aztec ruins are as alive as the Christian saints, and here, both have more power over men's thoughts than science and civilization. The twentieth century is easy to turn from when nothing is ever right, when the telephones don't work and the electricity is off and the polluted sky is a noxious brown. The modern world seldom works here longer than a tourist's camera snap, but the old world has always been there, reliable, ready, waiting.

These two faces of Mexico City wage constant war on one another, a daily battle between the primitive and the civilized, darkness and light—though who, it might be asked, is to say which is which?

It is a place that suited Adolfo de Jesus Constanzo well. Two sides, dark and light: The city was a mirror of the man.

There was the Constanzo who startled and amazed, the santero priest who had learned to roll a handful of seashells, stare at their pattern, then pin you to your chair with that dark, flat stare of his. He would read the shells and their intricate patterns and he would know things, secret things he could not have possibly known or guessed or paid to learn. Your hidden, dark truths, internal whispers you had scarcely told yourself, suddenly streamed from his lips.

Those sixteen little cowrie shells would tumble from his hand and he would seem to *know* you, completely, terrifyingly. His predictions would inevitably come true and then you were locked in. You kept coming back. You were his.

And slowly, so slowly, he led you away from the innocuous healing ceremonies, the spells for success and readings of the future. Little by little he revealed the true nature of his magic and the evil spirits he worshiped—a slow walk into darkness with this handsome, compelling man, until suddenly, without meaning it, your hands were bloody, too. And before you knew it, you were across the line. You were like him: part of the night, dark and soulless and free. Except you weren't really free.

You were his.

Omar Francisco Orea Ochoa was obsessed with the occult—had been ever since he was fifteen, when he begged an old gypsy to read his palm. The crone had gripped his hand in her rough claw and hissed his future: Omar would meet a powerful man some day, someone who would alter his life and determine his destiny. Be ready, the old woman told him. Beware.

By the time he had finished prep school, Omar had read every dusty library book he could find on astrology, magic, the tarot, and witchcraft, looking for clues to his future. Some of the books were so old they came apart in his hands as he eagerly turned the pages. His school notebooks were filled with obscure, mystical verses and strange drawings—occult doodles that absorbed far more of his attention than classwork.

In the spring of 1983, Omar left his parents' home in Puebla, a state capital sixty miles southeast of Mexico City. He entered the

National University, with plans to study journalism. But Omar's studies faltered when the young student, then barely eighteen, discovered the fast, dark life of the capital city's red-light district, the Zona Rosa.[1] He found it a place where occult worship was fashionable, and where his budding homosexuality stirred no comment.

Located near the broad greensward of Paseo de la Reforma, a boulevard cutting diagonally through the heart of Mexico City, the Zona Rosa is a curious mixture of tourist traps, street entertainers, fine restaurants, art galleries, fortune tellers, and sex for sale. For Omar, the zone was a dream come true.

Slight and waifish, almost elfin with his arched eyebrows and pointed chin, Omar quickly found a niche in the noisy gay bars of the Zona Rosa, where he soon became a familiar figure. One by one, he sought out the card readers and mystics who worked the zone, looking for the man he believed he was destined to meet.

Eventually, a gay former model named Jorge Montes, who, at age fifty still dyed his hair blonde, befriended Omar after reading his fortune in the cards. Years before, as his face began sagging with wrinkles and deep, sad pouches beneath each eye, Montes had given up the fashion business to become a witch. By the time he met Omar, he was an old hand at the city's flowing trade of mystics and card readers. He was known to most of his clients as Doctor Hindu because of his fondness for Indian artifacts and Buddhas, a motif that crammed his apartment on Calle Londres (London Street) in the once regal, now decaying neighborhood called Colonia Juarez.

Montes specialized in reading the Spanish cards, a forty-eight-card fortune-telling deck in which the suits are represented by wine cups, swords, clubs, and gold coins. He had adopted various aliases to suit differing clientele: Carta Brava for gays, Doctor Hindu for the housewives, and Doctor Salvador Antonio Villazo for underworld figures best kept in the dark about his true identity.

Once they were friends, Omar moved in with Montes for a time, passing himself off as the older man's nephew. Neighbors in the dingy apartment building at Calle Londres 31 assumed they were lovers, but no one was going to upbraid Montes. He had been a polite, helpful, and always discreet resident in the building for fifteen years, liked by all. He was known around the neighborhood simply as "the man with the dogs" because of his seven French poodles.[2]

A few months after meeting Omar, in April of 1983, Montes heard about a new card reader working the Zona Rosa. This newcomer was supposed to be something special, he told Omar.

"Let's go find him," Omar suggested.

It didn't take long for the pair to locate the new card reader holding court at a sidewalk cafe near the corner of Calle Londres and Genoa in the heart of the Zona Rosa.[3]

At a table close to the bustle of the street, they saw a tall, light-skinned man with dark, long hair, dressed impeccably in American sportswear, shuffling a deck of cards. With him sat two young women, all blonde hair and American giggles, eagerly watching his manicured fingers manipulate the deck. The card reader looked bored.

At his side was a young man, dark, short, muscular. This man never spoke, never smiled. He reminded Omar of the grim men in sunglasses who guard presidents and movie stars, their heads always turning to survey passersby, their mouths frozen in thin, humorless lines.

Omar and Jorge drew near to watch the throw of the cards. They could hear the *cartomatico*'s accented Spanish, the Florida-Cuban twang to it, as he shifted from their language to English for his customers' benefit. Omar could tell he was American.

Glancing up at Omar and Jorge, he nodded, inviting them to approach. Omar noted a peculiar look of recognition in the foreigner's eyes, as if he had expected them. Suddenly, Omar felt light-headed.

After a few minutes the reading was done, the girls handed over twenty-five dollars each, then left, looking a little disappointed at not being asked to linger. The man with the cards never gave them a second look as they drifted out of the cafe.

"Join us," the man said, looking at Omar, then gesturing to the two empty chairs across from him. "I am Adolfo de Jesus Constanzo."

He did not offer his hand. Constanzo rarely shook hands with anyone.

Omar and Jorge introduced themselves. Constanzo spoke for the silent man beside him, Martin Quintana Rodriguez, whom he described as his *mano derecha*, his right hand—a bodyguard. Martin merely scowled, obviously resenting the intrusion.

"I will throw the cards for you," Constanzo said abruptly, staring at Omar.

Then, flipping through the deck, he began turning up cards. In a disconcertingly disinterested voice, he began revealing subtle truths about Omar's past, his family, his ambitions, his desires. The drone of traffic and conversation at the cafe seemed to fade into a distant buzz as Omar listened, staring at this strange man who seemed, impossibly, to have known him all his life.

Omar, of course, was predisposed to believe, yet his was a reaction many experienced after Constanzo performed a reading—an eerie sensation of unreality, where the mental landscape loses its accustomed firmness. Somehow, Constanzo knew intimate secrets of others' lives.

This card reader did not speak in the ambiguous Jell-O talk Jorge used when reading the cards, where every prediction sounded like a fortune cookie—homogenized, pat, never wrong because it says nothing.

This was breathtakingly different. Adolfo knew where Omar was from, what he did at school, how his classes bored him, how he had suffered all his life. Who he was.

"It's been difficult for you, being different from others," Constanzo said sagely, a hint of sadness and, Omar thought, camaraderie in his voice. "I know what you feel. But soon that will change."

Sitting there, Omar forgot about Jorge. He stopped being aware of Martin's glaring presence, the waves of anger—or was it jealousy?—boiling off the silent right-hand man. Everything else faded, and Omar felt a deep attraction to this American, the beginnings of an obsession.

"You are about to fulfill a prophesy from your youth," Constanzo told him, looking up from the cards and smiling darkly, knowingly. "An old woman told you to be ready for this moment. She told you to beware.

"But there is nothing for you to be wary of now. Do you not feel I am right?"

And Omar remembered the palm reader from years ago, the old

gypsy who had given him hope through the painful years of adolescence, whose prediction had made livable the daily horror of growing up gay in this most macho of cultures.

"Yes . . . I've been waiting for you," Omar blurted, as Constanzo flipped the last card in the deck.

Adolfo smiled, almost gently.

"I know," he said.[4]

Once the cards were neatly stowed in their box, the men talked for hours at the sidewalk cafe. Even Martin relented in his initial hostility, though he did insult Omar numerous times until Adolfo scolded him for it. Then the young tough seemed cowed, like a child spanked by his father.

Adolfo explained to Omar and Jorge that he lived in Miami with his family, but that he was staying in Mexico City for weeks at a time in order to establish his business. He did not specify what that business was. "I'm just beginning to explore the city's . . . potential," he said.

During his recent visits to Mexico, Adolfo was living with Martin and Martin's mother on Calle China in nearby Colonia Popotla, he told Omar and Jorge.[5]

"I met Martin in this very cafe, just a few weeks ago," Constanzo told them. He made it sound as though the meeting was not accidental, but foretold. Just as he was attracting Omar with his ability to read the magical cards, so had Constanzo drawn Martin Quintana to his side. Using his apparently psychic abilities, Constanzo correctly sensed that Martin had recently broken off a troubled romance and was searching for someone new. The young fortune teller had been happy to fill the void.

"I am a santero priest. I can predict the future with the cowrie shells. I perform limpias on people, I cleanse their spirits."

Here in the Zona Rosa, though, he was merely playing the Spanish cards—just to make a few dollars from the tourists, he explained. It was a simpler, less refined method of seeing the future, but it worked, as Omar plainly could see. "The power of my religion is greater than anything you've ever imagined," Constanzo said.

Omar was fascinated. He knew little about Santeria and wanted

Adolfo to tell him everything. Constanzo promised that in time he would teach Omar, and Jorge, too, all his secrets.

When Constanzo mentioned his intention to move permanently to Mexico City in the near future to work, perhaps as a male model, Montes said he still had connections from his days as a model and a fashion designer. Perhaps he could help out Adolfo with his modeling—and refer some customers to him for limpias as well.

Constanzo was pleased at the prospect. In gratitude, he offered free cleansings to both Montes and Omar. And he offered more: He would bring them into his religion, teaching them how to use the power of the dead to their advantage. "You can learn all about my religion," he promised. "You will take part in ceremonies. You will be . . . initiated."

Montes was wary but Omar's enthusiasm was contagious. Jorge doted on his young friend, and they both agreed to take Adolfo up on his offer during the Cuban's next trip from Miami.

And so a cult was born.

Omar saw Constanzo constantly in the next two weeks before Adolfo returned to Miami. The mysterious visitor treated Omar to meals, took him to movies, bought him clothes, and flattered him constantly. Nearly every day they could be seen striding through the zone, hand in hand, as Constanzo explained the way of the santos to Omar, and how the African sorcery could be used to perform white witchcraft—or the black magic of Palo Mayombe.

Later, he threw the shells for Omar, predicting a bright future for the student. He correctly named all of his brothers and sisters and their occupations—stunning Omar anew with his apparent psychic powers. Then he predicted that Omar would become wealthy and an owner of great properties—if only he followed Constanzo's teachings and advice.

"Tell me how you know," Omar demanded.

But Constanzo declined to explain his powers, which only intensified Omar's curiosity and desire. And, for the moment, he refused to work any other sorts of magic, making Omar beg futilely for more. Constanzo only laughed and shook his head. Like his Haitian godfather before him, Constanzo had learned to bring people along gradually, first with white magic, then with spells that slowly grew more black and terrifying.

"In time," he told Omar. "In time."

After their first meeting, he gave Omar a gift wrapped in gold paper. It was a deck of Spanish cards, finely drawn, for Omar to practice making his own readings once Constanzo had shown him how. The box holding the cards was inscribed with a strange marking of arrows and other symbols—Constanzo's mystical signature, identical to the scar his padrino had cut onto his back. Constanzo also presented Omar with an empty notebook—a *libreta,* to be used for conjuring and magical spells.

Adolfo's generosity and charm overwhelmed Omar. Yet at the back of every compliment and prediction was a dark edge: the suggestion that Omar had to do as Constanzo said or disaster could strike. If Omar wanted access to the mysteries Constanzo seemed to command, then Omar had to submit.

Worse still, in Omar's view, if he did not do as Constanzo wished, his new love, the man he had awaited so long, might desert him. He was disturbed to find a peculiar coldness beneath Constanzo's mask of congeniality, making Omar strive ever harder to please the dark priest of black magic. They always went where Adolfo wanted to go, ate what he wanted to eat, yet Constanzo rarely seemed pleased.

At night Omar would listen to Constanzo on the phone with his mother, hearing the cooing love El Padrino reserved for Delia, and he would feel unreasoning jealousy. He wanted Constanzo to speak to *him* that way. Sometimes, in rare moments of tenderness, Omar got his wish. But the coldness at Constanzo's core, formed and hardened by his long years in Delia's foul home and the old Haitian's bloody shed, would always return. At such moments Constanzo would rage at the smallest transgression, and Omar would accept the scorn—even an occasional blow—without complaint, just as Martin had seemed cowed by Constanzo's ire on that day in the sidewalk cafe. Yet with it all, Omar genuinely loved Constanzo. And he believed Constanzo loved him back.

The young college student penned a poem to describe his roiling feelings for Constanzo early in their relationship. Even then, the dark side of his relationship, the pain and fear, seemed to come through:

I remember you like
something different.
Something special.
A light in my darkness.
I'm afraid of forgetting
that you gave me a hope.
I'm afraid of not forgiving
what time will erase,
what the wind will take.
And it hurts to imagine
that if I forget what hurts,
you won't be here any more.
You will be a mistake.
A failure.
A deadly obsession.
A desire of love.[6]

On the night Adolfo seduced Omar—a few days after their first meeting—he explained matter-of-factly that Martin also was his lover. But Constanzo said he had to have Omar as well. "This is how it will be," Adolfo pronounced with typical grandiosity. "Martin will be my man, and you, Omar, will be my woman. And both of you will become powerful and protected in my religion."

He didn't say protected from what; that would become clear only much later. Perhaps even Constanzo did not know at that time just how much protection he and his followers would need. And, in any case, Omar was too captivated to ask.

Still, Omar didn't like the arrangement—he wanted Constanzo to himself. But he could not say no to this man he had awaited so long. He agreed to everything.

"We did whatever Adolfo said," Omar would later tell the world. "We always obeyed. He could ask anything."

When asked why he obeyed, Omar's answer was simple: "I feared him. And I loved him."

Adolfo de Jesus Constanzo moved for good to Mexico City in mid-1984. For the first year, he lived in a series of rentals in stately old buildings around the Zona Rosa, where he went to work as a psychic, healer, witch, and sometimes fashion model.

By the end of the year, Martin and Omar had moved in with him, each with his own bedroom. Constanzo would alternate between the two, his "man" and his "woman."

The families of both young men were scandalized, but their protests led nowhere. Constanzo threatened to kill one of Omar's sisters, sending her from the home in tears after she tried to have police arrest Adolfo for corrupting a minor. Omar stood by and did nothing. Martin's family decided to attempt civil relations with Constanzo for Martin's sake, though sometimes it was through gritted teeth. Martin Quintana might have idolized Constanzo, but his brother, Alfredo, thought him a transparent fraud. Alfredo always believed he kept those feelings hidden, but during a family gathering in 1985, Constanzo let him know otherwise.

"I know what you think of me," Constanzo whispered, so low only the two of them were aware he had spoken. Constanzo wore a huge false smile at the time, hardly moving his lips to speak. "I don't really care what you think. I love your brother. But if you ever try to come between us, I'll cut your heart out and offer it to the spirits. Brother or no."

It wasn't the words Constanzo spoke that chilled Alfredo Quintana's heart. It was the cold stare and wide smile the man wore, as if he had just commented on the weather. Alfredo, who knew something of Constanzo's beliefs, had a sudden image of a grinning Constanzo ripping the heart from his chest. He almost dropped his drink.

Once he had been welcomed into Constanzo's household, Martin's life changed. He quit business school and stopped seeing his girlfriend, a woman named Mara from Veracruz, a center for witchcraft and mysticism in Mexico. Mara continued to visit, however. She was a self-proclaimed witch and, like Omar, wanted to learn the secret of Constanzo's psychic powers. Mara and Constanzo began sleeping together as well—though his preference was for men, Constanzo was willing to make the sacrifice.[1]

In his bedroom, Martin proudly displayed a card from Adolfo, written in red ink, which said, "You are my life. I cannot live without you." He taunted Omar with it, saying it proved Martin was the favored lover and Adolfo's best friend. The card drove Omar wild with jealousy, until Adolfo penned him an identical sentiment.

Omar and Martin would never stop their jealous bickering and rivalry for Constanzo's affections, yet the dynamic of a family, however skewed, had begun. Omar took on the role of Adolfo's homemaker, cleaning house, cooking, and waiting dutifully at home, while Constanzo and Martin took care of business. Omar continued taking college courses in journalism as a part-time student.[2]

Once they were moved in, Constanzo's charming facade seemed to slip a bit more. Sometimes he ordered one of them to dress as a woman; the pictures of Martin in drag, or lounging about in his panties with Constanzo, are hilarious. But he also required his two lovers to act as manservants, fetching his dry cleaning, polishing his shoes, laying out clothes for him. Omar never objected to the commands, but Martin and Constanzo quarreled often, always with the same result: Constanzo would beat Martin, while little Omar hid under the bed to avoid similar treatment.

Martin would never fight back during these beatings, though he was strong and muscular and fully capable of defending himself against any other attacker. He seemed to slip into the role of Constanzo's battered wife, putting up with the abuse for long periods of time, then finally just packing his bags and leaving to stay with his brother, Alfredo.

On such occasions, Constanzo inevitably would show up outside

Alfredo's house. He would lean on the horn, then scream that he would kill Martin or himself or both if Martin did not come out immediately. "You are my wife," Constanzo would yell. "You have to be with me."

Constanzo would loudly proclaim his love for Martin, oblivious to how he was shocking the neighborhood and passersby. He would cry and beat the steering wheel with his fists. Such scenes, however twisted, were Constanzo's greatest expression of love toward his male companions. The only time his emotional coldness seemed to slip, revealing his need for love and companionship, was when Martin threatened to leave.

After an hour or so of ranting threats and pleas from Constanzo, Martin invariably would shuffle outside with his suitcase and go back to Constanzo's embrace. Then a month or two later, the pattern would repeat.[3]

While Constanzo established this strange household in Mexico City, Jorge Montes made good on his promise to aid him with his modeling career. Constanzo soon began to accumulate a portfolio of modeling pictures, in which he sported gaudy fashions and draped himself on various granite monuments throughout the city. His family in Miami put together an album of four hundred such pictures; the police in the United States and Mexico have many more.

But the photos rarely, if ever, appeared in any publications, which was fine with Constanzo, because the modeling never really was intended as a major source of income. Modeling merely provided the sort of image he wished to maintain—and it proved a ready entree into the glitzy world of Mexican performers, stars, and rich hangers-on that Constanzo sought to cultivate with his witchcraft.

He would tell new clients and followers that, in addition to modeling, he and Martin were in the clothing business together, a cover he continued to use for years. Even his relatives, as well as Omar's and Martin's, believed there was such a business. It did not exist.

Instead, Constanzo became the fashionable witch for a fast-moving set of Zona Rosa regulars, a curious mixture of the famous, dilettantes, wealthy criminals seeking respectability, and equally wealthy criminals who cared nothing at all for respectability.

They were drawn from a Zona Rosa most tourists never see, the world of little clubs and nightspots on dark side streets, of hidden dens in unmarked walk-ups above gaudy souvenir shops. Constanzo plied this world as if born to it.

The card reader Jorge Montes proved invaluable in providing introductions to new clients—at first. But as Constanzo developed a reputation for startlingly accurate predictions and powerful brujeria, it was he that drew the customers and Jorge who got the referrals, a few crumbs spilling off Constanzo's increasingly full plate. There was just no competing with Constanzo—his predictions always seemed to come true. Even Montes, a seasoned veteran made cynical by the dozens of charlatans working the zone, found Constanzo's powers irresistible. He became Constanzo's eager helper.

"You are the only one who can help me with the sacrifices," Constanzo told Jorge, as he showed the older man how a santero offers the blood and flesh of chicken and goat to the orishas. "You, too, have power. I can bring you more."

Constanzo knew how to make his followers feel invaluable, as if only they could perform a certain, important task, cementing their loyalty by making them strive to please him. Omar was in charge of the house, Martin was the trusted bodyguard, and he made Jorge his assistant in animal sacrifices. Each of them competed to earn a smile on Constanzo's normally dour features.

With professionals like Montes swearing by Constanzo's powers, the ordinary customers seeking fortune tellers and healers in the Zona Rosa soon declared Constanzo a sensation. Word quickly spread about the man dressed in white who could stare at you over a table at a sidewalk cafe and see your whole life laid out in the cards. Starting with modest prices—a few thousand pesos for a card reading or a spiritual cleansing—Constanzo was soon able to demand payment in U.S. dollars, first in the hundreds, then in the thousands.

Adolfo had come to the Mexican capital with two suitcases of clothes, a box of herbs, and a few chipped ceramic statues of the Christian saints. But within a year he had closets full of the latest fashions, expensive gold necklaces, rings, and imported, jewel-encrusted watches—so much jewelry, he practically jangled when he walked. He drove a silver Lincoln Town Car luxury sedan, an uncommon sight on the clotted streets of Mexico City.[4] His success even seemed to surprise himself at times. He would marvel on the phone with Delia at the change in his fortunes, but she would assure him he was only receiving his due. "You are a star," she'd say.

Once he had money in his pocket, Constanzo was given to ostentatious displays of generosity, going through his cash without a thought, showering his mother, Omar, and Martin with gifts. He sent fur after fur to Miami, then he offered to buy new cars for each of his lovers. Martin chose a shiny black Thunderbird as a birthday gift from Constanzo, but Omar said he didn't need his own car.

"Take me shopping instead," he asked, and Constanzo obliged him with a broad smile and a fistful of cash. They spent $10,000 in a single day of clothes shopping in some of Mexico City's finest fashion salons.[5]

"He would tell rich people what to do, how to make things better," Constanzo's brother Fausto recalled. "And since what he would say would happen, they would pay him thirty thousand dollars or forty thousand dollars."[6]

One of Constanzo's earliest clients became one of his most ardent followers, a middle-aged real estate broker named Francisco. He was on the brink of financial ruin because of the devaluation of the peso and unstable property values when he came to Constanzo, begging for help. Constanzo read the cards for him, revealing, as he so often seemed to do, details about Francisco's past, family, and financial troubles without any apparent source other than psychic insight. Then Constanzo made what would become his standard pitch—one that sent some men and women screaming from the house, crossing themselves and wishing they had never come. But only some.

"If you accept the devil instead of God, if you give me your soul, I can help you," Constanzo told Francisco. He was echoing the words his own godfather had spoken to him, the promise one makes when accepting the power of kadiempembe.

Francisco did not run screaming from the house. Constanzo found there were many others like Francisco, who would gladly bargain with the devil—even if he charged forty-five hundred dollars in U.S. currency for the privilege. Francisco gladly scraped together the cash and paid.

In return, Constanzo performed a limpia and a reading of the cowrie shells for Francisco, then advised him to buy and keep a certain piece of decaying, seemingly worthless downtown property in Mexico City. Francisco sunk all the money he had left into the property—about twenty thousand dollars.

Six months later, on September 19, 1985, Mexico City was decimated by its worst earthquake ever—8.1 on the Richter scale—killing thousands of people, burying them beneath the concrete and steel rubble of hundreds of crumpled buildings. Seventy thousand people were left homeless. The business district was devastated and the government embarked on an enormous reconstruction program to restore homes and services in the sprawling capital city of twenty million.

Thanks to Constanzo's advice, Francisco made a quarter of a million dollars selling his worthless property to the Mexican government to construct a new federal building. After that, Constanzo could do no wrong in Francisco's eyes. He was his savior. Francisco's first purchase after closing the real estate deal was an all-expense-paid trip to the Mexican tropical resort of Acapulco for Adolfo, Omar, and Martin. Gripping Constanzo's hand and kissing it, he swore he would do anything Constanzo ever asked.

"I know that," Constanzo replied dryly.[7]

Another early customer of Constanzo's was Maria del Rocio Cuevas Guerra, an aging former model who had known Delia for many years through mutual friends in Miami.[8] She met Adolfo for the first time when he and his mother visited Mexico City in early 1983. Maria returned to him as a client once he was established in the capital city.

She had gone to him for a psychic reading in the winter of 1985, a rainy afternoon in a stuffy apartment. As she watched, Constanzo walked distractedly from his apartment for some air, then slipped from a balcony three stories high, tumbling into the void.

Maria raced down the stairs screaming, expecting blood and death to greet her. Instead, she found her mystical godfather striding into the apartment building lobby, dusting himself off. He brushed past her, unharmed, unfazed.

"Are you all right?" she cried.

"Of course," he answered, smiling that cold, mirthless smile of his. "I just . . . stepped out for some air."

As he climbed the stairs to his apartment, Maria began to doubt her vision—or her sanity. She walked outside and saw a buzzing crowd of men and women gathered in the cold drizzle, staring at a red car parked directly beneath Adolfo's balcony.

The car's roof was as bowed as a wok, as if a large, heavy object had fallen on it from a great height. Some of the onlookers kept glancing nervously up at Adolfo's balcony, then back at the car. One person crossed herself and turned away, her stiletto heels tattooing a steady beat as she walked off as quickly as she could, never looking back.

"Did you see a man fall?" Maria asked.

Three of the witnesses nodded. They had been in a sidewalk cafe across the street from the crushed car, one man said. They had seen it all.

"He wasn't even hurt," the man said, wonder in his voice. "Not a scratch. He should have been killed."[9]

Thus, reputations are built and stories spread of a man with great power. Perhaps he was not a man at all, but something else, something terrible, people would say.

Constanzo always denied the story, saying it never happened, laughing when someone brought it up, thereby cementing the legend. If it were a trick, he would have boasted of it, Maria always said, and no one would have believed. If it were true, he would not have to boast; belief would come of its own. And so it did. The story made Constanzo a minor legend in the Zona Rosa.

Thirty-seven years old at the time, Maria became an instant convert, asking Constanzo to become her padrino, another follower won over after witnessing a display of apparently superhuman powers. Frowsy and tending toward overweight, her blonde hair wispy from too much dye, Maria was overjoyed that Constanzo became her occasional lover. She tirelessly pitched his acumen as a witch, bringing him new customers and followers, often participating in the ceremonies that resulted. In return for her devotion, she asked Constanzo for help with her flagging modeling career and perennial bad luck with men, which he agreed to cure.

After performing dozens of spells and readings for her—accumulating a six-thousand-dollar bill—Constanzo announced that she needed a difficult and complex *cambio de cabeza* ceremony, literally, a change of head. The ruling orisha inside her—the equivalent of a guardian spirit—wished her ill, and therefore had to be cast out and replaced by another. Only that would banish her chronic bad luck, Constanzo prescribed.

Twelve animals—goats, chickens, cats, and tortoises—had to be sacrificed in a series of bloody ceremonies over a period of weeks, their hearts offered to appease the angry gods plaguing Maria. Her altar of saints and idols became crusted in blood half an inch thick. After the last sacrifice, Constanzo told her she was transformed, and that the spirits had informed him her true name was not Maria, but Karla.

"Luck will follow you from this moment on, Karla," he said.

Unquestioningly, Maria adopted the new name as her own. She decided she had been Karla in a previous incarnation, and that identity suited her much better than her given name. It seemed to ring true to her, just as Constanzo's predictions about her seemed to come true in the days to come: that she would find a new job, that she would find love, that she would find inner peace. Several modeling assignments came to her within two weeks and a new love affair began for her—with Constanzo. As a result, she did, indeed, begin to feel at peace.

"I had bad luck from the day I was born," Karla would later say. "That's why I went to him, so he could cleanse me. And it worked. Things got better. For a while."

Yet the darkness within Constanzo was always there, like the hidden face of Mexico City, hovering in the background. His charm and seeming patience with novices in his religion could erupt into unpredictable and terrifying rages. And even as he taught her the arts of Palo Mayombe, how to cast the spells of protection and destruction, he also warned Karla never to utter the secrets of his magic to outsiders.

"He said it could have a bad . . . effect on me."

The message was as clear as a dead chicken on a doorstep: Keep silent. Or die.

A third early-customer-turned-follower, known only as Damian, came to Constanzo seeking revenge against an enemy. Damian was a transvestite, who also went by the name Damiana, making a living as a female impersonator singing in gay clubs in the Zona Rosa. Damian went to Constanzo after a club owner failed to pay him for a singing engagement. When the entertainer became insistent, the owner, a flabby alcoholic, ordered a bouncer to beat him badly.

"I want worse for him," Damian told Constanzo, a sheaf of bills in his hand. He had heard of Constanzo around the zone; Omar and Jorge were instructed to talk him up at every opportunity.

For five hundred dollars, Constanzo prepared a coconut statue of Eleggua. He had Damian write the name of his enemy three times, douse the paper with a chicken's blood, then stuff it inside the hollowed-out coconut. Another piece of paper with the man's name on it was stuffed inside a doll, along with the chicken's head, and soaked in blood.

"Take this to a cemetery and leave it on a fresh grave," Constanzo told Damian. "You will have your revenge."

Constanzo then arranged for the nightclub owner to find a dead chicken on his doorstep, along with a series of bloody warning letters inside paper bags. A superstitious man who frequented curanderos, the nightclub owner grew badly frightened after finding the talismans. He started drinking even more than usual. Three weeks later, he was hospitalized with a heart attack. He died a week after.[10]

Damian became an instant convert.

Damian's curse would become the first in a long line of efforts by Constanzo and his followers to magically murder men and women. At first, the idea of it troubled Martin, Jorge, and particularly Omar, for they had assisted Constanzo in casting the spells for Damian and the other clients and therefore shared responsibility.

"I never wanted to hurt anyone, Adolfo," a shaken Omar said after hearing of the death of the nightclub owner.

"You didn't," Constanzo said, seeking to assuage his followers. It wasn't murder, he said, they hadn't used a gun or a knife. The man had died of a heart attack, right? And what's more, he had deserved it, hadn't he? This was justice. The gods always sought justice.

Omar nodded. The rationalizations were a balm. After all, most of the magic Constanzo performed was merely for aiding people in health and business, Omar pointed out. The curse had been a one-time event, right? And Constanzo was correct—they really hadn't done anything but make offerings to the orishas. That was no crime.

Constanzo let his followers rationalize. Only he realized they were but one step removed from out-and-out murder. Only he seemed to see that the leap from magically killing someone to actually performing the physical act was a very thin line indeed.

He wondered if he would ever cross that line. And what would happen if he did.

As Constanzo's clientele grew, he had to have formal assistants to carry out his spells, and to help him prepare for blacker magic. He needed more than followers. He needed initiates. He chose Omar, Martin, and Jorge Montes to form the nucleus of his cult.

Toward this end, Constanzo used a back room in Montes's apartment on Calle Londres, converting it into a shrine to Santeria and Palo Mayombe, a place where the hunter Ochosi guarded the door and the trickster Eleggua flashed his evil grimace on the gathering. Each of Constanzo's followers in turn was blindfolded and brought into the darkened room where Constanzo presided, speaking incantations in a mixture of Spanish and an African dialect he called Patua.

The windows were covered in black cloth to screen out the light. The atmosphere inside was a miasma of cigar smoke and a fine mist of rum, which Constanzo periodically gulped from a quart bottle, then sprayed from his mouth into the air. "The smoke and the rum will help summon the spirits," Constanzo told them.[11]

Just as he had been initiated by his padrino, so he initiated Omar, Martin, and Jorge into the mysteries of Palo Mayombe, one at a time.

For each, there was the sacrifice of a chicken, the spray of its hot blood on the initiate's back. Then the quick slice of Constanzo's knife raked their shoulders, making each of them rayado—making them his.

"I am your padrino," he told each of them. "This is your family. From this day on, you have no God. Your soul is dead.

"You have only me. And you must always obey."

To the bite of Constanzo's quick knife, each follower agreed, fervently, willingly. Fearfully.

They had seen him work magic, predict the future, bring down curses on people for the most minor slight. They knew he had true power.

Yes, Godfather, we will always obey, they answered.

Or die trying.[12]

9

Upon his arrival in Mexico City, Adolfo de Jesus Constanzo began compiling a gilt-edged libreta listing his spells, curses, clients, and followers—a mystic roadmap of the growth of the cult of Constanzo and its descent into darkness. This arcane journal reveals that Omar Francisco Orea Ochoa was the first person to be rayado by Constanzo's hand, cut into palo on October 12, 1983.

Many pages of instructions follow Constanzo's first journal entry on Omar, devoted to divining his future, his spells of protection, and his patron orishas, Eleggua and Oggun. To protect Omar from evil, Constanzo instructed his young lover to build a special cauldron of offerings: hearts of chicken, goat, cow, and cat. Omar prepared it himself, under Constanzo's direction, and dedicated it to the god of metal, Oggun.

After Martin and Jorge were initiated, the next rayado, according to the journals, was for a woman named Pilar, who mysteriously vanished a year later. That same year, a high priestess of the cult was anointed during a bloody ritual of animal sacrifice—Martin's former girlfriend, Mara, named a palera in Constanzo's journals. She lived for a time in the condo on Calle Pomona with Omar, Martin, and Adolfo, but she too eventually vanished, to be replaced by a new high priestess years later—by the name of Sara Aldrete.

Mexican police have searched without success for the two missing women, leading them to speculate that Pilar and Mara might have fallen from Constanzo's favor, then suffered the cut of his blade as sacrificial victims. There is no proof, though. Police say no one knows for sure what happened to Pilar and Mara.[1] They are simply gone. Two of thousands of unsolved missing-persons cases in the chaotic Mexican capital.

Not long after, Karla, Damian, Francisco, and several others were initiated into the cult, cut by Constanzo's knife as he loomed over them in a smoky, bloody room, declaring himself their godfather, sealing them with vows of obedience they did not yet begin to comprehend.

But no matter how many were brought in, Omar, Martin, and Jorge remained the inner circle of Constanzo's worshipers. The three were initiated not just as members of the cult of Constanzo but as *mayordomos de la prenda*—literally, caretakers of the jewel.

As such, each of them was empowered to assist Constanzo in constructing and using the evil and magical nganga—which El Padrino also called his *prenda,* his priceless jewel. After a year of practicing fortune telling and cleansings without an nganga, Constanzo decided it was time to put his darkest magical knowledge to work.

Together, in mid-1985, Constanzo and his three helpers invaded an old cemetery in a poor colonia in Mexico City, moving between rows of tombstones bleached white beneath a smog-hazed moon. At a certain grave, less than a year old, they scraped away the soft loam until they had uncovered a coffin. They pried open its lid and collected a human skull, tibias, toes, ribs, and fingers—which, in the literal magic of the Congo, would provide the intelligence, spirit, and soul of the nganga, its ability to walk, and its ability to grasp things. The thick smell of decay clung to the desiccated bones and the tattered flesh still attached. Long wisps of hair sprouted hideously from the leathery top of the skull.

Like all palo magic, the grave robbing and creation of the nganga could only be done when the moon was waxing. Constanzo was always greatly concerned with the phases of the moon, sometimes consulting astronomical calendars and almanacs while laying plans for ceremonies. Paleros fear the waning moon, during which all magic belongs to *ifa*—death. Any spell could end in disaster, turning against the sorcerer who cast it, if the moon was not propitious. This is an ancient principle, common to many religions and magical beliefs: the new moon and its growth is a time of power; the dying moon, a time of danger.

Not just any human remains would do, either. The unburied skull had to belong to someone who had died violently—a murder or accident victim—or someone who had lived violently—a criminal or an evil witch. Best of all was the skull of a violent man who died by violent means. Such a spirit would never shrink from committing evil at the palero's command, while its sudden death would so confuse the spirit that it could easily be bent to Constanzo's will.

Left behind at the grave were a small stack of pennies and a headless chicken, its small pool of blood spilled on the soil at the foot of the grave, payment to the spirits for what was taken.

Racing through the dark streets in his hulking American car, Constanzo brought the unearthed human remains, wrapped in a black cloth, to the altar room at Montes's apartment. He carefully placed them before the altar, then he threw himself to the floor as his mayordomos stood in a ring about him, chanting the Patua invocations he had taught them for this occasion.

Omar covered Constanzo with a white sheet, then surrounded him with four lighted candles, as if Adolfo was being laid out for burial. This is how the palero welcomes the dead inside him. One of the mayordomos then placed seven heaps of gunpowder on the blade of a sharp knife. He held the blade above one of the candles, then waited, motionless like the others in the room.

After long, tense moments, Constanzo's face contorted and turned red, while his body became rigid, veins swelling in his neck and arms. His fists clenched so hard, small moons of blood appeared under his manicured fingernails. His face became a sculptured mask of agony, skull-like and contorted.

The dead man's spirit was taking possession of him, moving from the dirt-caked skull to El Padrino. Constanzo had told his followers this would happen. Now, it seemed, they were witnessing spirit possession of their leader.

Quickly, as his padrino had instructed him, Omar addressed the spirit. "Do you agree to work for El Padrino, to live in his nganga, to serve him as your master?"

A voice unlike any of them had ever heard squeezed through Constanzo's clenched teeth in reply. The voice was rasping and sibilant, a wind blowing over tombstones, a rustle of faded funeral wreaths and dried bouquets—a voice no living thing should have.

"Yes," the dead voice spat through Constanzo's drawn-back lips. "I will serve."

Then the voice uttered a stifled bark, which Omar and the others recognized as a laugh, mottled and choking, as if Constanzo's mouth were filled with the same loamy graveyard soil that caked the skull's grinning jaws. Then the thing inside their godfather fell silent.

The three helpers stood transfixed, staring at their padrino. When the gunpowder on the knife ignited into hissing flames a moment later, Omar, Martin, and Jorge jumped like fearful children, while Constanzo suddenly awoke from his seeming spirit possession, his voice and features returned to normal.

Had the voice of the spirit said no, it would not serve, the skull and bones would have had to be reburied and the whole process begun again. And if the gunpowder had not burned all at once, a bad omen would have been signified, spoiling the potency of the magic.

But all had gone well. Happy and alert, Constanzo leapt to his feet, shucking off his funereal sheet and proclaiming the ceremony a complete success. "Bring the cauldron," he commanded, clapping his hands like a child with a new toy.

To his unnerved followers, he seemed remarkably unaffected by the experience. They interpreted this as yet another example of his remarkable strength and powers.[2]

With the spirit in agreement, its skull and bones were thrown into a black iron cauldron the size of an oven door. With it were placed coins for payment and a piece of folded paper with the dead man's name on it. Cemetery dirt, a roasted turtle, railroad spikes, a goat's head, a deer's antlers, peppers, spices, garlic, poisonous insects, coins, coconut shells, a boiled black cat, and a pile of other ingredients—each sprayed generously with chicken blood—were piled into the cauldron with the human remains, stocking the little universe with all the supplies the spirit would need or want.

Thrust into the center of the mixture were the twenty-eight palos from a variety of trees, carefully hewn earlier in sacred rituals. Searching through parks and wooded areas for just the right type of wood, Constanzo had asked each tree permission to cut a branch, then repaid the spirit of the tree with an offering of herbs and coins buried at its roots, along with the blood of Constanzo's ubiquitous chickens.

With this foul cauldron completed, it was now a proper home for the *nkisi*—the Bantu word for the human spirit occupying an nganga. From that day on, the nkisi had to be bargained with, tricked, or bribed with money, blood, and sacrifices so that it would empower Constanzo's magical spells. It would travel invisibly through the world, doing good or evil as Constanzo commanded. During ceremonies, Constanzo—like all paleros—would be addressed as *Tata Nkisi,* Father of the Spirit. His journals are filled with the term.

His nganga had to be inaugurated as one of two types. It either had to be devoted to the small, "good" branch of Palo Mayombe, or to the larger, more popular evil sect of the religion. The so-called good practitioners leave out the dead cat from their cauldron and add a crucifix and holy water, thus making themselves *Paleros Christianos,* theoretically incapable of working evil. The evil practitioners have no crucifix, and they are referred to by believers as *Paleros Judios.* The term equates evilness with Jewishness, not because of any quality of the Hebrew religion or people, but simply because Jews are not baptized with holy water, the universal antidote for curses in the Christianized Afro-Caribbean folklore.[3]

Though he often posed as a practitioner of "Christian" Santeria and Palo Mayombe—at least, during introductory sessions, when he was sizing up a potential client or follower—Constanzo's ngangas never included a crucifix or holy water.[4] As his journals clearly show, Adolfo's magic was dedicated to his personal guiding spirit, kadiempembe, the palero's version of the devil, devourer of souls. His nganga was built to inflict curses, sickness, and death, not for works of benevolence.[5]

The next day, Constanzo gathered his mayordomos in the darkened back room, with all present dressed in white. He squatted before the cauldron and sprayed it with rum and cigar smoke, then offered it blood from a sacrificed hen and a rooster. Later, during future initiations, the blood of those rayado would be poured into the mixture, for the evil nkisi always prefers to drink human blood, Constanzo told his followers.[6]

By grabbing the antler or one of the tibias thrust into the cauldron—playing with the nganga—Constanzo summoned the nkisi to obey his commands, to perform a *bilongo*, a magical spell. It was time for the nkisi to take on its first assignment, Constanzo told the gathering.

"We are a family now," he told the others. Then he faced the nganga and whispered hoarsely. "Protect our family from harm. Make us rich. Bring us new believers."

To Omar, Constanzo sounded more powerful—and more distant—than ever. In the hot, close room, he found himself shivering.

The spell seemed to work, though: The customers did come, faster than ever, with Montes and Omar out hawking Adolfo as if he were a god in the bars of the Zona Rosa. At the same time, Constanzo marketed his services to the models, photographers, and show-business types he met through modeling assignments and parties; they, in turn, helped spread the word about Tata Nkisi Constanzo.

Quickly, he gained a greater reputation for psychic powers and a seeming ability to bring luck, revenge, or whatever else his clients sought. And perhaps more important to the cynical yet superstitious star set he began to service, Constanzo's acquisition of the nganga—and the accompanying switch from the white magic of Santeria to the death religion of Palo Mayombe—gave him something he'd been lacking. He gained a reputation for putting on quite a show.

People with a certain taste for the occult, the same businessmen and housewives and celebrities who comb the aisles of the Sonora witches' market, were irresistibly drawn to Constanzo. They were fascinated by the dark, smoke-swirled rooms, the African chants, the gore of the animal sacrifice and, the real show-stopper, the grand finale: the sight of a man possessed, his face bloated and writhing as if he had, through some unfathomable sleight of hand, donned a mask.

Except everyone could see it was no mask. It was real. It was terrifying.

It made money.

Business was so good by early 1985 that Adolfo was able to buy a new, spacious condominium, an entire floor on Calle Pomona in

Mexico City's fashionable downtown neighborhood, Colonia Roma. He, Omar, and Martin moved in, the first in a long line of property acquisitions for the threesome. Before the condo was even partly furnished, an elaborate marble altar to the saints was set up, and a special side room was set aside for more secret ceremonies.

Constanzo called the room his *cuarto del los muertos*—his room of the dead. Always locked, it was the place where his most evil magic was performed. It was the room he took unsuspecting customers, terrifying them, sometimes cutting them with his knife and dousing the tiny wounds in the hot, stinging spray of raw rum. It was the place he kept his nganga.

Among the first clients to experience Constanzo's new level of black magic was Mexican pop singer Oscar Athie, a blonde, blue-eyed, and popular crooner, long a staple on Mexican television's endless array of variety shows. By 1986, though, Oscar's hair was thinning and so were his record sales and job offers. Oscar needed, he told a friend, a change of luck.

Word got around. One day, Athie just happened to run into a young college student with a bright pixie face while drinking in a bar in the Zona Rosa. The young man asked the singer for an autograph, and they began to chat.

"I know a man who can bring luck to anyone," Omar Orea Ochoa volunteered during a lull in the conversation. "He is a witch."

Oscar was intrigued. The singer soon accepted an offer to meet Constanzo.[7]

Omar brought Athie to a restaurant on Insurgentes Boulevard called VIPS (Mexicans pronounce this "Beeps," unaware the name is an English acronym for Very Important Person). VIPS is the Mexican approximation of an American Denny's, complete with orange plastic counters and seats, harshly lit by buzzing fluorescent lights and stocked with bland, greasy *hamburguesas* paired with ersatz French fries. The restaurant is very popular with affluent Mexicans, who seem to equate prosperity and modernity with all things American, even second-rate restaurant imitations.

VIPS was a favorite of Constanzo's, too, part of his endless passion for hamburgers—yet another contradiction in a man who otherwise gaudily pursued the trappings of wealth. He bought only the most expensive clothes, jewels, and cars, but he frowned on fancy food, preferring instead to down four Burger King Whoppers in a sitting (better yet, four with the works from a Texas fast-food chain called Whataburger).

In Mexico, he made do with VIPS. Constanzo and his followers often could be seen there, laughing and talking amid the acres of orange vinyl after an evening of black magic, washing down the blood with Cokes and coffees and burgers.

When Omar brought Oscar Athie to Constanzo's table one night in August 1986, the singer was immediately impressed by the stern and humorless brujo, who managed to be haughty even in the clatter and grease of a burger house. After a few cursory introductions, Omar faded into the background. Once they were alone, Constanzo pushed his empty plate away and said he could improve Athie's waning career a hundredfold, bringing in contracts, gold records, anything Oscar wanted.

"How?" Athie asked, almost laughing, then stopping himself, seeing in Constanzo's eyes that there was nothing at all funny here. "How will you do all this?"

"I will perform limpias upon you. Your spirit will be cleansed. Your luck will change. You will be . . . rayado.

"And it will not cost you much," Constanzo continued, not stopping to answer the question in Oscar's eyes at the unfamiliar term, rayado. Constanzo was too busy appraising the well-dressed entertainer, his custom-tailored suit and gold Rolex wristwatch.

"I will charge you only five million pesos. Only two thousand dollars."

Athie was taken aback. Of course, he had expected a fee, but he had been thinking a few hundred dollars at most, not thousands. "I don't have that kind of money," Athie replied. "I'm sorry. It's out of the question."

Constanzo seemed unperturbed, as if he had expected just such a reply. He nodded knowingly, sympathetically. "No matter. I will do you a favor. And you will do me one in return."

"What favor is that?" Athie asked.

"I like you, Oscar," Constanzo said, his face startlingly changed from his initial haughtiness into one of complete and unquestionable sincerity. The transformation made Oscar blink, as if another man had changed places with Constanzo. "I will cleanse your spirit for free, and your luck will change. In return, you bring me more customers. You know wealthy people in music, in the arts. Tell them about me. Introduce me."

"That's all?" Oscar asked.

For the first time since he walked into VIPS, Oscar saw Constanzo smile. He was not sure he liked the sight of that cold grin.

"That's all," Constanzo said.[8]

Limpias are a staple of Santeria, Mexican curandismo, and, in one form or another, almost every religion. Christian baptism is a variation of the same sort of ceremony, a washing away of spiritual evil through a physical cleansing—a vestige of a most primitive sorcery, sympathetic magic, which invests physical objects with invisible forces and spiritual powers.

Typically, a person receiving a limpia believes evil spirits or magic has contaminated his or her body, and that it must be "swept" clean by a magician. Glasses of water or a raw egg, symbolic microcosms of the world, often are used to entrap the evil, while bundles of herbs, leaves, branches, a chicken or dove, or even a broom can be used to sweep the infected person clean.

By the time Oscar Athie came along, Constanzo had moved most of his ceremonies from the back room of Jorge Montes's apartment to his upscale Calle Pomona condo with its room of the dead. However, for reasons Constanzo would not explain, the singer was brought from Constanzo's home to another address twenty miles away in the Mexico City suburb of Satelite.

When Oscar arrived for the ceremony, the singer was escorted to a darkened room. On the way he saw many votive candles burning on tables, decks of tarot cards spread out, and, crammed into every other available space, stereos, television sets, cameras, cassette recorders, and a host of other foreign goods—all new in the box—stacked to the ceiling.

Constanzo noticed Oscar eyeing the goods. He smiled. "Yes, I sell these, too. Be sure to tell your friends."[9]

Athie was left alone in a room with candles, figures of Christian saints, and strange altars he did not recognize. There was a smell he couldn't quite identify, an odor of rotting meat.

After fifteen minutes, Adolfo, Omar, Martin, and several others entered the room. Strong arms grabbed Athie, then someone blindfolded him as he sat in a chair in the center of the room. Constanzo began to chant in a strange language.

When the singer started to struggle, to ask what was happening, Constanzo commanded, "Be silent. Don't move."

Then he returned to his chanting. Athie could hear feet shuffling in the room, then the smell of alcohol and cigar smoke washed over him. Branches brushed up and down his body next, followed by a sharp, hot pain on his back, as if something was scratching it.

That was it. Constanzo pronounced him cleansed.

Much later, Athie denied any knowledge of Constanzo's crimes.[10] He said he was not a follower or a member of a cult; he had just sought a few spiritual cleansings in exchange for dropping Constanzo's name. Later, when Constanzo pursued him for more ceremonies and favors, Athie said he rebuffed him.

"He knew things, though," Athie said. "That's why people went to him. And the things he told me, they did come true. My career picked up after I went to him. No doubt about it."

Athie kept his word and passed on Constanzo's name to friends and fellow performers. Other Mexican celebrities Constanzo claimed were clients included a flamboyant actress and kiss-and-tell author, Irma Serrano; a film and television star, Lucia Mendez; and a celebrity hairstylist, Alfredo Palacios, haircutter to the stars, all of whom later denied knowing Adolfo.[11] All were supposedly drawn to his psychic and clairvoyant skills and, more importantly, to his ability to bring luck and success out of failure.

There were dozens of others with no name recognition but plenty of money: the owner of a chic jewelry store in the Zona Rosa paid him thousands for predictions before becoming a follower. Criminals, particularly drug traffickers, discovered Constanzo and sought him out for magical protection and revenge. One trafficker paid $40,000 over three years for Constanzo's magical protection.

Adolfo's journals document thirty-one regular customers and followers, some of whom paid as much as $4,500 for a single ritual of less than an hour—a throw of the cowrie shells followed by a prescription for appeasing the gods.[12] For his customers' convenience, Constanzo even developed a price list, a kind of magical menu. The small magic of sacrificing a rooster could be yours for only $6, he told them. A goat was $30, a boa constrictor was $450. The bigger or more exotic the animal, the bigger the price tag—up to $3,100 for a baby lion and $1,100 for an adult zebra, its head lopped from its shoulders into the laps of bug-eyed worshipers, Constanzo grinning all the while.

Constanzo's biggest client coup, however, involved no such extravaganzas, just straight fortune telling and cleansings. And it came from an entirely different sector than his show-business clients, in the form of a crusty veteran Mexican policeman named Florentino Ventura Gutierrez.

Ventura had been *primer comandante* of the Mexican Federal Judicial Police—the equivalent of FBI director in the United States. In 1985, he had become director of the Mexican branch of Interpol, the European-based international criminal investigation organization, making him one of the most powerful lawmen in Mexico. Respected by many U.S. drug enforcement agents for his tough stance against smugglers, he also had extensive contacts with the CIA. He was a natural cold-war asset for the U.S. intelligence community in Mexico City, where there were more KGB agents than any city outside the Warsaw Pact. The Soviet agents found the Mexican capital a perfect base of operations, a city close to the United States where the government imposed no restrictions on communist agents. Consequently, the CIA vies constantly with the KGB for the loyalties of certain influential Mexicans.

Ventura had been assigned to head the most politically explosive case of the decade for the Mexican government: the murder of DEA Agent Enrique "Kiki" Camarena. And Ventura was partly responsible for putting the alleged mastermind of the killing, Rafael Caro Quintero, behind bars after the DEA engineered his deportation from a hideout in Costa Rica, once again drawing praise. But there were also doubts about Ventura. Some U.S. agents believe he took part in an apparent coverup to protect high Mexican officials implicated in the Camarena killing.

Detractors and supporters alike agreed on one point, however: Florentino Ventura was by all appearances a classic, gruff, no-nonsense professional, fearless and fear-inspiring, a cop's cop. And that had made him one of the most powerful men in Mexican law enforcement.

That his colleagues had no inkling of his secret life only compounds the mystery surrounding Ventura. He hid his deeply superstitious belief in brujeria well. Few knew that he continually sought magical protection from his innumerable enemies. Few knew that quest had led him to the door of a certain apartment on Calle Pomona, to a man named Adolfo Constanzo.

Always with two bodyguards in tow, Ventura paid Constanzo thousands of dollars over at least two years, receiving cleansings, mystic protection from his enemies on both sides of the law, and prognostications of the future. Omar, the ever-faithful housekeeper, would usher the stern policeman into the apartment, then assist Constanzo during the limpias.[13]

Some investigators believe Ventura's payment to Constanzo for these services was not limited to money—that it also included information that benefited the cult leader's illegal enterprises. No one was in a better position to aid a drug smuggler than Ventura; no one else could make absolutely certain that Constanzo's advice to contrabandistas would never go awry. He could make sure a drug load got through or that an arrest was botched—insurance for Constanzo's predictions when he began catering to drug traffickers. Their relationship spanned several years, up until Ventura's death in 1988, and it coincided with Constanzo's entry into the drug business.

As head of Interpol, Ventura met extensively with leaders in law enforcement, and also, apparently, had access to some of Latin America's most notorious drug traffickers. These included Panama's former leader, General Manuel Antonio Noriega, a devotee of Brazilian forms of Santeria called Candomble and Macumba, now facing trial in the United States on narcotics and money-laundering charges.

Constanzo at times introduced himself to pricey clients and drug dealers as Alejandro de Jesus Ventura, Florentino's nephew. The name carried great weight with his customers.[14]

Whether or not Ventura was a source for it, there is no question that Constanzo received inside information and protection from Mexican police. Another of his early clients and most valuable of followers was a subordinate of Ventura's, a Mexican federale subcomandante named Salvador Vidal Garcia Alarcon.

Thirty-five years old when he met Constanzo in 1985, Salvador Vidal had been a butcher before joining the federales in 1983. He had worked first in Guadalajara, a notorious drug-trafficking city in west-central Mexico, lush and corrupted by Mexico's powerful drug traffickers. DEA Agent Camarena was kidnapped and killed there in 1985.

From Guadalajara, the tall, hulking agent moved to assignments in Monterrey and Mexico City, where Constanzo met him, then later to a distant border town across the river from Brownsville, Texas. A place whose name, translated into English, means "Bully." A place called Matamoros.

They met in early 1985, a time when Constanzo still was getting established in Mexico City, still hustling card readings for a few thousand pesos apiece. Jorge Montes had approached his new padrino about a friend, Sub-Comandante Salvador Vidal Garcia of the federal Antinarcoticos, a man who believed he was a witch but who was plagued by invading spirits.

"He is a very strange man, very troubled," Montes said. "Salvador has been scarred down the middle of his face, cut with a knife. It almost killed him. But instead, the knife gave him three faces.

"From the left side, because of that scar, he looks different than from the right. And from the front, he looks like an entirely different person again.

"He says he is possessed by separate spirits, one for each face—a Sioux Indian, a Cuban murderer and drug dealer, and an African witch. Each seizes control of him at different times, leaving the real Salvador lost. It makes him helpless, unable to perform as a policeman.

"I told him you could help, Adolfo."[15]

Constanzo grinned, sensing the opportunities such a man represented—a comandante in the Antinarcoticos, a man with access to drugs, drug dealers, and police intelligence.

He could practically see the dollar signs. This was the break he was waiting for, the good fortune his Palo Mayombe gods had promised years ago, before he had left Miami. Before he left mother.

"Of course I can help," he told Montes after a moment. "Set up a meeting for just the two of us: Salvador and I. Alone."

A week later, Constanzo threw the shells for Salvador. Again and again the little shells clattered on a carved wooden board—the ifa table—laid out in the dining room. This was the means of divining the future handed down, legend has it, from the Santeria god Orunla, who alone could see all of time, spread out like a fabulous quilt.

Constanzo's concentration was intense as he studied the patterns the shells made. After each throw, he scrawled cryptic notes in a tattered ledger on a page he captioned, "Salvador."[16]

Finally, he looked up, stared into the big policeman's deeply circled eyes, and said, "I see you have three spirits in you, one a Sioux Indian, one a Cuban murderer, the other an African witch. Is this not true?"

Salvador was captivated. A man eager for a cure is a man eager to believe and Salvador—all three of him—truly believed. It was magic: How else could Constanzo have known his secret? Finally, he thought, someone understood his anguish, his curse.

"It's a miracle," he whispered, clasping his new padrino's hand. Salvador became Constanzo's devoted follower from that day on, accepting his godfather's prescriptions for wellness, then taking orders for other, darker chores, never guessing the ruse that brought him into the fold. In time, he would become Constanzo's most valuable devotee as the young witch moved from fortune telling into the more lucrative business of the contrabandista.[17] Salvador was a clever and corrupt man, long a survivor in the backstabbing ranks of Mexico City's police, yet Constanzo had hooked him in a matter of minutes.

Not long after, Constanzo initiated Salvador and named him a palero. He marked Salvador's shoulders with the mystical symbols of *Siete Rayos*—Seven Lightning Bolts—the Palo Mayombe signature for Saint Barbara. With careful instructions from Constanzo, Salvador made daily offerings to his patron god and almost immediately, the troublesome Sioux, Cuban, and African spirits that sometimes possessed the drug agent seemed to flee to the farthest corners of his mind. He was overjoyed, though there was a price.

Siete Rayos is the harbinger of swift, violent death; its symbol is a double-edged axe, an instrument for beheading enemies. During the initiation, as the other followers pressed around inside that smoky room, Constanzo told Salvador Vidal he would become the cult's enforcer when Siete Rayos was offended. And there was only one person able to determine what Siete Rayos wanted: Constanzo.

"You will obey me, always," he told Salvador, like all the others, and Salvador agreed, selling his soul, offering up his future like a sacrifice to Constanzo.

In return for helping him conquer the spirits that possessed him, Salvador Vidal became one of Constanzo's sources of information on and introductions to drug dealers. The close relationship between Mexican police and drug traffickers is legendary. Many smugglers purchase police I.D. and badges directly from police comandantes, while hiring their off-duty men as guards for drug shipments. Salvador Vidal was no exception. One of his first tasks for Constanzo was obtaining police credentials for him.

Possessed people are revered as magical in Mexican folklore—Salvador had a reputation of his own as a powerful witch. Even before he met Constanzo, he already had contacts with traffickers inclined to believe in witchery. He began to introduce Constanzo to entire gangs and families of drug smugglers, starting in 1985. Most were provincials—growers and smugglers from the hinterland, new to wealth and big cities, with a long tradition of superstition and belief in magic behind them. They were perfect fodder for El Padrino.

Constanzo offered them mystical protection and guidance, advising them of propitious times to ship drugs, just as his old Haitian godfather had done in Miami. And he was an instant hit with the smugglers, eclipsing even his successes with the Mexico City star set.

But Constanzo found the stakes were far higher when dealing with these gangsters. If a prediction for Karla or Oscar Athie went awry, he could always blame them for failing to perform a sacrifice exactly as he prescribed (a standard dodge all santeros use to mollify dissatisfied clients). But the narcotics traffickers had millions of dollars in drugs at stake. They would not be so easily put off, and their toleration for error was bound to be slim.

At the same time, Constanzo knew if he remained a hit with the smugglers, the rewards would be far greater than anything his reputation in the Zona Rosa could earn him. The pressure on him was enormous. So Constanzo decided to hedge his bets. Just as he had used inside knowledge to win Salvador's faith, he was determined to do the same with the traffickers in order to ensure the success of his predictions.

When Omar, disturbed at the deception, timidly asked his godfather about it, Constanzo seemed not to understand the question. Being a true believer, he said, did not mean you couldn't be practical.

And so, when Constanzo was finished consulting the orishas on behalf of a trafficker, after the smoke and the rum and the blood had been offered to the nganga and the spirits of the dead, he made a quiet phone call to Salvador. The narcotics commander then made sure the right agents were paid off or ordered away from the route the trafficker was planning to use.

Success thereby was assured. When the loads kept getting through with Constanzo's blessing, his reputation as a magician was secured among the traffickers. He could charge almost anything he wished. And to the dealers, he was worth it, since a seized load of cocaine represented a loss in millions of dollars. What was $10,000 or $40,000 against that?[18]

Soon, though, Constanzo tired of being a consultant. It was hard to see all those drugs, all that money, yet earn only a tiny fraction. He wanted a bigger piece of the action. He wanted to be a partner.

Which is how Salvador Vidal came to introduce Constanzo to a powerful gang of Mexico City cocaine smugglers, the Calzada family.

It was also how Adolfo de Jesus Constanzo and his followers discovered the joys and profits of human sacrifice.

10

The Calzada family owned a small fire extinguisher company on Calle Barcelona in Colonia Juarez, not far from Constanzo's Calle Pomona condominium, and just a short ride from the verdant oasis and mossy granite monuments of the capital's centerpiece park, Chapultepec. F.M. and Associates occupied an unimpressive gray, two-story building at 27 Barcelona, marked by only a muted brown awning, a small sign, and no visible clientele.

Extinguisher sales were poor at best, yet business was never better: F.M. and Associates was a front for a cocaine storage center, a waypoint for drugs moving from South America to the United States.[1]

DEA agents refer to the trans-Mexican cocaine route generically as "The Trampoline," for the way drugs are shipped from Colombia to Mexico in one leap, then bounced over the border to Los Angeles, as well as to Houston, Tucson, New Orleans, New York, and other lesser ports of call.

The Calzadas, like virtually all Mexican cocaine smugglers, did not own the drugs they shipped. They provided merely a high-stakes hauling service for the white powder. Mexico produces no cocaine of its own. That task is the exclusive reserve of Andean regions in Peru and Bolivia, with the processing laboratories and the gangsters who own them located in neighboring Colombia. Still, Mexican smugglers found a lucrative role for themselves in the U.S. cocaine market in the early '80s. They cut a deal with the Medellin and Cali cocaine cartels that dominate and terrorize every facet of society in Colombia, offering the Colombian traffickers use of established marijuana-shipment routes, human "mules," and corrupted officials to move loads of South American cocaine north into the United States.

This proved an inviting alternative to the traditional seaborne route from Colombia into Florida, which had been suffering from increasingly frequent police seizures beginning in the early 1980s. For the Mexicans, profits increased wildly. A single kilogram (2.2 pounds) of cocaine is worth a hundred times its weight in marijuana, and the Colombians paid their Mexican contractors a handsome percentage for each load.

As a result, the entire international drug-smuggling landscape was transformed. In 1980, virtually no cocaine moved into the United States through Mexico. By 1989, at least one-third to one-half of the cocaine shipped to the United States was handled by Mexico-based intermediaries.[2]

Mexico City is not a primary stop on this drug-shipment trail. Smugglers prefer outlying areas, distant desert and coastal cities. Guadalajara's police and officials have been thoroughly corrupted by the traffickers, making it smuggler central for Mexico, the main leaping-off point for The Trampoline.

But the national capital remains a useful port of second choice for smaller shipments of cocaine brought in by rail, or hidden in luggage aboard commercial aircraft, or simply driven up from Colombia and other points south. And the city itself, with its concentration of wealthy, cosmopolitan Mexicans eager to embrace American culture—even a culture of drug abuse—along with a heavy dose of foreigners, is the only significant market in the country for cocaine street sales.

So the Calzadas did quite well bringing in multi-kilogram loads of the drug, then hiding the white powder inside fire extinguisher canisters, a perfect cover for shipment to the border and beyond. They were not major-leaguers, but they were big enough for Constanzo's purposes.

Through his police work, Salvador Vidal Garcia had come to know the leader of the family and co-owner of F.M. and Associates, Guillermo Arturo Calzada Sanchez. After Salvador became a follower of Constanzo, he introduced his padrino to Calzada in September 1986.[3]

Guillermo Calzada was a hard man, ruthless in his business dealings, as one had to be with the wild, violent Colombian traffickers. He was uneducated, barely literate, but there was a pugnacious intelligence glittering behind his small eyes, burning like twin pilot lights. Though innately superstitious, his mysticism was tempered by his utter distrust of everyone, a survival instinct that had served him well in two assassination attempts against him.

Yet Constanzo wormed his way even into Calzada's goodwill, as he had done with so many others who should have known better. He had learned to stay in tune with his audience, and Constanzo found the right role to play, the right mask to wear, to persuade this gruff, graying fire hydrant of a man to accept him. Constanzo knew his usual intimidation technique of stern curses and invocations of evil wouldn't work with Calzada. This man would not compete to please him as Martin and Omar did. Calzada called for a different sort of charm—he had to defer to the old smuggler out of seeming respect or even fear, Constanzo told his followers.

"You are a wealthy and powerful man," Constanzo intoned with the proper amount of awe, as he threw the shells for Calzada for the first time. "I will help you attain greater wealth, even more power."

Then, having been thoroughly briefed the day before by Salvador Vidal, Constanzo was able to tell Calzada about all the old smuggler's successes and problems in a well-rehearsed, dramatically delivered monologue. He listed Calzada's enemies and rivals in the drug trade by name and misdeed, including those who had tried to kill him. Then he promised to magically curse them into oblivion.

"You deserve no less, Señor Calzada," Constanzo said.

The old contrabandista couldn't help but be impressed. Once again, Constanzo seemed to know things he couldn't have known. Calzada found himself staring at this dark-haired brujo, with so much heavy gold jewelry and a face that would never be marked by smile lines. And he believed.

Soon Constanzo began receiving hefty fees for performing limpias to ensure the smuggler's business success and for the protection of his family and employees. In time, Constanzo's reading of the shells determined when Calzada's drug deals were closed, when cocaine was shipped, when payments should be delivered to suppliers—even when a load should be held up because Constanzo sensed (or was told by Salvador) that a police seizure was imminent.

The effect was as smooth and seamless as any of Houdini's greatest illusions: Calzada's business did, indeed, get better after Constanzo began working his magic.

And all the while, Constanzo was going to school, majoring in drug trafficking. Unwittingly the old smuggler was teaching Constanzo everything he knew about the business of drugs. During this learning period, the four or five thousand dollars a month Calzada threw Constanzo's way was enough payment to satisfy the young palero. But after a few months, Constanzo began to complain to his housemates Omar and Martin, pacing the condo and explaining that he really deserved more.

After all, it was his magic, his demands upon the nkisi, that made it all work for Calzada, Adolfo said, not to mention his contacts within the federales. He should be a full partner, he said. He should get half of everything.

Omar and Martin thought this sounded reasonable. They believed it was Constanzo's magic, not Calzada's smuggling skills, that really mattered.

But Calzada didn't see it that way. When Constanzo showed up one day, demanding a half split in exchange for continued magical protection, Calzada said no. He felt satisfied with the way things were.

At first Adolfo remained deferential, diplomatic as always with Calzada. He thought he had explained his position reasonably, but he tried again, standing in the older man's living room and speaking slowly, as if instructing a backward student.

But when Calzada continued to refuse to see reason, Constanzo flew into a rage, the old petulance of his childhood creeping to the surface. He screamed at Calzada that he had to agree. And still the smuggler declined. He shouted right back at Constanzo, told him to get out, to never come back.

Stunned into silence, Constanzo stumbled out of the room, away from the old man, numb with fury, unable to cope. No one had ever talked to him that way, not without paying dearly for the impudence. Or so Constanzo told himself.

Yet, as he walked stiffly to the door, Calzada's hulking bodyguard, Federico de la Vega Loustalot—El Titi to his cronies—guffawed at Constanzo, compounding the humiliation. In a searing moment, the all-powerful Tata Nkisi had been stripped of his self-image. He had been reduced to the outcast, friendless boy of his Miami days, the one who had been bullied and laughed at by the other children, who ran to his mother to have her fight his battles with curses and dead chickens on doorsteps. Constanzo the laughingstock, Constanzo the failure. It was unbearable.

None of his followers had ever heard of this past, of course. When he spoke of his youth to Omar and Martin, he replaced those memories with tales of his prowess, his macho bravery. All his followers had heard how he had fought off ten thugs at once, idiots who had taunted him in Miami when he was fifteen. He pummeled them with the hammer fists of Siete Rayos.[4]

Here in Mexico City, Constanzo had created the image of a potent magician none would dare cross. He had remade himself, and everyone deferred—Constanzo's greatest magical feat of all: He had made a mask that never came off.

Then Calzada threatened to spoil everything, making a fool of a man he should be down on his knees thanking. Constanzo knew he had to do something to save face, to preserve his mask, to wreak revenge. The lessons his mother had passed on to him kept ringing in his head. The nonbelievers are animals, she had told him, worthless animals.

And then there were the teachings of his padrino, who had said in blood there was power—particularly in human blood. By the time he left Calzada's building, his ears still ringing with El Titi's laughter, Constanzo had decided on a course of action.

He didn't speak a word as he climbed stiffly into the car where Martin Quintana waited behind the wheel. Martin took one look at the awful expression on Constanzo's face and he knew something terrible had happened.

And that something even more terrible would follow.[5]

In the months leading up to this humiliation, in early 1987, Constanzo's followers began to see a change in the man—a descent into utter ruthlessness and violence. Three years after his arrival in Mexico City, Adolfo's devotion to the religion gradually started taking a backseat to a consuming obsession with accumulating wealth—houses, cars, clothes, jewels. He couldn't get enough, and he would do anything to get more. He was always talking about how much he could charge a new customer, or how he could sell a certain person on some new ceremony, as if he were a car salesman trying to hawk optional whitewalls or leather bucket seats.

And when he felt slighted, when a client refused him or no longer wished his help, Constanzo would curse that person. Vile, horrible, fatal curses, things he had never uttered before in front of his followers, would spill from his lips like a stream of sewage. He would sometimes cut these "ungrateful" clients, torturing and terrifying them in his stinking room of the dead before finally letting them leave, as Martin and Omar looked on uneasily. Gradually, as they got used to the blood and the screams, Constanzo's lover-helpers grew hardened to the terror their godfather inflicted. He said the vibrations of fear charged his nganga, and he really wasn't hurting them that badly. In time, they came to believe that Constanzo was only dishing out what people had coming.

"If you obey—and pay—he never hurts you," Martin would tell other followers. "But once you give up your soul, you can't expect to get out, not easily. You'd better obey."[6]

One woman, Consuelo, who had come to Constanzo for a simple cleansing, was sent screaming from his house when he threatened to take her soul, her god, and her life. In the background, as the woman fled, she could hear Constanzo laughing with contempt, still clutching Consuelo's hard-earned money in his fist.

"He changed," Karla later recalled. "I became afraid. But I didn't dare leave him."

With singular determination, Constanzo began to accumulate properties throughout the city. Soon, in addition to the Calle Pomona place, he had acquired a luxury condo in a secure building on Calle Jalapa. The place cost 150 million pesos—$60,000, a fortune in Mexico City. Constanzo paid cash, in three installments over six months.

Then came a sprawling, two-story house in the affluent suburb of Atziapan, a white five-bedroom home surrounded by a high wall, bristling with security cameras and motion detectors installed to ensure Constanzo's privacy.

Elaborate altars with life-size saints were set up for sacrifices at each of the new homes, and another room of the dead was set aside and another nganga created after grave robbing under a full moon.

The corrupt real estate speculator Francisco, forever in Constanzo's debt, helped him acquire the property at cut rate, as he had with six or seven other apartment buildings and condos in the space of two years. The properties allowed Constanzo to launder his growing drug earnings.[7]

For transportation he acquired an $80,000 Mercedes 500 SL—a car rarely found anywhere in Mexico—along with another new black Thunderbird, another Lincoln Town Car, a Ford Crown Victoria, and several other cars. He developed a habit of rewarding followers with new cars when they had pleased him, making gifts of them to Martin, Karla, Salvador, and others.

Constanzo furnished his homes by shopping at some of the most expensive boutiques and department stores in the city, always swirling into the store with an entourage, his white clothes blinding, spending thousands at a stop, always paying in cash. He and Omar would sweep into a fashion salon and the two men would buy dozens of shirts, pants, and jackets at a time.

His witch's earnings paid for much of this, but, as time passed, more and more of the support for his life-style began to come from drugs.

In early 1987, Constanzo, Martin, and Salvador had gone to the policeman's old stomping grounds in Guadalajara, where, posing as U.S. Drug Enforcement Administration agents, the three men raided the office of a dentist who was dealing cocaine on the side. They beat and robbed the dentist, taking his drugs.[8] The five pounds of cocaine they took from the dentist paid for the first installment on Constanzo's new Jalapa condo. And it was so easy. He had used the knowledge and contacts gained from working for Calzada.[9]

Next they recruited a corrupt comandante in Monterrey, Mexico, whom Calzada had dealings with. Constanzo arranged to purchase cut-rate cocaine and marijuana that the corrupt policeman had seized from other dealers. Salvador, in turn, sold some of these drugs to contacts he had in Matamoros, while Constanzo smuggled cocaine to Miami for quick sales to some wealthy gay dealers he knew. They made nearly $100,000 that way.[10]

When Constanzo saw the stacks of bills, a tabletop covered with glorious green bundles of it, he couldn't believe what a few paltry bags of white powder had brought him. "It's time to change things," he had told Martin and Salvador. "Why protect some trafficker's goods and money with magic when I could be protecting my own?"

So he had tried partnership, approaching Calzada with a most reasonable plan. Too reasonable, Constanzo realized later, as he sat fuming in the back of his Lincoln Town Car, cruising away from the humiliating scene in Calzada's pitiful little storefront factory. Calzada was nothing, Constanzo told himself. He was small time, like all the other dealers Adolfo knew.

They weren't customers, they were his rivals, he realized. He had been stupid to make them rich. They should be cursed, not helped. They should be attacked with magic, driven into ruin. Then he would take their business and the riches he deserved.

Or even better, he could fulfill his Haitian padrino's legacy. He could cross the line from magical attacks to real ones, and his enemies could be sacrificed. An image of El Titi suffering under his knife filled Constanzo's head as Martin drove them toward home.

His padrino had taught him long ago about the dark powers human sacrifice could bring, infinitely greater than the magic of slain animals. Human sacrifice was drastic, terrifying. It might drive his followers away from him in terror. It could land him in jail. It could separate him from his beloved Delia forever. But what choice had that bastard Calzada left him? Didn't the old man deserve whatever he got? Constanzo balanced the equation during the half-hour ride home, then reached a decision. He was entitled to the old man's drugs, his blood, his money. His soul.

"It's time for a new ritual," Constanzo told his driver-bodyguard-lover. "Will you follow me?"

Martin looked at Constanzo, hearing death in his voice. He hesitated, sensing a terrible step lay ahead of them. But the habit of obedience and the desire to please his harsh master were too ingrained to allow any objections.

"Yes, Padrino," Martin said quietly. "I will follow you."[11]

A few days after their argument, Constanzo telephoned F.M. and Associates and spoke to Guillermo Arturo Calzada Sanchez. Humbled and apologetic, Constanzo asked the drug trafficker's forgiveness. He had been all wrong, far too presumptuous.

Constanzo said he didn't know what had come over him—an evil spell, probably, from a rival palero. It left him momentarily mad, but it had passed.

Because this evil spell might have been intended for Calzada too, Constanzo said he wanted to perform a special ceremony, a limpia, for Calzada's whole family, his workers, and his business. As a precaution and an apology, he wanted magically to cancel out any remnants of the evil spell.

There would be no charge, of course, he said. "It will be my gift."

Calzada agreed, glad to have his hotheaded magician back, feeling magnanimous in the face of Constanzo's abject apology. They arranged to meet the next day at Calzada's office building–home.

"Bring your whole family, everyone," Constanzo said.

That Thursday evening, April 30, 1987, Constanzo arrived with a crate of eggs, several figures of the saints, and a pair of live chickens. The bodyguard, El Titi, watched Constanzo suspiciously, drawing near and examining his paraphernalia. He saw nothing harmful and receded silently as Constanzo bustled about, setting up an altar.

He explained that a special cleansing ceremony would be held in which the powers of Santeria would drive evil from each participant's body, depositing it into the eggs.

"Everyone must take part, or the magic cannot work," Constanzo announced. He shot a look, blank as a blackboard, at El Titi. "You, too."

When his preparations were complete, they gathered around him in a circle in the Calzadas' large living room, a total of seven people: Calzada; his wife; his mother; his teenage maid; El Titi; Calzada's business partner, Jose de Jesus Gonzalez Rolon; and his secretary at F.M. and Associates, Celia Campos de Klein.

Candles were lit and the lights were dimmed. The atmosphere

in the room was hushed and expectant. Most of those present had seen Constanzo's states of spirit possession before and they were eager to see it again.

Constanzo's eyes were wet, flat stones as he began chanting in his strange African dialect, rhythmically tossing his thick black mane back and forth. He was dressed entirely in white, the traditional garb of the palero, and he seemed to glow in the orange candlelight.

In his raspy, sensual voice, he called to the orishas to give him strength, appealing to the power of Siete Rayos to strike down his enemies. Perhaps the ring of watchers around Constanzo thought it strange when he pointed at each of them when he hissed the word "enemies," but they had no chance to question it.

Suddenly a gleaming blade appeared in Constanzo's hand and two of his loyal followers burst through the door, as if on cue. Leading the way was Martin Quintana, dark and thick, a look of uncertainty on his face; he still was not certain what was about to happen.[12] Soon it would become clear: Their souls, mortgaged to Constanzo so long ago, finally were about to be collected.

Each of the followers held a machine gun, leveled at the gathering.

As he stepped toward his smuggler-patron, Constanzo's blank expression slowly became a smile.[13]

The next day, May 1, 1987, Mario Klein Allencastor called the police to report his 39-year-old wife, Celia Campos de Klein, missing. She had gone to a religious ceremony at the office where she worked, he said, and told him not to wait up for her. But when he awoke in the morning, Klein realized she had not come home.

He was supposed to have gone with her to attend the ceremony, which he described as a spiritual cleansing, but he had to back out that afternoon because of a late business appointment. Now he cursed himself for not going, for not being there to protect his wife.

He did not know the details of the ritual, or who might have conducted it. But he was certain something was wrong. "She's never been gone like this before," he said.

The two policemen who were dispatched later that morning to

the Calle Barcelona address to check on the missing Mrs. Klein found a crowd already milling outside the building. The first hint that a crime had been committed was the Volkswagen microbus, belonging to F.M. and Associates, parked at the curb. It had been set aflame and completely gutted, reduced to a pile of blackened metal and melted tires.

The door to F.M. and Associates was unlocked. The policemen entered cautiously, calling out to anyone who might be home. No one answered. Inside, the patrolmen found broken eggs scattered across the floor and the carton that contained them upended. Several statues of Christian saints lay broken amid the eggshells and dried yolk.

At the foot of a staircase leading up from the living room, a thick, wide puddle of some dark liquid, still tacky, was spreading across the carpet. One of the policemen touched the spot, then looked at his fingertip: It was a reddish brown color all policemen know.

"*Sangre,*" he whispered, then crossed himself. Blood.

Small craters pocked the plaster walls in different places, which the police recognized immediately as bullet holes.

The officers combed the entire house and business, looking for bodies. There were none. Whoever had bled on that carpet was gone, along with the gunmen.

Detectives who came to the house later that day first suspected some kind of religious ritual killing. But they started drawing other conclusions when they saw scales, bulk quantities of plastic wrapping, and other paraphernalia more suited to drug smuggling than to the fire extinguisher business. Further searching turned up a small cache of cocaine and bits of drug residue on some of the implements. F.M. and Associates had been uncovered as a front for drug dealers.

With that discovery, investigators forgot all about the religious ceremony of April 30. Obviously, they were dealing with a drug kidnapping and, probably, a drug assassination case. There was more than ample motive for murder: Based on records found in the house, police estimated that the assailants had made off with between $100,000 and $200,000 in cash and drugs.

A quick canvas of the neighborhood informed the police that the entire Calzada family—husband, wife, mother, and maid—was missing. But none of the neighbors knew what had happened or who was responsible—not the kidnapping, not the shooting, not even the burning of the VW.

In the next few days, more missing-persons reports filtered in—for the bodyguard, El Titi, and for Calzada's partner, Jose de Jesus Gonzalez Rolon. They, too, had gone to attend a cleansing ritual on Calle Barcelona, never to be seen again.

Seven people had vanished without a trace, except for a puddle of blood and a few bullet holes. It had all the signs of a drug killing, maybe even a Colombian hit team at work, the Mexican detectives theorized. They had seen it before.

This opinion was only reinforced five days later, on May 7, when two bound and mutilated bodies were found washed up along the trash-choked riverbanks of the Rio Zumpango north of the city.

The naked bodies, bloated and blackened with decay, had been tied with rough cord, then weighted down with rocks to make them sink. Still, they had washed to the surface to be discovered by riverbed scavengers. The bodies had been savaged beyond recognition. One of them, a male, had its fingers cut off. In the cavity that had been the right index finger, a rolled U.S. $20 bill had been inserted, in some sort of arcane symbology. Toes and ears were also sliced from the body. The man had been shot, bludgeoned, stabbed, and castrated.

The throat of the other body, a female, had been slit so thoroughly that the head was nearly severed. The woman's heart had been removed, leaving a ragged opening in her chest, as if she had been carved up by the Aztecs of ancient Mexico. Because of a prosthesis in her breast, police were able to identify the woman's body as Celia Campos de Klein, Calzada's secretary. The other body was identified as that of Calzada's bodyguard, Federico de la Vega Loustalot—El Titi.

During the next week, five more naked bodies were found washed up in the Zumpango, the nearby Tula River, and the *Gran Canal* that flows through the city, fed by both rivers. All were mutilated. All showed signs of torture, with fingers, hearts, sexual organs missing, throats slashed, and chests hacked open. Vertebrae and a portion of the spinal column were removed from one body. Two had their brains removed.

Only one more of the bodies was positively identified: Gabriela

Mondragon Vargas, the Calzadas' seventeen-year-old maid. The other four were too injured in life and decomposed in death to be identified. Police believe, but cannot prove, that they were Calzada, his partner Jose de Jesus Gonzalez Rolon, his wife Rosalie Ibarra de Calzada, and his mother Guadalupe Calzada Sanchez.

Two years after the events at Calle Barcelona, the four remained on the Mexican police rosters as officially "missing and presumed dead." The bodies were buried in pauper's graves, marked only with the date and location of their discovery.

Investigators remained convinced that the killings were drug-related but, as a matter of routine, they questioned several practicing brujos in the area in hopes that one might be a witness. None, however, knew anything of the killings or the Calzadas. The name Constanzo never came up.

More promising and logical seemed the theory that a Colombian hit team, angry over some cocaine deal gone awry, had been dispatched to kill the Calzadas. Colombian traffickers were notorious for killing whole families in revenge against a single person, using torture and mutilation as a means of avenging misdeeds—and terrifying others who might consider crossing them in the future.

Mexican police conferred with DEA agents at the U.S. embassy, hoping that U.S. authorities had encountered similar killings in the past. A lengthy records search led nowhere. With no new leads and no witnesses, the agents were stumped. The case was left open, put on the inactive list, along with hundreds of other unsolved crimes.

Soon, it was forgotten. But only for a while.

The Calzada killing marked a dreadful turning point for Constanzo, though he had not realized it until after the blood had been spilt and his unreasoning anger against the old trafficker had been spent.

In the past, his path always had been chosen for him, not by him. Delia and her vile home life had made him an outcast child. His godfather had presided over his training in black magic and his squalid deflowering in the bloody shed. The young apprentice had little choice there. And Constanzo's headlong rush toward success and wealth in the volatile business of drugs and magic had made a violent confrontation with one trafficker or another inevitable at some point. It couldn't be helped.

But now Constanzo was master of his own fate. He saw he could choose his own path. He could turn away from the killing, write it off as a just revenge, a moment of passion never to be repeated—and move on. It would be easy.

Except it wouldn't be so easy. Constanzo had found that killing was not so bad—that, in fact, it excited him with its mixture of fear and power. He had got carried away with the violence in an almost sexual way, breathing hard, seeing red. It was not much different from the grave robbing—cleaner, really, without the stink and dirt, and the blood flowed hot and red, full of power for his nganga. The killing had grown easier with each slash of his knife, with each screaming victim, and his mind had drifted back to his padrino's vague prediction that he would some day discover the awesome power of human sacrifice.

Reflecting on all this, safe at home after a night of blood, Constanzo realized he did not want to turn away from murder. He wanted to embrace it. There was uncertainty and fear, of course—fear of being caught, fear of others' vengeance, fear of failure. But Constanzo couldn't shake the feeling that had seized him: He had found his path. He would bide his time, and he would kill again.

The others, he knew, would have to be brought along slowly, carefully. They might not feel as he did. So he made sure to implicate each of them with guilty knowledge, binding those who had not actually taken part in the killings by making them accomplices after the fact.[14]

Martin was already compromised. He had not known they would kill until his godfather thrust the knife into Calzada, then he had cried and puked and embarrassed Constanzo. Adolfo had punished his bodyguard by making him carry the severed fingers and organs back to the apartment, retching all the way. Still reeling from the violence, Constanzo then forced Martin into bed when they returned home and nearly raped him, so violent was his excitement over what they had done. Martin wept again, but said no more about the killing. When Omar asked what had happened, he refused to speak of it.

Martin shuddered the next day, though, when Constanzo described the ritual in ecstatic terms to the group. Constanzo promised the others that, in time, they all would have blood coursing hot down their arms as they joined him in the joy of human sacrifice.

They listened uncertainly when he told them he had seen it all in a vision as the Calzada family's hearts and fingers and other severed organs were placed in the nganga—where the victims' spirits would not be dead, but would live on, magically, in a new and better existence through Constanzo's power.

"Think of it that way," he told his followers. "Human sacrifice is not murder. Their spirits have not died. They exist now to serve us.

"Do it, kill, and then your souls will truly be dead, like mine," he said. "And you will have no fear, no weakness left in you. Just power."

Perhaps some of his followers disbelieved him then, thinking that all his talk about killing was just that—talk. Only Martin reluctantly admitted seeing these supposed murders, and he had kept strangely silent except when pressured by Constanzo. In any case, none of Constanzo's closest followers—not Martin, Jorge, Omar, Salvador, Maria del Rocio, Joaquin the jeweler, Damian the witch—let their leader's talk of murder or his actual deeds drive them away in May 1987, or any other time. No one dared object. Awe of his power and desire for his blessings kept them loyal. And fear of his blade kept them silent.

11

A month after Constanzo stocked his ngangas with various parts of the Calzada family, Salvador Vidal Garcia was promoted and transferred from Mexico City to a new assignment in the city of Matamoros. He was ordered to report to Comandante Guillermo Perez, whose corruption and complicity with the top mob bosses on the border were already legendary.[1]

Constanzo quickly saw the possibilities such an assignment offered. Matamoros was where the real narcotics trade flourished, in the wide-open border region where carrying drugs across a few feet of muddy water called the Rio Grande would double their value. The concept staggered Constanzo in its simplicity. That's where he needed to find a drug-trafficking partner—not in Mexico City, but on the border, someone with good contacts, a plentiful supply of drugs, and, most important of all, not too many brains.

He clapped Salvador on the shoulder when it came time for the big Mexican agent to leave, offering words of encouragement and a reminder that El Padrino was still his master, no matter where Salvador went. "I know you'll find the one I seek, Chava," Constanzo said, calling Salvador by the nickname he had given him. "I have foreseen it."

Salvador agreed to do as Constanzo wished. He was fully under El Padrino's spell. He had helped him get close to the Calzadas, he had stolen and sold drugs—his hands were as dirty as Constanzo's. How could the accomplice refuse his master?

A few weeks later, in mid-July 1987, Salvador telephoned Constanzo from Matamoros with good news for his godfather. "I have learned of a family of drug traffickers here. They have a good source of drugs and they once had very strong protection. The biggest mob boss in Matamoros is behind them, the same one who owns my new comandante."

"That doesn't sound like what I asked for, my friend," Constanzo replied crossly. "If everything is so good for them, there will be no room for me."

"Ah, but you didn't let me finish, Padrino. I saved the best for last. Just seven months ago, in January, the leader of the family was killed. Their new leader is barely in his twenties. He is stupid and violent. The family is in trouble, their business is failing."

Constanzo chuckled. This was just what he wanted. "Tell me more, Chava," he said.

"Well," Salvador began, "their name is Hernandez . . ."

A few weeks later, on July 30, 1987, Sara Maria Aldrete Villareal was out in her father's battered green Impala. She cut a swath through the thick, breezeless Matamoros afternoon, windows rolled way down, vinyl seats sticky with the heat. She cruised down the wide, tree-lined boulevard of Avenida Alvaro Obregon in the dusty heart of Matamoros as the summer swelter boiled up from the ground. Every Mexican town has a broad main street like this one, cutting through town to the central square, leading to all the important places—the old stone Catholic church, the battered city hall, the plaza and its mandatory, dust-choked fountain.

Passing Matamoros's central plaza, Sara squinted into the white light of summer and looked for something, she wasn't sure what. She only knew she deserved better.

Sara was twenty-two years old, a failed marriage behind her, an uncertain future ahead. Nice Catholic girls in Matamoros didn't get divorced and there had been talk, but Sara's parents, if somewhat wearily, had welcomed her back into their small home on Calle Santos Degollado—the Street of the Beheaded Saints. Now she was back in school at the two-year college in Brownsville, taking a course load heavy on physical education classes. The year before, she had used a phony Brownsville address to get the financial aid she needed—a standard ruse on the border—and she had parlayed that white lie into one of the top grade point averages at Texas Southmost College. She talked of becoming a teacher and her professors assumed she soon would switch to the Brownsville campus of the four-year Pan American University for her bachelor's degree.

Still, she felt a longing for something more, a desperate need to escape the tired border streets and the tired dreams of mere survival they bred. There had to be more to life than making a local "Who's Who" list at a broken-down junior college within spitting distance of the Rio Grande—on the very site of the original Fort Brown, where Union troops and the Mexican army had traded cannon shots over who could claim this flat, ragged edge of Texas. Every day, Sara coldly surveyed the crumbling brown brick and adobe remnants of that fort, now used to house part of her college, and she knew she would rather die than end up spending her whole life on the border. "There has to be more," she would tell her friends. "I deserve more."

It was the standard refrain of all Sara's friends, the lucky few who could afford a little more than the bare essentials of survival on the border—a stereo or a color TV, an occasional trip to Houston. They had just enough to realize how much more there could be, and how far they were from having it.

And so, like everyone else aimlessly driving up and down Avenida Alvaro Obregon in the universal, small-town ritual of cruising, Sara was looking for something different that day in July. But all she saw were the same old taco stands and tourist traps creeping by her windows, the same people who waved to her and honked. Still, she peered through the windshield, feeling, somehow, a change had to come her way.

Dimly, she heard a man's voice calling from a car tailgating her, asking her to stop. She ignored him—men were always calling to Sara when she went out cruising. She glanced at herself in the rearview mirror, checking her makeup, wondering which of her boyfriends she would see for dinner that night.

"Hey, watch out for that guy," Sara's younger sister, Teresa, cried out from the passenger seat. Teresa pointed out her window at a huge silver Lincoln Crown Victoria that had sped from behind them, then raced around their car at a side street to make a U-turn. Now it was bearing down on the Impala, its rear end fish-tailing with lunatic acceleration.

Sara slammed on the brakes and the Impala skidded to a halt. They had been doing no more than fifteen miles an hour in the heavy cruising traffic, but Sara was still jarred and angry from the near collision. The big car, blindingly new, screeched to a stop in front of Sara's car, half in, half out of the traffic flow, blocking her way. The low afternoon sunlight bounced off the Lincoln's tinted rear window, hammering her eyes. The license plates bore the inscription, "Dade County, Florida."

Another stupid gringo bad driver, Sara thought, and she started to roll her eyes at her sister. But then she noticed a man emerging from the passenger side of the car making her forget for a moment what she had been about to say.

First she saw his head pop out, his long, shiny black hair combed back from a smooth forehead, then the rest of him, tall and slim and firm, unfolding gracefully from the Lincoln. Watching him, she thought of the grace of a panther, sleek and deadly.

He was as blinding in the sunlight as his car, dressed in white from shoes to shirt, impossibly spotless amid a sea of aging, dirty cars and seedy storefronts. Sara found herself checking the rear-view mirror again to see if her hair looked okay.

"Hey," she called, leaning out the window, now as angry at her own vanity as at this maniac driver in front of her. "Can you move it?"

He just stared at her. Horns began to sound behind her as traffic backed up, first one honk, then a chorus.

"Can you move it?" she repeated.

The man in white smiled, shook his head. "No. Can you park? I want to meet you."

Teresa giggled. Sara fumed. "No. Are you crazy? Just move it!"

"No." And still he smiled, perfectly calm, his tone as mild as Sara's was irritated. The man's voice sounded throaty, raspy—not deep, but sensual, like a lover's whisper. "You should have stopped when I called you before," he added, with a hint of reproach, as if this raucous traffic jam were all Sara's fault.

Sara got out of her car then, fists balled. She was an intimidating figure, tall for a woman in any culture at six feet, one inch, but in Mexico she was a giant, with long, strong legs from teaching aerobics and playing volleyball at college. She had towered over all the boys from grade school on and she was used to getting her way.

Sara Aldrete would have no truck with the traditional Mexican female obeisance. Sara was used to men doing what *she* wanted.

Now she strode toward this rude, presumptuous man, a good two inches shorter than her. Sara practically shouted in his face. "Are you going to move your car, or do you want me to move it for you?"

The man leaned against the door of his car and shook his head. Sara peered inside and through the tinted glass, she could dimly see another man at the wheel. By then the honking behind her had reached a deafening, discordant crescendo. People were leaning out of their cars, yelling and waving madly. Sara gave them a furious look. As if any of them had anywhere to go other than up and down this stupid street, she thought.

"Won't you please move?" Sara asked, humiliation finally dissipating her anger, making her plaintive. He had called her bluff.

"Why don't you just stop and talk to me?" the man responded, leaning back with his arms crossed, relaxed. He seemed to feel he had all day, seemed not to even hear the horns. "I just want to talk to you."

"Talk to him already, señorita!" someone shouted from a car behind Sara's. "*Por favor*. Please."

Sara finally nodded, acknowledging defeat. A small chorus of cheers welcomed her concession, a brief harmony for the honking. "Okay, okay," she sighed. "Just get out of my way and we'll talk. Who are you, anyway?"

The man smiled, his teeth as white and gleaming as his clothes—white like bone, Sara thought.

"Adolfo," he said. "Just call me Adolfo."[2]

After they parked and Sara's sister had driven off with some friends, Adolfo and Sara finally talked. Or rather, Adolfo talked, Sara listened.

For nearly an hour he spun a fascinating tale of foreign lands and great wealth as they sat inside his air-conditioned luxury car, oblivious of the time. Sara's initial anger and wariness slipped away, pierced by this strange man's charm and the feel of soft leather seats beneath her hand. That raspy, hypnotic voice held her.

Gesturing expansively, he told Sara he was a Miami lawyer vacationing in Mexico. His family was Cuban and very wealthy, he said. His clients were very wealthy, too. "Colombians," he said, arching his eyebrows. "You know what I mean."

Sara nodded. She had some friends who did business with the Colombians, too, she told him. She watched Adolfo nod, as if he knew that before she told him.

How odd, how different he is, Sara thought. How enigmatic. It was a word Sara would come to use often in describing Adolfo and her strange attraction to him.

Adolfo told her he found the border fascinating. Too bad he could only stay a week or two. He would be sorry to leave. "Perhaps you can spend time with me while I'm here?" he asked. He was almost telling her, not asking her.

Yet for some reason—Sara couldn't quite put her finger on why—Adolfo didn't come across as a boastful jerk to her, though he certainly was haughty and full of himself. He had hardly asked a question about her, yet the slight hadn't bothered Sara. She found herself nodding yes, she would spend more time with him before he left.

Sara interrupted Adolfo's monologue about himself only once, by pointing to a strange, multicolored beaded necklace around his neck and asking, "What's that?"

At her gesture he pulled away slightly, almost shyly. Sara found this sudden bashfulness endearing. "It's part of my religion," he said.

The beads were small and shiny, colored red, black, green, and white. Sara had never seen anything like it. "What religion?" she asked.

"Just my religion," Adolfo replied, refusing to be more specific. Sara asked several times more, to no avail. Cryptically, he said he would tell her more when she was ready.

"Let's get something to eat," Adolfo said abruptly. "Do you want to eat?"

Sara said she did.

They ended up in the upstairs bar and restaurant at Garcia's, a half-block from the international bridge. The bar was dark and noisy with strumming mariachis, a typical Friday evening. Sara,

Adolfo, and his driver ordered light meals and drinks—piña coladas for the men, Sprite for Sara.

"I don't drink," she explained. Adolfo again nodded as if he already knew all about it.

At Garcia's, Adolfo finally introduced Sara to the man behind the wheel, who had remained silent and still in the front seat of the Lincoln throughout Adolfo's conversation with Sara. "This is Martin. He's my partner in the clothing business."

Sara shook Martin's hand. Handsome, dark, and short, Martin was also very Mexican-looking, not at all like Adolfo's pale-skinned, foreign good looks.

"I thought you were a lawyer," Sara commented dryly.

"I have more than one business," Adolfo replied, his face suddenly expressionless.

"And you, Martin, are you from Miami, too?"

"Yes," he told her in the unaccented Spanish of a Mexican native. When Sara raised an eyebrow, he quickly amended, "Well, I'm from Mexico City originally, but I live in Miami now. I moved there."

"Uh-huh."

Sara figured she was being fed a line, but she didn't care. The border and its men seemed to her so rough and uncivilized at times, so uncouth. Adolfo, though, with his stern good looks and obvious wealth, seemed to Sara deliciously smooth, a thorough departure from her usual boyfriends. Who cared if he was something of a liar?

Still, she didn't want to appear too easy. Sara decided to ignore Adolfo a bit and to talk with Martin, the same way Adolfo had ignored his friend when talking with Sara in the car earlier. She and Martin began discussing sports—soccer, volleyball, baseball, tennis. Suddenly the dour Martin was gabbing with Sara like an old friend. It turned out he, like Sara, was a passionate sports fan.

Adolfo was not. He had no knowledge of or interest in sports. He sat, miffed and forgotten, drumming his fingers on the table as Martin and Sara spoke animatedly about the championship women's volleyball team at Texas Southmost.

"I'm in charge of the team's booster club," Sara was saying when Adolfo finally interrupted.

"Hey, remember me? I'm here, too." He seemed a trifle petulant and Sara smiled at her victory.

Martin, though, looked stung. Shamefaced, he mumbled, "I'm sorry."

"Do you still want to know about my religion?" Adolfo asked Sara, back on center stage. Sara's gaze had kept drifting to those flashing beads around his neck throughout the evening, even during her sports conversation with Martin—he must have noticed, she realized.

She nodded. "Yes, I'd still like to know about your religion."

"Then meet me for lunch tomorrow."

Sara looked at Martin, not understanding why he was staring morosely at the tabletop like a scolded child. Something was strangely unpleasant about all this. All the same, she wanted to know more. She wanted to be with this enigmatic Cuban from Miami. She put aside any reservations she might have felt. "Lunch tomorrow," she said.[3]

Lunch, sans Martin, turned into dinner the next night, and dinner turned into meeting the next morning for jogging, and without really meaning to, Sara ended up spending almost every day for the next two weeks with Adolfo.

At that first lunch, Adolfo—who said at the time his last name was Alejandro—told Sara the two of them were destined to be more than just friends. They would be lovers, he said. They would "go together." His use of the adolescent phrase seemed endearing to Sara at the time, a rare boyish note within an otherwise somber personality.

"You want to go with me," he said, again making a statement out of what should have been a question.

"No I don't," she replied, feigning irritation. "We just met. And besides, I have a boyfriend."

"Well," he insisted, "I want more than a friendship."

Despite herself, Sara was flattered. She started to say, "We'll see," then thought better of it and changed the subject. "Why don't you tell me about your religion, like you said you would?"

Instead of being annoyed by the switch of topics, as Sara had expected, Adolfo seemed pleased. He began to tell her about Santeria and Palo Mayombe, providing a straightforward, simple explanation of his magical religions—with some significant omissions. He did not mention human sacrifice, dedication to evil, or men without souls. That would come later, long after the time for objections had passed.

For the moment he explained only that his religion revered the Christian saints as personifications of ancient African deities. He described to her the power of Eleggua, Oggun, Ochosi, and the others, and how each controlled a different aspect of nature and man's destiny. He told her that, in order to succeed, these gods had to be appeased with an offering of fruit or the blood of chickens and goats, killed in ritual sacrifice. In gratitude, each saint provided the worshiper a different sort of reward. Failure to appease them would bring financial ruin, sickness, even death, he said.

"Every day, I must make a sacrifice."

Sara told him his religion sounded barbaric. She could never kill an animal, she said.

Adolfo laughed. "You eat chickens, don't you? You eat beef. It's no different."

In a way, he said, his religion was less cruel, because a creature killed for Santeria serves a far higher purpose—it becomes blessed.[4] Sara found herself nodding. There didn't seem to be any harm in it.

"Sacrifices will bring you luck and power," Adolfo told Sara, shooting her a penetrating look. "My religion can give you what you want most. A way out."

And once again, she saw that familiar nod, as if Adolfo was reading her mind. Yes, she almost said, biting her tongue, I want a way out.

At eight the next morning, Adolfo appeared uninvited at Sara's door to go jogging with her. He had expensive white sweats on, new white running shoes and, incongruously, all his heavy gold jewelry. Sara said fine. She ran every day and figured she could dust Adolfo, something she would enjoy immensely.

To her surprise, Adolfo not only kept pace with her through one mile, then two, then three, but he showed no sign of tiring. Long after Sara began to pant and her legs started cramping, Adolfo didn't seem to be even running out of breath. The miles slid by, the street's hot tar soft beneath her sneakers, but Constanzo wouldn't wear out.

Finally, Sara had to admit through gritted teeth that she was the tired one. "That's enough."

"Okay, we can stop," Adolfo said with a grin. His thick gold jewelry had swung with every step they had taken. He clanked to a halt. Gasping, Sara looked him over. She could see no sign of sweat on the man. "I never get tired," he said blithely. "It's because of my religion."

Much later, when Sara heard about Adolfo falling three stories unhurt or besting ten men in a fight, she didn't doubt the stories a moment. In fact, she would compound the legend of Adolfo Constanzo, superman of Santeria. "He can run forever," she would tell Omar and the others. "He never tires."

After their run, he asked her once again to "go around" with him. "Let's go over to my apartment," he said. "We can be alone."

Sara shook her head. He would ask her the same question every day for the next two weeks, always getting the same reply: no. Yet he remained undaunted, knowing, he said, that Sara's no would become a yes.

As the days passed and they continued dating—only as friends, Sara later insisted, because at night, she kept seeing her boyfriend, Gilberto—Adolfo told her more about his spiritual odyssey. He talked more about Palo Mayombe and the spirits of the dead, but what really caught Sara's attention was his revelation that he could use seashells or cards to tell the future—anyone's future.

"Read the cards for me," Sara demanded immediately. She guessed this must be how he seemed to read her mind at times. "Please. I have to know the future."

Adolfo, however, said she was not ready. Whenever she'd ask, he kept saying, "Later," and then he would schedule their next date, stringing her along. She knew what he was doing, that it was part of his relentless need to control her, but whenever she tried to refuse a date he became petulant again. The suave Miami drug lawyer seemed transformed into a temperamental child. Inevitably, she would relent before his disappointment and the masterful Adolfo then would reappear, telling her he had known all along she would come around. It bothered Sara, but she just couldn't help herself.

Nearly two weeks after their first meeting, Sara and her boyfriend, Gilberto Sosa, ran into Adolfo while strolling through the Sunrise Mall on the north end of Brownsville. Adolfo was out shopping with Martin, who, as usual, kept silent except to say hello to Sara. For his part, Adolfo seemed brusque and uncomfortable at the meeting, and when Sara's boyfriend offered his hand, Adolfo would not shake it.

"Who is that jerk?" Gilberto asked Sara after Adolfo had stomped off with Martin.

"Just a friend," she replied, staring uncertainly at Adolfo's receding white shirt.

The next day, Adolfo went jogging with Sara. As they raced over the cracked and weedy sidewalks of Matamoros, he remained uncharacteristically silent and grim. Finally, he stopped after the first mile and told Sara that she had to break up with her boyfriend.

"Why should I do that?" she asked.

"Because I said so. He's not right for you. He's a criminal."

Sara knew Gilberto was, in fact, a drug dealer, descended from a long line of drug dealers. But how did a lawyer from Miami know that? Sara wanted to know. "And what are you still doing here? Your vacation is supposed to be over. Why aren't you back in Miami?"

"Well, the thing is, I don't live in Miami, I live in Mexico City," Adolfo said. "And my name isn't Alejandro, it's Constanzo. And I'm not on vacation."

"So why lie?"

"Because," Constanzo said, "I couldn't tell you the truth. I'm not a lawyer, either."

He pointed across the street to a black Ford sedan with antennas bristling from its trunk—an unmarked police car. "That's mine," Adolfo said. "That's how I know about your boyfriend. I'm a cop. I'm working here undercover."

He pulled a leather wallet from one of his pants pockets, flashed it open to Sara. She saw the gold badge inside and on it the words, "Federal Judicial Police."

"You're a federale," she whispered.

Adolfo nodded silently, putting a finger to his lips. "I only tell you this because I trust you." And he took Sara's hand in his.[5]

A few days later, Sara's boyfriend called. Gilberto was upset by an anonymous phone call he had received the night before. "Somebody called and said you are seeing another man, Sara. It's true, isn't it?"

Gilberto said he had watched the way Adolfo acted in the mall the other day. He had been suspicious then, and this anonymous call only confirmed his fears.

"And you believe that?" Sara asked. "Even if I tell you it's not true?"

"Yes."

Perhaps Sara felt genuine outrage at this lack of trust. Or perhaps Sara had found just the excuse she was looking for. In any case, she told Gilberto they were through and slammed the phone down in disgust.

The next day, she couldn't hide her depression over the breakup when Adolfo showed up in the morning, uninvited yet expected. He said he wanted to take her to breakfast. Listlessly, she agreed to go with him, and they crossed the bridge to Burger King in Brownsville, Adolfo's eternal affection for fast-food, even in the morning, dictating their choice.

"You want to talk about it?" he asked after they had ordered and sat down.

"About what?"

He munched a French fry, carefully chewing the bit of food before speaking again. "About how you broke up with your boyfriend."

For the hundredth time, it seemed, Adolfo had shown he knew things he couldn't know. Sara asked him how he did it, how he knew about Gilberto.

"Well, I saw it in the cards."

"You what? You read my cards without me?"

"Of course, why not?"

Sara looked wounded, but Adolfo laughed. "I guess you are ready now. We'll go to my apartment and I'll show you. I'll read the cards for you."

Before, Sara had always resisted Constanzo's invitations to his apartment, but this time she let herself be coaxed into driving there with Constanzo.

"You think I just want to get you to my apartment so I can try something funny?" Constanzo asked solemnly, then laughed. "I would never do anything like that. Besides, Martin will be there—your little chaperone."

Sara had to laugh. On the way to the apartment, her hand seemed to slip into Adolfo's almost without her realizing it as he drove the big car one-handed.

Constanzo and Martin shared a large apartment in central Matamoros, near the city's finest hotel. It was a bright, sunny day, but all the blinds were drawn. As her eyes adjusted to the gloom in the living room, she saw a huge altar along one wall, with a clay pot containing a coconut draped in red and black beads—the colors of Eleggua. Several large statues of Christian saints stood nearby, with candies, glasses of water, fruit, and plates of offerings before them. One terra-cotta dish held a decapitated chicken, its glassy-eyed head on a separate dish, its white feathers painted with blood.

"What's that smell?" Sara asked. Something stank, like sweepings from a butcher shop. Embarrassed, Martin hastily grabbed an aerosol can and started spraying in the living room, surrounding Adolfo and Sara in a cloying mist of artificial pine scent.

"Chickens," Adolfo said, leading Sara to the kitchen. He reached down and held open a large plastic trash bag half full of headless chickens, their feathers blood-clotted. The apartment otherwise was spotless. Countertops shone, not a dirty dish was in sight. What kind of bachelors are these? Sara wondered.

Adolfo excused himself to change from his running clothes. When he emerged, dressed in his usual white clothes, he wore a gold amulet Sara had not seen before, in addition to his normal poundage of jewelry. He stood close so Sara could study the amulet, a golden likeness of a beautiful woman bearing a chalice in one hand, a sword in the other, with rubies and diamonds set into the gold. It was Saint Barbara, behind which lay the fearsome god

Siete Rayos. "I usually wear this under my shirt," he said. "But I never take it off. Not even to bathe. It gives me power."

They sat at the kitchen table opposite each other. Constanzo produced a deck of Spanish cards, shuffled them, and then arranged the cards in rows. After studying them, he gathered them together and told Sara to place her hand in the deck three times. From each spot she chose he pulled a card.

He looked at the three cards she had picked, then told her he would make three predictions for her immediate future:

"You're going to get some money from your school for next semester. You're going to get a call from someone you haven't seen in many years, an old friend. And another old friend, someone you once dated, is going to come to you with a problem, but that won't happen for a few weeks."

He stared at the cards again, then said he knew she had been married for five months in 1983. "The man hit you," Adolfo said. "So you left him."

Sara nodded, captivated, listening as he described events from her childhood, courses from her school, things even she had forgotten. He knew her father was a retired electrician, that her mother liked to dance but stopped because of frail health, that she had two younger sisters, both in school in Brownsville—things Sara had never told him. Adolfo seemed to know things about her he couldn't have known. It was, Sara insists to this day, magic.

"I know what's going to happen to you. I can know everything about you," Constanzo said. He tapped the deck of cards. "It's all right here."

"How?" Sara whispered. "How can you know?"

"I can know anything."

In the days that followed, Constanzo's first two predictions came true with stunning accuracy.[6]

First, a letter came from her college informing her that she had qualified for a scholarship of four hundred dollars a semester. Sara had never applied for such a scholarship; the college admissions office had done it for her. There was no way she could even have inadvertently tipped Constanzo. The letter left her breathless, standing in her parents' living room, hearing Adolfo's half-whispered words echo in her ears: "I can know anything."

Two days later, a childhood sweetheart who had long since moved away telephoned and said he would be in Matamoros for a few days. Could they meet for old times' sake? Sara could barely contain herself, cutting the man off almost rudely so she could call to tell Adolfo that two of his predictions had come true.

"Of course they came true," he replied disdainfully. "You doubted it?"

"No, no, of course not," she said quickly. "But what about the third prediction, Adolfo? When will that happen?"

"Soon," he said. "Be patient."

When Adolfo asked her again to be his woman—"It's the last time I'm going to ask," he said unnecessarily—Sara said yes, all hesitation gone. She embraced Constanzo and his beliefs, fascinated by him as she had never been captivated by a man before.

"I'm glad you finally see," he told her. "Now, let me tell you something about me. The truth."

"What?"

"The truth is, Sara, I am a witch. Reading the future is how I make my money. I perform limpias, I change bad luck into good, I protect people. I am a brujo. I make more money with a little magic than a year's pay from the police."

A week earlier, Sara would have thought him crazy for saying such things. She would never have agreed to go out with someone who thought he was a witch. She would have fled. But Sara had seen him foretell the future. She had no doubt he was for real. Any worries about his strange series of lies leading to this startling admission were all cast aside in the fervor of a convert and the burning desire to learn more about this man and his mysterious religion.

Soon Sara had a small altar of her own, with statues of the saints, candles, small pots of fruit and herbs, and a frowning Eleggua statue. Adolfo brought these things to her, explaining the significance of each item. Santo Niño de Otoche was really Eleggua. Saint Peter was the metal god, Oggun. Saint Francis of Assisi was the goddess Orunla, patron of fortune tellers. And Saint Lazarus was really Babalu Aye, who could banish or inflict sickness—the title subject of the Cuban folk song "Babalu" that Desi Arnaz made famous on the *I Love Lucy* show. Adolfo even helped her make an offering at her altar to ensure her good grades in the coming semester. As she looked on, the spirit of an orisha seemed to claim Adolfo's body, making him shake, gasp, then grow deathly still.

"It is good," Adolfo told her in his trancelike voice, his eyes closed, the blood of a freshly killed chicken staining his hands. "I am Eleggua. It shall be as you ask."

When, a moment later, Adolfo seemed to come to, no longer a god but a man, Sara hugged him in gratitude.

In back of Sara's new altar, the whitewashed wall gradually became spattered with the dried blood of chickens and goats. At first the blood bothered her, but after a while, she no longer noticed.[7]

Adolfo would drop Sara at her parents' house at night after dinner or dancing or a ritual, telling her he would see her for jogging in the morning. They would kiss good night, but he was curiously chaste, Sara thought. She wondered why he seemed so disinterested in sex after pursuing her so avidly. She wondered if she had done something wrong.

Adolfo would never come in the house at such times. He always had some excuse for not meeting Sara's parents. Instead, he would toot his horn and wave and be off, leaving Sara at the gate and her father peering through the window at the retreating car.

After leaving Sara, Adolfo did not always return to the apartment he shared with Martin, as he said he would. Several nights a week he journeyed to a dark, ramshackle bar deep in the city's most unpleasant barrio, a place that stank of urine and spilt beer, where questions were never asked and faces never remembered. There, he would meet with Salvador Vidal Garcia, who had given him a badge and a police car, then spent weeks gathering information on the Hernandez family, the Matamoros drug trade, and a certain exceptionally tall, young Mexican woman named Sara Aldrete.[8]

Yes, Constanzo had made two uncannily accurate predictions, but, once again, he was not content to rely on his faith alone. Salvador had already told Adolfo all about Sara's ill-fated marriage, her family, her school. The most basic of investigations had mined invaluable information for use in his card reading and predictions. Constanzo's own peculiar insights provided the rest. And the prediction that remained unfulfilled, the arrival of a friend with problems, also came thanks to Salvador's hard work, combined with an educated guess by Constanzo.

Salvador had learned not only that Elio Hernandez once dated Sara before she was married, but that he still carried a torch for the lanky señorita six inches taller than him. Poor little Elio, Salvador explained to Adolfo, was trying to run the family drug business, thrust into a role of leadership for which he was eminently ill equipped.

"This is perfect," Adolfo told Salvador at one of their late-night meetings, barely hiding his glee. "Sara will bring me to Elio, and the little smuggler will be mine. We will make him rayado. We will take over his business."

Adolfo had told Sara the truth about very little, but about one thing he had been honest. Their meeting on Avenida Alvaro Obregon on the last day of July 1987 had been no accident. Constanzo had come to Matamoros to meet Sara. Through her he was going to enter the border drug trade.

12

When Sara's friends asked about the exotic, dark-haired stranger they sometimes spotted striding across campus with her, she deflected their questions, masking a growing obsession with Constanzo and his religion behind the cheerful, friendly, A-student demeanor her friends knew so well. "Just a guy," she'd say, waving a large hand with carefully lacquered nails. "It's nothing serious."

For the next year and a half, Sara skillfully concealed the depth of her relationship with Adolfo and the double life it entailed. By day, she remained the hard-working, Brownsville honor student, president of the soccer booster club, voted the school's outstanding physical education student. Perhaps she didn't go out with the crowd after school anymore—"Gotta study," she'd always say—but who could knock her for that? It seemed to be just one more affirmation of what everyone at Texas Southmost College knew: Sara was going to make it some day.

By night, though, her studies concerned not English Lit but the dark powers of kadiempembe, the demon god of Palo Mayombe. The pretext of Christian Santeria had quickly vanished as Constanzo introduced Sara to black magic. With a Cuban-American witch at her side, she learned to slice the heads from chickens with a single, quick stroke, offering the spurting, hot blood to primitive gods, feeling their shadowy presence swirl around her like cobwebs. She, too, knew Sara Aldrete was going to make it in life, but it would be through asking those dark deities for good grades, for wealth and power, for all the things she had craved and couldn't have as a Mexican girl whose family had barely scratched its way into the middle class.

At night, after the rituals were finished and their hands had been washed clean of blood, she listened raptly as Adolfo explained his plans to build an empire on the border—and her role in it. He was El Padrino, and she was to be his La Madrina, the godmother. Together, they would rule.

Much later, friends and teachers would decide that yes, after all, they had noticed a few subtle hints of change in Sara, their all-American girl, especially after she met Adolfo in late 1987. For one thing, there was that peculiar secretiveness about a necklace of red beads Constanzo had given her, beads she would never take off. They seemed redder on some days than on others—as if they had been dipped in something, dye or paint, that later dried and faded. She had warned a friend never to touch them.

And now and then outside the classroom, she made offbeat, impassioned remarks about magic and Santeria, and how the movies always got it all wrong, leaving people in the athletic department where she worked slightly bemused at her vehemence. At the same time, though, she was utterly conventional in her anthropology class, which included a lengthy discussion of primitive, Afro-Caribbean religions and magic. In fact, the professor later recalled, she didn't say a word during that discussion. Funny, because she usually took part in class debates.[1]

"She never gave an inkling that she had any special interest or knowledge of the occult," Professor Anthony Zavaleta remembered. "Obviously, she was concealing things. But we had no way of knowing."

When pressed by girlfriends eager to hear about her gorgeous new boyfriend, Sara would finally give in, in the process displaying a talent for turning a story around, for placing herself at the heart of things without regard for the truth. Sara was the kind of girl who always broke up with a boyfriend; no one ever heard Sara say a boyfriend broke up with her. So when the questions about Constanzo would fly and she could no longer ignore them, Sara would state airily, "Adolfo is obsessed with me."

Then, with just the right hint of embarrassment tinged with pride, Sara would go on to explain how Constanzo was consumed with passion for her. He wanted to possess her, to dominate her, to dedicate his life to her, Sara would say. Even after her arrest more than two years later, Sara still talked about how her dark Cuban lover would fly into rages if she even suggested spending time without him.[2] She said he would phone her dozens of times a day, dunning her at work at Texas Southmost, where she was a part-time office clerk in the athletic department. He called so often she couldn't get her work done and her bosses started getting angry.

She said it was all very flattering, almost overwhelming to be courted with such force, but it was getting out of hand. Adolfo began to demand strict accountings of her day, minute by minute. Every date became an interrogation. "He was always asking, 'Who was that I saw you with?' " Sara recalled with a crooked smile. "He didn't want me to have a life."

But others remember differently. They recall a girl willing to do anything to be with her beloved Adolfo, not the other way around. Constanzo's followers say it was Sara who, once her dependence on him had been firmly established, began a relentless pursuit of the distant and uncommunicative godfather. She wrote him endless love letters begging him to sleep with her, long after he had lost interest—that is, long after she had served her purpose on the border and he had returned to the arms of Martin and Omar.

"I can't believe how much my heart pounds when I'm near you," reads one unsigned letter written in English and, according to Mexican police, written in Sara's handwriting. "I long to have your arms around me and feel your body against mine. I know you don't feel like I do, which is why I don't have the courage to sign this. But I just love you more than words can say."

The letter ends with "XXX OOO XXX." Hugs and kisses.[3]

Sara's teachers and coworkers in the athletic department at Texas Southmost can't remember her being hounded by phone calls from Constanzo or anyone else. They say it never happened. They remember only that she was a fine worker, an excellent typist, always on time, dependable and smart. But for a financial aid student with a part-time, minimum-wage job, she always had a wad of cash on her after the fall of '87. She was constantly buying lunches and breakfasts for everyone, picking meals up on the way to work, then refusing to accept money, even on occasions when she came bustling into the office with five or six bags of fast-food.

"You're a generous kid," one of her coaches said one day, watching her plop a bag of burgers on his desk, then flee from the five-dollar bill he held out to her. "How do you do it?"

"Don't worry about me," she called back over her shoulder. "I've got plenty."

"I can see that," the coach said under his breath. "But from where?"

Even more puzzling was her new dark blue Ford Taurus with its sophisticated car phone. Where had that come from? Sara would never say.

And finally, she began to tell lies—a constant stream of seemingly meaningless little lies. One day she came to work in a neck brace and said that she had wrecked her new car. The next day she showed up driving that same car, which had not a scratch on it.[4] "Oh, the accident wasn't as bad as I thought," Sara said when someone noticed the discrepancy. The neck brace came off suspiciously fast, too.

Another time she showed up at school bandaged and hobbling on crutches, accompanied by a ridiculous, ever-changing explanation about dog attacks or assailants in the night. Sometimes she seemed to lie out of simple habit.

No one guessed her newfound secretiveness was a commandment of her new religion, or that her strangely red beads had been soaked in blood, or that her injuries were the products of violent states of spirit possession, in which she would writhe and whirl before Constanzo's satisfied stare. They never knew her money and car came from Constanzo's witchcraft and drugs, and when the revelation finally came, everyone who knew her at the college was stunned.

At the time, though, friends figured she was merely eccentric, that she had a strange sense of humor or just liked to make up stories. They liked her so they let it ride. After all, she was one of the school's top students. Everyone knew Sara would make it big some day.

The day after she agreed to "go around" with Adolfo, the two of them went shopping together at the Sunrise Mall. Constanzo wanted to look at some gold jewelry for himself, but then Sara mentioned that the following day was her birthday—September 6. She would turn twenty-three.

To Sara's surprise, Constanzo, who had grown indifferent whenever Sara tried to discuss her interests and concerns, seemed ecstatic at this bit of news. Then the reason became clear: it had nothing to do with Sara.

"Really?" Adolfo exclaimed. "That's my mother's birthday. This is incredible! We have to call her."

As he dashed to a pay phone, dragging Sara by her hand, he asked what time she had been born. Sara said she thought it was around half-past three in the morning.

"Even better," Adolfo exclaimed as he hastily dialed. "The same as my mom." Not only did this mean great things for his and Sara's relationship, he went on, but it also meant that Sara would have the same magical abilities his mother possessed. They only had to nurture them with a few ceremonies to bring them to the surface.

"Hi, Mommy," Constanzo said brightly into the phone, his voice and face transformed with childlike joy. Sara was shocked. Her stern Adolfo never used endearing terms like "sweetie" or "honey" with her, and here he was addressing Delia as "Mommy." She felt a vague unease she couldn't quite justify.

"Mommy, I met a girl who was born the same day as you," he said. Then he added, almost as an afterthought, something he had never mentioned to Sara. "We're in love."[5]

After chattering happily about the details of their birthdays, Constanzo pronounced Sara and his mother "astral twins." Then he insisted that Sara talk to his mother, thrusting the phone at her eagerly.

The two women chatted awkwardly for a while. Delia politely told Sara that she had to visit the family in Miami, but Sara didn't miss an edge of resentment. Mommy doesn't want to share her Adolfo, Sara thought.

"This is more than I could have asked for," Adolfo said when Sara had hung up, more to himself than to her. "I couldn't have planned it better."

"What do you mean?" Sara asked.

Adolfo looked at her blankly a moment, as if he didn't recognize her, then smiled broadly, his voice robust again. "I just meant, isn't it something that the two women I care most for in the world were born on the same day! We must celebrate tomorrow. I'll take you to the best restaurant in town for your birthday."

Constanzo's ebullient mood died, though, when Sara said he was being very sweet, but that she had some long-standing plans to spend her birthday with some girlfriends.

"You'll cancel, of course," Constanzo said.

"No, I can't," Sara replied. "I made those plans a long time ago. I told you about them yesterday."

"Yes, but you weren't my girlfriend yesterday," Constanzo fumed. "Now you must do as I say." He went on to shout that he didn't care about her friends, that they were worthless and she should realize that. He had no friends, and was glad of it, he proclaimed. Yet beneath the sudden petulant fury, Sara thought she sensed a note of desperation, even envy. She found herself wondering if anyone had ever thrown a birthday party for Adolfo.

However, in Sara's recollection, she decided to stand firm against Constanzo's bullying this one time. She told him she would not continue dating him if he was going to try to control her life. "I told him he wasn't my boss, he was my boyfriend," Sara later recalled.

On this first day of their new romantic relationship, the normally tyrannical Constanzo backed down for once—unwilling to risk a breakup that would spoil his plans. "I'm sorry, Sara," he said contritely, his face bearing a wounded look, though his eyes remained flat and dull. "Of course you should go see your friends. I just don't want to lose you."

As they left the mall, Adolfo added, "You know, I really should meet some of your friends. That way, I wouldn't feel so jealous."

Again, Sara was surprised. Previously, Constanzo had shown nothing but disdain for her friends. "Okay," she said. "You can meet my girlfriends tonight, maybe after dinner. We're just going to the Drive Inn on Avenida Obregon."

"Actually, there's someone in particular I want to meet. Don't you know some boys from Matamoros whose father is a rancher?"

Sara thought immediately of the Hernandezes. "Yes. But how did you know?"

"You forget what I do for a living," he said, smiling and patting the shirt pocket where he kept his wallet badge. "I know what business they're really in. And it's not growing corn."

Sara nodded. She had seen their new cars, the big houses, the wads of money they stupidly flashed in the bars near the bridge, letting everyone know what they did for a living—and not caring. She, too, knew what the Hernandez family did for a living. Sara used to date Elio Hernandez, poor little Elio, pudgy shrimp that he was. But he had money, Sara had to give him that, and he had always been like a puppy around her, giving her anything she wanted.

"You're not going to arrest any of them, are you?" she asked. Her alarm was not out of any concern for Elio, but because acting as an informer, even an inadvertent one, was as sure a way of getting killed on the border as leaping into traffic.

Constanzo put his arm around Sara possessively. "Of course not. I just want to . . . help them."

"Well," Sara said, "I know Elio Hernandez. I can call him for you . . ."

"No, no, that won't be necessary," Adolfo said, ushering her into the Lincoln, parked by itself in the vast, empty parking lot surrounding the mall. "Remember my third prediction?" he asked. "About the friend who would come to you with problems?"

"That's Elio?" Sara asked, her long neck swiveling to watch Constanzo as he started the car.

Constanzo nodded. "That's Elio. He'll come to you with a problem. And you'll tell him you know a man who can help. You'll say, 'I know a witch with great powers you should meet.' "

Sara was shocked. "He'll think I'm crazy. I can't say that."

Constanzo flashed her a smile as warm and human as the grille on his Lincoln. "I think you can," he said, still grinning, as if he had already seen it happen. "I know you can."[6]

By October 1987, Sara was ignoring her studies to learn the ways of Palo Mayombe, thoroughly under Constanzo's spell. She no longer objected when Adolfo told her what she could do, where she could go, whom she could see. She soon realized he was involved with drug trafficking, not policing, but it didn't seem to bother her. In Sara's world, the life of a contrabandista could be an honorable one.[7]

Adolfo, meanwhile, had adopted the habit of introducing Sara as his wife to people they met on the street or at dinner meetings with people he called "businessmen"—men with bodyguards and expensive suits and eyes like cloudy ice. Drug dealers and gangsters, Sara knew. Their names were infamous. At these dinners, Constanzo would kiss her hand and, with feeling in his voice, ask all present whether they agreed that Sara was the most beautiful girl in Matamoros. Her heart would melt and the men at the table would politely, sometimes heartily, voice their assent. But when they were alone, this romantic side of Constanzo faded from view, leaving Sara deflated and disappointed. It was all part of Constanzo's show.

One Sunday afternoon, while they were walking near the main plaza in Matamoros, Sara watched a dark, hulking man with a terrible scar rippling across his face walk toward them and greet Constanzo. Adolfo introduced him to Sara as Salvador Vidal Garcia, a sub-comandante of the federal Antinarcoticos. Once again, Adolfo referred to Sara as *mi esposa,* my wife, but before Sara could say anything, he and the policeman had walked several paces away for a whispered conference. When they parted, the grim-faced Salvador continued on his way across the plaza. "He works for me," Constanzo explained with a wink.

"Why did you tell him we were married?" she asked. She felt an unreasoning fear of the scar-faced man. "I don't like his looks."

Constanzo laughed. "So he'll know never to hurt you," Adolfo said without further explanation, increasing Sara's uneasiness. "Salvador and I are working on something together."

Despite all his pretensions of marriage and his courtliness in the presence of others, Constanzo was rarely affectionate toward Sara. He never called her beautiful or said how lucky he felt to be with her, and his disinterest in sex still confused her. He traveled between Matamoros and Mexico City every week or so, but when he and Sara parted or reunited, there were no longing kisses, no fevered hugs. She began to think something must be wrong with her.

So Sara started fixing her straight brown hair elaborately, dying it auburn and putting it up in a swirling mass on top of her head, making her look even taller. She took to wearing sleek black outfits of lace and silk, with gold lamé slippers on her feet, all to entice Constanzo. Adolfo, though, never seemed to notice. His kisses remained almost brotherly, and in bed he was mechanical and quick.[8]

As he had with other lovers, Constanzo attempted to make up for his chilly personality with lavish gifts, spending thousands on Sara during daylong shopping jaunts to Houston and San Antonio. In the short time they had been dating, he had filled Sara's jewelry box three times over. Her home had been equipped with a new stereo, a color television, and a video recorder, bought by Sara with Constanzo's cash. And he had financed a $7,000 addition to the Aldretes' house as well. With his money, Sara built a separate upstairs apartment, where she could live—and practice her new religion—in privacy.

The answer to her lover's curious indifference was not long in coming. During their month-long courtship, Sara also became friendly with Martin, in some ways forming an easier, closer relationship than she had with Adolfo. On lazy afternoons they would watch soccer matches on television together, cheering themselves hoarse while Adolfo buried his head in a newspaper. One day, while Constanzo was out conducting business—exactly what he did remained unclear to Sara[9]—Martin even gave her a nickname: *La Flaca*. The Skinny One. In time, all of Constanzo's followers would call Sara La Flaca.

Late in October, after watching TV, Sara asked if Martin had a girlfriend. When he looked startled by the question, Sara apologized for prying, but said she just would like to meet her sometime. She had assumed the handsome and manly Martin had a girl, if not several. "Maybe Adolfo and me could double-date with you," she suggested.

Martin said that would be fine. But afterward, whenever Sara broached the idea with him or Adolfo, they always changed the subject.

Finally, when Sara came by Constanzo's apartment one evening after school, Martin greeted her at the door. His face was flushed, his expression anguished. Sara guessed he and Constanzo must have had a fight.

"Flaca, Adolfo has something he has to tell you," Martin told her abruptly, as he pulled on a jacket and fled through the open door.

"Don't you even say hello?" she called after him. "What's wrong?"

"Nothing is wrong, Sara," Constanzo said, startling her. He was standing half in, half out of the shadows, and she hadn't seen him. The living room, as usual, was lit only with candlelight. He shut the door and sat Sara down, then he brought her a soda. They chatted for a while, but Sara grew impatient and demanded to know what was going on.

"I wanted to tell you this before," Constanzo said softly, "but I didn't want to hurt you. Martin didn't want me to say anything, but it's time."

As he paused, groping for words, Sara found her heart racing all of a sudden, as if she had run to Adolfo's house, rather than driven.

"You see, there are . . . others in my life."

"Oh my god," Sara said. "You're married, aren't you?"

Now it was Adolfo's turn to look startled. Then he almost laughed. "No, nothing like that."

"Well, what, then?" Sara demanded.

"I have two lovers. In Mexico."

"So, what's the problem?" Sara answered. "If you're not married, then you can break up with these women. Right?"

"You don't understand," Adolfo replied. "They're not women."

"What?"

"They're men."

Sara just stared at him. Several minutes passed as she kept asking if he was joking. He kept saying no. Patiently, talking Sara through her shock, he explained that he was a familiar face in the gay bars of Miami and Mexico City, even in the little gay community of Brownsville. She just gaped.

"Sara, how could you be so blind, anyway?" he exclaimed, getting irritated by her continuing shock. After all, he had bedded the gay son of a prominent Brownsville city elder—it was all over town, he said. What's more, he was always hanging around Brownsville's historic, Spanish-style City Hall, which doubled as a bus depot and, by night, as a showcase for the city's small flock of transvestites. They strutted their stuff up and down Main Street like rouged and florid peacocks, awaiting pickups and tricks. Constanzo was a regular there, a sometimes rough but always generous customer, known to some as Alfonso, to others as Alonso.[10]

It was all too much for Sara. She had seen Constanzo as the essence of manhood. He was her man, her future, but now it all was slipping away. "And I suppose," she finally blurted, choking back the tears, "that one of these two lovers of yours is Martin. That's why he couldn't look me in the face today, right?"

Constanzo said she supposed correctly. But it didn't change anything as far as he was concerned. He still wanted to be with Sara, he said. He needed more than one person, and she should understand that. He was sorry he had hurt her, but he had finally spoken out about his bisexuality because, he said, he loathed pretending to be something he was not.

"I didn't think I had to pretend with you anymore, Flaca."

Sara's head whirled with images. She saw herself in bed with Adolfo, then imagined her friend—her friend!—Martin slipping into her place when she left, rustling under the same covers, still warm from her body. It made her sick to her stomach.

"Oh yeah?" Sara said, her tears flowing now, streaking her face with trails of mascara. "Well let me tell you—you and me are through."[11]

She got up to leave, but Adolfo rose too, reaching across a coffee table to grab her wrists. Sara tried to yank free, but his grip was like iron. She felt the power in his cold hands, and her will slipped away. She realized she didn't really want to leave. Despite it all, her fascination with the enigmatic magician still held. She still loved him.

Sara felt used and betrayed, and yet some secret part of her still hoped she would win in the end, that she could change him somehow, make him hers. She could do it, she thought.

"We're not through, Sara," he said calmly, staring into her hazel eyes with his penetrating black gaze. "You know that. We'll never be through."

Despite her grief, despite the sick feeling welling within her chest, Sara found herself nodding.

It was true, she knew. They would never be through.

Sara, wait a minute," a voice called, its sound whipped across Avenida Alvaro Obregon by a brisk November breeze, a cool taste of autumn. "Sara, wait."

Across the street, a young black-haired man in a denim jacket was waving at her. She waved back and smiled, but a terrible feeling of *déjà vu* had struck Sara at the sight of the man. The smile was forced.

Sara had been buying a taco from her favorite food stand after a day at school. Adolfo was away in Mexico City and she was alone, seeking solace in a lonely meal, missing him and the lessons in black magic he was slowly imparting. A month had passed since he had told her he was gay, yet still they were together. Now and then she had left love notes on his desk, his pillow, in his car. He never mentioned them.

As the man in blue denim waved to her and dashed across the street, Sara felt Constanzo's grim presence beside her, a chill wind blowing down her collar. He had predicted this would happen.

"Hello, Elio," Sara said as the short, stout leader of the Hernandez family puffed to a stop in front of her.

"Hi, Sara," he said with a broad smile. "I haven't seen you in a long time."

Though she knew what he would answer, Sara had to ask the question. "How have you been, Elio?"

A sad look passed across the little man's face, his small, thick mustache twitching beneath his nose. His narrow shoulders seemed to slouch even more than usual, and his head seemed too large for his plump little body. Sara found herself wondering how she could have ever gone out with Elio. "Oh, Sara, you don't want to know," he said, waving his hand with what passed for macho bluster. "I am not well at all. I have problems. Big problems."

There it was, just as Adolfo had said. The third prediction had come true. Sara had a sudden impulse to just leave, to turn away without another word. This would be her last chance to get out, she realized. Once she had become Constanzo's recruiter, there would be no turning back. Get out while you can, part of Sara screamed silently.

"I won't trouble you with my grief," Elio was saying uncertainly now. "It's just that since my brother was killed, everything's fallen apart. Now I think they're trying to kill me."

Sara noticed that his gaze had shifted to her breasts as he talked. Stupid little Elio, she thought.

"Don't be silly," she heard herself say, in a voice that was little more than a croak. "Tell me all about it. I may know someone who can help."

"Really? Who?"

"Don't laugh," Sara said, resigned to her role now, almost beginning to relish it. "But he's a witch."

Elio didn't laugh.

13

The initiation would take place during Holy Week, the third week of March 1988.

Constanzo liked the irony. He would bring new members into his cult of death during a week in which everyone else in the city celebrated rebirth and resurrection. Let them pray to their stupid God, who never answers a single prayer. Fools! His gods were real, you could touch them, suck them inside you, feel their power. All it took was unflinching dedication to evil. And to blood.

Constanzo had returned to Mexico City in November and had not been back to Matamoros since, except for a brief Christmas visit. He and Sara, however, had talked on the phone almost daily as he coached her on how she should prep Elio with tales of Constanzo's powers.

After nearly a month of swapping messages on telephone-answering machines, Elio Hernandez and Adolfo de Jesus Constanzo finally connected directly. By then Sara had awed Elio thoroughly with stories about Constanzo's great strength, his clairvoyance, his access to dark forces. She flirted with Elio throughout, although she always pulled back in the end, sending him home in disappointment to his wife.

Sara informed Elio how Constanzo had known he would come to Sara with his problems. She explained how her success in school was guaranteed magically, through the blood rituals of Santeria. "He can help you, too," she told Elio.

Uneducated, superstitious, and, most of all, desperate in the wake of his brother Saul's death and their failing business, Elio was inclined to take a chance. On the phone, Adolfo offered simply to protect Elio's family and make his business better with magic. All the young trafficker had to do was come to Mexico City. "We can discuss the terms in person when you get here," Constanzo had said.

Elio had murmured his assent.

Elio Hernandez had no idea just how thoroughly Constanzo would change things for his family and his business. But elaborate preparations had been underway long before the two men ever met—preparations that had nothing to do with magic. The key to Constanzo's plan for the Hernandez family was Salvador.

Salvador worked for the corrupt comandante of the federal police in Matamoros, Guillermo Perez—who, in 1989, would become a fugitive, with five million dollars of dirty money left behind in his desk. In 1988, however, Perez was still making a fortune on drugs, with no one to challenge him.

Perez, in turn, was a hireling of the notorious Juan Garcia Abrego Mexican drug-trafficking organization, the largest criminal gang in the Rio Grande Valley, the de facto government of Matamoros.[1] Perez had grown rich stealing millions of dollars' worth of drugs seized from small-time traffickers, locking them up, then reselling the dope for the gang. Only members of the mob organization and those who paid protection money to it were safe from Perez.[2] This same ruthless crime organization Perez worked for—and by extension, Salvador worked for—also had employed Elio's murdered brother, Saul Hernandez.

Salvador had heard the whole story and told Constanzo: Juan Garcia Abrego had met Saul Hernandez ten years before and befriended him. The Hernandez family had been dirt-poor farmers when one day Saul used his tractor to pull a stranded truck free of the mud. The truck, so the story went, allegedly was piled high with Garcia Abrego's marijuana.[3] In gratitude, Hernandez was given a menial job in the mob organization—driving, making deliveries, odd jobs. All the same, it still paid more in a week than Saul and his brothers normally earned in a year.

A few months later, an assassination attempt left Juan Garcia Abrego's brother hospitalized in Matamoros. Saul volunteered to guard the brother from a second murder attempt, and he spent a week at the wounded man's side, vowing to protect him with his life. When Saul left that hospital, he had not only earned Juan's complete trust, but also a spot high up in the mob organization, trafficking in drugs. Saul and Juan became inseparable friends.

As a result, the Hernandez family seemed set up for life. Saul brought his brothers into the business, and together they middled deals for the organization. The Hernandez boys, puffed up with machine guns and tough hired hands, would move the mob's drugs across the border, sell them to stateside dealers, pay off their mob bosses, then keep a tidy markup for the family. They made huge profits without having to put any money up front, all because Saul and his rusting tractor had earned a powerful man's trust. Not that the money wasn't well-earned. The Hernandez family took on the dirtiest, riskiest end of the mob's smuggling operation, insulating the organization's loftier members from direct involvement in moving drugs to the U.S. side of the border, where cops were not so easily bought.[4]

But the business was shattered—and a door opened for Constanzo—on the night of January 7, 1987, when Saul was gunned down as he and a notorious crime figure, Tomas Morlet, left an equally notorious restaurant in central Matamoros, called Piedras Negras. The owner of the restaurant was Juan Ñ. Guerra, usually referred to simply as Juan Ñ. (pronounced EN-yay). A legendary figure in Brownsville, he is allegedly the godfather of Matamoros and the uncle of Saul's patron, Juan Garcia Abrego, who had allegedly inherited day-to-day control of the crime organization from the old man years before. Saul, the trusted aide, was a fixture at Piedras Negras.

Saul's companion on the evening of January 7, Tomas Morlet, had been a comandante in the Federal Security Directorate, a Mexican police agency so corrupt the government eliminated it in 1985 for routinely giving police badges to drug traffickers, among other illegalities. It had been created with the assistance of the CIA. As part of that organization, Morlet had been a powerful figure in Mexican law enforcement, once assigned to maintain security for Secretary of State Henry Kissinger and, later, the exiled Shah of Iran. Morlet's official downfall came in 1986, when Mexican prosecutors accused him of murdering Kiki Camarena, the DEA agent tortured and killed in Guadalajara in 1985. Morlet was released a few days after his arrest "for lack of evidence," and began a new career as a drug trafficker, feared and hated by many, yet still largely untouchable.

As the two men left Piedras Negras, a black car slid to a stop in front of the restaurant and an unidentified gunman unloaded a machine gun's full clip into Morlet. Saul just happened to get in the way of a stray bullet, catching one in the groin. It opened an artery and he bled to death before help could reach him.[5]

Saul's body hardly was buried before his brothers began bungling. First of all, Serafin Hernandez Rivera, the eldest brother, was busted within a month of Saul's death while waiting for a dope load at an isolated airstrip. Elio's taking command only made things worse. He was a hothead, Salvador had reported to his padrino, a victim of little man's complex, always ready to shoot it out over nothing, drawing attention and trouble wherever he went. Even in the macho world of Mexican mobsters, there was such a thing as prudence, and Elio had none. The gangsters thought him stupid and dangerous, in every way the opposite of his brother Saul, who had been refined, charming, even sedate—yet deadly when he needed to be. The professionals wanted nothing to do with Saul's little brother Elio, and they cut off the supply of drugs to Rancho Santa Elena like a spigot gone dry.

Constanzo stood ready to fill that void. Through Salvador and his boss, Comandante Perez, Constanzo had a direct link to the largest, most powerful criminal organization in the Rio Grande Valley—the very same people who had forsaken the Hernandezes. Constanzo would tell Elio he could use magic to bring back the protection and the business, knowing he had the contacts to back up his promise.

At the same time, the Matamoros mob had its own use for Constanzo. It had lost a valuable and reliable trafficker in Saul Hernandez and a vacuum had been created, an enticing avenue for rival smugglers with none of Saul's loyalty. Constanzo was ready to fill that void, too. He let it be known via Salvador that he would provide the brains the Hernandez gang sorely lacked, while at the same time pushing out the rival traffickers who had settled like carrion birds around Saul Hernandez's corpse.[6]

Constanzo's carefully planned pitch had something for everyone.

The mob would have a loyal family again for moving drugs across the border, while at the same time clearing the decks of unwanted competition. For the Hernandez clan, the drug pipeline would open again at Rancho Santa Elena. Knowing nothing of the behind-the-scenes wheeling and dealing by Salvador and Constanzo, the instant change in the family's fortunes would seem nothing short of magic.[7]

As the meeting with Elio approached, Constanzo became sure his plan could not fail. He had seen it in the shells; he had stared into the rot and stink of his nganga and saw it clearly. And as he considered the rival smugglers who might have to be eliminated to reestablish the Hernandez drug business on the border, another plan began to take shape, one he had not considered before but which now seemed as obvious as it was intriguing.

Perhaps he could attempt another ritual. Like the one he had held for the Calzadas.

On the morning of Wednesday, March 23, 1988, Sara Aldrete took the train from Matamoros to Mexico City. She passed through the harsh border country villages where hollow-eyed peasant children stared mutely at the passing train, on to the outskirts of Mexico City, where mile upon mile of tin-roofed hovels fronted streets with raw sewage flowing through open ditches on either side. These makeshift neighborhoods housing poor immigrants from the countryside finally gave way to the more genteel inner city and its staid architecture, as the train creaked through the aging heart of the most densely populated city in the world. At the train station, marked with a half-century's worth of smoke and grime, Adolfo, Martin, and Omar met Sara.

She and Omar, meeting for the first time, immediately hit it off. They began chatting together in the backseat of Adolfo's Thunderbird like two teenage girls. Sara had adjusted to her place in Constanzo's "family"—he was still her ticket out of Matamoros, gay or not.

Sara told Adolfo that Elio planned to drive to the city with his wife the following day, which was fine with Constanzo. Sara had to be prepared for the next day's ceremony with a ritual of her own.

They drove away from the city, reaching in a half-hour the newly paved boulevards and trees of the suburb Atziapan. Adolfo wanted to show off his new house to Sara, who had never visited him in Mexico City before. He, Omar, and Martin stayed in Atziapan most of the time, though Constanzo still maintained the two condominiums in the city on Calles Jalapa and Pomona.

As they pulled to a stop, several young women emerged from neighboring houses to greet Constanzo. Sara thought they were practically hanging on him, which amused her, given what she knew of his sexual preferences. Constanzo, as usual, introduced Sara as his wife. "It keeps them off my back," he whispered to her, making her laugh.

The tour of the place Constanzo gave her both impressed and frightened Sara. The ten-foot walls and well-tended greenery bespoke wealth, but the elaborate security system featuring five remote-controlled, closed-circuit television cameras covering all avenues of approach to the house suggested Adolfo had enemies as powerful as his magic, Sara thought. Backing up the cameras, a radar-activated security system cast bright spotlights automatically on the street whenever a car passed in the night. Out by the garage, "the boys," as Sara called them, had constructed a pistol range and its target, Sara could see, had been pimpled many times by bullets.

As Adolfo showed her the grounds and lectured her about the need to maintain security here—he didn't say why—Sara grew uncomfortably self-conscious. She could feel the cameras watching her, and she imagined Constanzo leaving her to leer over the screens, playing back the tapes, looking for some telltale sign of her betrayal. But that was ridiculous, she told herself, she would never betray Adolfo. Then she realized he had stopped talking and was staring at her curiously.

"Now, don't ever forget, you must lock the gate behind you whenever you come and go," Constanzo said. "I know you would never . . . betray my trust in you."

Sara was certain he had emphasized the word "betray." He had read her mind! She was sure of it. Suddenly she felt like a traitor, not for something she had done, but for something she might do in the future. Something he had foreseen. But that was crazy, Sara told herself. She'd never betray him.

Suppressing an overwhelming urge to cough nervously, Sara said as calmly as she could, "Of course not, Adolfo. I'll lock the gate."

But he had already turned away.

After an excellent lunch prepared by Omar, the foursome drove into the city. It was time, Adolfo said, for Sara to become rayado, like Omar and Martin and all the others. She would be the first to be initiated into the border branch of the Church of Constanzo, he told her, laughing at his little joke.

They drove to the apartment on Calle Pomona, then clambered up the steps to the third-floor flat. "This is where I do my trabajos," he told Sara.

Upon entering, the first thing Sara saw was an array of statues of saints ranging from a foot tall to life-size, vividly painted and surrounded by candles—tapers stolen from churches, Omar whispered in her ear. Every saint Sara had ever heard of, and some she had not, was there, staring at her with hard ceramic eyes, like a frozen congregation. Scattered around the figures of the saints were the butts of Cuban cigars smoked to varying lengths, hot peppers, bottles of rum and other liquor, and glasses of water. At the sandaled feet of the figures, soup tureens held offerings to each god: dead chickens, candy, a dark viscous liquid Sara guessed was blood, coins, and many strings of beads, each one different, made up of colors associated with the orishas inside the saints.

There had been two smaller but largely identical displays in the Calle Papagayos house in Atziapan, though instead of sitting on the floor, as in the apartment, they had been set upon great altars of marble. Custom-made, Adolfo had boasted.

Once again, Adolfo gave Sara a complete tour. She saw the living room was lavishly furnished with white leather couches and chairs, with glass and chrome coffee tables between them and plush carpeting on the hardwood floor. The dining room had a huge antique oak table with room for ten. Yet, despite all this luxury, the immaculate condo still stank of death, a foul smell that invaded Sara's nostrils, clinging even after she left, making her wonder if she could ever get used to it. She would have to, of course, and even begin to like it, for only then would she enter the world of the nkisi. Constanzo's world.

Adolfo showed her every room except one. "What's in there?" Sara asked, pointing to the closed door.

"You mustn't go in there," Adolfo said sternly. "That is where I do my work. If you go in there without me, something will get you."

He called it his room of the dead. "Later, when the moon rises, you will be initiated there. You'll see for yourself what lies behind that door. But for now, stay away. I must go out to make preparations." He leaned to give her a brotherly kiss on the cheek, then he and Martin left.

Sara sat down in the kitchen to chat with Omar for a while, and was surprised to find that he was not just some sexual plaything, cook, and housekeeper, but that he had studied all sorts of magical beliefs in his youth, not just the Santeria and Palo Mayombe that Constanzo had mastered. She guessed, correctly, that he probably was the second in command after Adolfo when it came to religious matters, even before Martin. "But Adolfo, he is the most powerful magician I have ever heard of," Omar said. "I have no powers, just knowledge."

While Omar busied himself making dinner, Sara drifted back down the hall, drawn to the closed white door and the mysteries that lay behind it. She hesitantly pressed an ear against the door, imagining somehow that she would hear the power of Adolfo's nganga behind it, humming like some fantastic dynamo charged with magical current. But she heard nothing except her pulse roaring in her ear as she pressed against the door.

After staring at the doorknob, she reached out slowly and tried the door, fearing that it would open yet unable to stop herself. The door was locked. Sara was more relieved than disappointed.

When Constanzo returned an hour later, Sara was curled up on the glove-soft leather couch, watching television in the living room. He stood before her, arms akimbo, closed his eyes for a moment, then gave her his patented stare. "What were you doing at the door?" he asked.

Sara saw he knew what she had done. There was no point in denying it. "I'm sorry, Adolfo," she said abjectly, cowed once again by his apparent mind reading.

Then Constanzo laughed, breaking the tension. "I only warned you for your own good."

She laughed, too, and Adolfo reached out, putting his hand on Sara's shoulder. But the squeeze he gave her was ungentle, a warning that he might not be so understanding next time.

"Let me explain what will happen now," Adolfo said, still gripping her shoulder. "After dinner, you will come into the room of the dead, where my prenda lies. The others will be there to assist."

"What others?" Sara asked, but Constanzo ignored the question.

"I am their padrino and you will be their madrina. We must do this now, because I need you for Elio's ceremony tomorrow. When Elio is initiated and you both go back to Matamoros, you will be bound together, and he will have to obey you, his godmother."

Sara raised an eyebrow at this. She would be in charge? She hadn't anticipated that.

"Of course, to become a palera and a caretaker of the nganga, you must give up your God and your Catholic Church, with its lies about the great reward awaiting you in death." He paused, suddenly seeming to tower over Sara as she sat on the couch before him. Now her delight faded to a nervous excitement. "The only reward is here, now, in power and magic. Not in some Catholic heaven. We take that power in us, to be one with the spirits, to make them serve us. That is the meaning of Palo Mayombe. Everyone else, all the outsiders, are animals. Now you must welcome kadiempembe as your guiding spirit. You must let your soul die. You will be one of us."

During this impassioned, terrifying speech, Adolfo seemed to loom larger with every word, and his face seemed to become kadiempembe's as Sara watched. "Are you ready?" he asked.

For the first time, the enormity of what she was about to do struck her fully. Yes, Constanzo had explained this to her before, but abstractly, in terms of what he had done. Now she had to turn her back on twenty-three years of hard-core border Catholicism welling up inside her in protest. She had to give up God?

"Answer me, Sara!" Constanzo demanded.

Then she thought of her long years of going to church and praying for change, never getting an answer. Yet in a few short months with Constanzo, she had seen his magic work—for him and for her. His gods listened. They rewarded those who believed, and the rewards were tangible, immediate.

And then she thought of being in charge back home, of being Elio's boss, of being La Madrina. Her dilemma suddenly was solved. "I'm ready, Adolfo," she said, voice quavering but clear. "I have been for a long time."[8]

Dinner was a subdued affair, punctuated only by three separate rings of the doorbell. Each time the bell sounded, Omar rose silently, answered the door, then Sara could hear the sounds of muffled conversation and of footsteps accompanying Omar to the room of the dead. Then Omar would return and sit down to resume eating, saying nothing.

After dinner, Adolfo brought Sara to a bedroom where clothes had been laid out for her: white pants, white shirt, white shoes—the only color suitable for palo rituals. Constanzo told her to wear nothing under the shirt and pants.

When she reappeared in the living room, ghostly and pale, Adolfo was gone. Omar stood alone in the dim candlelight, dwarfed by the statues of the saints. He, too, was dressed in white, a flicker of brightness in the shadows. "Come," he said, taking her hand and leading her to the closed room. At the door, he stood on his tiptoes and tied a white blindfold around Sara's eyes. Then the door opened and Sara was drawn inside.

Immediately, she was assailed by suffocating clouds of cigar smoke billowing around her head. She was told to breathe deeply of it, which she did, sending her into a fit of coughing. As she gasped, she became aware of a new smell, the brackish stink of a coarse rum being sprayed at her. It was *Aguardiente de Canoas*—literally, Firewater of the Cane, a cheap Mexican liquor known for inflicting brain damage and hallucinations in large doses. It was favored in all of Constanzo's ceremonies.

As that smell faded, a more persistent odor invaded her nostrils, the one Sara thought most appropriate to el cuarto de los muertos. She smelled the stink of decay, of rotting meat and congealed blood. She smelled death.

Someone gently pushed her back several steps. Feeling her legs bump a chair, she sat and waited. The bottle of cane liquor suddenly was thrust against her lips, banging her teeth as it was upended. Before she could react, the burning alcohol coursed down her throat, setting her head roaring, choking her. Gagging, she tried to push the bottle away, but someone held her arms and she was forced to keep swallowing. She heard Martin whisper she should drink, that it would help the spirit enter her. She was allowed to breathe for a moment, and the fierce burning subsided, becoming an almost pleasant warmth inside her. The bottle was returned to her lips. This time, she drank greedily.

Constanzo began chanting in Bantu to summon the gods and the spirits of the dead. He had taught Sara some of the words, and she understood much of what he was saying. Except it didn't sound to Sara like Constanzo's voice. It was a horrible, rasping whisper, the voice of the nkisi speaking, the spirit inside the nganga. Normally, the nkisi was under Constanzo's dominion. But at this moment, when it was being asked to open the dark world of the dead to Sara, the nkisi entered Adolfo. Now it was in control, she believed. "You seek power from the dead?" it whispered in her ear, its breath reeking of the rum. "Well, I *am* the dead!"

She heard four or five strange voices chanting then, several she did not recognize. The room seemed filled with spirits, and she began to panic. Where was Omar? Or Martin? She imagined a possessed Constanzo wildly swinging a glinting knife. A cold, fevered sweat coated her body. Her head spun from the liquor. Almost, she cried out. But before a sound could leave her opened mouth, a hand clamped on it and Omar hissed, "Be silent. Say nothing."

Sara nodded against his hand, biting her lip until the bitter taste of blood filled her mouth.

The Constanzo/nkisi was chanting in Bantu again, telling her to pray to the *Siete Potencias,* the seven most revered and powerful orishas. She would become a priestess to one of them before the ceremony ended—if the nkisi agreed to admit her into the mysteries of Palo Mayombe.

A clucking chicken was brushed up and down her body, then its head was severed in a spray of blood, hot liquid hitting Sara in the face, spattering her white shirt in red splotches. Something heavy was dragged before her next, something struggling, as if it was being held or bound. She heard a muffled bleat, the brush of fur against her leg—it was a goat, Sara realized. The bottle was at her lips again. She swallowed until she could hold her breath no longer.

Constanzo's chanting reached a crescendo: He was speaking of blood and power and of appeasing the world of the dead by feeding the nganga blood and life. He told Sara that the powers were about to enter her, that she, too, would become magic.

She heard a swishing sound then, like a baseball bat swinging, and an ugly, fleshy thump. Then a gout of hot blood spilled on Sara and though she could not see it, she knew Constanzo/nkisi had just decapitated the goat at her feet. Blood was everywhere. She was dripping with it, inhaling it along with the smoke and the rum, feeling its warmth. And, she realized with a queer quickening of her pulse, part of her was enjoying it, finding comfort in its heat. Reeling with drink and the stench of death, she felt an almost sexual thrill, as if something really was entering her. Something powerful and dark.

At that moment, someone roughly ripped open her shirt and pulled it down to her waist. Buttons popped, the animal blood streaming down her chest. Then she felt something burning on her back and shoulders—Constanzo's knife, she realized. She was being made rayado, her flesh was being faintly marked by a series of crosses and Xs that symbolized her acceptance by the nkisi.

"You are one of us now," Constanzo said, still speaking in the spirit's graveyard voice. "There is no God for you now. Your soul is dead." Then, in his own voice, with the spirit returned to its nganga domain, Adolfo said quietly, "Your orisha is Oshun. Pray to her."

Oshun, Sara knew from Adolfo's lessons, was an African deity hidden inside the Catholic image of Our Lady of Charity. Very powerful, she was master of money and love, marriage and sex. Oshun could turn a family against itself, or bring love out of hate.

With the sweat and blood cold and drying on her fevered skin, Sara nodded to herself, then slowly smiled, feeling drained and tired. She imagined the powers of Oshun protecting her, nourishing her, and felt content.

"Now," she heard Constanzo say, "you are La Madrina."

The blindfold came away. Sara blinked in the candlelight, peering through the swirls of smoke into the reddish light. She saw Omar and Martin and Adolfo, and in back of them the nganga, with its sticks and innards wet with blood. Some of it was hers, Sara knew, feeding the greedy nkisi, binding it to her.

With them stood three other cult members she did not know. They were introduced to her as Jorge Montes, Juan Carlos Fragosa, and Damian, who used no last name. Sometimes, the girlish Damian explained with a wolfish grin on his bloodstained face, he became La Damiana. He looked at Constanzo as he said this.

So he was a transvestite, Sara thought with a mental shrug. So what? After this ceremony, the deviancy seemed trivial.[9]

Only when she rose to greet them did she realize her shirt hung in tatters around her waist. Martin placed a clean white bathrobe around her shoulders, allowing Sara to cover herself. Strange, she thought, but she had felt no modesty or shame at standing half-naked before these men. The robe was just to keep her warm.

"They are your family now, Sara. They took part in your initiation. They witnessed your acceptance by Tata Nkisi," Constanzo told her. "I am their godfather. And now you are their godmother. After me, they will obey you. Nothing in this room can hurt you now. Now, you have the power."

Dreamily, she said, "I know." Then she walked from the room without waiting to be told and headed for a hot shower. After she had cleaned up, she decided she would tell Adolfo that it was time she knew his plans for the border. All of them. She wanted to know everything.

She was, after all, La Madrina.

14

Elio Hernandez had left Matamoros a skeptic, headed to Mexico City out of desperation. Three days later he returned a believer with Constanzo at his side, initiated into the cult just as Sara had been, possessed of a cocky confidence and painful mystical symbols carved into his shoulders and back.

Constanzo had wined and dined him, then awed the little contrabandista with secret knowledge and displays of power. Elio was amazed when his new godfather had stared at the cards, then saw how the Hernandezes had earned the trust of the mob, how the family had entered the drug business, then how they had fallen from favor after Saul's death. On a more practical level, Constanzo made certain Elio met the hulking Salvador, so the young trafficker understood he would help the Hernandez family not just with magic but with followers in high places. By the time Constanzo finished with him, Elio was practically begging to be taken into the room of the dead. He could sense salvation awaited him inside, even if he didn't understand Constanzo's mumbo jumbo.

Once inside, the neophyte was blindfolded and filled with cane liquor, made witness to innumerable animal sacrifices, then cut with Constanzo's sacrificial knife—not small scratches, like those he had placed on Sara's back, but deep bloody arrows scoring Elio's shoulder until the man cried out in agony. Satisfied with the bloodletting, Constanzo had welcomed Elio into the cult, pronouncing him a part of mysteries he didn't begin to comprehend. When Elio said as much, Constanzo told him not to worry, since Sara would act as his spiritual guide, his godmother. "Obey her. She is your family now." Elio had nodded his assent, eyes spinning with pain and alcohol.

Afterwards, settled in at VIPS, Constanzo explained how he would magically protect and restore the Hernandez drug business through rituals and spells. In exchange he asked for half the profits. Even with such a split, he assured Elio hastily to blunt any skepticism, business would improve so much that the Hernandez family would be making more money than ever. And if it didn't, he promised to forgo any payment. That's how confident he was: magic, with a money-back guarantee.

Before Adolfo had even started wolfing his second hamburger, Elio had agreed to everything. He realized he had nothing to lose and, besides, he sensed Constanzo was the genuine article. "When do we start?" he asked.

Constanzo laughed. "We already have."[1]

Back on the border with Elio, Constanzo wasted no time. He and Martin began what would become weekly trips to Matamoros, quickly building a new branch of his religion.

"Who are your most loyal men?" Constanzo had asked Elio, knowing that anyone the little trafficker controlled was certain to be wild, violent, and weak-minded. What other kind of person would serve Elio?

Constanzo was not disappointed. Soon, five new acolytes were brought before El Padrino, all friends, gunmen, and smugglers working for the Hernandez family. These first five would be converted to form a nucleus of followers, Elio and Adolfo decided. Then, with the strength of numbers behind them, Elio could bring his more skeptical brothers into the religion as well.

First among the new believers was Alvaro de Leon Valdez—nicknamed *El Duby*—the violent *pistolero* known for his swaggering boastfulness and for shooting up the cantinas of Matamoros. As a child of ten, he had found a gun in his father's dresser, loaded it, then climbed a tree, from which he happily began taking shots at the neighbors. He had grown up with a fondness for hurting others, and the vicious Duby found himself fascinated with the bloody rituals of Palo Mayombe. Constanzo pegged him as a natural for the role of mayordomo de la prenda.

With Duby came his friend and sidekick, Carlos de la Llata, another thug and coke dealer who worked the tourist bars, selling one-hundred-dollar grams, amply cut with sugar, talcum powder, laxative, rat poison, or whatever else he could find to foist off on the gringo college students.

Aurelio Chavez, the brutish foreman at Rancho Santa Elena, became a crucial early convert, eager to belong. Also among the first batch of converts was a young homosexual cousin of Elio's, Sergio Martinez Salinas. Nicknamed *La Mariposa*—The Butterfly—Sergio had helped the Hernandez family with some nighttime drug loads in the past. Constanzo had other nighttime activities in mind for the effeminate young man; bringing Sergio into the fold was his idea, not Elio's.

A small, bright, and ruthless friend of Elio's, Malio Fabio Ponce Torres, rounded out this first group of followers in Matamoros. From a wealthy family, Malio was a student in a college in Monterrey, Mexico. Slim and dangerous, given to carrying a stiletto knife he wielded with a cobra's speed, Malio caught Adolfo's eye immediately. Nicknamed *El Gato,* The Cat, Malio was far smarter than the others. Sensing a kindred amoral spirit in Malio, Constanzo decided to make him Elio's superior in the cult's hierarchy.

Constanzo pulled the converts aside one at a time, making a different offer to each. Instinctively he appealed to their most fundamental desires.

To Malio, Constanzo offered power over the Hernandez drug operation. Yes, he told El Gato, it was covert power, rule through manipulation, but it was power nonetheless. "You will be my captain here. I will trust only you, Malio," Constanzo told him while the others were out of earshot at the London Pub in downtown Matamoros.

Malio leapt at the chance.

For Chavez, he offered a chance to be more than a hired hand for the first time in his life. As part of the religion, he would become an equal to his employers, something he had never dreamed possible before.

He vowed to do anything for his godfather.

Sergio's reward was access to Constanzo's bed, while Carlos, who simply wanted to belong to a gang no one could push around, was offered the protection he sought, both magical and physical.

El Duby's inducement was the most basic of all. "Do you want to make money?" Constanzo whispered to him during the first ritual in Matamoros, a bloody initiation. "Do you want to kill?"

Constanzo had taken one look at Alvaro's ferretlike face, the pointed chin and narrow eyes that seemed to disappear when his thin, cruel bark of a laugh sounded, and he knew Duby didn't give a damn about Santeria or ngangas or religious precepts of any kind. All this young psychopath cared about was unlimited money and unlimited cruelty, Constanzo saw. And he promised Duby both.

"My godfather is a very serious man. I'd do anything he told me to do," Duby once told a childhood friend. Then he laughed. "I'd even kill you, Jose."[2]

The living room of Sara's new upstairs apartment became the new group's cuarto de los muertos on the border. But because the reeking nganga Constanzo promised to create for Elio could not be set up there, only limited ceremonies were possible until better quarters could be found. In the beginning, though, those were all that was needed.[3]

Throughout the first weeks of April, Sara and Adolfo used the apartment to school the new converts in Santeria and Palo Mayombe, conducting what Sara called their "classes." When the witchcraft lessons were through and each convert vowed his loyalty, they were initiated in a ceremony of candlelight and blood, during the week of April 15, 1988.[4]

Once again, Constanzo proclaimed them all a family, and he warned that his word was law. Disobedience meant death, horrible and lingering. "Your family comes before everything. You must always obey."

Though most of the acolytes were barely grazed by Constanzo's blade, Alvaro was heavily marked, as Elio had been, with bloody runes that resembled the feathered shaft of an arrow. This symbol, Constanzo whispered to them both, empowered them to kill for their new religion.[5] At the time, his statements sounded more symbolic than literal.

All five received necklaces of beads, each colored for a different orisha, their guiding spirit. After they were initiated, Constanzo sacrificed three goats, three chickens, three cats, and three tortoises to the gods, asking them for protection. He invoked Ochosi, the favorite of drug traffickers, to ward off the police, then fell into a state of spirit possession. Sara spent the next morning scrubbing furiously, but still the blood of goats and chickens and men stained her apartment, caked thick on the altar and floor.

Prancing around the apartment in wild gyrations, Constanzo shouted in his weird graveyard voice that he was Ochosi, and that he was willing to protect the gang if they remained faithful. In the fluttering candlelight, Constanzo's face seemed to elongate into a demon's face. Sara and the boys drew back, stricken by the face of a god, glaring crazily at them from Adolfo's eyes.

"You shall have your protection," he shrieked at them. "But you must remain faithful. You must obey." Then Ochosi whirled through the room, knocking over the candles, plunging the room into darkness. Someone yelped in fear—it sounded like Sergio, Sara thought. Then Duby struck a match and relit a candle.

When their eyes adjusted to the gloom, they saw Constanzo sitting calmly, his legs crossed, the spirit possession over. He stood up. "Now that you are rayado, there are three rules you must obey. Or you will die."

The first rule was to obey El Padrino's orders without question. Sara would take his place when he was gone, and she would report any disobedience. "My gods have no mercy with the unfaithful," he told each. "Nor do I."

The second rule was to accept the orishas, the spirits of the dead, and, most important, the power of kadiempembe. "For you, there is no more church," he ordered. "Christians are animals."

Finally, he forbade his believers from taking drugs. They must remain pure, Adolfo said. Or die.

As he always did when he wished to convince others of his powers, Constanzo spent the night conducting limpias and card readings for his new followers, showing them his peculiar ability to know their innermost secrets, while Elio and Sara looked on knowingly. And if these weren't enough to make them believers, the promise of money and power was. Soon, Constanzo vowed, they would construct the most evil and powerful nganga ever made, dedicated to kadiempembe, protected by Ochosi and empowered by the blood of their enemies. Then they would be unstoppable.

His next order of business was to find a place to house the cauldron. He quickly became dissatisfied with Sara's apartment, finding it too cramped and too accessible to Sara's well-meaning parents, who would be horrified to learn what went on behind their daughter's locked door.

Elio and Chavez soon brought him to the isolated fields of Rancho Santa Elena, where they followed a pair of tire tracks to the back of the spread. The path took them to a rundown shack standing on a cement slab next to a corral. Constanzo was ecstatic.

"This will be our temple," he announced the moment he saw it. "It is just as I pictured it, just as the shells told me it would be." He made a sweeping, inclusive gesture with his right arm, then fixed wild eyes on Elio. "Do you know what we can do here?" he shouted, his words caught and carried by the wind, making him seem far away, even though he stood just six paces from Elio.

Elio shook his head.

Constanzo turned away, facing the shed again, as if he could see something in the crumbling wood and corroded metal that the others could not. "It doesn't matter," Constanzo said, more to himself than Elio. "I do."[6]

At the same time Constanzo indoctrinated his new followers with animal sacrifices, he and Salvador were working behind the scenes to restore the Hernandez dope trade. By mid-April, immediately following the Ochosi ceremony in Sara's apartment, corrupt federales in Matamoros made a ton of marijuana seized from other traffickers available to the Hernandez boys.

Constanzo had "predicted" the arrival of the dope, how much it would cost, and how much the gang would make on the deal. After they stashed the drugs at the ranch, Constanzo told Elio who would buy the dope. Although the name of the buyer had been supplied by the Matamoros mob, Constanzo told Elio that he had divined his identity through the cowrie shells.

Constanzo's magic had worked, Elio told his brother Ovidio, who was less than enthusiastic about giving Constanzo half their profits. Look at the evidence, Elio said, and Ovidio had to concede that their lot had improved drastically with Constanzo's arrival. The dope train had all but dried up for them, but as soon as Constanzo came along they had more marijuana than they had ever seen in one place. The warehouse at the ranch was full.

"We've never done this well, not since the federales burned the ranch in Oaxaca," Sergio told the others, as they moved the bales across the border, moonlight gleaming silver in the river's black water.

"It's El Padrino," Duby whispered, fingering his beads. "It's black magic."

After a quick sale in Houston, handled by Old Serafin, the family made a $200,000 profit on the marijuana load. Half went to Constanzo, as agreed. No one complained. It appeared he had earned it.[7]

Adolfo immediately gave a $5,000 "signing" bonus to Sara for bringing Elio into the religion. Elio, in turn, expressed his gratitude to Sara for introducing him to Adolfo by giving her the new Ford Taurus, complete with cellular phone. "Adolfo said I had to take care of you," Elio told Sara shyly when he presented her with the car keys. But when he tried to take her in his arms, Sara danced away.

"Thank you, Elio," she said, running her hand over the car, thinking what a toad Elio was, trying so obviously to buy her. "It's beautiful, but you know, I am La Madrina. I can't be with you. I belong to Adolfo."

They went for a ride then, but Elio sat silently fuming as Sara chattered to a girlfriend on her new car phone. He would have to talk to El Padrino about this. Constanzo would understand his needs. Later, though, after the business got settled.

Throughout the next five weeks, Constanzo directed Elio to run several more loads of marijuana and cocaine, obtained through the federales or directly from the Matamoros mob—and all blessed through dark rituals of protection. Elio followed every order.

By this time, though, the crime figures wanted Constanzo to fulfill the second part of his bargain. He was taking control of the Hernandez family, but he had yet to deal with any of the upstart traffickers.

Late in May, Constanzo explained to Elio that, though the Hernandez family had lost its old source of dope through Saul, other avenues were open to them. "Why should we pay others good money for drugs?" Constanzo asked. "Why give them our gold when . . ."

"When we can give them lead?" Elio said, finishing the cliché.

Constanzo rewarded Elio with an icy smile. They were ready for their first rip-off.

And their first murder.

The white sun of late May punished Moises Castillo's naked back as he worked the small field, uncooled by an ineffectual breeze that merely carried the odor of asphalt from the road to Matamoros a half-mile away. Castillo wiped the dusty sweat from his brow and stared up at the sun a moment, thinking that at fifty-two, he was too old for this backbreaking toil.

Moises had moved to Houston from Matamoros seven years before, determined to escape the endless grind of peasant farming. His twelve children, all grown now, had joined him in the big city, with all its promise of future, and they had given him twenty-nine grandchildren. As Moises Castillo was fond of saying, he had made it to the middle class.

But his aged father, Hidalgo, all gristle and gray mustache, still lived here in Matamoros, still farmed the hard, depleted soil next to the foul Rio Grande. He still wore the white straw hat and white pants and white shirt that Mexican dirt farmers have worn for generations. Hidalgo Castillo was seventy-three now, stooped and hard as a tree stump, yet he refused to retire. Whenever his son suggested it, Hidalgo would say the day he stopped planting was the day he would be planted in the ground himself.

So every year Moises came back to help his father, returning to the memories he had tried so hard to leave behind. Moises could never say no to his father. Unfortunately for Moises, he couldn't say no to the contrabandistas, either.

Every farmer blessed with land near the Rio Grande knows of the opportunities to make big money for little effort. Hidalgo's land was not only on the river, but far enough from the highway to make it a perfect spot to transport dope in the night. Certain contrabandistas were willing to pay a thousand to two thousand a trip to do just that, and Moises, without telling his father, was happy to oblige. All he had to do was let the traffickers stash their plastic-wrapped bales on his land for a few days, keep an eye on them, then make himself scarce when the time for the dope run arrived.

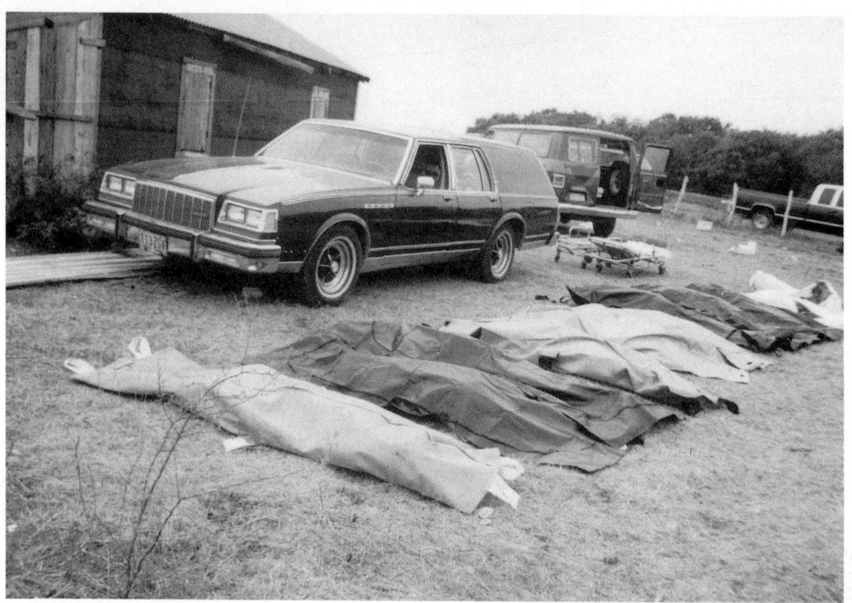

Body bags lay ready for transport to funeral homes after police stumbled on a mass grave at Rancho Santa Elena. *(Courtesy: Joe Hermosa)*

Gravediggers unearth fourteenth and fifteenth sacrificial victims of Constanzo's cult, this time from an orchard near Rancho Santa Elena. *(Courtesy: AP/Wide World Photos)*

Comandante Juan Benitez, commander of federal antinarcotics in Matamoros. He discovered the bodies and broke the case.

Assistant Federal District Attorney General Federico Ponce Rojas, who led the investigation in Mexico City.

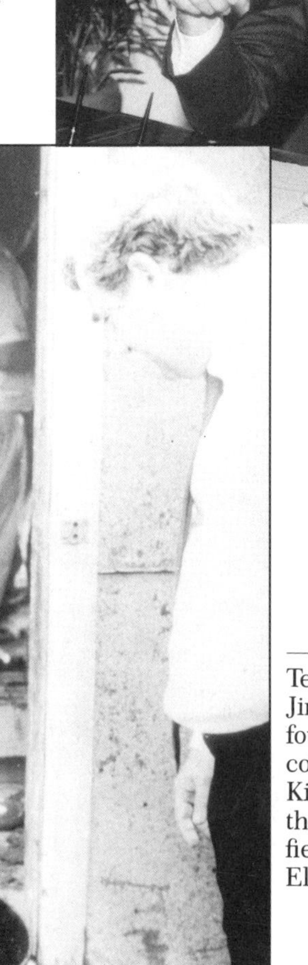

Texas Attorney General Jim Mattox peers into the foul cauldron which holds college student Mark Kilroy's brain, one day after the discovery of a killing field at Rancho Santa Elena.

Adolfo de Jesus Constanzo, wearing his ever present magical necklace and amulet, posing in his Atziapan home. From Omar's photo album.

Omar Francisco Orea Ochoa, cult member and lover of Adolfo de Jesus Constanzo. From Constanzo's "family" album.

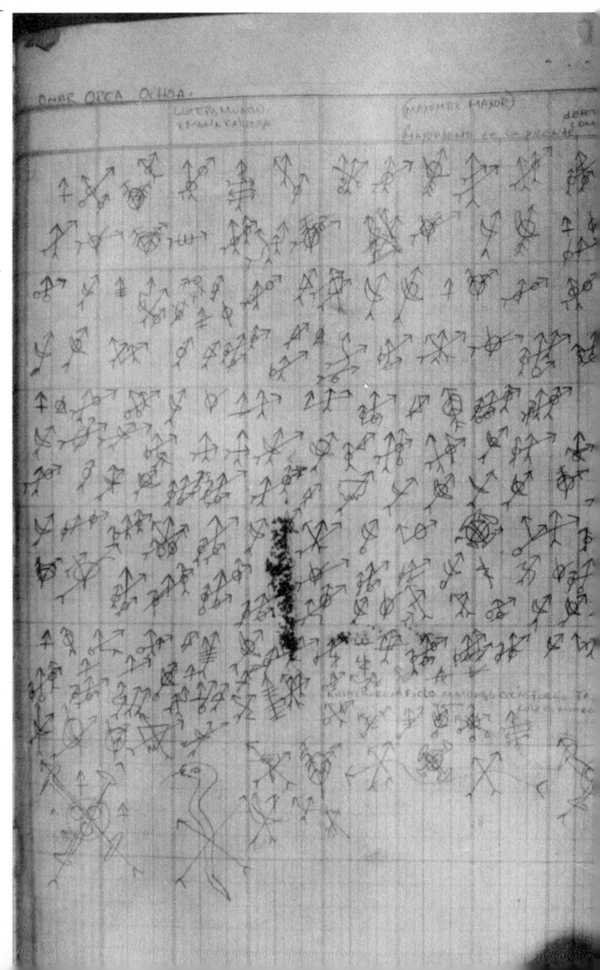

A page from Constanzo's *"libreta,"* his book of black magic dedicated to the Afro-Caribbean religion of Palo Mayombe. This page is dedicated to Omar, who is identified at top left as a *"mayordomo de la prenda,"* keeper of the jewel, which means he had access to Constanzo's darkest, most secret magic—the dreaded cauldron of death, the *nganga.*

The symbols on the page record a series of throws of magical cowrie shells used to divine the future and the wishes of the gods. Through them, Constanzo made magical prescriptions for Omar to bring him wealth, luck, and power.

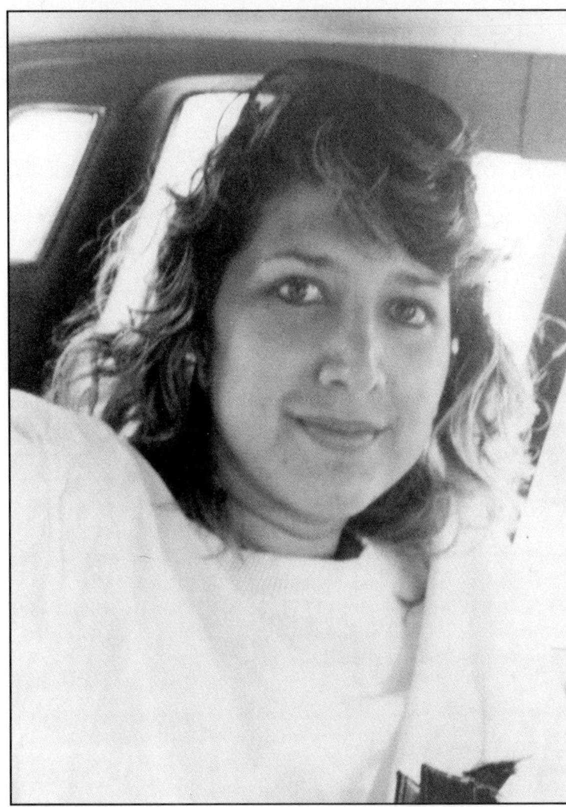

Sara Maria Aldrete Villareal, during an outing in Constanzo's Lincoln Town Car. From Constanzo's "family" album.

Martin Quintana Rodriguez, Constanzo's bodyguard and lover.

Left: Serafin Hernandez Garcia, "Little Serafin," Brownsville college student and devoted follower of Constanzo. He confessed to kidnapping Mark Kilroy, then witnessing his torture and dismemberment and death. *(Courtesy: Candice Leek and Rafael Martinez, Institute for Police Technology and Management) Right:* Elio Hernandez Rivera, leader of the Hernandez drug-trafficking organization, handcuffed at Rancho Santa Elena on the day of his capture. *(Courtesy: Candice Leek and Rafael Martinez, Institute for Police Technology and Management)*

Cult members Ovidio Hernandez (left) and Alvaro de Leon Valdez, alias El Duby, during a party in Matamoros.

Omar, Constanzo, and future sacrificial victim Ramon Paz Esquivel, alias La Claudia, posing in the Mexico City apartment of cult member Jorge Montes.

Constanzo's luxurious home in Atziapan, a suburb of Mexico City, complete with satellite dish and close-circuit video surveillance system. *(Courtesy: AP/Wide World Photos)*

James and Helen Kilroy address their church congregation during their son Mark Kilroy's funeral. *(Courtesy: AP/Wide World Photos)*

Mark Kilroy, twenty-one, tortured and killed in black magic rites.

Brownsville Customs chief Oran Neck, Texas Attorney General Jim Mattox, and Cameron County Sheriff Alex Perez speak to the press after the killings were uncovered. *(Courtesy: AP/Wide World Photos)*

Mexican district police haul cult member Alvaro de Leon Valdez—"El Duby"—into custody at gunpoint moments after a furious gun battle outside Constanzo's Mexico City hideout.

Bow and arrow symbol of the god Ochosi, hanging at the door to the shed at Rancho Santa Elena, where Constanzo conducted most of his human sacrifices. Among Ochosi's powers is the ability to ward off police and arrest. *(Courtesy: Candice Leek and Rafael Martinez, Institute for Police Technology and Management)*

The *nganga* is burned by police during an exorcism at the Rancho Santa Elena shed used in Constanzo's human sacrificial rites. The cross was left by peasants to ward off evil. *(Courtesy: Candice Leek and Rafael Martinez, Institute for Police Technology and Management)*

The shed at Rancho Santa Elena—Constanzo's temple of death—burns during an exorcism staged by Mexican federal police Comandante Juan Benitez Ayala. *(Courtesy: Candice Leek and Rafael Martinez, Institute for Police Technology and Management)*

Some of the contents of Constanzo's *nganga*, on display. Anthropologist Rafael Martinez dismantled the cauldron just before the exorcism, finding twenty-one blood-soaked sticks, fourteen horseshoes and railroad spikes, a roasted turtle, animal corpses, and the rotting remains of human organs and blood. Afterward, Martinez was ordered to restore the contents to the *nganga* so it could be ritually burned during the exorcism. *(Courtesy: Candice Leek and Rafael Martinez, Institute for Police Technology and Management)*

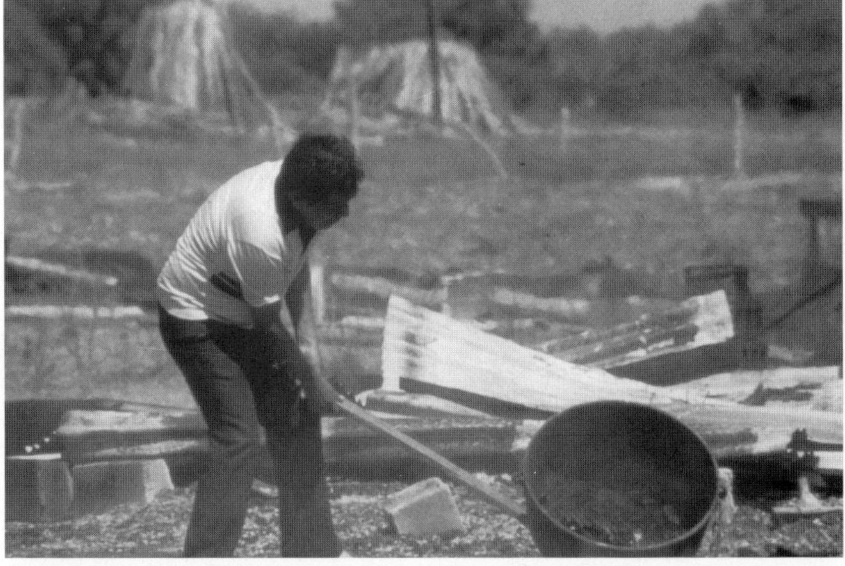

Eluterio—a *curandero* or white witch—hired by Mexican federal police to exorcise Constanzo's temple of human sacrifice, examines the charred remains of the *nganga*. Using fire to cleanse the evil, the *curandero* destroyed the shed and the human organs and dead animals inside the cauldron. *(Courtesy: Candice Leek and Rafael Martinez, Institute for Police Technology and Management)*

Statue and religious artifacts seized from cult members' apartments.

Wax skull and other black magic objects seized from cult members after the shootout.

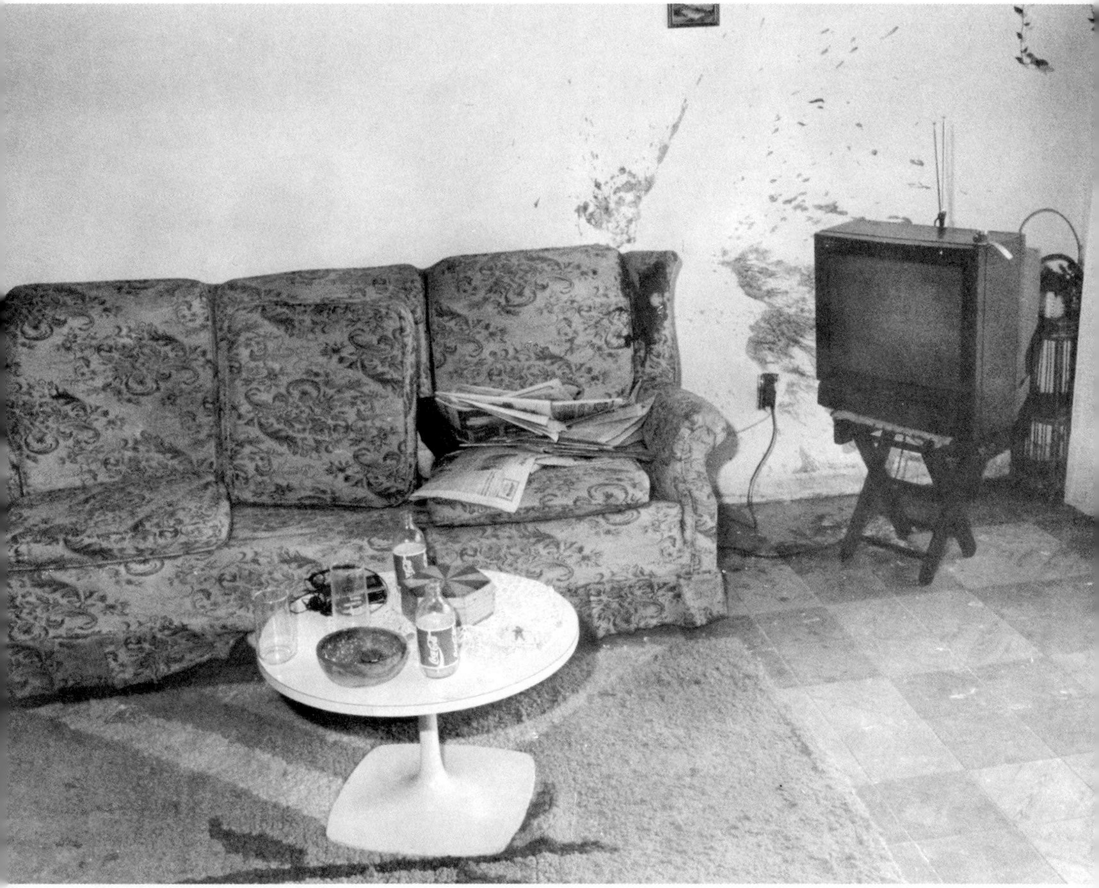

The decrepit living room of the cramped apartment on Rio Sena in Mexico City, scene of the shootout and Constanzo's death.

Constanzo's final hideout: The apartment building on Rio Sena. The third floor corner windows were Constanzo's.

Sara Aldrete at the press conference: "Adolfo would order you to do something, and you would do it. I don't know why. . . . He had a power."

The press conference after Constanzo's death. *Seated:* Mexican Prosecutor Federico Ponce, cult member Omar Francisco Orea Ochoa, prosecutor Abraham Polo Uzcanga. *Standing in center:* Comandante Rodrigo Martinez—"Superman"—and beside him, Sara Aldrete.

A Mexican federal policeman escorts gang member David Serna Valdez at the death ranch. *(Courtesy: Joe Hermosa)*

Cult members lined up for the press after the shootout and Constanzo's death. Left to right: Sara Maria Aldrete; Maria del Rocio Cuevas Guerra, alias "Karla"; Omar Francisco Orea Ochoa; Dr. Maria de Lourdes Bueno Lopez; Alvaro de Leon Valdez, alias "El Duby."

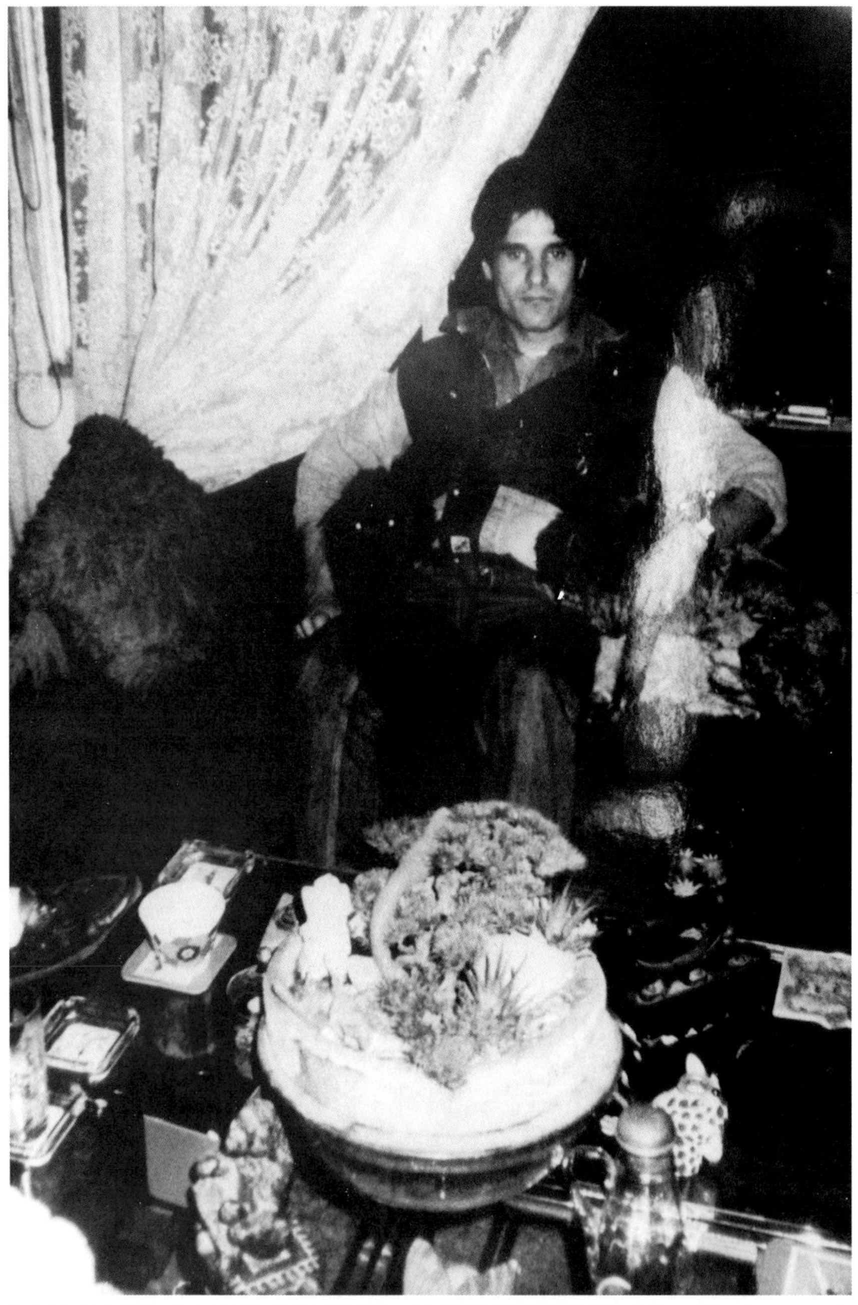

Adolfo Constanzo, El Padrino, poses in the Mexico City apartment of his follower Jorge Montes and the transvestite La Claudia in 1986. Two years later, El Padrino and his henchman tortured, killed, and dismembered La Claudia during black-magic rites.

That year there were plenty of new smugglers in town, each trying to claim a piece of the turf, and they were eager to make use of the Castillo farm. Moises was no criminal at heart, but he found ample ways to rationalize his complicity with the traffickers. For one, it really wasn't his marijuana, so he wasn't really hurting anyone. Then, too, it was the only way he could afford to take off from construction work in Houston to come help his father. Besides, they were moving dope up the road at Rancho Santa Elena all the time. The Hernandez family was making a fortune and everyone around knew it. Why shouldn't Moises get some, too? Not just for himself, but for his family, for his father, for his grandchildren to go to college.

On May 28, 1988, Moises was babysitting some three hundred kilograms of marijuana belonging to a small-time Matamoros trafficker named Hector de la Fuente, who had hidden it there several days before. Moises had known de la Fuente for years. He and the thirty-nine-year-old contrabandista had an easy relationship, with several years' worth of hidden loads and secretive crossings between them, bringing a measure of mutual trust.

As he worked the field beneath the merciless afternoon sun, Moises glanced nervously at the small shack where the drugs were stored, knowing he really didn't have anything to worry about but worrying anyway. De la Fuente had told him the drugs were supposed to cross that night, which would be a relief. He would just stay in the wretched ranch house he lived in when in Matamoros, let the *narcos* do their deal, then de la Fuente would bring him his money. Simple, he told himself.

Behind him, the ranch house was swallowed by afternoon heat shimmers, as if it had been enveloped by waves of water. Moises could see hawks and buzzards soaring high overhead a few miles west, riding the thermals pulsing from the ground like the sighs of some great, huddled creature built of dust and heat.

Looking down, he saw a trail of dust passing behind a stand of scrubby trees. A truck was approaching on the dirt road that led to his father's small farm. De la Fuente, Moises supposed. He walked over to greet him.

When de la Fuente's pickup truck ground to a halt in front of him, Moises noticed its bed was full of strange men, but he didn't suspect anything unusual at first. Nor did he see the guns bulging beneath their shirts and waistbands as the men leapt from the truck. Instead, he waved at de la Fuente, who jumped from the truck's cab, black snakeskin boots flashing beneath his black pants.

His smile of greeting slowly faded as he saw the look of fear on de la Fuente's face. And de la Fuente wasn't holding his hands behind his back; they were bound with gray duct tape. Moises's legs felt suddenly weak. He thought of running, but the men were all around him now. Some of them held guns.

Only one of the men smiled, a light-skinned man dressed in white clothes, with long black hair, styled and fluffed, and four necklaces of beads and gold around his neck, making him rattle as he walked. The man's smile held no warmth, only malice.

"Who are you?" Moises whispered, his eyes fixed on the dark-haired man.

"The devil," Adolfo de Jesus Constanzo replied. "Come for your soul."[8]

Moises Castillo's undoing came in two parts, both beyond his control:

First, he had agreed to help a trafficker who had no protection from police or mobsters, leaving both of them vulnerable. And second, the little ranch house he lived in while farming for his father just happened to lie next door to the home of Rancho Santa Elena's foreman, Aurelio Chavez.

Chavez, like the other new initiates, was eager to make his mark in the new cult. He had been told to be on the lookout for strangers moving drugs—trucks moving in the night, any sort of furtive activity in isolated areas. The Santa Elena foreman had spent every night combing the highways, his headlights off, looking for signs. He slept only an hour or two at dawn. He found nothing.

But late in May, after he had returned from another fruitless surveillance, he heard de la Fuente's truck in the distance. He crept outside, and there, practically in his own backyard, he saw a truckload of dope being unloaded onto the Castillo farm. The next day, he excitedly told his padrino.

Grabbing the unsuspecting de la Fuente on the way to town that afternoon was a simple matter. Elio's men forced him into a truck and made him drive the gang to his stash. Everyone but

Sara came that day: Adolfo, Martin, Sergio, Duby, Elio, Malio, and Chavez all were on hand for the gang's first big rip-off. "Bring shovels," Constanzo had commanded, and the men exchanged looks, wondering if they were going to be unearthing something. Or burying it.

While some of the men kept their guns trained on de la Fuente and Castillo, the others quickly loaded the marijuana onto the pickup truck. They would be moving it only a few miles to Rancho Santa Elena along back roads, and a simple tarp thrown over the bales would be enough to hide them.

After the marijuana was driven to Rancho Santa Elena, the gang marched its prisoners to an orchard a quarter-mile away, to a co-operative farm called Ejido Morelos. "This will do," Constanzo said, looking at the dusty trees of the orchard with approval.

Later, he would come back on a moonlit night, muttering Bantu prayers, removing branches from these same trees. They would become his palos, thrust into his new nganga—cut from trees appeased with human blood.

Standing in the empty orchard, Constanzo called everyone to his side, facing Castillo and de la Fuente. Then Constanzo asked for a gun. When little Elio handed him a silenced 9mm automatic pistol, Constanzo methodically checked the magazine, sighted idly down the barrel, then let the gun dangle at his side. When he looked up, everyone's eyes were fixed on the gun, captives and captors alike.

"Are you good Christians?" Constanzo asked the two prisoners, his voice mild.

De la Fuente just stared at the barrel of the black handgun. He said nothing.

"Are you good Christians?" Constanzo repeated, his voice still smooth and calm.

Castillo's lips trembled, then he whispered, "Yes, I am a Christian."

Looking at his followers, Constanzo said, "Didn't I tell you all Christians are animals?" Then he reached out, and with two quick pops from the silenced weapon, mere puffs of sound in the warm air, he shot both men in the head. As their skulls exploded in clouds of blood and their bodies crumpled to the ground, Constanzo said serenely, "We sacrifice animals."

His followers, even Elio, stood transfixed. Someone threw up.

They all had guessed the two men were to be killed. That was understandable. But for these young drug traffickers, violence and anger had always been inseparable. You worked yourself into a frenzy, ranting, screaming, frothing, and then you did it, almost without thinking, with fists or knives or guns. Only later did you think about it. But this had been different. Cold, emotionless murder, like the bite of a poisonous snake. Constanzo had killed them with a smile. He had enjoyed it.

One of the bodies still twitched spasmodically. With a bored look, Constanzo put another bullet into the head. Someone gagged again, drawing a sharp glance from El Padrino.

"Why did you kill them?" Sergio finally asked.

"I didn't kill them," Constanzo replied. "We killed them. And we did it so you would all learn."

"Learn what, Padrino?" Duby asked. Of all the new followers, Duby alone seemed eager to learn Constanzo's way of thinking.

Constanzo smiled. "To get used to it. Now, dig a hole for these. It's time to go."

Duby and Sergio grabbed shovels from the truck and set to work, Duby cheerfully, Sergio pale and sweaty. The others looked on uncertainly. Elio felt particularly troubled. This was not part of the bargain he had made with Constanzo. Those two men had been nobodies, people who lacked the firepower and the protection to be any real threat to the Hernandez clan. Elio even knew Moises slightly from his years on the farm. There was no reason for Constanzo to have killed them. The gang could have taken their dope with impunity, without fearing any retaliation. Why had he done it then? It bothered even hotheaded Elio, because only one answer made any sense: Constanzo did it because he felt like it. Elio tore his eyes from the bodies and looked at Constanzo with a new sense of awe, fear, and, despite the queasiness rocking his gut, admiration.

The hard soil yielded itself unwillingly to the grave diggers, making their backs ache and their hands bleed. They gave up after the hole reached four feet. The two bodies were dumped unceremoniously into the ground, locked in a twisted, dead embrace.

A year later, investigators excavating corpses at Rancho Santa Elena would puzzle over these two deaths at the nearby orchard, for they did not fit the pattern. There was no mutilation, no removal of organs, no bizarre rituals, as in all the subsequent murders.

The reason for this was simple, though, as any student of Palo Mayombe could explain. It was necessary for Adolfo to kill the traffickers and steal their marijuana before de la Fuente moved the drugs that night. But no ritual was possible that day, because the moon was waning—and Palo Mayombe magic cannot be invoked unless the moon is waxing.

"This time, we merely kill them," Constanzo had told his cult, as darkness gathered around them. He looked at them solemnly, each glassy eyed after witnessing the murders, yet strangely exhilarated by it all. He knew they soon would feel as he did—above the law, untouchable, superior. And since they were participants in murder, he knew they would be bound to him by guilt and complicity, and made loyal through fear of his gun and his blade. He was finally fulfilling his destiny. He had his own temple and his own following, and he had learned the darkest lesson of all: He found he could use killing to control the living. And he was learning to love it.

"Next time," the godfather said, "we will have a ritual. And then we will be protected forever."

15

While Constanzo began to search for a soul to enslave inside a new nganga, the ranks of his followers along the border swelled. Rumors of the twin killings in the orchard had spread in certain circles, attracting a certain sort of man to his side. They all had heard of the violence and power of El Padrino, and they wanted to be part of it.

A month after the killings, Constanzo initiated the man who, much later, would play a pivotal role in bringing down the cult with a lugubrious ride through a drug checkpoint. But at the time, Elio's nephew and helper, Little Serafin Hernandez Garcia, seemed the ideal follower, gladly submitting to the pain and fear of a bloody rayado in Sara's apartment in June 1988.[1]

Little Serafin seemed of particular value to the gang. While most of his relatives and all of Constanzo's other followers were Mexican nationals, Little Serafin was a U.S. citizen, and therefore could cross the border with far greater ease, becoming the perfect courier. Born in the tiny border town of Weslaco, Texas, he had been raised in Houston, then moved to Brownsville with his parents, becoming one of the few Hernandez boys fluent in English. He was nicknamed *El Chaparro,* which can mean either a small, scrubby oak tree or a short, chubby man. Either interpretation seemed to fit. Pale and short, his most distinguishing feature was a large, droopy mustache that seemed out of place on his small, sallow face.

Little Serafin was a college student—a law-enforcement major, no less—at Texas Southmost College in Brownsville, Sara's school.

He told college counselors and professors he wanted to be a policeman or a drug agent. Quiet, almost invisible in class, Little Serafin metamorphosed once he became a godchild of Constanzo, becoming a loud and boastful big shot around town and a would-be lady's man, given to proposing marriage to strange women or offering them expensive dates in exchange for sex. He believed Constanzo's magic made him a sure hit with the women, and the fact that he was almost universally turned down never seemed to deter him. Suddenly a big talker, Little Serafin was buoyed by the new money in his pocket and the tough, merciless gang members who surrounded him. He and Duby became instant pals, and Little Serafin admired the young thug's violent propensities. When Elio whispered to his nephew warnings of Constanzo's murderous side, suggesting he might want to be cautious in his devotions, Little Serafin shrugged it off. To him, the violence seemed no more real than a slasher movie on television. Who cared if strangers died?

Though he was little more than a gofer, the youngest Hernandez served another useful function: he proved to be an able recruiter for the gang. Within a week of meeting Constanzo, Little Serafin brought a friend into the cult, Jorge Valente del Fierro Gomez, a young cokehead who turned out to be the least serious devotee, just in it for kicks. He also recruited David Serna Valdez, a gay college student nicknamed *El Coqueto,* The Flirt. Serna, a friend and lover of Sergio's, was rayado with Little Serafin in Sara's apartment in a twin initiation ceremony.

With Little Serafin spreading the gospel, Constanzo's followers on the border soon numbered an even dozen.

Of all the smugglers in the Hernandez family, only Old Serafin Senior, the eldest brother, Little Serafin's dad, remained aloof from the cult of Constanzo. He would work on the drug deals, he would meet with El Padrino, but he avoided the ceremonies. His wife, a devout evangelical Christian, helped him resist the pull of black magic and murder, and he kept insisting to Elio that he wanted no part of Constanzo—though he did nothing to dissuade his relatives from joining. "I'm a drug dealer," he would later say. "I have been for years. But I don't kill people."[2]

Old Serafin was distressed that his son took part in the rituals, but his only response was to impose one rule: "Don't tell me about it, Fino. I don't want to know."

"Don't worry, Papa," Little Serafin replied. "It's just so I get good grades and all the girls. It doesn't mean anything."

And even Old Serafin had to admit Constanzo had brought success. The gang was swimming in drug money, driving a fleet of new cars, strutting boastfully through the downtown bars, unafraid and cruel. For his part, Elio's doubts and fears began to evaporate as soon as the memory of the orchard killings began to fade. After all, the drugs were flowing, as were the profits,[3] and Constanzo had positioned himself perfectly to take credit.

Each deal was the same. First, Constanzo would get a phone call from one of his police sources, telling him about a new load waiting at the police station. Other times he would be told where he could find some small-time trafficker with drugs ripe for ripping off.

Then Constanzo would gather his followers at the ranch. Of late, the rituals had shifted from Sara's apartment to the remote, windswept fields of Rancho Santa Elena. There, the wide-eyed converts would circle the new altar and its layers of caked animal blood, awaiting a demonic blessing. Ringed by candles, chanting in that awful voice of possession, Constanzo would then predict their next drug deal, telling who, what, and where, guaranteeing success.

"Do you doubt me?" he would ask, staring them all in the face, one at a time, until they averted their eyes and murmured no, no.

Then they went off to move more drugs and make more money. After a few performances like that, the gang members were willing to do anything he asked. Who cared if it was magic or not, or if any of them really understood the bizarre things Constanzo whispered and shrieked about? The point was, it worked. That was what counted.

Once the drug business was running along smoothly and the initiations were complete, Constanzo began to plan the central event of the summer: the creation of a new, powerful, supremely evil nganga at Rancho Santa Elena. Using the blood-fed branches taken from trees near the graves of Moises Castillo and Hector de la Fuente as his magical palos, Constanzo gradually built a miniature universe for a new nkisi in a huge, black iron cauldron hidden in the little shed at the ranch. Once again, the spiders and scorpions and railroad spikes and spices were thrown in the cauldron. Once again, a black cat was boiled and placed inside with animal blood, a roasted tortoise, and the glassy-eyed head of a goat.

Then it was time to find the proper nkisi—the skull and brain of a dead man. But this time Constanzo had no intention of relying on grave robbing. There would be another ritual. It was time to fully realize the predictions of his Haitian padrino.

The incomplete nganga was buried at Rancho Santa Elena to begin its all-important rot, while Constanzo waited for the moon to become propitious, and for the right victim to come along.

His plans were interrupted, however, when his predictions of murder spurred his most bloodthirsty follower, El Duby, into a fatal, drunken gunfight on June 23, 1988, leaving Duby a marked man in need of Constanzo's special protection. He had shot down Lauro Martinez, scion of a prominent Brownsville family and a reputed narcotics smuggler.[4] It had been just one in a long line of senseless, hothead shootouts that seem to rend the streets nightly in Matamoros, but now Duby feared a contract had been put out on his life by a vengeful relative of Lauro's.

The shooting had occurred in a sleazy border saloon called Los Sombreros, a favorite hangout for the Hernandez gang—and a year later, a stop on Mark Kilroy's fateful last night of partying. After drinking heavily and swapping insults and glares, Martinez and Duby lapsed into a turf battle over who could sell grams of coke at the bar. Duby, typically haughty, said his padrino claimed the bar as his territory. Lauro laughed and told Duby to go screw his old witch of a godfather, then slapped the diminutive Duby around the bar.

"Get out of here, you psycho," Lauro spat at the pistolero, then, with a cousin's assistance, shoved Duby out the door.

People were already slipping out of the bar at this point in the argument. The locals had heard unpleasant rumors about this godfather character, and they knew for a fact that Duby was crazy. Sure enough, the hotheaded Duby, slap marks still vivid on a face otherwise ashen with anger, ran to his car, then stormed back through the bar entrance with his gun blazing. Martinez went down, dead on the spot, while his younger cousin was wounded. On the other side, cult member Carlos de la Llata was fatally shot, his aorta nicked by a bullet intended for Duby, who then ran from the bar, leaving his dying friend slumped on the floor of Los Sombreros.

Although there were plenty of witnesses to the shooting, nothing ever came of the case. One of Duby's relatives was a high official at a local Mexican police agency, and the man intervened on Duby's behalf, quashing any attempts to prosecute.[5]

Afterwards, Constanzo raged at Duby for acting without orders, threatening to flay him alive for his stupidity. It had been a wasteful killing, Constanzo screamed. The gang had not only lost a member, but an opportunity for a ritual. Duby's enemy could have made a perfect sacrifice to his nganga.

"Do you understand?" Constanzo berated his follower, and Duby had nodded fearfully, expecting to die at any moment, totally cowed by his padrino. Instead, Constanzo calmed down and decided that Duby would come live with him in Mexico City as his second bodyguard. He would be safe from a revenge killing there. Duby babbled his gratitude, though, in truth, Duby became not a bodyguard but the lowest of flunkies in the Constanzo household, feeding the dogs and washing the cars, relieving Omar and Martin of those menial tasks.

Within a week of the Sombreros shooting, Adolfo, Martin, and Duby traveled to Mexico City as promised. Sara joined them a few days later, as did Salvador, who had been transferred back to Mexico City. This suited Constanzo's plans well. Since Salvador was no longer needed on the border, his position in the capital would allow him to pass on key intelligence on narcotics traffickers and enforcement efforts, keeping El Padrino's magical predictions on target and the Hernandez smuggling operations safe. To celebrate their good fortune, they all dined together at Salvador's new apartment on the Fourth of July.[6]

Upon his return to the home on Calle Papagayos in Atziapan, Constanzo found Omar angry at being left alone so long. Employing his usual tactic, Adolfo promised to bring Omar to Brownsville in August for another shopping extravaganza, but he was not so easily bought off.

"I feel like you're drifting away," Omar complained, finding Constanzo colder and more distant than ever, obsessed with his drug running and with finding the right victim for his new nganga. "You've changed."

His words seemed to have an effect on Constanzo, who softened a bit, allowing some rare moments of affection in place of domination. He took Omar out for a fancy dinner for just the two of them, then devoted the next several days to Omar, shopping and seeing movies together, making Martin and Sara jealous, but in the end appeasing Omar.

All the while, though, Constanzo was thinking of the cult's next ritual. He had decided it had been a mistake to insulate his young lover from his blackest magic to date, the ritual killing of the Calzada family. He had decided to change all that, to mold Omar into a man with no soul, as he had Martin. He had been planning to choose his victim during the upcoming shopping trip to Matamoros, but then Jorge Montes came along, and inadvertently offered his godfather the perfect opportunity to settle the matter right then and there. The perfect victim had practically fallen in Constanzo's lap.

Ramon Paz Esquivel, a surly transvestite who sold antiques for a living, at one time was Jorge's lover. Lately, though, he was just an unpleasant and unwanted tenant in the maid's quarters in Jorge's flat. Esquivel also answered to the alias Edgar N. (he had a police record for burglary and theft under that name), and when he wore his red dress and high heels, he was known as La Claudia, a slim and diminutive, if not very attractive, drag queen.

Disliked by all the tenants in Jorge's building, La Claudia would flout Jorge's affections by bringing young boys home with him, and they would drunkenly cavort on the stairs and landings within earshot of the scandalized neighbors. Then he would rise late, brutally hung over, and refuse to admit Jorge's clients for fortune telling. Jorge and his tenant argued constantly, though nothing was ever resolved.

Slovenly in every respect, La Claudia was fanatically fussy about only one thing: his antiques. He showed them daily in the nearby London Market, then hauled them back home to Jorge's place, polishing them painstakingly, fretting over the slightest scratch, constantly rearranging them in the apartment. He continually admonished Jorge never to touch the furniture, making Jorge feel like an unwelcome guest in his own apartment.

On July 16, 1988, Esquivel launched into a violent tirade against Jorge, accusing him of stealing one of his beloved antiques. Jorge, well aware that his roommate had just been questioned by police for a neighborhood burglary, was outraged by the little thief's accusations. What was he trying to do? Set him up? Would he denounce Jorge to the police next?

"You dare call me a thief, you little whore?" Jorge screamed, loud enough for the neighbors to hear through the thin, cracked plaster of the decrepit apartment building. "Get out. I want you out of here! Now!"

"I will not," Esquivel shouted back. "This is my home as much as yours. Who picked the furniture? Who pays half the rent, even though I live in your stinking maid's room? Why should I leave because you steal from me?"

The little man began to storm through the house, knocking things over in a rage. Then, seeing one of Jorge's beloved poodles eyeing him curiously, Esquivel lashed out with his foot, kicking the small dog across the living room. "And keep your damn dogs away from me. Get them out of the house. Or you'll be in trouble."

Jorge's face went white. He prized those dogs above all else. He had always suspected Esquivel of abusing them. Now he knew. "You'll pay for that, Ramon," Jorge hissed, then left the apartment, his mind consumed with one thought: "Wait until I tell Adolfo."

Ten minutes later, he stood breathlessly at the door to the condominium on Calle Pomona. When Constanzo had heard the story, he smiled and shook his head, his expression a study of understanding and compassion. Constanzo had met La Claudia before and had never hidden his disdain for the little transvestite. He had mocked Esquivel openly in the past, and now he launched a tirade against Jorge's stubborn tenant. But by then Jorge's anger was spent, and he began to wonder if coming there had been such a good idea after all.

"So, Jorge, you want to get rid of La Claudia?" Constanzo asked. "You want me to take care of it?"

Uncertain, Jorge held his tongue.[7]

"Good," Constanzo said brightly after a moment, a wolfish eagerness behind his smile. He reached into a drawer and drew out a knife that was almost as long as a machete. "Let's go."

Jorge and the others looked alarmed. Omar asked, "What are you going to do, Adolfo?"

"We're going to evict La Claudia for Jorge," he said with an innocent smile. "That's all."

Omar looked to Martin for confirmation, but he would not meet Omar's eyes. Seeing the hesitation, Constanzo felt his control slipping and lapsed into bullying. "Don't question me. I said let's go!" He whirled and headed for the door.

"It'll be all right, won't it?" Jorge whispered to Omar as they filed out after Constanzo. But Omar remained silent.[8]

Adolfo, Jorge, Martin, Omar, and a fourth follower of Constanzo's, Juan Carlos Fragosa, returned that night to Jorge's apartment on Calle Londres for a ceremony. Sara waited back at the condo.[9] Once there, candles were lit, the white clothes were slipped on, the power of the dead was invoked. Constanzo offered a prayer to kadiempembe, asking the dark god to guide him this night. Then they sat back and waited. The four followers stared nervously at one another while Constanzo sat serenely, cradling his knife in his lap, cross-legged on the floor, masked in shadows.

At last, La Claudia's footsteps sounded on the stairs, his key scratched against the lock. Esquivel entered, drunk and groggy. When he saw the candles and the men all in white, he stopped, blinking in surprise. "What's going on?" he slurred.

He was wearing a dress and a wig slightly askew, and his large, mannish hands flapped like lost birds in his confusion. He remained baffled even as a smiling Constanzo approached him with a glittering knife and a voice unlike any Esquivel had ever heard. "Hello, senõrita." And then Constanzo laughed.

They bundled him from the living room into the bathroom, squealing like a pig. Suddenly, he was cold sober. The awful witch who Jorge hung around was going to do something to him, he realized. He was muttering some strange language, staring at Esquivel with hungry eyes. Panicked, La Claudia sought Jorge's eyes with his own teary ones. Montes wouldn't meet them.

"I'm sorry, Jorge, I'm sorry," he blubbered. "Just let me go. I'll move. I promise. I'll pay you. Anything."

"Too late," Constanzo said.

They dropped Esquivel into an empty bathtub. Constanzo barked an order and Martin bound the little man's wrists with duct tape, then plastered a strip roughly across the man's mouth, lipstick smearing into a wide crimson stain. Then Martin began ripping away the transvestite's garish dress.

"What are you doing?" Jorge asked. "Why the bathtub?"

Constanzo grinned at him, pushing the drain plug in place. "To catch the blood, of course."

"You're going to cut him?" Omar shouted, alarmed, but Constanzo ignored him.

Esquivel's eyes bugged. He puffed his cheeks out and the tape gave way. "What do you want?" he wailed.

"Your soul," Constanzo replied. And the knife flashed.

Shocked at the sudden and unexpected bloodletting, Jorge and Omar asked to leave the room, unable to watch. Adolfo looked away from his work just long enough to instruct them to scatter one of Esquivel's antique paintings and several other small pieces in the lobby of the apartment building, as if the man had been mugged and abducted.[10]

"You don't want to be a suspect, do you, Jorge?" Constanzo asked.

Jorge shook his head and fled with Omar.

"I had hoped you'd be stronger than this," Constanzo called after Omar as they pounded through the living room. As Constanzo had commanded, the pair dutifully lugged the antiques downstairs and placed them where neighbors would find them the next day. Then they decided to walk the dogs.[11]

Martin remained at his godfather's side, however, grimacing at the carnage but resolutely following his lover's orders. He had never imagined himself a violent man before meeting Constanzo, and he took no pleasure in watching Esquivel die. But he had already been compromised by the Calzada killings, sucked in unknowingly, much as Jorge and Omar had been duped into participating this time. Martin had enjoyed the look of revulsion on his rival Omar's face—and the look of disappointment on Constanzo's that accompanied it. That alone made all this worthwhile to Martin. He would do anything to score points against Omar in their battle for Constanzo's affections.[12]

Juan Carlos Fragosa, meanwhile, was puking his guts up, just as Martin had a year before. He, too, would now become part of the inner circle, loyalty cemented by complicity.[13]

Only one neighbor heard Esquivel scream that night. The neighbor dismissed the loud, inarticulate wail, though, thinking that the little drunk was up to his usual escapades on the stairwell.

In the crowded bathroom, blood sprayed. Constanzo cut off the man's fingers, his toes, his penis—all while he lived. Martin and Juan Carlos watched from behind, eyes bright and frightened, mesmerized by the awful butchery. Juan Carlos had never seen Constanzo in action, had never witnessed the fevered violence. He shook as he watched.

"Don't worry," Martin whispered, consoling the neophyte with a pat on the shoulder, though he never took his eyes from the thing in the bathtub that once was La Claudia. "I was afraid the first time, too. But it gets easier each time. Believe me."

Even with the tape slapped back in place, the man made too much noise when Adolfo started to remove his skin, curling it back like a hunter skinning a deer. So he finally slit La Claudia's throat, satisfied that he had inflicted enough pain to make Esquivel's spirit into the angry, cursing demon he desired for his cauldron.

He stroked Esquivel's throat with his knife—that's how Constanzo thought of his blade's touch, a stroke, almost a caress—then stood back as the man's feet clattered against the porcelain of the bathtub. As the transvestite's life bubbled away through the gaping wound, breath gurgling wetly, Adolfo leaned close. "You are mine," Constanzo whispered, staring into his eyes, where consciousness was ebbing but still present. Constanzo saw recognition in those eyes. He was sure of it. It was the perfect sacrifice, just as he had prayed for.

He leaned still closer, whispering his parting words to the dying man. "You will serve me in hell, Ramon. I'll come for you."

Then it was over. The eyes dulled, the feet stopped kicking. A last, wet wheeze, then silence.

Constanzo became businesslike then. The blood went into a jug, so it could be carried to the nganga on Calle Pomona. It would be a powerful offering to the spirits to protect him during the next drug deal. Fingers, toes, genitals, and a shinbone were saved for the new cauldron in Matamoros. And finally, the brain was removed with a sickening chop of Constanzo's huge knife, spattering blood and bone in all directions. That, too, would make the long drive to Matamoros with the gang. "To help the nganga think," Adolfo explained as gore dripped from his fingers.

What was left of La Claudia was then shoved into three Hefty trash bags, along with the killers' bloody clothes. When Omar and Jorge returned, Constanzo snarled an order at them, and they set to work scrubbing the bathroom until it sparkled.[14]

Early the next morning, across town, three boys watched a black Lincoln race to a stop in front of a vacant lot. A man leapt out, ran to the back, and hurled some bags from the trunk. Then the car sped off.

The boys looked inside the bags, vomited, then called for police.

Another mutilated corpse was added to the files, another unsolved murder, just like the Calzadas the year before, though police found no connection at the time, despite the grisly similarities. The victim's roommate had reported the man missing after neighbors found antiques scattered in the lobby of their apartment building. The police went out to question the roommate, Jorge Montes, as soon as the body was found. He seemed very upset, the detectives thought.

"Isn't it terrible?" he asked the detective in charge. "Do you think you can solve this?"

The detective could only shake his head. "Who knows?"[15]

16

They never even asked his name.

He was just a dusty stranger headed nowhere in particular when a new silver Chevy pickup stopped on the shoulder of the road to Matamoros. Elio Hernandez leaned out the driver's window, squinting into the late-afternoon glare.

"Need a ride?" he called, a slight quaver in his voice.

The man didn't notice Elio's nervousness. He just shouldered his bundle—a pack of clothes wrapped in a blanket—and jogged on worn shoes to the pickup truck. "Thanks, amigo," the man said. "Where are you headed?"

"To my ranch," Elio said, trying to keep the fear he felt hidden, all the while feeling utterly transparent. "You know, I might have some work for you there, if you need some. You interested?"

When the hitchhiker said he was, Elio wasn't sure if he should be glad or despondent. Sure, it was what padrino had ordered, and Elio was too frightened of Constanzo by this time to refuse. But he was also scared to death of what was about to happen. What had he gotten himself into? Gritting his teeth, he jammed the truck into gear and headed back toward the turnoff to Rancho Santa Elena. There wasn't much time. It would be dark soon, and Constanzo had said they needed a sacrifice quickly. He commanded Elio to find anyone, anywhere, as long as it was fast. Whomever he found would become the gang's first ritual sacrifice on the border.

Minutes before, Elio had fled the ranch in a panic, leaving Constanzo and the others preparing the new nganga with parts of La

Claudia. This first rite wasn't supposed to be so hasty, but they needed a ceremony right away—a plea to the gods to save Elio's brother, Ovidio. Something had gone terribly wrong.

Ovidio had been kidnapped.

Secretly, Elio considered the kidnapping to be Constanzo's fault, though he was too cowed to say so. The Cuban magic had brought back the business and the money, but his latest drug deal had gone awry, and now Ovidio was paying the price, his life being held ransom. Constanzo said he could fix everything with the right ceremony—a human sacrifice at the ranch. The whole Hernandez family was crazed by the kidnapping, desperate, and at a loss to save Ovidio. But human sacrifice? Still, when Elio had exhausted more conventional methods of rescuing Ovidio and could think of no other solution, he had turned to Constanzo, placing his fate in padrino's hands.

Elio glanced at his unsuspecting passenger, slumped against the passenger door, dirty and tired. He would do, Elio thought. Wouldn't he?

"This is it," Elio said, bumping the truck off the highway and onto the rutted dirt road to the ranch. He rolled his window closed against the cloud of dust that billowed up.

"What kind of work do you have here?" the man asked, eyeing the ominously desolate ranch.

Elio smiled for the first time, the cruel smile of a pudgy Mexican bully. "Nothing too hard," he answered. "Just a little digging."[1]

Ovidio had been kidnapped the day before, the end result of El Padrino's biggest drug deal yet, as he moved the Hernandez boys from marijuana to cocaine, where the real money could be found. Salvador had stolen seventy-five kilograms (about one hundred and sixty-five pounds) of cocaine from traffickers in Mexico City, which Constanzo arranged to sell for nearly a million dollars to traffickers in Mission, Texas. The problem was, Constanzo's plan called for taking the money without handing over the drugs, and Ovidio had been kidnapped in the melee that ensued.

All had gone deceptively well at first. A week earlier, the first week of August 1988, they had all come to Brownsville—Adolfo, Duby, Omar, and Martin. They had checked into the comfortable

Holiday Inn on the freeway, five minutes from the border, and began making final arrangements for the big deal.

Omar had decided to cope with his terror over the La Claudia murder by pushing it from his mind, burying the secret for good. He loved and feared Adolfo too much to leave him or turn him in, and besides, he was an accomplice in covering up the crime. He quietly resolved to avoid similar ceremonies in the future, but otherwise, he continued as part of Constanzo's "family."

Sara joined them at the motel and they all went shopping, buying more clothes than even Omar wanted—five suitcases full—hitting nearly every men's store in town as part of the promised shopping expedition. Constanzo once again seemed especially solicitous toward Omar, and decided not to pressure him into taking part in the creation of the new nganga. After shopping, they met Elio, Ovidio, Little Serafin, and Malio, and all nine trooped over to Matamoros for dinner and music.

On the way, Elio brought them to his street in Colonia Bancaria, where he proudly showed off five new stolen cars he had obtained at Constanzo's direction. They were for Salvador, compensation for his efforts to obtain the cocaine. Later, the cars would be sold for cash and used for bribes.[2] "Well done, Elio," Constanzo said, watching the little man swell with pride.

Later, at a large table in the rear of a quiet Matamoros restaurant, the remains of their meal spread around them, Constanzo told them his plans. "Salvador and his men will be here tomorrow with the seventy-five kilos," he said. "The buyers from Mission will come a little later—they used to do business with Saul. Elio knows them."

Elio nodded. He had been in charge of setting up the meeting. "*El Gancho* will be coming," Elio said. "He works for the man in Mission. It'll be fine."

El Gancho—The Hook—was a distant relative of Elio and Ovidio, a *concunio*—the brother of an in-law.[3] In Mexico, a concunio relationship is considered close, worthy of trust.

Constanzo, however, proposed to betray that trust. "El Gancho and his partners will have eight hundred thousand dollars for us," he said. "First we have to show them the drugs, to prove we have them, then El Gancho's partners will bring the money. And then we have them."

Elio and Ovidio exchanged surprised looks.

"What do you mean, Padrino?" Ovidio asked, his round, dark face perplexed.

Constanzo looked annoyed. "What do you think I mean? We take the money and keep the drugs. Then we do what we want with the men."

Bristling, Ovidio turned to Elio. He was not yet a believer like his little brother, and though he was glad to have the drug business resuscitated, he did not yet share Elio's confidence in Constanzo. And the idea of stabbing a concunio in the back was too much. "Brother, you never said anything about this. We can't do anything to El Gancho."

"Yeah, he's right, Padrino," Elio piped up. "Why don't we just do the deal like I told them we would?"

Constanzo waited a moment, expressionless. Then he reached out and slapped Elio once, lightning fast, stunning the diners at the table. The godfather's air of charm had become cold rage in an instant, as if a mask had fallen away. "Shut up," Constanzo hissed. "Don't tell me what to do. You do as I say. Or aren't you interested in making four hundred thousand dollars?"

Everyone was silent for a moment. Elio's face slowly turned crimson. He saw Sara and Martin glaring at him angrily, as if he had committed sacrilege. Omar and the others were intently studying the leftover refried beans on their plates. Ovidio's initial anger looked more like fright.

"Well, it's just that El Gancho is family," Elio volunteered after a moment, speaking barely above a mumble.

"No!" Constanzo yelled, banging the table, rattling plates and drawing stares from the handful of other patrons in the restaurant. "This is your family. Here, at this table. Don't you remember your vow to me?"

Elio said he remembered. The scars on his back tingled with the memory of it, the moment when he turned his soul over to Constanzo.

"If we keep the drugs, we double our profit. Even you can understand that, can't you?" Constanzo demanded, his eyes burning into Elio, making him look away.

Now Elio imagined Constanzo not just marking him with a knife, but thrusting it deeper, making him a sacrifice and smiling all the while—as he had done with La Claudia. Sara had told him all about the transvestite's death.[4] That's what you get for crossing Constanzo, she had said.

If Ovidio had spoken up then, or one of the others, perhaps Elio might have joined in objecting. He didn't want to double-cross his relative. But no one came to his aid. Finally, Elio found himself nodding.

"Don't worry," Constanzo was saying now, calm again, seeing the fear in Elio's and Ovidio's eyes. "We won't hurt your precious El Gancho."

"Thank you, Padrino," Elio whispered.[5]

But Constanzo did want to hurt El Gancho. Ovidio's and Elio's feelings meant nothing to him. He had other plans.

The next day, they all met to finalize the deal. El Gancho met Constanzo, Martin, Elio, Ovidio, and Old Serafin in a pancake house in Brownsville a few stops down the freeway from the Holiday Inn.

"We'll do it at the ranch," Constanzo insisted. "It's safe there."

Ovidio and Elio exchanged frightened looks. They guessed Constanzo had more in mind than taking the drugs. Despite his promises, Adolfo planned to make El Gancho and his partners the gang's first human sacrifices on the border.

But Constanzo was to be frustrated. El Gancho, survivor of dozens of drug deals, refused to set foot on Rancho Santa Elena. He was adamant. He trusted his concunios, but he had to be sensible: No matter how much you trusted someone, in the drug business you never made yourself totally vulnerable. That ranch was so desolate and isolated, anything could happen there.

El Gancho said the deal would be done at a shopping mall, out in the open, or not at all. The drugs would be brought to one mall and the money to another. "We'll exchange, give the word over the car phones, then go our own ways," El Gancho said.

Reluctantly, Constanzo finally agreed, then stormed out of the restaurant without another word. El Gancho's life would be spared.[6]

Early on the evening of August 8, Constanzo went to the Sunrise Mall, just off the freeway, where he met Salvador. The federale commander, with two police assistants, had driven up from Monterrey with the drugs. They were stowed in the trunk of Salvador's Thunderbird, piles of snow-white plastic bags—his police credentials getting him across the border with little effort.

Constanzo greeted Salvador warmly, climbing from a new white Lincoln Town Car, bought just the month before in Houston for $20,000 in cash. He and his helpers—Martin, Little Serafin, Ovidio, and Elio—briefly admired the trunk's contents. By the time the drug made it to the street, cut up into hundred-dollar-a-gram packets, it would net more than $7 million for dealers in Houston, Los Angeles, and Chicago.

Constanzo saw the Uzi submachine gun nestled among the bags of cocaine and nodded approvingly. Salvador and his assistants would stay with the drugs, while Constanzo and the others met El Gancho with the money.

They regrouped in the desolate parking lot at the Amigoland Mall, Brownsville's second shopping center, a squat and ugly complex close to the border, walking distance for international shoppers. The big attraction at Amigoland is the mall's cut-rate Wal-Mart—the one branch of that bargain department store chain that carries all the defective and returned merchandise rejected by other Wal-Marts, foisted on the Mexican shoppers at low, low prices.

Surrounding the mall is a vast parking lot, far larger than needed, flanked by a shaggy, palm-tree–lined boulevard leading to an empty field. Until a few years before, that field was to be the Amigoland Amusement Park, full of rides and attractions, but the project had died with the peso.[7] Now Amigoland is mostly a weedy field, a perfect empty place for covert meetings and unobtrusive drug deals.

In a far corner of the lot, Constanzo and his men waited for dusk to gather, their car engines slowly cooling, ticking away like bombs. Just after sunset, as orange light bled into gray, Ovidio's car phone rang. It was Salvador. An anglo partner of El Gancho's had arrived to inspect the drugs. Satisfied, the anglo had called El Gancho to tell him to deliver the money.

As soon as the man hung up, Salvador's two assistants appeared with guns to take the anglo hostage, preventing him from leaving with the drugs. "Everything is set," Salvador told his padrino.

Just then, El Gancho drove up. He climbed from his car and

shook hands with Elio and Ovidio, confident and trusting in his concunios. He believed his partner had the drugs and, after all, in the last few months, they had handled several smaller deals with the Hernandez boys without problems. Why suspect any now? He wasn't even armed.

El Gancho started to hand Elio a suitcase, but Constanzo spoke up. "No, bring it here."

El Gancho turned, saw a dark-haired man with gold chains around his neck slouching against a white Lincoln, and shrugged. He brought him the suitcase, setting it on the Lincoln's hood so they could open it together.

Constanzo's eyes glistened as he stared at the wads of fifty and hundred dollar bills. "It is all here?" Constanzo asked, snapping the case shut and handing it to Martin, who climbed into the Lincoln with it. Little Serafin, Elio, and the others also started getting into the cars.

"Sure," El Gancho said, eyeing Martin, feeling the first, vague alarm bells going off. Something wasn't right. "Like always."

El Gancho walked to Ovidio, the only one who hadn't moved. Ovidio looked shamefaced.

"We'll be leaving now," Constanzo said pleasantly. Suddenly he had a gun pointed out the open window of the Lincoln directly at El Gancho. He started to move, but stopped when he heard the sound of the gun being cocked.

"Thank your concunios here that we're only taking your money," Constanzo said as the big car pulled away, his electric window sliding into place, muffling his last words. "There are more valuable things than money we might have taken."

Then he was gone.

"Ovidio, what is this?" El Gancho asked.

"I'm sorry, El Gancho. There aren't any drugs. We didn't give them to your compadre. It was a trick. I didn't want to do it, but there was no choice. It was El Padrino."

El Gancho stared at him a moment. Then he threw up. His boss in Mission was not a forgiving man, especially when it came to losing nearly a million dollars. "I'm as good as dead, Ovidio," he gasped, the bile still rising in his throat. "You might as well just kill me." Ovidio left him there, retching and gagging in the empty parking lot.[8]

El Gancho's boss, the owner of the money Constanzo snatched, was Manuel "Poncho" Jaramillo of Mission, a self-styled narcotics godfather of the Texas border country—a la Don Corleone, not Adolfo Constanzo. Wealthy and feared on the border, Jaramillo had married into the notorious Herrera drug-trafficking family of northern Mexico. In the States, he was accused of being a major source of narcotics for organized crime in Chicago, linked to reputed Chicago mob boss Albert Caesar Tocco.[9] He has been indicted for cocaine and marijuana trafficking.[10]

After confirming with his partner that there were no drugs, El Gancho reluctantly called Mission. His orders were harsh: to kidnap one of the Hernandez boys and hold him hostage until the cash was returned. If the money was not given back, the hostage would die. If El Gancho and his partner failed, *they* would die.[11]

It was Ovidio's bad luck to be the one member of the gang caught alone with his guard down three days later. Of all places, he was captured at the same Amigoland Mall where the rip-off had occurred.

Ovidio had taken his two-year-old son, Chato, to do some shopping. El Gancho and his anglo partner, David Lynn McCoy, flanked him as he returned to his truck, forcing Ovidio and the boy into another car.[12]

A few hours later, Elio got a call on his car phone. "Elio," Ovidio said, his voice panicky. "They want their money back by tomorrow. Or they will take me and the boy."

Elio blanched. He had only his share of the money, and he had already spent a good deal of it, leaving only about $100,000. Constanzo had the rest.

"Whatever you have, they want you to take it to McDonald's in San Benito. Six o'clock sharp. And alone. And no policemen.

"And nobody should do anything, Elio."[13]

The telephone went dead.

Elio tried to reach Constanzo at the Holiday Inn, but he had checked out. Even if they had reached him, Elio knew he would never return the money.

Elio and his brother, Old Serafin, talked it over and decided that they'd only expose themselves to being kidnapped or killed as well if they met with El Gancho. So they took an extraordinary step for members of an outlaw drug-smuggling gang. The next morning, they went to the police.

The two brothers, accompanied by Little Serafin as a translator, went to the Brownsville Police Department. They were interviewed by two men—a lieutenant with the city police department, and the chief investigator he called in from the sheriff's office, one Lieutenant George Gavito.

"They have our brother—and his little boy," Elio told the heavy-set Gavito. "Something bad is going to happen." Then he began to cry.

The two policemen exchanged looks. Amusement, not sympathy, flickered across their faces. They knew what the Hernandez family did for a living, and what it must mean when one of their number was kidnapped.

"So, what happened, Elio?" Gavito asked, his small, shrewd eyes measuring the little man. "One of your dope deals go bad?"

Serafin and Elio expressed indignation then. They didn't know anything about drugs. All they would say was that their concunio, El Gancho, had kidnapped Ovidio and was demanding money. They described El Gancho's car and where he usually stayed in Matamoros. "That's all we know," they said.

"We're desperate," Elio added. He genuinely cared for his brother and young nephew, fearing for their lives. "It's not just Ovidio. It's the boy."

Gavito and the other policeman called them liars, though, telling the brothers that if Ovidio and his boy ended up dead, it would be their fault for not coming clean.[14] The Hernandezes left the police station more distraught than ever, feeling no better off than when they arrived.

"Now what?" Old Serafin asked.

"I keep looking for Constanzo," Elio said wearily. "What else can I do?"

They didn't know it, but within a few hours, the police began secretly monitoring and recording all the family's car-phone conversations.

The kidnappers, meanwhile, altered their demands. A third Jaramillo employee, Michael Habiniak, arrived to help straighten the mess out, and they formulated a new plan. Instead of bringing the money that night to McDonald's, either Elio or Old Serafin was to turn himself over to a group of corrupt Mexican federal police who had come in from Guadalajara to serve as enforcers for the kidnappers. The Mission traffickers had many dealings in Guadalajara, and they had called in some favors.[15] Ovidio would then be released with his little boy, while the new hostage would remain captive until the stolen money was returned.

"Turn yourself in, Elio, you or Fino. They won't do anything to you, please, brother," Ovidio begged. "Don't do it for me. Do it for the child."[16]

Elio, however, remained pragmatic. "Why should we turn ourselves in?"

It went on like that all day, with Elio hemming and hawing and making excuses; he couldn't turn himself in because he had to sell the ranch and the trucks to raise money. And no, Serafin couldn't do it, either, because he had to cosign the sales slips. They couldn't do that if the federales had them, Elio told his brother.

On the phone, Ovidio grew increasingly frantic. He kept telling Elio that the kidnappers were becoming impatient. Their boss's do-or-die deadline for the hostages was fast approaching. Something had to break.

Something did, late that afternoon of August 12, thirty-six hours after Ovidio was kidnapped. Constanzo's Mercedes glided to a halt in front of Elio's house.

El Padrino would fix things.

"It's time," Constanzo said, "for a ceremony."

A few hours later, Elio's truck skittered to a stop near the shed at Rancho Santa Elena, an unsuspecting drifter on the seat at his side. The gang members slowly ringed the truck. Constanzo emerged from the shed, his expression beatific, his white clothes already splashed with animal blood.

"Bring him," he said. Duby, Malio, Little Serafin, and Valente del Fierro dragged the stranger from the pickup, wrapping his hands and feet and mouth in duct tape, then carrying him to the shed.[17] Inside, surrounded by votive candles, the new nganga bristled with sticks cut from the orchard, a human skull at its center, the rotting remains of La Claudia buried deep inside. Strange symbols were scrawled on it in white chalk. This language only Constanzo knew, and the marks exactly matched the scars on his shoulders, carved by the old Haitian so many years before.

They brought the prisoner before the cauldron and forced him to his knees. Sweat streamed down his face and his eyes grew wide at the sight of a dead chicken and a severed goat's head on plates on the dusty floor. Spatters of blood were sending the flies into a frenzy. The room was stifling from the afternoon sun and the tiny room stank unbearably.

When the door was shut on the little temple, only Elio stayed in the shed throughout the ceremony with Constanzo, acting as mayordomo de la prenda, assisting as El Padrino's machete flashed, removing fingers and ears for the nganga. The victim's muffled screams made the tape on his mouth bulge. The others stood outside, waiting, listening, wondering what they were missing, relieved to be missing it—except Duby, who had asked to stay inside. Constanzo promised him that, in future ceremonies, each of them would be allowed to file into the temple to join in the torture.

With each offering of blood and flesh tossed into the cauldron, Constanzo pleaded to the gods and the dead for protection and invulnerability. Free Ovidio, crush our enemies, Constanzo said, over and over. Elio watched in sick fascination, shaking at what he was seeing, trapped in the horrible shed with a madman. When Constanzo asked for a bottle of raw rum, Elio almost dropped it, his hands were so unsteady. It took all he had not to run from the shed in terror. He kept telling himself this was for Ovidio. For little Chato.

When the torture and the feeding of the nganga finally were ended, Constanzo spewed rum and cigar smoke on the victim and into the cauldron, littering the floor with damp ashes and butts. Blood ran down the sides of the nganga, blurring the chalk marks there. "You, too, will serve us in the nganga," Constanzo told his victim, gripping the man's lolling head and shaking it until the clouded eyes focused on his tormentor.

Then Constanzo sent the pale and nauseous Elio from the shed and slammed the door shut on the makeshift temple. In a moment of obscene privacy, the priest of Palo Mayombe ripped his victim's clothes off and began a ritual rape of the man.[18]

Later, Constanzo told his followers that the mutilation of victims before killing conditioned their spirits to serve in the afterlife, inside the nganga. Evil death breeds evil deeds, Constanzo said. Torture was essential. "They must die screaming," he told them.

But there was no denying another, simpler reason for the torture: Constanzo enjoyed it. None of the followers missed it. Seeing that fierce joy on El Padrino's face at another's pain was the most fearful thing of all, worse than the killing itself.

More than anything else, that murderous look made all of them try their best to please the dark Cuban sorcerer. Anything short of total obedience, they knew, might put one of them behind the closed door of Constanzo's temple on the border.[19]

Afterward, when Constanzo had rearranged his white clothes and his sacrifice lay supine before him, bleeding, naked, and helpless, El Padrino hefted his machete high over his head. "Guide my hand, kadiempembe," he said.[20] Then he swung with all his might.

All those gathered outside the shed heard the unmistakable wet crunch of metal parting flesh and bone. Then the door to the temple opened, and as the others crowded around to watch, they saw Constanzo cupping the man's brain in his red-stained hands like the most precious of jewels, then deposit it in the cauldron.

In the candlelight, they also saw a pan had been placed under the man's head to catch the blood. Later, as the cult became more proficient at killing, the method would be perfected by stringing the bodies from the ceiling with wire, so that the blood could run down efficiently into the nganga.

After they had stared for a while at the body, Constanzo directed Elio to slice open the man's chest and place his heart in the cauldron next to the brain. "It will make the spirits strong, unstoppable," he explained. "And it will make you strong. It will kill your fear."

Elio's eyes, however, were filled with fear. He looked pleadingly at the others, but there was no help for him there. They shuffled nervously and now Constanzo began glaring at him, pointing at the body. Hesitantly, Elio approached the corpse, and as Constanzo loomed over him, he set to work with a large knife. The others pressed forward to watch.

Soon, far more easily than Elio had ever expected, the pinkish gray heart, still warm and bleeding, lay next to the brain, a quivering offering to the dead riding atop the mass of rot and filth in the cauldron. At Constanzo's urging, the others hacked and cut at the corpse, adding to the rot inside the nganga. The hands of the cult were awash in blood.

It was their rite of passage. And Elio realized that Constanzo had been right: The fear and revulsion that first welled up in them were fading. It was the damnedest thing, but as he sawed and cut and the body of the stranger gradually stopped looking human, he had begun to feel better. And he had begun to feel a kind of power.

The body of the nameless man no longer looked even real. Constanzo had said it was just like killing an animal—"only better." And it was! Elio could almost feel the power inside the shed now, as if an electric charge had been pumped in by the killing, stoking the magic, feeding the spirits.

"Your fear is gone," Constanzo told them. "Your souls are dead."

Elio stared at his knife, red and slick, and saw that his hand no longer shook. "What about Ovidio?" he asked, hearing his voice, amazing himself by sounding normal and reasonable.

"He will return soon. The spirits of the nganga will see to it. Now dig a hole. But first, take this and wrap it around the man's spine."

Constanzo handed Elio some stiff metal wire.

"Leave the wire sticking out, Elio," he instructed. "Later, we'll pull it out and you'll really see something."

The next day, August 13, Ovidio and little Chato came home unharmed. The kidnappers had released him and fled town without their money.

The overjoyed Hernandez boys called the police and said everything was fine, they should drop the case. The kidnappers and the Hernandez family had settled their differences. When the police brought the brothers back to the station anyway, insisting on a more thorough explanation, Elio and Old Serafin eventually admitted Ovidio was kidnapped because of the $800,000 drug rip-off.[21]

There was no mention of Constanzo; Elio and Serafin knew

better than that. And of course, no one said a ritual murder had been the solution to the dilemma. Even Old Serafin didn't know about that, distanced as he was from the cult side of the business.

Elio knew, though, oh yes. Even as he spoke to the police, the incredible scene at the ranch still filled his head, horrifying him, yet at the same time exciting him, making him feel powerful and strong.

Frustrated at the Hernandezes' lack of cooperation, investigators seized Ovidio's new pickup truck, claiming it was bought with drug money. Earlier, they had impounded El Gancho's abandoned car, and a 1982 pickup also apparently abandoned by the kidnappers; documents and two telephone pagers found inside the vehicles eventually were traced to El Gancho, McCoy, and Habiniak.

But they could do little more. Ovidio would not press charges. He would deny the whole thing happened if it was brought to court.

Constanzo's magic, meanwhile, received the credit for Ovidio's miraculous return. What else could explain it?

Later, police would theorize that the kidnappers had no stomach for murder, especially when a little boy was involved. Or perhaps the police seizure of the kidnappers' truck and car panicked them into abandoning their plan, certain that they could be identified and charged with murder if they killed Ovidio. El Gancho would say simply that, "There are some things you kill for. Money is not one of them. At least, not to me."

If the federales from Guadalajara had got hold of one of the Hernandez boys, things might have turned out differently. But El Gancho and his two partners were no killers. They decided to go into hiding from a wrathful boss rather than obey his orders to kill.

Elio, Ovidio, and the others, though, knew what really had happened. Magic, pure and simple, had done it, they agreed. They had seen the power of human sacrifice at work, and they believed.

Constanzo had performed the ceremony and said Ovidio would be freed. Then it happened, just as he said it would. And they still had the money. The drugs had been resold in Houston for another $800,000, all profit. All it had cost was some hitchhiker's life—a bargain by Elio's new system of accounting.

That night at Sara's house, Constanzo performed a spiritual

cleansing on Ovidio, removing the last shreds of vulnerability. He announced that they were all protected, this time for good. "Nothing can touch us now," he said.

They went out and celebrated, a stack of stolen money buying a night on the town for them all.

17

In November 1988, El Padrino personally selected his next victim on the border, one of the gang's own, chosen for disobeying the godfather's commands. Constanzo hoped his death would help mold the rest of the gang into a fear-driven machine that obeyed without question and killed without remorse.

Jorge Valente del Fierro Gomez was the chosen one, having had dared to use cocaine, a violation of Constanzo's prohibition against using drugs. To make matters worse, the cocaine he had consumed was stolen from the gang's own drug supply, which Valente was supposed to be selling, not snorting. When Constanzo learned of the treachery, he decided to make an example of the man.

Once, years before he joined Constanzo's following, Valente had been a city policeman in Matamoros. He quit the force to start dealing drugs. Later, he was hired as a madrina by Matamoros's corrupt Comandante Perez. In Mexican police parlance, the term *madrina* is not the same as in Palo Mayombe. As a police madrina, Valente was a combination criminal contact, informant, and cop with a badge but no listing on the official payroll—perfect for collecting bribes and issuing threats.[1]

At thirty-five, he had been a valuable addition to Constanzo's mostly young and inexperienced band on the border, aiding his relations with the police and the mob while helping to target other traffickers for rip-offs. But then he flouted El Padrino's commandments, and he did it in front of Sara. La Madrina dutifully reported the transgression.

A week later, early in November, Constanzo returned from Mexico City. Without saying why, he summoned his followers to Rancho Santa Elena that same night. When the group had assembled near the shed and the candles had been lit, Constanzo began a ceremony to strike out magically at the gang's enemies.

He killed a chicken and then a cat, the sacrificial animal most preferred by the dread devil god kadiempembe. He chanted and knelt before his cauldron, dribbling the blood inside. Then, with his hands red and sticky, he turned to his followers crowded outside the tiny shed. "We have an enemy in our midst," he pronounced. "One who has disobeyed, who has stolen from us, used our drugs, and laughed behind our backs."

Involuntarily, Valente took a step back from the group, his guilt and fear suddenly on display. The others' heads swiveled toward him, any sign of kinship on their faces fading as they listened to their leader's accusations. The fact that he was not a relative of the Hernandez clan made Constanzo's lesson that much easier to conduct.

"It's you, Valente," Constanzo said. He sprang at him and in one fluid motion, struck his head with the flat of a machete, breaking the man's jaw with a sickening crack.

Del Fierro had no time to react or even scream before the machete hit home. He crumpled to the ground, moaning and writhing. The others started to shrink back from the sudden, unexpected violence, but Constanzo would not let them withdraw. He ordered his followers to take part in the ritual torture of their friend. Elio hesitated, but only for a moment, having tasted blood and realizing it wasn't as bad as he had thought it would be. The others, however, seemed frozen. Little Serafin was aghast. Valente had been his recruit, his friend. What were a few grams of cocaine measured against a life?

"It's not how much he stole," Constanzo said suddenly, his eyes locked on Little Serafin, eerily in tune with the young trafficker's thoughts, making him shudder. "It's the fact that he stole at all. And that he has offended the gods. That's why he must die. That's what you must remember—or die yourselves." He spoke to the entire gathering but continued to stare at Little Serafin, who, wilting under that merciless gaze, was only too happy to stand aside as Duby eagerly pushed forward toward Valente, kicking and punching the prone cult member.

Duby's willingness to participate in the torture broke the spell of horror that had rooted Little Serafin and the others in place. Without a word, they moved forward as one, allowing the comfort and anonymity of the mob to insulate them from the horrors they proceeded to commit. One by one, they broke each of del Fierro's ribs, stabbed his stomach and chest with long knives, and finally beat him until his face was a pulpy, unrecognizable mass.[2]

Breathing hard—not from his exertions but from blood lust—Constanzo then picked up a hammer and swung with all his might. Del Fierro's skull cracked open at Constanzo's feet, the hammer buried to the handle in gore. "That is what happens to children of kadiempembe who disobey," he said, as the dead man's blood drained into a plate, more food for the ever-hungry nganga. "Do you understand?"

To a man, they nodded. The lesson was clear. If any members of Constanzo's following had not understood the need to obey before, they understood it now. The godfather had to smile at his accomplishment: He was molding his following in his own image. Some of them would become like him, with conscience buried deep beneath the desire for blood. For the others, fear and the allure of dollars would persuade them to pretend they had reached the same depths. As far as Constanzo was concerned, either would do.

At his order, Little Serafin, David, and Sergio set to work digging a new grave.

The cult continued to feed on itself for its next two victims, as Constanzo continued to hammer home his lesson of obedience or death. In December, the lives offered to Constanzo's evil gods belonged to Salvador's two police assistants, the same men who had helped the gang with Constanzo's $800,000 cocaine rip-off. Though they had been initiated as followers in Mexico City and accepted Constanzo as their godfather, Salvador grew to distrust Joaquin Manzo and Miguel Garcia.[3] Constanzo decided to make examples of these wayward godchildren as well.[4]

Sent to the border on a fool's errand, the two police assistants were met at the McAllen airport by members of the gang. They climbed into a new Thunderbird and disappeared.

When their bodies were uncovered later at the ranch, the coroner found that forty-year-old Manzo had a fractured jaw and that his heart had been ripped from his chest. Before he died, his eyes and mouth had been covered with gray tape, then he had been shot once in the mouth.

His partner, Garcia, had his throat slit. Blood pumped from his opened jugular into Constanzo's cauldron.[5] He was castrated, then his heart was carved out as well, placed next to Manzo's in the nganga as a twin offering to the gods.

When the ceremony was done, Constanzo turned to their first grave and pulled the wire from the ground. He stared at the grisly thing dangling from its other end—the accordion coil of a man's vertebrae. "Clean it up, Elio," he said with a smile, "and you'll have a necklace that brings you luck forever."

Without hesitation, Elio reached for the prize.

A fourth member of Constanzo's following died violently in 1988, though this time it was not the cult's doing.

On September 17, Florentino Ventura, the head of Interpol for Mexico, spent a day drinking and partying in Mexico City with his best friend and their wives. By the evening, however, Ventura and his wife fell into a violent argument. Ventura drew out a gun and killed his wife, then shot his friend's wife for attempting to intervene. Then, according to the best friend, who was not injured and who provided the account to police, Ventura turned the gun on himself, firing a single bullet into his head.

Constanzo was not present at the shooting, though he was in Mexico City at the time. Ventura's motive for committing the double murder–suicide remains unclear, but he had become increasingly devoted to Constanzo in the months before his death, seeking more and more magical protection from his padrino's bizarre ceremonies. He even helped Salvador obtain the seventy-five kilos of cocaine brought to the border for the August rip-off ploy.[6] But though the frequency of his cleansings and readings picked up, they brought Ventura little peace.

His last act for the cult was to intercede on Constanzo's behalf when El Padrino and his brother, Fausto Rodriguez, visiting from Miami, had a run-in with police near Constanzo's suburban home in Atziapan. Constanzo had been arrested for lacking proper import and ownership papers for his new Lincoln Town Car, which the local police wanted to appropriate for their own driving pleasure. Constanzo, nervy as ever, marched into the U.S. embassy and filed a complaint, railing about injustice. Then he got his friend Ventura to make a call. The police in Atziapan, who couldn't care less about the U.S. embassy, quickly backed down after a few words from the powerful Interpol chief. Constanzo got his car back.

Four days later, Ventura was dead.

Some investigators found the tale of Ventura's murder-suicide suspicious, suggesting someone else might have had a hand in the man's death. The witness's story was never shaken, though, and the investigation was soon closed.

Constanzo stopped calling himself Ventura's nephew that same week. He never spoke of the veteran policeman again.

Constanzo, Martin, and Duby continued shuttling between Matamoros and Mexico City through the new year. In the winter, they brought Omar and Sara along for vacations in Acapulco and Matzatlan, where Constanzo wore his gleaming gold chains even on the beach. Sara took dozens of pictures.

El Duby gradually lost his fear of assassination over the Los Sombreros shooting and began frequenting the bars in Matamoros again, trying to recruit friends to enlist in Constanzo's cult. He had taken to carrying around what he called "souvenirs" of the gang's human sacrifice—visual aids to show prospective members.

"Would you like to join us?" Duby kept asking his boyhood friend Jose every time they'd run into one another in some beery saloon. "Would you like to see an ear? How about a finger? I've got them in my pocket."

Jose, who had known Duby for ten years, always laughed it off, as if he thought Duby was kidding. Jose sensed it was no joke, but he didn't want to know for sure. And he never wanted to see what Duby had in his pockets.

"C'mon, Jose. In our religion you can have anything you want. We take people's drugs, we take their blood, we take their souls—everything. Then we are protected."

"Sure, sure, Duby," Jose always answered, rolling his eyes, then changing the subject. He thought once about calling the police, but then came to his senses. Jose didn't want any of his parts ending up in Duby's pocket.

"They were crazy—all of them. But especially Duby," Jose later recalled. "Duby was always nuts. I saw him climb up on a light pole and just sit there once, waiting for someone to shoot at. And he was just a kid then. He liked to kill. He plain loved it."[7]

The following October, Elio finally approached Constanzo about his desire for Sara—right in front of her, while the three of them were in her apartment. "You said we were a family," Elio complained. "But Sara will not sleep with me. Can you marry us in the cult?"

Constanzo was amused, but Sara snapped, "Don't be stupid. You're already married, Elio."

"Well, Elio, as far as I'm concerned," Constanzo said after a moment, malice in his voice, "you two already are married in the eyes of our religion." Constanzo looked at Sara, whose face slowly turned crimson. Elio was beaming. "Sara," Constanzo said, "if Elio wants you, he should have you."

Furious, Sara demanded to speak to Constanzo alone in the next room. She couldn't understand why Constanzo was doing this to her. He listened calmly to her protests, then said he had made up his mind—she would sleep with Elio. Period. "We'll control him even more afterwards, Flaca," he said. "Do it."

Sara shook her head and stormed out. But she couldn't say no to Constanzo. There was too much she wanted, too much fear, too much guilty knowledge for her to risk a falling out. That night, she let Elio into her bed.

After that first time, she fended him off with excuses as much as possible. Finally, his jealous wife put an end to the affair by threatening to leave Elio if he refused to stop his obvious and humiliating courtship.[8] Sara found, though, that Constanzo was right: Her control over Elio was greater than ever. He showered her with gifts and consulted her on his drug deals and purchases whenever Constanzo was out of town. She made him account for every penny he brought in, and he never complained.

At the end of the year, the cult that practiced black magic and human sacrifice celebrated a different sort of rite: a traditional Christmas party at follower Maria del Rocio Cuevas Guerra's house.

Karla's home in the Mexico City suburb of Echegaray may have been filled with magical herbs and the trappings of Palo Mayombe, but Christmas there came complete with an American-style tree and decorations, lavish gifts, and a holiday turkey feast.

Holiday snapshots, just like any family's, captured the festive decorations and the whole gang celebrating—a leering Ovidio mugging for the camera, Elio caught surprised while bending over something in the kitchen, a beaming Duby wearing a T-shirt proclaiming "I Am a Virgin."

The only note of discord during the holiday came when Sara, who had stayed home with her family in Matamoros, called to wish Adolfo and the others a Merry Christmas. Karla answered the phone. The jealous sniping began almost immediately.

For his own dark reasons, Constanzo took a perverse pleasure in making certain the two women would be at odds. Shortly after arriving for the Christmas visit, Karla had abashedly admitted to Constanzo that she was seeing another man. She hoped he would be jealous and begin sleeping with her again, for it had been almost a year since they'd been together. "You're hardly ever with me anymore," she complained.

Constanzo gave her a cold smile and said, "That's just as well, Karla. Because I've been meaning to tell you, I'm married. Her name is Sara, and we've already had a child—a daughter born on your birthday."[9]

Now it was Karla who was bitterly jealous, devastated by Constanzo's lie. He had deftly turned the tables, assuring himself by her reaction that he, not her new boyfriend, still controlled her. Karla fled the room, weeping, while Constanzo laughed quietly.[10]

"What's with her?" Sara asked Constanzo the next day, after getting a freezingly rude greeting from Karla on the telephone.

"Nothing," Constanzo replied. "She's just mad because I sleep with you, too."

Sara, almost as smooth as Constanzo, barely hinted that she had heard that "too." She blathered on about her Christmas gifts and plans, and how much she had loved the gold necklace Constanzo had given her. But both of them knew the message had been received.

In Sara's mind, it was one thing to compete for Adolfo with two men, quite another to have a woman for competition. She made up her mind to do something about this Karla. Some day, she knew, she would get the chance.

For the time being, though, little more came of this seed Constanzo planted. But later, the jealousy he initiated with such glee would play a pivotal role in his downfall, in ways even he couldn't foresee.

The Christmas celebration took a different tack on December 27, when Ovidio underwent the bloody rayado ceremony in the Calle Pomona condo. Constanzo's jeweled dagger sliced Ovidio's back and shoulders in the dark and smoky room of the dead, and the twenty-six-year-old Hernandez brother emerged proudly bearing the arrow-like scars of Constanzo's minions. He, too, became empowered to kill for the cult, just like his brother Elio and El Duby before him.[11]

Unaware at the outset that the Christmas holiday in the capital would lead to a black magic ceremony, Ovidio had brought his wife and children with him. Later, he was forced to hide from his wife the purpose of his visit to Constanzo's condo, telling her that his back was injured in an accident. It troubled him to have to lie, though. Ovidio had always been the family man among the brothers. From an early age, he had urged Elio to settle down and have children and, once Elio followed that advice, Ovidio had ordered him to salt money away for his children's education. Elio might be the leader of the family's drug business, but Ovidio's word was final on matters of family. He took great pains to shield his own wife and children from involvement in his drug trafficking and black-magic pursuits, and told Elio to do the same.[12]

Nevertheless, by February 1989, Ovidio was back in Matamoros and ready to test the new powers that rayado had granted him. It would be the cult's bloodiest month ever.

Early in the month, Ovidio and Elio were approached in the Los Sombreros bar in Matamoros by one of the border town's small-time drug smugglers, a small, nervous man named Ezequiel Rodriguez Luna. Elio had known him for years as *El Chequel,* but had little to do with him in the past. Now the twenty-seven-year-old trafficker was telling the Hernandez brothers he had made his biggest score ever. He had eight hundred kilograms, nearly a ton, of high-grade marijuana stashed nearby.[13]

Elio and Ovidio exchanged a quick glance, setting their bottles of beer down on the table in unison. "Why tell us?" Ovidio asked, an edge to his voice, his normally pleasant round face without expression.

"You think everyone in town doesn't know what you do for a living?" El Chequel said, laughing. "With your boys, even your nephew, in here all the time, talking about all the cops you have on the take, all the money you're making?"

"Where is this stash?" Elio interrupted.

"You think I'm stupid?" El Chequel asked. "Your guys talk about other stuff, too, you know. Weird stuff. About torture and cutting off ears and magic rituals. Duby carries the stuff around in his pockets. He says you kill people."

Elio and Ovidio were silent a moment, then burst out laughing, shaking their heads as if that were the funniest thing they'd heard in years. Even in February, sun and warm air streamed into the bar through open windows, making those dark words seem almost funny, even ridiculous. After a moment, El Chequel started laughing, too.

"Pretty stupid talk, huh?" Elio said, wiping a tear away, then slapping the little dealer on the back. "That was a good one."

"Yeah," El Chequel said. "You ought to tell those guys to watch what they say. Things like that hurt business."

At that, Ovidio and Elio started giggling again.

After allowing the Hernandezes to buy him a beer, El Chequel handed Elio a small plastic bag of marijuana under the table. "See what you think. I want four hundred thousand dollars for the eight hundred kilos." Then he gave the brothers an address in Matamoros where they could find him with their answer, drained his beer, and left.

The smiles evaporated from the Hernandez brothers' faces. They went out to their car and made a long-distance call to Mexico City.[14]

Constanzo, Martin, and Duby returned to the border a few days later, on February 14, 1989. When they met up with Elio, Constanzo said, "Let's have another talk with your friend Chequel. If he's so interested in our religion, perhaps we can give him some firsthand experience."

At Constanzo's instruction, Elio called the dealer to complain about the price and the quality of the marijuana. As Constanzo anticipated, El Chequel was outraged—the quality of the marijuana actually was very high, as was obvious from the sample.

Elio commiserated with El Chequel, explaining it was his partner, Adolfo Constanzo, who was displeased. "Maybe you should talk to him," Elio suggested. "Can you meet us?"

El Chequel then made the last decision he'd ever make. He said yes. Elio suggested a nearby cafe, and El Chequel agreed.

Three members of the gang were waiting for him there in ambush. They sprang at the unsuspecting trafficker as he walked toward the cafe, hustling him into a car, disarming him, then binding his hands with duct tape. They took him to the ranch, where Constanzo waited, greeting the captive as he was pulled from the car. "You'll tell us where the marijuana is hidden, won't you?" he said pleasantly. Then he brandished a large and crusty pair of tin snips, opening and closing them in front of the face of his terrified captive.

By the time a single finger had been sheared off with Constanzo's rusting metal scissors, El Chequel was ready to tell him everything. But because Constanzo was enjoying himself so much, he cut off two more fingers for good measure. And then he snipped off one of the man's nipples.

Little Serafin stayed back near the truck with Malio and Sergio during this torture, but the rest of the gang gathered around, fascinated. Most still had little stomach for prolonged torture, but one by one they were being inured to the horror, partaking of it like a rite of passage. For his part, Ovidio, a fervent convert since his rayado, picked up a knife to join in. But Constanzo gestured him away, silently mouthing a single word: "Later."

As a gout of blood coursed down the man's chest, Constanzo listened patiently. His weeping victim babbled directions to a Rancho Caracol, about fifty miles southeast of Matamoros, near the small town of La Pesca.[15]

"And who is watching the drugs?" Constanzo saw a gleam of hope in his captive's eyes at the question, a dim thought that partners guarding the drugs might somehow bring salvation. But El Padrino raised his tin snips again, and the look died. Constanzo knew his prisoner would speak the truth.

"Two men," El Chequel said. "They are armed."

Constanzo patted the man's cheek and smiled. "Good," he said. "Then you won't have to die alone."

El Padrino said they should travel in force. Martin, Malio, Little Serafin, Elio, Duby, David Serna, and Sergio Martinez piled into their cars and trucks and sped with Constanzo to Rancho Caracol, machine guns at the ready. Ovidio stayed behind, watching the prisoner.

An hour later, they turned onto the Caracol ranch from the highway, heading directly to a storage shed that El Chequel had described. Constanzo sprang out, brandishing his federale badge.

"You're under arrest," Constanzo yelled as the two guards, faced with eight heavily armed "policemen," dropped their guns and put their hands up.

As farmhands watched from the distance, the two men were led to Constanzo's silver Gran Marquis and shoved in the back. Then the caravan of vehicles left for Matamoros, spewing dust in its wake—but not enough dust to obscure the license plate on Constanzo's car. The farmhands wondered why a Mexican policeman would be driving a new car with Florida license plates.[16]

One of the captives was Ruben Vela Garza, a thickly bearded, thirty-year-old farm worker from Matamoros. He had been living at the ranch, earning more money than ever before in his life just for sitting in a warehouse full of dope. "Easiest hundred bucks you'll ever make," El Chequel had said, and Ernesto had agreed.

But an hour after he had been thrown into Constanzo's car, he was standing next to a bleeding, bewildered El Chequel, staring into a hole they had just been forced to dig at gunpoint at Rancho Santa Elena. The hole looked suspiciously like a grave.

Next to him was the other guard, Ernesto Rivas Diaz, who had come up from Monterrey, Mexico, with the marijuana, guarding it for El Chequel. The twenty-three-year-old Rivas's pregnant wife was in Matamoros with friends that day, the only bright spot in an otherwise very bleak picture. At least his wife and baby would be all right, he knew, staring with grim fascination at the bloody holes where El Chequel's ears used to be.

With the digging finished, Constanzo walked toward the three men, stopping at the other side of the hole. The ugly, blunt, boxy shape of an Ingram Mac-10 machine gun poked from the crook of his arm like some malignant growth. Moving slowly and deliberately, he screwed a stubby metal tube on the end of the gun's barrel—a silencer to quiet the passage of the .45-caliber slugs that the Mac-10 could spew at a horrific rate.

"Shall we cut them before we shoot them? Or after?" Constanzo asked idly, looking at his followers.

He shrugged. Then, still looking bored, he sprayed the three traffickers with bullets, making them jitter and writhe.

"After, I suppose," Constanzo said, pulling out the machine gun's empty magazine, its barrel smoking. Bright brass cartridges lay at his feet in a small pile. He still looked bored. Some of his followers laughed and pointed at the comical way the bodies had tumbled into the grave. Constanzo nodded with approval—they were coming around. Soon they would become men whose souls were as dead and buried as his own seemed to be.

At his godfather's instructions, Ovidio leapt into the hole and began hacking at the bodies, his first real act of violence for the cult. His vehemence surprised even Elio. The victims may have been dead already, or still clinging to some shred of life. It didn't matter to the gang.

With blows from Constanzo's machete, Ovidio cracked two of the men's skulls, removing one brain after another, cupping the bleeding masses in his hands and, his eyes spinning crazily, passing them out of the grave to Elio and Duby. Then he climbed out and other gang members fell on the corpses, scrambling over one another to remove hearts and penises, each wanting a trophy to place in the nganga.[17]

Covered with blood, they gathered around the reeking temple as darkness fell, Constanzo chanting and allowing the spirit of the evil kadiempembe to speak through him: "I am pleased. You will be protected."

Then they cleaned up, covered the bodies over with dirt, and left again for Rancho Caracol, where nearly a ton of marijuana awaited them. When they arrived, they found the farmhands had fled—driven away, Constanzo said, by his magic.

They took the bales of pot, challenged by no one.

Nine days later, with eight hundred kilos of marijuana safely stowed in the Rancho Santa Elena warehouse, Constanzo told his cult that they needed yet another sacrifice right away.

Their magic, he explained, was like some huge engine that used blood for fuel. When the motor was idling, only a little fuel was needed, a sacrifice every month or so. But now, with drugs and money pouring in and traffickers being knocked off, the need for protection was never greater. The engine was racing, and the blood had to keep pace with the money.

"We need a sacrifice. Tonight," Constanzo told Elio. The request no longer made him cringe.

Constanzo, Elio, and Malio drove to a cafe that afternoon, then randomly grabbed a stranger as he walked out the door, thrusting a gun in his ribs and forcing him into a car. At a stoplight, though, in the middle of heavy traffic, their captive started screaming for help, making so much noise Constanzo became fearful they'd be found out. He ordered Elio to shoot their prisoner with a silenced pistol.

Elio shot him in the head without hesitation. Then they shoved the body down out of sight.[18]

Constanzo was furious. "The sacrifice is ruined," he raved. "Take me to the ranch. Then we have to find someone else."

Night was falling by the time they arrived back at the ranch. Clouds glowed golden on the horizon, but the cult took no joy in the sunset's beauty. All they could do was dump the body of the stranger into a hole as Constanzo cursed his soul, wishing him eternal torment.

A few of the cult members stabbed listlessly at the corpse, but after a few minutes they covered him over with the hard clay soil inside the corral, next to the little temple. They didn't fill the hole all the way, though. There would be another body that night, and there was no sense in digging more than was necessary.

Constanzo called Duby, David, and Sergio to his side. "Bring me someone," he said, the hunger in his voice making them run to their cars. Then El Padrino turned to his mayordomo de la prenda, Elio. "And you, Elio, will have the honor of making this sacrifice." He handed Elio his machete, sharpened to a razor edge.

Constanzo had always done the killing before. This would be the final descent into hell for Elio, from which there could be no turning back. The godfather had drowned his own fears long ago in the need to maintain an air of bravura and ruthlessness for his followers—until, finally, he found he had no fear left at all. Only the sick, sexual thrill of the kill remained. He wanted Elio and the others to feel that way, too—to be like him. By sheer coincidence, their next victim provided the gang its ultimate depravity, transforming them at last from peasants and students into men with no souls.

Two miles away, Jose Luis Garcia Luna walked along the Reynosa-Matamoros highway, returning home from the ranch where he worked tending the chickens, goats, and cows. It was good work for a fourteen-year-old boy on the border, and his family desperately needed the money.

Jose lived in a two-room, dirt-floor, plywood-walled hovel with his parents, seven sisters, and three brothers. Two of the sisters had children of their own—squawling infants with barely enough to eat. The shack had two rooms only because of a rough muslin curtain slouching through the middle of the shack, offering a porous illusion of privacy. A crusted propane stove and chipped Formica table marked the part of the house designated the kitchen. They had no lights, no electricity, no running water. Like all the ramshackle houses in the flatlands outside Matamoros, poverty lay like a blanket of dust in Jose's barren front yard, with its rusting car parts and scraps of wood. It showed in the premature weight of years etched into the blank faces and staring brown eyes of his little sisters.

But Jose had never given in to hopelessness. Alone among his family, he had completed sixth grade. This achievement was spoken of reverentially by his family—indeed, by the entire tiny village of Ejido La Barranca, where they lived. Sixth-grade graduation in Jose's world is tantamount to a doctorate in the United States, and represented a monumental effort by a child who worked a full-time job and lived in such terrible squalor.

His mother, Herlinda, was a stout, quiet woman with a natural dignity even poverty could not defeat, and large, penetrating brown eyes—eyes that thin, quick Jose had inherited. She called Jose her *coyotita,* her little coyote. His graduation certificate was her most prized possession.

On the morning of February 25, Jose had left for work, promising to be home for dinner. "I'll see you at five, Mama," he had said, kissing his mother good-bye, his thin frame swimming in an oversize green and gray football jersey. The shirt was his favorite thing, his one frivolous possession.

Jose ran a little late that night, though. It was a few minutes after five and he was still a mile from home, since the animals had taken more time to bed down for the night than usual. He walked along the highway, listening to the tires singing, gazing idly at the line of trees toward the horizon. Those trees marked the near bank of the Rio Grande and the United States beyond—the place where, in Jose's mind, so many possibilities existed, where riches could replace poverty. As darkness enfolded the landscape, turning greens and browns into shades of gray, Jose glanced at the large and prosperous ranch he was passing. Someday, Jose had once told his mother, he would cross the border and grow rich, then buy a ranch like their neighbors, just as big and just as nice as Rancho Santa Elena.

He was about to leave the highway for the dirt path to his hamlet—a path that also led to Rancho Santa Elena—when a truck pulled onto the shoulder, cutting him off. Jose immediately recognized the shiny new vehicle as one of the Hernandez ranch trucks.

He started to speak, but before he could say a word, a man jumped from the truck and threw a burlap sack over his head, while another man hit him with both fists. Doubled over in pain, Jose was bundled into the truck. It spun wildly around, then roared back from the highway to the ranch.

Moments later, the truck screeched to a halt in front of the tarpaper shed. All the Matamoros followers were gathered there except for Sara, who was waiting for them at home. Constanzo had promised to take her to dinner later.

Elio, meanwhile, had worked himself into a frenzy for his first human sacrifice, hoping to silence the nauseous fear gnawing at him still. As Duby hauled Jose from the truck, Elio shrieked, "Bring him here!" Still dazed, Jose was thrown to his hands and knees in front of Elio.

Constanzo looked on calmly, approvingly. "It is time, Elio," he said.

Elio reached down with one hand and ripped the sack off the

boy's head. Then, without hesitating, without giving the boy a chance to look him in the face, he lifted the machete high over his head with both hands, then brought it down with all his might, screaming in red-faced incoherence all the while.

He had planned to take off the top of his sacrifice's skull, but he missed. Or maybe Jose moved at the last second, throwing off Elio's aim. As a result, the boy was completely decapitated, blood gushing forth from the severed neck, the head rolling to a stop in the dirt at Elio's feet, face down.

Then the madness passed from him, and Elio for the first time noticed the shirt his victim wore. He knew that gray and green jersey somehow. His nausea flooded back with tidal-wave force.

His hand shaking, Elio reached down and picked up the head of his victim. He no longer looked like the fierce killer of a moment ago. He looked scared. He brushed the bloody dirt from the face of his victim, then stared at it, fear welling inside him, fear he thought had been banished from him with his soul. But he had been wrong.

He had killed Jose Luis Garcia Luna. His cousin.

"Padrino!" he wailed. "He is family. What have I done?"

Elio began to cry. Ovidio rushed to console his younger brother. The others stared, shifting their feet uneasily. Was this a bad omen? Were they in trouble?

Constanzo, however, was unmoved. He calmly picked up Jose's head where Elio had dropped it, placed it on the ground, and struck it again with the machete, lopping off the top of the skull. Then he withdrew the brains and brought it to the nganga. "Bring the body," he said. "Pour the blood into the cauldron."

Slowly at first, then with a halting renewal of confidence, the others moved to obey his commands, even Ovidio, leaving Elio standing alone, weeping, his face in his hands. After a moment, Constanzo called to him. "Come, Elio, this is your ceremony. Your cousin shall live on in the nganga. Come."

Elio wiped his eyes, and after a moment, he shambled into the shack.

"This will make you strong, Elio," Constanzo said, handing him a knife.

At his godfather's insistence, Elio, still weeping, bent over the headless corpse and sliced open Jose's chest, removing heart and lungs for the nganga. Then the head was skinned, baring the skull.[19]

The hell of it was, when he was done, Elio realized he really did feel better. Just like the last time.

When Jose did not come home on time that night, his mother worried, but she decided he must have gone somewhere with his father. When her husband came home at eleven o'clock without Jose, though, Herlinda knew something was terribly wrong. She had heard stories of men being abducted on the road to Matamoros, and now she had a sinking feeling that the same might have happened to her Jose.

The next day she walked to the tiny police substation in nearby Ramirez. The policemen there said they would like to search for the boy, but they had no gasoline for their truck and no money with which to buy it. Perhaps she could go to Matamoros?

Herlinda's family had no car. So she had to walk and beg rides to travel the sixteen miles from her home to Matamoros, finally getting to the police station at four o'clock in the afternoon. The policeman she talked to was not helpful.

"Your son's not lost," the policeman said. "He just crossed over the river. He went to the United States to work. It happens all the time." He showed her a book full of the names of missing people. "They're all over there. That's what happens."

Herlinda shook her head. "He would never do that without telling me." Then she gave the policeman a picture of Jose. "Please look," she said. "Find my son. Find my little coyote."

The policeman's glare seemed to soften. He took the picture and said to come back the next afternoon.

Herlinda spent the following day searching, as did her husband and children. They talked to dozens of people, all of Jose's friends, his employer, the neighbors. No one had seen or heard from Jose.

Then, at four o'clock, she wearily returned to Matamoros, only to find a different policeman, who denied that she had left a picture of her son the day before. He said there was no report of a missing boy on file named Jose Luis Garcia Luna. "And it's too late to file one now. Come back tomorrow."

Herlinda left in tears. But the next morning she was waiting on the police station's doorstep from four in the morning on. When the police opened up at seven, they yelled at Herlinda for being there too early. Then they told her to leave.

They would not look for her boy, they said. He had just crossed over the border, they said. Stop bothering us.

"But somebody took him," she wailed as a policeman slammed the door on her. "Somebody took him."[20]

18

By mid-March, the streets and saloons of Matamoros overflow with college students on spring break. Their daily migration across the murky Rio Grande jams the narrow Gateway International Bridge with long lines of traffic and hot clouds of carbon monoxide. Every day during spring-break season, starting an hour before the muggy border sunset, a procession of new cars winds its way through the seething mass of street sellers and revelers at the Mexican end of the bridge. As their stereos blast American music, the students' sparkling cars and trucks provide a stark contrast to the rusting, smoking relics common in Matamoros, secondhand castoffs from the States, held together with scavenged spare parts and a cardboard box of tools in the trunk.

Husky young Americans in neon shorts spend the late afternoon slogging down Margaritas in the tourist sector's airless bars, bantering with one another, looking for dates with obsessive desperation. Outside, knobby-kneed Mexican teenagers, thin legs jammed into frayed sneakers, hustle shoe shines for a few pesos from students who stare not at them, but through them.

A few mariachi bands strum with weary eyes and forced smiles, their guitar cases open on the sidewalk, a plea for coins from the passing students. Most of the American kids just roll their eyes at the traditional Mexican ballads, smirking to one another or cranking up the dial on their Walkman stereos, drowning out the annual clash of cultures that is spring break in border country.

The gulf between two nations is never more apparent than during spring-break season. The narrow Rio Grande never seems so impossibly wide. It has been this way for years, for as long as anyone could remember.

But in March 1989, a new element was injected into the mix, and spring break became more than a mere clash of cultures. It became a crowded, noisy cover for black magic, drug dealing, and murder.

Constanzo was back after a two-week hiatus in Mexico City. He had returned to the capital a few days after Jose Luis's sacrifice, satisfied this latest ritual had served its magical purpose. In the days that followed, he seemed equally pleased that the Mexican police had done nothing about the missing peasant boy—and that his followers in the Hernandez family had stayed in the fold after their brief bout of concern over murdering a relative.

"The police cannot touch us," he told a rapt Elio and Little Serafin upon his return to the border on March 10. "And if the police did come, they could not see you. So long as the magical shield of blood is in place, their bullets cannot pierce you and to their eyes, you will be invisible."[1]

Elio remained silent at this pep talk of Constanzo's. He was a man of little imagination, and the concept of invisibility eluded him. But Little Serafin nodded vigorously. "Invisible," he whispered, imagining all the perfect crimes he could commit. His literal interpretation of his padrino's words would become all too apparent in the weeks to come.

Constanzo had returned to Matamoros to help arrange the cult's next drug sale. He knew he had to keep the narcotics moving and the money coming in, for he was responsible for feeding, clothing, and giving an "allowance" to Martin, Omar, Sara, and Duby. Elio felt the pressure, too, since he had to support his brothers, his henchmen, and their families in Matamoros with the share Constanzo granted him.

That was no small task. Constanzo and his band continued to spend money wantonly on clothes and cars and properties. The gang did not use bank accounts or credit cards. All their assets were liquid, wads of cash kept in boxes and safes. Cash flow was crucial to maintaining the profligate life-style Constanzo craved, the shopping sprees, the gold jewelry, the ridiculous furs for his mother. And the drug flow made the cash flow.[2]

The eight hundred kilos of pot ripped off in February were still in storage at the Hernandez ranch. The drugs represented a potential $300,000 profit for the gang, and Constanzo wanted to move it soon.

While a sale was arranged—Old Serafin told Elio it would take another week, possibly two, to set it up with buyers in Houston—Constanzo decided another sacrifice was needed. He wanted to enhance the cult's magical protection while they sought a buyer. "It will keep us safe," he told Elio and his other followers.

By then, the followers of Adolfo de Jesus Constanzo accepted their godfather's explanation without question. They didn't seem to realize the killing had little to do with religion anymore, that Constanzo's Palo Mayombe had been perverted into something new, something far more evil by his fascination with human sacrifice. They had never been exposed to a mainstream palero, whose gravest crime should have been grave robbing, not murder. They thought Constanzo's way was the only way, if they thought about it at all.

In truth, though, the sacrifices rapidly were becoming less and less about magic and more about satisfying El Padrino's bloodlust.[3] He had gradually stopped his lecture about how they really were not murdering victims, but liberating their spirits for eternal life in the nganga. The need for rationalizations had passed; he found that the more he killed, the more he wanted to kill—needed to kill. The satisfaction he felt after a murder once had lasted months. A year had passed between the Calzadas and his feverish dismemberment of La Claudia, and that had seemed like enough. But lately he seemed to desire a new, gruesome death within days, sometimes hours, of a ceremony. The craving for the torture and the blood—and for the moments alone in the stinking squalor of the little shed, when he rammed himself inside his naked victim even as he raised his machete for the death blow—had become overwhelming. So he continued to feed his endless appetite for blood and money, and his cult following was only too happy to oblige.[4]

"We must have a sacrifice tonight," Constanzo told his men on March 13, after consulting the orishas in a ceremony at Sara's bloody altar. "Bring him to me at the ranch."

As they had on other nights, eight of the godfather's followers fanned out through town that evening, searching for the perfect victim. And they thought they found him: a young Mexican drug dealer peddling grams of cocaine in one of the bars the Hernandez boys claimed as their turf.

The dealer was a stranger, a lone operator who had followed the spring breakers into town, his eyes on their thick wallets. He was looking for some quick sales of cocaine he had diluted so much with powdered laxative that there was little drug left. The drunken gringos would never notice, even after the laxative sent them to the bathroom five or six times in a night. They'd just blame "the water" and come back for more.

Little Serafin, David, and Sergio caught up with him on a dark sidewalk after he had made a furtive sale, and forced him into their car, whisking him off to the ranch. Constanzo waited there, naked under a white robe, a dagger in his hand. The familiar dance of blood and death began, each cult member slicing and cutting and kicking in turn, before Constanzo slipped into the shack with his sacrifice.

But then the ritual followed a strange, unfamiliar path. As the followers waited outside the little temple, listening for the final blow from El Padrino's machete, they realized something was missing.

Their victim wasn't screaming.

The tough little drug dealer they had snatched, whose name they didn't even know, had remained silent under the knife. There were no wails, no pleas for mercy, no screams—except, in the end, their godfather's shouts of frustration. The cult members looked at each other nervously. The ceremony had been a failure. The sacrifice was useless.

When the door to the shed swung open, they saw Constanzo had begun to skin the man alive, and still he had not screamed. And if the sacrifice didn't die in confusion and pain, if he didn't scream from the depths of his soul, then his spirit would not serve the cult. The nkisi could not be fed. The protection would evaporate.

Constanzo hid his frustration—and his sudden, inexplicable fear—from his followers' questioning eyes. He had to swallow the bitter taste of failure, along with the memories of his outcast past they evoked, and move to put things right.

"Next time, bring me an American," he growled, standing in

the doorway of the shed, candles burning at his back, the bloody corpse behind him in shadows. His eyes were black holes in the dim light. His expression seemed to tell his followers that the failure was theirs, not his, as he commanded them to find him a gringo, a college student. "Someone blonde and soft."

First Little Serafin, then the others, nodded and said, "Yes, Padrino." They would do it. The next night, they would do it.

"Bring me someone I can use," Constanzo said. "Someone who will scream."[5]

As the blood of his nameless victim drained into plates behind him, Constanzo vowed to his followers that this next sacrifice would be the most important of all, the one that imbued their nganga with great intelligence and guile. The spirit of a gringo college student would make their magic supreme in the United States, as it already was in Mexico.

"We will not fail," he told them, staring into each of their eyes, one by one. Seeing their fear of him made him strong again, erasing his doubts and the bitter taste in his mouth.

His followers nodded in assent.

Mark Kilroy was just one of two hundred and fifty thousand students who flood the Rio Grande Valley every year during March and April. Spring break at colleges throughout Texas and the Midwest unleashes a horde of book-weary students headed to the Texas coast for beach and booze. The beach can be found on South Padre Island, a white-sand, warm-water oasis on the Gulf of Mexico, almost as southerly as the Florida Keys and just as deliciously sweltering.

Padre lies about twenty miles northeast of Brownsville, whose only attraction for the spring breakers is its fast-food restaurants and its Gateway International Bridge to Matamoros, which is where the booze side of the spring-break equation can be found. After a day on the beach, the raucous drink factories on Avenida Alvaro Obregon are the students' destination of choice. The bars stay open late, they're reasonably priced, and, most important, the only identification papers the bartenders need to see have American presidents printed on them.

On Friday, March 10, the same day Constanzo arrived back on

the border, Mark Kilroy finished an exam in one of his junior-year pre-med classes, grabbed a travel bag, and left the lush, green campus of the University of Texas at Austin behind.

His boyhood friend, Bradley Moore, on break from Texas A&M in Bryan, came to pick him up. Together they made the long, bleak, flatlands drive south to their homes in Santa Fe, Texas, a small town about forty miles outside Houston—hot, flat, and devoutly religious.

Once in Santa Fe, the pair met two other old friends, Bill Huddleston and Brent Martin. They, too, were on spring break from different campuses around the state. All were high-school buddies, all former basketball and baseball players on the Santa Fe school teams. Kilroy had known the others for most of his twenty-one years. The four had planned this spring-break vacation for months, probably the last they would ever have together, for next year they would graduate and begin to drift apart. They piled into Brent Martin's Oldsmobile Cutlass and drove through the night to South Padre Island, seven hours of looking forward to a week-long party.

The islanders have mixed feelings about this onslaught every spring. The kids are notoriously obnoxious, hooting from open car windows, playing loud music at all hours. The crash of hurled beer bottles on the sidewalk is common, as is the sight of drunken students peeing and puking in restaurant parking lots. Vandalism runs rampant. Highway 4, leading to Brownsville, has been nicknamed "Blood Alley" because of the inordinate number of drunk drivers who crash carloads of teenagers shuttling between Matamoros and the island. Every spring, the *Brownsville Herald* carries the inevitable tragic stories of young out-of-towner lives snuffed prematurely in some hideous car wreck.

On the other hand, over this five-week period, the spring-breaking students pump ten to fifteen million dollars into a local economy desperately in need of any boost. In the past few years, the area had been shattered by a devastating hurricane, a disastrous collapse of a downtown Brownsville department store, and the devaluation of the peso, drying up cross-border business overnight. Two of the five poorest counties in America now lie nestled in the Rio Grande Valley. In those counties, contaminated water supplies in unregulated barrios make hepatitis an epidemic. People still suffer from polio, tuberculosis, even leprosy—all the Third World diseases unheard of elsewhere in America. One of these is Cameron County, home to Brownsville and South Padre Island.

And so the students are welcomed royally, with banners and contests and beach parties sponsored by beer companies. The ever-popular Miss Tanline contest is the chief attraction, a yearly, organized ogling and drinking fest at the island, in which hundreds of young males hoot at bikini-clad women, urging them to remove their tops, erupting into near riots when their pleas are heeded. Popular sport on the beach involves groups of men holding young women upside down with the spigot hoses from kegs of beer jammed in their mouths—to see which girl can drink the most brew in such an unusual posture. Young people staggering drunkenly on the beach, sometimes pitching headfirst into the sand, are as common as seashells in the surf.

On Saturday morning, March 11, the four boys from Santa Fe checked into the South Padre Sheraton, a gathering point for spring breakers. They slept a few hours, then spent the afternoon on the beach, watching the Miss Tanline contest. They partied on the island that night with some girls they met at the hotel.

The next afternoon, the boys left the beach behind and drove to Brownsville, where they parked the car, then walked across the bridge to Matamoros with four different girls. Mark, the only one of the four who had been to Matamoros on spring breaks past, served as tour guide. They spent the night drinking at a dance bar called Sergeant Pepper's, then made a bleary, early-morning drive back to the hotel, sans girls.

Monday, March 13, the four decided, would be a repeat of Sunday: first some hangover recovery on the beach, a little Miss Tanline, then Matamoros.

The lush, tree-lined tourist zone of Matamoros near the bridge was packed with spring breakers that night—ten thousand young men and women cramming the bars and spilling out into the street, lining up to drink immense frozen Margaritas and prowling Avenida Alvaro Obregon in search of action.

As thudding music poured out of the bars, traffic jammed to a standstill on the avenue. Streetside sellers were out in force, bearing legal curios and illegal substances, one big open-air market. It was a hustler's paradise, and those who knew enough to do so shifted wallets from back pockets to front.

Kilroy and his friends ended up spending most of the night in two bars. First came the scarred tables and sawdust floor of Los Sombreros, near the bridge, packed with college students, pulsing with rock music and bright neon—the place where El Duby had shot it out with a rival dealer, claiming it as his and his padrino's turf. That night, however, Sombrero's belonged to the students. If Duby and the gang were there—which is likely[6]—no one would have noticed; and if they had, no one could have heard them, no matter how many fingers and ears Duby raved about. It was impossible to talk over the music and babble inside the crammed bar.

After a few get-loose rounds, Mark, Brent, Brad, and Bill left to look for something better. They ended up in a nearby bar, the London Pub. For spring break, the cantina's management had decided to practice a little trademark infringement by renaming the place Hard Rock Cafe, pirating the name and insignia of the popular Los Angeles–based chain of theme bars. The tactic made the pub the most popular stop on the street that night.

If anything, the new saloon with its sweating, densepack crowd was more deafening than Sombrero's, and the crowd was getting wild. Guys on the balcony kept hurling plastic cups of beer on the crowd below. Later, they graduated to chucking whole bottles. Down on the floor, waitresses couldn't move through the pack. Dancing became an exercise in forced intimacy as the crowd pressed in.

Mark—tall and fairly good looking—was the lucky one that night, his friends would later recall. Overcoming his usual shyness with Margarita-stoked courage, he cornered a contestant he had seen at the Miss Tanline contest. The two slipped outside to talk, then they danced and drank and talked some more. After a while, though, Mark reluctantly returned to his friends. The girl said she had to leave.

By two o'clock in the morning, the crowd began to thin. Suddenly the place seemed shabby in its emptiness, too bright, too loud. The four friends, exhausted and drunk, decided to head back.

Out on the street, the cool, damp night air near the river was a welcome relief. As the bars disgorged their throngs of sodden students, car engines revved and people ambled toward the bridge, a steady flow beneath a long line of hazy yellow street lamps, each surrounded by brown, whirring halos of moths.

By day, Avenida Alvaro Obregon is a pleasant stretch near the bridge, lined with neat, whitewashed homes and stores—a stark contrast to the crumbling buildings and cratered streets that mark much of Matamoros. But at two in the morning, with the blaring music gone and the streets moving with shadows, the city seemed dark and forbidding.

The four young men walked back toward the bridge in a loose group. Most of the time, they walked shoulder to shoulder, though at some points, they drifted ten or so yards apart. Huddleston was closest to Kilroy, just behind him, until they passed Sombrero's, the first bar they had hit that night.

In sight ahead was Garcia's restaurant, with its tourista store crammed with crafts and glassware strategically placed to be the first spot travelers pass once clear of the bridge. At that point Bill glimpsed a Hispanic man, short and dark, leaning against a brick wall and gesturing to Mark. Huddleston only caught it from the corner of his eye, only paid half attention. He heard something in English, like "Didn't I just see you somewhere?" He didn't notice if Mark responded.

The man was wearing a blue shirt and seemed to have a small, round wound on his face, still fresh. There was nothing threatening about the man, and that was all Bill saw or heard because at that moment, he decided to jog ahead to Garcia's, where he could relieve himself behind a tree. He figured he'd be done by the time the others caught up with him.

Brent and Brad walked by just as he was zipping up and stepping back to the sidewalk. "Where's Mark?" one of them asked.

Startled, Bill replied, "I thought he was with you."

They looked behind them, drunk and blinking like owls. They had been apart less than a minute. The three friends stood there, trying to clear their heads.

People were still walking toward the bridge, moving in from the chill shadows, then moving past. Mark Kilroy was not one of them.

The man with the scar on his face turned out to be nobody of importance, a detail in the account that would mislead, not help, police. Rather, it was a call from a passing red pickup truck that followed a moment later that was crucial. But neither Bill nor Mark's other friends heard it. Mark Kilroy heard that call.

At Constanzo's command, Little Serafin and Malio Fabio Ponce Torres had set out in Serafin's truck to find a suitable new victim. Serafin drove, while young, tough Malio scanned the streets for someone drunk and alone and easy to snatch.

A month later, Little Serafin would describe the moments that followed in a videotaped confession: "We were riding around, it was like two in the morning, one thirty in the morning. We were going toward the bridge, near Garcia's. We were riding slow and Malio told me stop, and I heard Malio say, 'Do you want a ride? Do you want a ride?'

"And Mark said, 'Yes, yes.' Mark said, 'I'm drunk. I'm so fucked up, I drank too much.' I forget what he said exactly, something like he wanted to go to Silverado's and drink some more. We said okay, but let's go take a leak first, we've got to use the restroom."

Kilroy said fine and climbed into the truck with Serafin and Malio, reeling from too much drink and grateful for the good Samaritans who had picked him up. He looked around for Bill Huddleston, to tell him to climb in, too, but his friend already was jogging ahead, fumbling with his fly. Mark decided to just take the ride. His long night at the Hard Rock Cafe had made the walk across the bridge seem much too far. Now he could cruise across, then meet his friends on the other side, smiling.

Avenida Alvaro Obregon spills onto a plaza just after Garcia's. Walking or driving straight through puts you on the international bridge. Turning right dumps you onto a bumpy street that parallels the river, with a high dirt levee rising on the left.

Serafin, Malio, and Kilroy cruised to the plaza and turned right, then stopped in an empty, ill-lit lot in back of Sergeant Pepper's, the bar Mark had visited the night before. They really did stop to pee, Serafin said.

Kilroy must have sensed something was wrong. Suddenly the good Samaritans didn't look quite right to Kilroy. He started running in the direction of the border, drunkenly lurching toward the levee, not realizing that there was no way to cross at that spot. He just wanted to get away.

Little Serafin's smile is burned into the videotape as he recalled this moment: There they were, Malio and Serafin, the big, bad drug smugglers, caught helplessly with their pants undone and their parts in hand while their captive tries to flee. "We were, ah, using the restroom," Serafin primly put it, chuckling. "So we couldn't chase him."

Unfortunately for Mark Kilroy, more than one group of followers had been out looking for a sacrificial victim for Constanzo that night. When Kilroy climbed into Little Serafin's truck, The Butterfly and The Flirt—Sergio Martinez Salinas and David Serna Valdez—fell in behind as backup, driving the gang's blue Chevy Suburban.

They were all the same age as Mark, with college and sports and ambitions shared among them, much like Kilroy and his friends. But this foursome had been recruited into Constanzo's cult, hardened witnesses and participants to brutality. They were ready to obey, ready to kill. And they had a plan rehearsed for just this moment.

"They chased after Mark and yelled, 'Freeze,' " Serafin said. "They didn't hit him, they just told him to freeze."

The fake cop talk apparently was enough to fool the befuddled Kilroy. Thinking his assailants were Mexican policemen, Mark stopped in his tracks and, without a struggle, allowed himself to be hustled into the blue car. Only when they were speeding down the Reynosa highway, to the solitude of Rancho Santa Elena, did he realize his mistake.

Once they arrived at the ranch, Little Serafin looked in the back of the Suburban and saw Kilroy lying curled there, his hands, eyes, and feet bound with gray duct tape. When Mark asked what was going on, Serafin said, "Nothing's going to happen. Everything's okay."

Continuing to reassure the panicked youth, telling him he would be released unharmed, Serafin fed him some crackers and water. It was almost three in the morning by then, and all four of the young gang members left, leaving their prisoner alone, blind and immobile in the back of the car.

Back in Matamoros, Little Serafin telephoned Sara Aldrete. "We've done what he asked for," Little Serafin told her.

Sara said that was fine. She told him they should all be at the ranch the next day for a ceremony.[7]

Serafin passed this on to the others, then they all went home to bed. Little Serafin was pleasantly exhausted and had no trouble sleeping.

Early the next morning, while the gang still slept, Domingo Reyes Bustamante arose from his caretaker's shack and prepared a plate of eggs to feed to Kilroy, as he would later tell police. He felt sorry for the poor gringo, but not sorry enough to let him go.

The ranch foreman, Chavez, brought Kilroy out of the Suburban and placed him in a hammock strung between two small, dusty trees. He was still bound and blindfolded. The caretaker gave Mark the food, feeding him patiently. Kilroy spoke to him in English, words Domingo couldn't understand, for which the caretaker was grateful. He didn't want to comprehend his pleas. Still, he knew the gringo was asking for help he dared not give.

When Kilroy finished eating, Domingo returned to his shack and stayed there. He wanted nothing to do with what was about to happen. He was telling the truth later when he told the police he did not see what happened to Kilroy.

But he knew. He couldn't help but know.

By noon, everyone was at the ranch, according to Little Serafin's recollection: Constanzo, El Duby, Elio, Ovidio, Sergio, David, and Malio. Also, Martin Quintana, lover and bodyguard, was there at Constanzo's side, as always. By the time Little Serafin arrived half an hour later, Constanzo, Elio, and Martin were inside the little chapel with Kilroy.

Less than twelve hours before, Mark and his friends had emerged blearily from the Hard Rock Cafe. Now, while his three worried and hungover buddies walked Avenida Alvaro Obregon, hoping to find him unconscious in some alley or, better, holed up in some bar, Kilroy was sixteen long miles away, spending his last moments in terror.

"It was quiet. We were outside," Serafin recalled during his confession. "Then all of a sudden we heard a sound like when you slice a coconut. Bom!

"At first we thought it *was* a coconut. Then we stayed outside a little bit longer, and Adolfo came out and said, 'Go in there and take him out.' "

The four cult members who had abducted Kilroy dutifully filed into the reeking shack with its strange religious altar, its plates and bowls of coconut, cigars, rum, and dead animals. Inside, sprawled before Constanzo's magical cauldron of sticks and blood, was Kilroy's naked body.

He had been sodomized and castrated, though Serafin said he heard no sounds of torture prior to the sound of the coconut being sliced. Except, when they saw the body, they knew it had been no coconut.

It had been Kilroy's head cracked open, three inches of his skull chopped cleanly away. The bloody machete lay next to the body, a crescent moon of metal reflecting eerily in the flickering candlelight.

Serafin could see Kilroy's brain had been scooped out and placed in the cauldron. An American college student's brain would make the spirits in El Padrino's cauldron more intelligent, more capable of carrying out intricate, evil plans. "That was why Adolfo killed him. To make the spirits smarter," Serafin said.

In the harsh afternoon light, Constanzo's followers gathered around Mark Kilroy's battered, naked body, uncertain what they had brought down on themselves by taking an American. Even reckless, bloodthirsty Duby looked frightened, staring dazedly at Kilroy's shattered skull, then at the brain sitting obscenely in the center of the nganga.

But El Padrino knew what to do next. "Alvaro," he said, handing Duby a bloody machete. "I want you to cut off his legs."

Duby blanched. Despite his bragging in bars and brandishing of severed fingers, he had always stood back for Elio or Constanzo or one of the others when it came time for the actual killing and hacking. The things he carried in his pocket were little things, some given to him by the others. Duby had killed before, yes, but that was in a bar fight, a moment of passion. This was different. Even with Kilroy already dead, Duby sensed it meant crossing some terrible line, a point of no return. He had seen the others cross the same line and change for good.

"Do this and your fear will go away," Constanzo prodded. "He's a Christian. He's an animal. Do it!"

"Do it, Duby," Elio urged, his eyes wide as saucers.

Duby hefted the machete, gauging its weight, as two cult members dragged Kilroy's body from the shack. Then Duby set to work.

At first he grimaced and swung woodenly. But after a few blows, a warm glow filled Duby's insides, a feeling almost of being outside himself, hovering above, watching dispassionately. His ears roared, drowning out other sounds, and he fell into a hacking frenzy, cutting Mark's feet off at the ankles, then his legs off at the knees. The others gathered close in fascination, no longer fearful either. Some even joked, punching each other on the shoulders like athletes after a particularly skillful play. Constanzo had brought them further: They knew now that there was no outrage they could not commit with impunity.

"You're right, Padrino," Duby said when he was finished, panting from the effort, face flushed. "I am no longer afraid."

Calmly, then, Duby seized Constanzo's jeweled ceremonial dagger, an Aztec relic stolen from a museum in Mexico City. Then Duby cut Mark Kilroy's heart out. "My soul is dead," he said, holding up his prize. "I am not a human being."[8]

When the cauldron had been fed and a possessed Constanzo finished chanting and capering about the little temple, Kilroy's spine was cut away from the body and wired to produce a necklace, like the one from their first sacrifice. Then the body was dumped into a shallow grave and covered over with dirt, a small hump of dark earth beneath the iron-gray sky of the border.

19

By April 1, the so-called Mark Kilroy investigation had foundered. The University of Texas student's disappearance two weeks before remained a mystery. Police on the U.S. side of the border had pumped unprecedented manpower into the case, broken all the international rules—and had come up empty.

Every day, Cameron County Sheriff's Detective Ernesto Flores left Brownsville, drove across the bridge, and dutifully made a check of the Matamoros jails, hospitals, and morgues. These daily searches were mechanical and hopeless gestures though, as was his periodic questioning of inmates in Brownsville jail cells, waiting for a lucky break, a rumor in the cell block.

So far, he and two Customs investigators assigned to the case had sprung one spring breaker languishing in the Matamoros City Jail on a drunk and disorderly charge—not Kilroy—and had solved several unrelated crimes. They had hauled in some 127 known criminals for questioning or arrest, some of whom were fugitives in other cases. But none of them knew anything about Mark Kilroy.

It all seemed so futile. The investigation really had no official standing anyway, since it was supposed to be a Mexican matter. Neither U.S. Customs nor the Sheriff's Department had any jurisdiction to investigate crimes on Mexican soil. Usually they didn't.

Three days before Kilroy vanished, a Texas student had been badly beaten and robbed in Matamoros near the bridge. And a day later, a woman from the University of Texas was gang raped close to the same spot. The U.S. authorities had left those cases to the

Mexicans, which was to say, next to nothing would be done. Flores hated that, but if you're an American cop, you just shrug and tell yourself, that's the border, and you go on. It was their country.

But the Mark Kilroy case was different. His uncle was a U.S. Customs supervisor in Los Angeles, and strings had been pulled. At the urging of Customs officials in Brownsville, an informal group of agencies with no jurisdiction in the case immediately sprung up to search for the missing youth. Sheriff's detectives, Customs agents, DEA investigators, and others signed on. The Sheriff's Department put Flores on the case, though higher-ups dealt with the public and press.

Flores quickly learned the city and state police in Matamoros were worse than useless. They actively impeded the investigation, claiming Kilroy had crossed over and disappeared on the U.S. side of the bridge, conveniently absolving Mexico of responsibility. Never mind that eyewitness testimony showed Mark must have vanished on the Matamoros side. At the federal level, Comandante Benitez helped, but there was only so much a Mexican drug agent could do in a kidnapping case.

After the first week, no one really believed that the young student would turn up alive. Except, of course, for James Kilroy, Mark's father, whose hope could not be erased, whose belief in his son's survival was as relentless as the fast-approaching South Texas summer. Looking at Mark's father made Detective Flores work even harder, despite his doubts—it was unbearable to do otherwise.

Leaving his home and job in a suburb of Houston, Kilroy came to Brownsville shortly after his son vanished and refused to return home. Instead, he became a constant presence at the Sheriff's Department, staring over shoulders, always questioning the detectives and Customs investigators crammed into a spare office at the department. His second-guessing tried everyone's patience, but what could anyone say? What father wouldn't do the same?

When James Kilroy wasn't at the Sheriff's Department, he was handing out fliers on the international bridge between Brownsville and Matamoros, just a few hundred yards from where his son vanished. He'd bake for hours at that packed and rickety river crossing, a pale, sad, middle-aged man towering above the beggars and sellers who tug at all passing tourists but who quickly learned to ignore Kilroy as a no-sale. The bridge denizens moved around the rumpled father as if he were invisible, parting like schools of fish before some vaguely annoying but harmless obstacle.

Only when James Kilroy was out on the bridge would Flores and his colleagues discuss their best guess of late: that Mark had been arrested by corrupt policemen seeking bribes and that the requisite beating had gotten fatally over-enthusiastic. The theory fit the facts. Mark's friends said he had been very drunk that night, making him a target for all sorts of mayhem. The attitude of the Matamoros city cops, insisting Mark had crossed to Brownsville that night, only reinforced the suspicions. But it was just a theory. No one really knew.

The investigators had been over and over the case, reenacting the disappearance, looking for something they missed, even allowing the television tabloid show, *America's Most Wanted,* in on the case—part of an overall media blitz engineered by the head of Customs in Brownsville, Oran Neck. Neck's quiet manner and hangdog expression became staples on TV and in newspapers throughout Texas as the Kilroy case drew more and more publicity. Not since the disappearance and murder of DEA agent Enrique "Kiki" Camarena four years before had a crime against an American in Mexico drawn such unprecedented attention.

The massive press coverage was a potent weapon, threatening to undo the tourism Mexico depended upon. It ensured cooperation from at least some of the Mexican authorities. And Neck got the response he desired: Once dozens of articles and TV spots appeared, the calls poured in. But they were all cranks, crazies, or people full of sympathy rather than information.

Mark's friends endured reliving the night he disappeared for an *America's Most Wanted* camera crew, stiffly moving from bar to bar as the spring-break revelry swirled around them. Drunken students mugged for the camera in the background, unaware of the nature of the drama being repeated in their midst. When the five-minute segment was broadcast in late March, it too provoked hundreds of tips but no answers. The moment Mark vanished remained elusive, like a dream in the first moments of waking—almost within grasp, yet faded beyond reckoning. Even a hypnotist hired to enhance Huddleston's alcohol-fogged memory added nothing to investigators' meager body of knowledge in the case. No one had seen the critical moment when Mark disappeared.

From his chemical engineer's salary, James Kilroy put together a $5,000 reward for information on his son. The Brownsville business community, genuinely sympathetic—and well aware that an unsolved disappearance like Mark's could devastate tourism—passed around the hat and bumped the reward to $15,000. Again, calls flooded in, again without result.

Next, Border Patrol helicopters flew the length of the river near Matamoros, looking for a corpse washed up on the banks. All they spotted were weeds and illegal immigrants scrambling for cover at the thump of the helicopters' rotors. James Kilroy kept news of this airborne search from his wife until the helicopters returned, so he could call that night and say, "Good news, Helen. They didn't find a body."

The investigators spent days hunting for the man with the scar on his face and the woman from the Miss Tanline contest, figuring he was a kidnapper and she might have seen something. The man was never identified. The woman was finally found, but she knew nothing. She had said good-bye to Mark on the street and watched him walk off with his friends.

At one point, Flores took Bill Huddleston to Matamoros to look at mug shots, hoping to find the man with the cut on his cheek inside some musty police photo album. A state police *jefe*—chief—pulled Flores aside as the student flipped through blurry Polaroids of suspects. In a harsh whisper, the Mexican policeman told Flores that the three kids who were with Mark must know what really happened—they just weren't talking. The boys must have been doing a drug deal. And when they crossed the border, something went wrong and Kilroy got kidnapped, probably killed. It was all so obvious, the Mexican jefe said. Why try and blame this thing on Mexico?

"Leave him here with me for an hour," the police official said, staring coldly at Bill Huddleston. "I'll get the truth."

"The only thing I knew," Flores said later, "was that I was not going to leave him alone with that cop. Not for a second."

By the first week in April, the phone tips were down to the hard-core crazies who perennially call police with bizarre bits of fiction. There had been psychic predictions, phony confessions. Flores had wasted an entire day searching Matamoros for a certain spot where three palm trees formed a vee, supposedly marking Kilroy's grave.

Flores continued making his daily checks but, finally, he and the Customs agents assigned to the Kilroy disappearance stopped working on it full time. They felt defeated. Other cases beckoned. You hate to do it, but this is the border, Flores told himself: You shrug and go on.

Only Kilroy's deeply religious parents remained hopeful. They were buoyed by friends, relatives, and, perhaps most of all, by strangers in Brownsville and Matamoros. Through their churches and synagogues, dozens of men and women in those two cities had begun praying for the Kilroys daily, raising money to fuel their search, even helping them pass out James Kilroy's endless stream of yellow fliers with a blurry Xerox photo of Mark, offering a reward for information on his disappearance.

"I feel he's going to come back to us," Helen Kilroy said in one of countless press interviews. "We don't have any anger. . . . We just want Mark back. With everyone praying like this, I don't see how the Lord can refuse us."

In a strange way, the young man's disappearance had brought the community of Brownsville together in a manner few residents had seen in the past. There were bake sales and prayer meetings and a genuine wish to help the brave and stoic parents they saw in the papers and on TV.

Amid this outpouring of sympathy, no one paid much attention to the strikingly tall, thin young Mexican woman carrying a stack of fliers and a stapler through downtown Matamoros, a strange look on her smooth, unlined face. She was the only volunteer who could have known what really happened to Mark Kilroy, yet there she was, clutching those fliers as if she didn't know the search was hopeless.

With two quick slaps of the stapler, Sara Aldrete posted the flier with Mark Kilroy's smile high on a telephone pole. She looked at it a long moment, then La Madrina walked away.[1]

Constanzo had not anticipated the publicity that would be generated by the disappearance of a lone college student. It wasn't as if he had killed one of the DEA agents who were always coming over to Matamoros—the ones who used to think they could work with corrupt Comandante Perez, and instead had their pictures taken secretly, so that they could be passed out to the comandante's drug-dealing partners. So much for undercover work, Constanzo had laughed. Yet Mark Kilroy, a faceless nobody in Constanzo's reckoning, had become the subject of a massive manhunt. His disappearance had become an international outrage.

He should have anticipated this, Constanzo told himself. He should have known that kidnapping a gringo would have a very different impact than kidnapping a Mexican. It wasn't fair, it didn't even make sense, but he should have known. It was one more nagging misjudgment, one more thing to make him question himself, like the man who wouldn't scream.

Nonetheless, with all their press coverage and task forces, the police had not come close to discovering the cult. Little Serafin and Malio had captured Kilroy on a street filled with revelers, yet no one had seen them, not even Kilroy's three companions. Ironically, for Little Serafin the kidnapping provided firm evidence that he really was invisible, that the magic was unstoppable.

For Constanzo, it had been the best sacrifice ever, a memory he savored and relived in his mind over and over.[2]

Although U.S. Customs agents and sheriff's deputies began prowling around Matamoros the very next day, and Constanzo had lost his corrupt comandante to Benitez, he still had his sources of information. And he used the cards and the shells and the Ochosi, his means of reading the future, and he would sometimes tell his followers he could feel the law reaching blindly in their direction. But no witnesses came, no leaks came from within his band, there was no hint to the police that the ranch was involved in Kilroy's disappearance—or that a killer named Constanzo roamed free. They were safe.

"You see," he was able to say days after Kilroy was killed, "they search everywhere for him, and still they cannot touch us."

The publicity really was tailor-made, Constanzo eventually decided. It became one more reason for his cultists to blindly follow his commands. Yet, in the back of his mind, the man who wouldn't scream still troubled him. He sensed it might be an evil omen.

"Make sure you keep your passports and visas ready," he told Duby and Martin late in March. "We might have to leave in a hurry."

20

Two weeks after Kilroy died, Constanzo had grown edgy enough to kill yet again. Another sacrifice was needed, he announced. It was time to reinforce their magical protection.

The deal to sell the eight hundred kilos of stolen marijuana was finally set up, but only after many delays. With all the rip-offs the gang had committed, buyers were getting hard to find. Apparently, word of the cocaine and marijuana thefts had spread. At last, though, a man known as Chacho, representing a Houston drug trafficker, offered to take delivery of the entire load. Constanzo decided to do a straight deal—no rip-offs, no tricks, just plenty of powerful magic behind them.

In preparation for the sale, Constanzo decided the next sacrifice would be Gilberto Garza Sosa, the man who had dated Sara before El Padrino had come along. Of late, Sosa had been making new overtures to Sara. Elio and the other gang members had found out and even teased her about "her new boyfriend." Then they told Constanzo. He was not amused.

When he told Sara not to see Sosa anymore, she argued with him, claiming Constanzo shouldn't care what she did. "You don't care if I'm with Elio, why should this bother you?"

Constanzo merely smiled at this admission. Sara unwittingly had chosen his next sacrifice. Under his constant glare, her protests soon dissolved into compliance, and she helped set Gilberto up for sacrifice. With Little Serafin, David, and Malio waiting at her apartment, Sara called Gilberto at his Brownsville home on the night of March 28 and invited him over.

Gilberto eagerly came. But as he reached to open the wrought-iron gate to Sara's house, Malio jammed a gun into his ribs, then forced him into a car. The three cult members took Gilberto to the ranch, where the rest of the gang had assembled.[1]

They fell upon Sosa like hungry wolves, out of control. No longer satisfied to remain a bystander, Duby cut off one of Sosa's little toes, then thrust it into his pocket, while the others ripped off their victim's clothes, flailing at him with fists and knives. Later, after Constanzo had cornered his screaming, bloody prey alone in the shed for a time, Malio was invited in. Constanzo gave him the honor of slitting Sosa's throat.[2] Then the body was draped from the shack's rafters, allowing the blood to pour directly into the nganga.[3]

As usual, Constanzo, Elio, and Little Serafin spent a few hours relaxing at Sara's house after the killing, the blood on their pants and shoes drying and peeling as they chatted and sipped Pepsis. Thoughtfully, Constanzo had stopped to pick up a bag of hamburgers, fries, and sodas on the way. After they finished eating, they made offerings at Sara's altar, asking the orishas to protect the movement of drugs set for April 8, ten days away.

Two days later, Little Serafin set the cult's downfall in motion on April Fool's Day, with his "invisible" ride through the Mexican federales' drug checkpoint. Though certain U.S. officials would later claim their search for Kilroy was responsible for flushing the cult, it was the drug investigation Serafin inadvertently triggered that day that set in motion the grisly discoveries at Rancho Santa Elena.

Yet even as the police began to close in, the gang made another sacrifice: this time, a likable gangster by the name of Victor Saul Sauceda, targeted for murder as an enemy of the cult.

Victor had spent April Fool's Day searching for El Duby, a search that had gone on for months. Victor planned to kill El Duby. "He's a punk," Victor would say over and over. "I want him."

Victor Saul Sauceda had been a Matamoros city cop a few years back, but after six months of poverty-level wages and corrupt police jefes, Victor turned to a more profitable (and, by local standards, more respectable) line of work: He became a pistolero for the reputed godfather of Matamoros, businessman and restaurateur Juan Ñ. Guerra.[4]

He was only twenty-two, but Victor seemed older. He was smart, tough, and humorless. His sharp brown face was well known around Matamoros, where he earned respect not only because of his mob connections but because of his savvy. When Juan Ñ. Guerra gave the nod, he even helped U.S. detectives track down the occasional suspect or witness hidden in Matamoros. Shopkeepers and street people who wouldn't give an American cop the time of day practically begged to help Victor.

He had particularly impressed Sheriff's Detective Ernesto Flores in Brownsville. A year before, Victor had helped Flores when the detective needed to find one of the faceless kids who hustle Chiclets and clean tourists' windshields for pennies on the four-lane international bridge.

With T-shirts flapping and worn sandals slapping on the asphalt roadbed, these *chicle* kids swarm like locusts on gringos' passing cars, when, inevitably, they have to stop in the border's heavy traffic. The kids take a couple of swipes with oily rags at undefended windshields, then thrust a dirty brown hand, palm up, into the driver's window, mutely demanding money. Newcomers always pay; experienced border crossers offer the money *before* the kids smear an otherwise clean window.

The boy Flores sought was the sole witness against a man accused of molesting several of the chicle kids, then taking one to Brownsville, dousing him with gasoline, and setting him afire. Flores had been unable to find the boy after two days of searching.

It was the kind of crime even a mob boss abhors, and Victor Saul Sauceda was sent to help. What had been a hopeless case for Flores became a three-hour chore for Victor. He made the rounds with Flores, questioning some, threatening others, getting crisp replies from the same people who had given Flores blank looks when he was alone. Shortly, Victor was handing Flores a skinny kid in a dirty white T-shirt and walking them to the border.

"Victor was very professional," Flores recalled later. "You could tell by the way he questioned people he had police training. He was good."

Now, a year later, Victor was a man with a different mission. He had been a friend of the late Lauro Martinez, the reputed narcotics smuggler El Duby shot to death in July 1988 at the Los Sombreros bar. Victor had sworn revenge.[5]

Lately, Victor had been drinking in the Hernandez gang's favorite hangout, deriding the family's weird religion and describing gleefully how he planned to do El Duby in. Word got back to Duby. And to Adolfo de Jesus Constanzo.

On the evening of April 1, just a few hours after Little Serafin returned from the ranch and his ride through the checkpoint, Victor Saul Sauceda drove to Avenida Lauro Villar near the city's north side. Lauro Villar is a residential avenue lined with simple, whitewashed homes and apartments. It is a quiet, out-of-the-way street of dusty shade trees—a perfect cover. One of the homes belonged to the Hernandez family. Innocent-looking from the outside, the safe house was heavily stocked with weapons, drugs, and communications equipment behind its locked doors and shaded windows.

Victor had heard about both the place and that Duby had been seen there recently. Victor's plan was to stake out the house and wait for his target. But shortly after he arrived there, two Matamoros policemen lured Victor into their patrol car with a story about the chief wanting to see him. The two had parted on bad terms, but he still agreed to accompany the policemen back to headquarters.

As soon as he climbed in the patrol car, Victor the hunter became Victor the prey. The plot against him had been well planned, right down to making sure he heard about the house on Lauro Villar through a deliberate, well-timed informant's tip. The two policemen had been waiting for him that day, paid by Constanzo, who engineered the whole plan. Victor never had a chance.[6]

They drove him to a deserted alley and, before he realized he had been duped, pushed him from the squad car and drove off. Three armed men he had never seen before were waiting there for him: Little Serafin and two of Elio's helpers, all members of Constanzo's bloody cult.

Blindfolded and bound hand and foot, Victor was driven to Rancho Santa Elena in one of the family's Chevy Suburbans.[7] Victor couldn't figure out who was kidnapping him or why. On the way out of town, he kept asking, "Don't you know who I work for? What do you want with me? Who are you guys?"

"You'll see," one of his captors smirked. They behaved like kids soaping windows on Halloween—it was all so funny. "You'll see."

Soon the car turned onto a bumpy road, then stopped. Victor could smell dust rising through the windows from the road. He was out in the country, he knew, out where screams and gunshots would summon no one. Outside the car, he heard more people approaching to greet the new arrivals.

Then he heard a woman's voice, sweet and clear, speaking in the unaccented Spanish of a native. As the others addressed her, she seemed to answer to several names: La Flaca, La Madrina, and, finally, he heard someone address her by a real first name—Sara.

After a moment Victor felt her lean close to him, reaching through the car window to run a cool hand over his cheek, a touch both gentle and appraising, like a shopper caressing a melon.

"Is it him?" a raspy man's voice asked in strangely accented Spanish.

"Yes, Padrino," Victor heard one of his kidnappers reply. "I recognize him."

Then he heard the woman's voice again, harsh and flat this time, saying: "Bring him."[8]

Dragging Victor from the car, they brought him to the shed that stank of decay and death. Victor instinctively recoiled at the graveyard stench, falling to his knees. They dragged him across the rough floor.

Little Serafin had lit several candles on the floor in preparation for this moment. They cast a flickering light on a room filled with strange idols, plates containing severed animal heads stained with blood, and the cauldron crammed with sticks and filled with its vile black rot.

"Welcome to the house of the devil," Victor heard the raspy-voiced man called Padrino say. Then a strong hand gripped the blindfolded man's face, and the voice suddenly was very close, the breath smelling of rum. "Your soul belongs to me now."

They sat Victor down in a chair, still blindfolded and tied. After a brief, tense silence, he heard footsteps, someone else entering, then a familiar voice, letting him know why he was there, letting him know there was no hope.

"Do you remember what you said?" El Duby whispered. "Do you remember what you said?"[9]

Then Duby moved closer, a knife in his hand. In back of him, Adolfo Constanzo's grin glowed in the candlelight, voracious as a crocodile's, ready to devour a soul.

The same city police department whose officers were later implicated in Victor's kidnapping would duly open a missing-persons case on him. At his father's behest, they searched the city for him. Police reports say they found nothing.

A few weeks later, when Victor Saul Sauceda's body was unearthed at Rancho Santa Elena, dozens of stab wounds were found peppering his body, ragged slices made slowly and carefully, meant to hurt, not kill. His killers had chopped his fingers off one at a time with a machete. The same with his ears. Most of the skin was carved from his face and upper body. They castrated and gutted him, removed his heart and stomach, cracked his skull wide open.

The autopsy report, in clinical understatement, describes how Victor suffered from "an absence of brain."

Later, Little Serafin would coolly recall how Duby, Constanzo, Elio, Ovidio, and other cult members slowly tortured Victor, each taking turns going into the "little house" while the cult's tall and beautiful madrina, Sara Aldrete, patiently waited outside, listening to Victor's screams, the one sacrifice Serafin was sure Sara attended.

Sara did not often participate in the violence, Little Serafin said, but this time Constanzo had commanded her presence. She did not directly participate in the cutting, however, by Little Serafin's recollection. The young student, who, like his Uncle Elio, had a deep crush on Sara, also minimized his own role in the killings. Though he freely admitted participating in more murders than he could remember, he adamantly denied torturing Victor or anyone else.

"No, I didn't torture him," Little Serafin would say in his videotaped confession, expressionless as the tax man, giving the most hardened agents in the room shivers. "All I did was kick him in the face once and cut off a nipple. That's all."

Even the slaying of Victor Saul Sauceda couldn't undo the damage done by Little Serafin's ride. A few days later, the police questioned the pudgy ranch caretaker, Domingo. Word got back to Constanzo, and he knew his sense of an ill omen had been correct. Soon he would leave Matamoros for good.

All the same, Constanzo went ahead with the drug deal. The dope moved safely in darkness on April 8, and the gang made its $300,000, even though U.S. Customs agents had staked out the point on the river where the deal took place.

But the next day, Little Serafin, Elio, David, and Sergio were busted by Comandante Benitez as drug smugglers. They were in jail before Constanzo got the chance to take the $300,000 from them.

Ovidio Hernandez, already working on a new drug deal in Monterrey, was the first to hear about the arrests when a panicked relative phoned him. He immediately called the Brownsville Holiday Inn, spreading the word to Constanzo, Martin, and Duby. Then he called Malio with a similar warning. The car phones had paid off. In minutes, the entire gang was warned.[10]

They all agreed to go into hiding—Ovidio and Malio near the border, the rest to Mexico City. Constanzo knew he had to hurry. In the hands of the Mexican federales, he assumed it was only a matter of time before the Hernandez boys broke and the police came for him. After hanging up on Ovidio, late on the night of April 9, he made his last call: Sara.

"Elio and the boys have been arrested, Flaca," Constanzo told her.

"Oh no. For what?"

"Don't ask," Constanzo said. "Especially on the phone. Just get over here. Now. We'll meet you at the bridge."[11]

Twenty minutes later, a tall, gangly woman stood on the U.S. side of the international bridge, towering over the last straggling shoppers and tourists, waiting for her ride. Across the street, in front of Texas Southmost College, where she had just abandoned her classes for good, Constanzo's Mercedes ground to a halt.

"Get in, Flaca," Martin hissed. Duby sat next to him, his face pinched and fearful. "Adolfo is waiting back at the hotel. Hurry!"

They brought Sara to the Holiday Inn, where Constanzo had her make airplane reservations for the four of them to Mexico City, then to Miami. Records would show the reservations were made at 3 A.M. on April 10, by Sara Aldrete.[12] They did not use aliases. The flights would leave later that morning.

Once in Mexico, they would decide how bad things were. If leaving the country was too difficult, they might try for Acapulco rather than Florida.

As they discussed their plans, drinking Cokes and coffees in their air-conditioned motel room, Constanzo seemed annoyed by the arrests but not panicked. His lack of concern calmed Sara.

"What do you think happened, Adolfo?" she asked.

"I think someone was stupid," he answered. "If I find out who, I will kill him. Or her."

"What if Elio tells them everything?" Duby asked as the hour of their flight approached. They had to leave soon, and he did not share his godfather's seeming confidence that they would escape. "Or Serafin? What if they talk about the bodies?"

"The boys know better than to talk," Sara said. She turned to Constanzo. "They know what you'd do to them."

Constanzo said nothing. Instead, he picked up the phone and dialed long distance, then waited as his call went through. "Mommy," he said into the phone. "I have to run. The police are after me."

Twelve hundred miles away, Delia Aurora del Valle inhaled sharply and gripped the phone until her knuckles turned white. "Why? What's wrong, Adolfo? Why must you run?"

"Because I have to. I am innocent, but I have to hide. Don't believe what you're going to see on television, all the terrible things. I can't tell you any more. I'm sorry.

"I love you, Mommy."[13]

As he hung up, Sara and the others couldn't help but stare at him. Duby's mouth had dropped open. Constanzo's voice had slipped into that childish, lilting manner he adopted with his mother, a change as dramatic as any spirit possession they had seen grip him. He almost had whined when he proclaimed his innocence.

When he set the phone down, though, his face hardened. When he turned back to his followers, there was nothing but iron in his voice. "*Vamanos,*" he said. "Let's go."

They didn't dare risk crossing over to claim their share of the drug money. The cops hadn't gotten it—Ovidio and Malio had seen to that. He'd have to trust them to give over his share later. Trusting others was the one thing Constanzo loathed more than anything else, but he had no choice. They had to drive to McAllen to make the flight Sara had booked.

As they left the motel and climbed into the Mercedes, though, Sara realized she had not brought her Mexican passport or travel visa for leaving and entering the States beyond the border area. The others already had theirs, but Sara would have to go back to Matamoros. Constanzo cursed her loudly, making Sara flinch. Then he said she would have to travel on her own. They were leaving without her.

"You take the next flight. It will be safer for us to separate anyway," Constanzo said.[14]

Reluctantly, Sara agreed. They dropped her back at the bridge, urging her to be careful. Then the Mercedes glided off, just a few hours ahead of the police.

In Matamoros, Elio, Little Serafin, and the others were just beginning to spill their guts about Adolfo de Jesus Constanzo and the buried secrets of Rancho Santa Elena. But not quite soon enough.

PART III

CAMBIO DE CABEZA

(Change of Head)

To die for a religion is easier than to live it absolutely.
—Jorge Luis Borges, *Labyrinths*

You will need to sacrifice:
Five goats
Five cats
Five chickens
And the soul of an innocent—
A girl, age 1 to 10 years.
—Journal of Adolfo de Jesus Constanzo, on appeasing angry gods

21

On the Texas map thumbtacked to Armando Ramirez's wall, the border between Mexico and the Lone Star State is a firm, black line, clearly drawn, telling you exactly where you stand. But in the humid sunlight outside his air-conditioned DEA office, that seemingly clear boundary becomes a blurry thing, sand shifting in a capricious breeze.

Families, businesses, jobs, whole economies—everything overlaps, washing away the cartographer's lines as easily as an incoming tide erases a child's sand castle. The real border has nothing to do with maps. It is a hazy, ever-changing middle ground, a merging of Third World and Main Street, U.S.A., creating a separate place that is neither Mexico nor United States, but what locals wryly call "occupied Mexico."

Here, immigration laws are flouted daily—thousands of times daily. Men with their pants wet to the knees from crossing the shallow Rio Grande shop unself-consciously in downtown Brownsville, assured of not being molested.

In Brownsville, every Anglo family that can afford to hires illegal immigrants to clean house, to baby-sit, to garden. The locals consider it an entitlement, payback for the stagnant economy, the nonexistent public services, the oppressive weather. The federal authorities don't try to stop it for the same reason state troopers give you a ten-mile-an-hour cushion above fifty-five—in both cases, enforcement by the book would bring the system crashing down under its own weight.

Brownsville's survival—and, because they are so thoroughly interdependent, Matamoros's fate as well—relies upon this official head turning. There is little in the way of professional day care in the desperate economy of Brownsville, and if there were, most people couldn't afford it. The illegal immigrants fill that vital need. More important, if the Mexicans can't cross to work, they can't cross to spend, and that would shatter an entire downtown Brownsville—an entire economy—that caters to shoppers from Matamoros. Wet pants or not.

But the border's flimsy barrier—more figurative than real—carries an enormous cost as well. For the police, especially for those whose business is battling the narcotics trade, frustration and ambiguity are the hallmarks of life along the border.

The contrabandistas cross the line with impunity—with planes, with four-wheelers, with phones, and FAX. Their families live on both sides, their investments are international, their friends and protectors are legion north and south. The smart ones do their dirty work on one side of the border, then hide behind respectability on the other, grinning and untouchable, with their gaudily luxurious homes rising overnight in dusty barrios, paid for with briefcases of untraceable cash.

The banks of the Rio Grande Valley swell with their billions—the only place in Texas where the branches of otherwise failed savings and loans continue to thrive with enormous cash reserves. Elsewhere in the state, the banks have gone belly up, but not in Brownsville. Everyone knows where that money comes from, but proving it is like fetching water with a colander. The banks dutifully file the cash-transaction reports required by federal law when more than $10,000 changes hands, but there are rivers of such forms, and only a handful of agents to check them.[1]

To the drug barons, it's all so laughably easy. The border is nothing to them. They know they can cross that muddy little river at will, secure in the knowledge that it poses an impenetrable, two-thousand-mile barrier to their pursuers in the Drug Enforcement Administration.

For the border is anything but fictional to Armando Ramirez and his small cadre of DEA agents in Brownsville. Unlike the smugglers, his fourteen agents have to respect the sovereignty of foreign nations and the marks they legislate on his map. In Mexico, DEA agents are barely tolerated interlopers, reluctantly admitted under a long-standing treaty, then barred from making arrests, from carrying weapons, or from doing much of anything without an escort of Mexican officials, who may or may not be in the employ of the very traffickers the DEA is trying to investigate.

On the best of days, Ramirez's job is monumentally frustrating. On April 12, 1989, the day after Rancho Santa Elena disgorged its bodies, things got worse for the veteran DEA agent. Much worse.

That was the day Ramirez took charge—at least, in theory—of the stateside manhunt for Adolfo de Jesus Constanzo and his men. Tall and balding with a bushy black mustache, the deceptively easygoing Ramirez seemed to fit the dusty, slow-paced, hard-times town of Brownsville. He'd spent most of his forty-three years along the Rio Grande, nineteen of them with the DEA. But the discovery of the twelve bodies at Rancho Santa Elena shattered Ramirez's customary calm. Before the day was out, he would be popping Rolaids like candy.

The city, the valley, the entire state of Texas had become consumed with the case, justifiably fearful and horrified at the mass murders in their midst. Everyone seemed to be looking over the shoulders for a stately woman called La Madrina and her priest of death, Constanzo, dressed all in white. Everyone spoke of it, debated it, scanned the lurid headlines. A horde of newspaper and television reporters from nearly every state and a dozen foreign countries, accompanied by numerous self-proclaimed cult experts, descended on Brownsville and Matamoros, creating an overnight international sensation. "Devil's Ranch," headlines screamed. "Voodoo Satanic Drug Cult Killers."

The legitimate practitioners of Santeria, fearing a dangerous backlash, came forward to denounce Constanzo and to describe their religion as benevolent, not at all like the evil perversion practiced by El Padrino. Despite their best efforts, Santeria inevitably was confused in the press with satanism, and pulpits throughout the region were pounded over the irrelevant dangers of devil worship and heavy metal music. Unfounded rumors of child sacrifices flew up and down the valley. Gun sales rocketed. False reports of Constanzo and Sara sightings poured in from throughout the state.

All had been dumped in Ramirez's lap. He had to pursue the cult members with a drug indictment, hunt down witnesses, search homes, seize cars, gather information at Sara's college.

There were hundreds of people to talk to, and thousands of documents to sift through—not to mention the sickening revelations arriving hourly from Ramirez's friend, Comandante Juan Benitez Ayala, as he continued his Tabasco-laced interrogations and excavations.

A dozen mutilated bodies had been found in the ranch's secret graveyard, and Elio Hernandez and four of his fellow traffickers-turned-murderers were in custody. Ramirez knew the comandante was doing his part, piecing together the drug-smuggling cult's operation in Matamoros, but he knew investigating the U.S. side of the gang's business was crucial, too. There was the possibility Constanzo or some of his gang had run north to hide, and it was Ramirez's responsibility to find them.

Of course, there was supposed to be a task force sharing the legwork in the hunt for the killers, an outgrowth of the search for Mark Kilroy. DEA, Customs, FBI, sheriff—everyone was supposed to be pulling together under Ramirez's leadership. But they didn't. And there lay another grim reality of the border, the biggest frustration of them all. It wasn't enough to have to police an impossibly huge and open frontier. The nation's War on Drugs was also poisoned by bitter rivalries among federal agencies, which compete for budgets, for agents, for seizures, and, worst of all, for arrests. In keeping with this unfortunate tradition, the search for Constanzo had degenerated into interagency warfare, in the end aiding the killers' escape rather than their capture.

The rivalry and enmity were especially keen between the Drug Enforcement Agency and the U.S. Customs Service—the two agencies that needed to cooperate most if the Matamoros cult case was going to get anywhere on the north side of the border. Going in, there was an institutional rivalry dating all the way back to 1973, when the DEA was created by Congress with four hundred agents and exclusive domain over domestic drug cases. Up until then, the agents and the mission had belonged to Customs. From that day on, Customs agents throughout the nation saw the DEA as violators of their turf, upstarts who hadn't earned their stripes; while DEA agents saw their Customs counterparts as incompetent cowboys who lacked the savvy to make cases stick against major traffickers.[2]

The cult case stoked these nascent bad feelings like a furnace.

Customs agents griped that, once again, the DEA was playing the usurper, snatching the case from those who had done the dirty work searching for Mark Kilroy—and who therefore deserved the credit and the glory. The U.S. Attorney's Office in Brownsville said otherwise, putting the DEA in charge of the case for what prosecutor John Grasty Crews called obvious reasons. No murders had been committed by the gang in the United States, only drug deals—and the DEA, not Customs, has jurisdiction over investigating trafficking cases. Furthermore, DEA agent T. K. Solis and his boss Armando Ramirez had already been assisting Comandante Benitez on the Hernandez drug investigation when the case broke open. The logic was inescapable, Crews told the task force members: DEA should lead the case. Unstated were concerns within the U.S. Attorney's Office about corruption and ineptitude within the local Customs operation and their frequent partners, the Cameron County Sheriff's Department—making them unlikely choices to lead such a massive and important undertaking.[3] Rational arguments didn't matter, though. Wounded pride left Customs agents furious that DEA drew the lead role in the case.[4]

Ramirez had hoped he could use the momentousness of the cult killings to ease the interagency rivalries, but it was not to be. While Ramirez struggled to take control of the task force, working with Comandante Benitez and devising a strategy to hunt for Constanzo, others took control of an equally powerful tool: headlines. Cooperation never had a chance.

While the bodies were still being uncovered at Rancho Santa Elena on April 11, Customs head Oran Neck, Sheriff's Lieutenant George Gavito, and his boss, Sheriff Alex Perez had rushed from the ranch to Brownsville, leaving behind their subordinates to deal with the case. The three men staged a hasty press conference on the Cameron County Courthouse steps.

The mystery of Mark Kilroy's disappearance, Oran Neck proclaimed, had been solved. Their search had paid off, he and the others said, implying that the U.S. investigation of the student's disappearance, not Benitez's drug case, had led to the awful discovery at the Rancho Santa Elena.

"Turning up the heat on this worked to our advantage," Lieutenant Gavito told reporters.

The next day, as the DEA inherited control of the case, Neck, Gavito, and Perez staged a second, larger press conference on "their case." They were joined by Texas Attorney General Jim Mattox, who had not the remotest involvement in the investigation other than a few phone conversations with the Kilroy family. However, he was at the time a candidate for governor, and the opportunity for exposure was irresistible.

The press conference was a circus, with Neck, Gavito, Sheriff Perez, and Mattox seated at a long table in a meeting room crowded with reporters. As a long line of video cameras pointed at them, lights glaring, Gavito and Perez, in their gleaming white Stetson cowboy hats and shiny cowboy boots, once again credited their search for Mark Kilroy as key to cracking the case. Almost as an afterthought, the officials added that the Mexican authorities had been a big help. Nevertheless, the misimpression that Neck and Gavito had led the investigation and that Kilroy lay at the center of it was cemented for good that day, repeated over and over in news accounts nationwide. Though they had played no real role in storming the ranch or uncovering the bodies, these four U.S. lawmen would be the ones to receive credit—and they would be the only officials quoted in the U.S. news media for the next two days.

Partly because these officials were not at the forefront of any aspect of the investigation, much of the information made public during the next twenty-four hours was incorrect. The errors were magnified further because they would be repeated in ensuing news stories as if they were gospel. Even a year later, the press accounts would remain stilted and incorrect, so ingrained was the initial account making heroes of Neck and Gavito. Over the next few days, the gang was accused falsely of practicing cannibalism, satanism, and of basing their religion on a horror movie about Santeria called *The Believers*. The crimes were sensational enough without adding these additional horrors to the tale, but the self-appointed spokesmen in the case could not seem to stop themselves. Oprah and Geraldo were on the phone, and they were only too happy to oblige.

Comandante Benitez, not surprisingly, was outraged at being

portrayed merely as a helper on the case. "It's my case," the comandante complained to DEA Agent Ramirez after watching television news coverage of the case. "We were chasing drug dealers, not your college student. You know that."[5]

The DEA chief spent an hour on the phone trying to assuage the angry Mexican comandante, whose continued cooperation was essential to the task force's success. Ramirez had forged an unusually good working rapport with his Mexican counterpart—clashes, not cooperation, between U.S. and Mexican police departments are the norm on the border—and he eventually calmed the man down, assuring him that steps were being taken to correct any misimpressions.

Benitez was especially rankled because he had welcomed Oran Neck and George Gavito to his office, allowing them to take part in his own press conference in Matamoros on April 12. After the big press briefing in Brownsville, all the reporters had trooped across the border in a traffic-jamming caravan to Benitez's headquarters, where the comandante trotted out his suspects onto a balcony for the gathering. The reporters, more than one hundred, shouted their inquiries while the suspects made deadpan confessions, their faces peaceful, almost serene, as they publicly admitted to mutilation and murder.

"We did these things because El Padrino told us to," Sergio Martinez intoned.

"It was because of our religion," Elio told the rapt gathering of reporters as the cameras whirred and clicked.

Then Benitez pulled his suspect's shirt down and showed the tiny arrows Constanzo had etched into Elio's shoulder—marks, the comandante said, that were Elio's license to kill for the cult. Elio stood there posing for the cameras, then said, "We were told that the sacrifices would protect us against police, that bullets wouldn't enter our bodies. I blindly obeyed whatever El Padrino ordered."

Did he regret the killings? someone cried.

"Yes," Elio replied, a thin smile on his lips. "But it's too late."

When the reporters grew too unruly, shouting all at once in a multilingual babble, it was the American, Gavito, who leaned out over the balcony and demanded everyone shut up or the press conference would stop.

"Like he was running things," Benitez later complained. "He

and Oran Neck talk like it was the Americans' case. That upset us. It wasn't the kidnapping that broke this case, it wasn't Kilroy. It was drugs. It was Little Serafin.

"It was luck."

Loose talk to the press not only offended Benitez, it also hurt the investigation. On April 12, when DEA Agent T. K. Solis received a tip from an informant that Constanzo and his entourage were en route to Miami, Oran Neck took it on himself to announce the new development during a press briefing. "They're quite possibly in the United States," Neck told reporters. "We're looking in Texas and in the Miami, Florida, area."[6]

The next day, to Ramirez's horror, news reports told everyone—including any cult members who picked up a paper or watched TV—that authorities knew Constanzo and company might be headed to Miami. Tipped off, the gang would almost certainly change their plans, investigators knew.

"I think we could have gotten him in Miami if people had kept quiet," Ramirez said after Constanzo failed to make the trip to Florida. "The idea is to catch the bad guys, not warn them."[7]

Angry at the lapse and at the possibility of alienating the comandante, Ramirez, Assistant U.S. Attorney Crews, and FBI officials told task force members to make no more statements to the press. The plea was ignored. Neck and Gavito, citing their leadership in the failed search for Kilroy, continued to act as spokesmen for the case.

Civic leaders, meanwhile, began laying plans to present the pair with awards "for solving the cult case."

With all the press briefing, neither Gavito nor Neck bothered to mention one of the biggest fiascoes in the case: Gavito's own sheriff's department had allowed one of the cult members to escape.

The deputies had been assigned by the task force to watch one of the Brownsville addresses listed in Hernandez car-phone bills. Some time during their surveillance on April 12, the deputies spotted a young man at the house, knocking on the door. When no one answered and he drove away, the deputies followed him, then stopped him after a few blocks. Before them stood Malio Fabio Ponce Torres, Constanzo's smart and vicious lieutenant on the border—the man who lured Mark Kilroy to his death by offering him a ride.

The deputies let him go.

"I'm a student. I'm on my way to Monterrey University," the boyishly handsome El Gato explained. "Is there a problem?" He smiled and nodded and expressed bewilderment at being stopped by the police, an entirely disarming performance. He had stopped at the house to see if a friend was home, that's all, he said. The deputies, figuring they had no evidence of wrongdoing by Malio, told him he was free to leave. They walked back to their cruiser and watched Malio smile, wave, and drive off.

Malio had been named as a suspect by Benitez on April 11—a full day before he was stopped by the deputies. Everyone in local law enforcement should have known about Malio by the next day.[8] Yet the deputies said they had never heard of Malio—at least, not until they returned to headquarters and saw a list of fugitive cult members with Malio's name and picture near the top. But by then, El Gato was long gone. A frantic search was launched, far too late.

In all his press interviews trumpeting the capture of Elio and Little Serafin, Sheriff's Lieutenant Gavito never mentioned the cult member who got away.

The final blow to the task force created to hunt down Adolfo de Jesus Constanzo came four days after the bodies were found. That was the day Customs agents began pursuing leads on their own—hiding a witness crucial to the case when DEA agents sought to question him.[9]

The witness was none other than El Gancho, concunio of Elio, the victim of a Constanzo rip-off and near human sacrifice. He was a potential gold mine of information on the fugitives' movements.

But before Agent Solis and other task force members could get to him, Customs agents, accompanied by sheriff's investigators, picked up El Gancho on their own, brought him to a secret safe house, questioned him, then refused to let DEA or FBI agents speak to him.[10] Instead, they offered Ramirez a tape of El Gancho's debriefing, in which the man spoke in a halting voice, as if from a script, and at one point asked, "What do you want me to say?" Key questions were left unasked—and unanswered—by the obviously coached El Gancho. As evidence, the tape was useless, Agent Solis and prosecutor Crews decided.[11]

When Ramirez angrily pressed for access to the witness, he was told El Gancho was spooked and only wanted to talk to Customs agents. Later, a Customs agent told Ramirez that El Gancho had left town owing to a sudden illness in the family. Besides, Ramirez later complained, the agent added that Oran Neck had forbidden a debriefing by DEA or anyone else.[12] Neck, however, angrily denied any improprieties. He complained that DEA agents had dragged their heels, so he had his men, accompanied by sheriff's deputies, question El Gancho, then hide him for his own safety. Had he not acted, El Gancho might have vanished, Neck said.

The situation finally came to a head, because the safe house in which Customs had stashed him turned out to be an apartment maintained by DEA for protecting endangered informants. Ramirez and Solis easily learned their quarry was there and drove to the apartment, where a startled El Gancho greeted them in the doorway, saying he had no sick relatives and, as was plain to see, he had not left town.

"Well, that's great," Ramirez told him. "Because you can pack up and leave now."

"What? What are you talking about?" El Gancho answered, panic raising his voice an octave. "What am I supposed to do? Where am I supposed to stay?"

"Go stay with Oran Neck," Ramirez replied angrily. "You don't want to talk to DEA, why should we do you any favors?"

"Wait a minute," El Gancho whined, fearing an eviction might amount to his death warrant. Both Constanzo and his ex-boss, out $800,000, probably wanted him dead, he knew. "I wanted to talk to you guys at DEA all along. But Customs wouldn't let me. They said not to."[13]

El Gancho became a star witness for DEA on the spot. And he did prove to be a wealth of information, firming up drug charges against the gang. A solid narcotics case against them in the United States was vital if Constanzo and his followers were captured north of the border, since the Mexican charges might not be enough to hold them in a U.S. court.

Upset at what he saw as duplicity in the matter, Assistant U.S. Attorney Crews fired off a caustic memo to task-force members, pointedly reminding them that the cult investigation was under DEA control and that all information had to be shared. Customs' angry response was to withdraw the computers and the eleven agents Oran Neck had contributed to the task force, then refuse to take part in any other ongoing drug investigations with the DEA.[14] Instead, Customs and the sheriff's office would pursue their own leads in what they called the Mark Kilroy Investigation. And Gavito and Neck would keep talking to the press, no matter what Ramirez said. "They took their balls and went home," Crews said at the time.

Although the daily press never caught wind of it—preoccupied as it was with revelations of mass murder and mutilation—the task force hunting the killers was shattered within ten days of its formation. Chances to capture Constanzo in Miami and Malio in Brownsville had been squandered. The U.S. end of the cult investigation crumbled in disarray and the investigators ended up stabbing one another in the back—yet another enterprise poisoned and corrupted by the pervasive influence of Adolfo de Jesus Constanzo.

22

While U.S. investigators bickered and back-stabbed, Comandante Benitez's men methodically continued their investigation, carefully searching gang members' homes in Matamoros, looking for clues to Constanzo's whereabouts. They found weapons, drug caches, and strange occult altars stashed throughout the city, but no sign of the fugitives.

In the four days since Domingo Reyes nodded at Mark Kilroy's photograph and Little Serafin had led them to the bodies, the case had come to a standstill. Only a few of the bodies had been identified, while the rest sat rotting in Matamoros funeral homes. Benitez wasn't even sure what to call Constanzo's religion. Was it devil worship? Voodoo? Black mass? His suspects had used all those terms and more, but they did nothing to help him understand Constanzo's motivations. And he had to understand his quarry to catch him.

Then, on Thursday, April 13, the case progressed in a way Benitez could have done without: The craggy, cement-colored soil of Rancho Santa Elena yielded up another body. Two days earlier, Little Serafin had been the federales' unwilling coolie, forced to help unearth a dozen victims at the ranch. Now it was Sergio Martinez Salinas's turn to dig.

During one of the countless interrogations after the discovery of the bodies, the chubby young cultist known as The Butterfly remembered a thirteenth victim, a sacrifice he had buried three months before. Sergio said he was sure that particular body had not been exhumed during Little Serafin's expedition at the ranch.

When Comandante Benitez asked why they hadn't found the body the first time, Sergio shrugged. Maybe Little Serafin had been unaware of this particular killing, Sergio said. Or, more likely, he had simply forgotten. "There were so many," Sergio said, smiling at Benitez, infuriatingly smug just like all the other cultists in his jail. "I can show you where it is," he added helpfully.

"Show us, then," the comandante said, fighting the weariness that had crept into his voice and posture over the past four days.

By this time, Comandante Juan Benitez's cult investigation was suffering its own peculiar problems—far different from the internal collapse of the U.S. task force, but just as beleaguering. On one side, the young comandante had to fend off interference from the corrupt state and local police in Matamoros, who blocked his investigation whenever possible, just as they had insisted a month earlier that Mark Kilroy had not vanished in Mexico.[1] At the same time, Benitez had to soothe jumpy bureaucrats in Mexico City pressing for arrests. For them, the case was a national embarrassment that threatened to shut off the flow of badly needed tourist dollars. They wanted a quick resolution. They wanted Constanzo.

Finally, Benitez had to deal with the damn gringos trying to take credit for his case. He had swept into town a mere two months before, a thirty-five-year-old wunderkind amid the patronage and back-stabbers of the federales, and he had taken down every one of the agents stationed in Matamoros under the last corrupt comandante. And now he was repaid by having to worry about the Americans sticking it to him as well.

Feeling besieged, Benitez had slept three hours in the two days since finding the bodies. His sleek black hair was unkempt, his smooth Indian face was blotched and puffy, his large brown eyes—"Bambi eyes," a writer for *Texas Monthly* aptly described them—were swollen and rimmed red.

And if all these headaches weren't enough, he had to endure the giggles and smirks from the cult members.

No one in their right mind laughed at the federales—not tourists, not peons, not drug dealers. Everyone knew they could lock you away and lose the key, or stick you in a cell with a crazed, demented killer, or put your head in a plastic bag until your face turned blue.

Things happened. And even when they didn't, the federales did little to discourage the stories people spread, knowing a fearsome reputation was every bit as good as being fierce.

Yet Elio, Sergio, and David didn't care. They were still laughing, still saying they would be magically liberated by their padrino. They knew he was still out there, still plotting. Only Little Serafin, the lone American, the pampered baby, had fallen apart. And even he was recovering the gang's trademark cockiness, talking about how the magic had helped him with his grades and with women. It was enough to make Benitez sick.

But of all of them, Elio remained the hardest, thoroughly conditioned by Constanzo's violent programming. During the fourth day of interrogations, with Elio still giving Benitez lip, the comandante finally lost control. He grabbed Elio's handcuffs and hauled him out to the lot in back of the Antinarcoticos headquarters. He dragged Elio to an area of charred dirt and ash, where the agents periodically burned bales of seized marijuana, sending great clouds of the highest-quality pot smoke billowing into the surrounding barrio. Benitez jerked his prisoner so hard that the cuffs bit into Elio's wrists, making them bleed. When he let go, Elio spun to the greasy black ground. Then Benitez barked an order to one of his agents. "*Cuerno de Chivo!*" he shouted. Horn of the Goat. "Bring it."

The agent handed Benitez one of the Chinese-made AK-47 assault rifles confiscated from Elio's home. Benitez pointed the heavy rifle at Elio's face, the tip of the ugly black barrel a mere two inches from his forehead. Benitez waited.

"*Chinga tu madre,*" Elio spat after a moment. Fuck your mother. Then the stubby trafficker, his dark eyes hollow and filled with contempt, stared into the barrel and added, "I told you I'm protected. Your bullets can't hurt me."

Without uttering a word, Benitez pulled the trigger of the automatic rifle. He twitched the barrel to the left a few inches as he fired, just enough to send three slugs screaming past Elio's ear—instead of through his brain. They pounded into the dirt in three small explosions of dust.

The report of the combat weapon so close to his head almost deafened Elio, sending him crashing to his knees in disbelief and pain. Two of Benitez's agents leapt forward in alarm, certain their comandante had just murdered their prime suspect.

Then Benitez pointed the rifle directly at Elio's head again. "Now what do you think of these bullets?" he screamed, making sure Elio could hear each word above the impossible ringing in his ears.

Elio nodded. He was ready to talk.[2]

Some of the most valuable bits of information given up by the four prisoners quickly followed: two street names in Mexico City: Calle Pomona in Colonia Roma, and Calle Papagayos in the suburb of Atziapan.

"Padrino owns those houses," Elio said, describing his rayado in the Pomona apartment. "It is where he has his rooms of the dead."

Even though Elio could not remember the exact addresses, the search for Constanzo and the others still was given an enormous boost. Benitez quickly relayed the information to the federales in the capital.

Although Elio quickly regained his smug self-confidence, the episode with the combat rifle helped make all the cult members a bit more pliant. Sergio's admission of a thirteenth body followed, though he had brought it up casually, as if commenting on the weather.

Benitez, his agents, and the Americans all had suspected there might be more bodies somewhere at the ranch or nearby. They were considering bulldozing the entire spread. Witnesses who had heard gang members bragging in bars months before hinted disturbingly about other burial sites, other murders. Supposedly, there was even an attempt to form a ring of peasant women who would become impregnated for pay, then give up their newborns to Constanzo's nganga. The plan, Benitez learned in his interrogations, had never gotten off the ground.

"He needed more time," one of the cult members said. "A few more months."

Yet Benitez could not be sure. A pair of child's sneakers found at the ranch graveyard, and baby clothes and pictures found amid the refuse near Sara's bloody altar, would always leave room for doubt.[3] And though it was quickly taken away before the press could photograph it, a small skull—possibly a child's—had been found inside the nganga during the first day police searched the ranch. Benitez later denied its existence, but witnesses described it in detail.[4] The ominous possibility of child sacrifices by the gang would never be resolved.

Sergio's revelation about a new body brought on an instant replay of the first digging scene at the ranch—with one major difference. With Little Serafin directing the digging, the only observers present had been police and a few fearful peasants. During round two, with young Sergio wielding the shovel, there were sixty to seventy reporters, photographers, and TV crews on hand, pens scratching on notepads furiously, cameras clattering frantically like a horde of angry insects.

A television crew from Tokyo had just arrived at the desolate ranch for some standups at the grave site when Benitez and his men swept onto the property, a media caravan trailing behind a quarter of a mile long. The Japanese reporters, expecting a quiet afternoon of journalistic catch-up alone at the ranch, were startled by the sudden mass arrival. The Japanese TV crew members wore bright white surgical face masks to guard against the odor of decay, and they looked like a lost troop of hospital workers as the police roared to a stop twenty yards away.

The ranch was just as the federales had left it two days before, though no guards had been stationed. Benitez knew few of the locals would venture there alone. The one brave soul who had entered the ranch of the devil had left a crude pine cross set up at the door of the reeking temple. The agents eyed it approvingly: you could never be too careful.

Next to the cross, Constanzo's evil cauldron of rotting blood, human organs, and dead animals still bristled where Little Serafin had dragged it. Bloated blue flies and maggots crawled obscenely over its mottled surface. As Sergio hacked away with his shovel nearby, the men and women of the international press poked around and shouted questions at him. "I didn't kill anybody," Sergio kept saying. "I just buried them."

Little Serafin and Elio had implicated Sergio in the kidnapping of Mark Kilroy and fourteen-year-old Jose Luis Garcia Luna, as well as the torture and killing of Duby's enemy, Victor Saul Sauceda, and Sara's unfortunate suitor, Gilberto Sosa. Sergio had been one of the friends who had teased Sara the most about her affair with Sosa, egging Constanzo on in his decision to kill Gilberto.[5] Yet when he was arrested, Sergio had claimed he was just a farmhand, a peon Elio had hired to work on the ranch. He knew nothing of killings or torture. But at twenty-three, Sergio had no calluses on his hands, no muscles beneath his shirtsleeves. He wore designer jeans and a chic blue-striped shirt. When the federales handed him a pick and a shovel, he looked vaguely uncertain about what to do with them.

"Can't you get a tractor to do this?" he asked at one point, squinting at the hot sun overhead.

"You'll dig with your hands if you have to," an agent growled.

The federales uncuffed Sergio's right hand, and the handcuffs dangled noisily from his left wrist when he pointed out the grave. "It's over here," he said. "Behind the hay."

The cult's graveyard spread around the little temple in a rough crescent shape. Eight of the bodies had been buried in five graves inside the corral, with the rest scattered nearby. Two hay mounds and a pile of refuse ringed the makeshift cemetery.

As Sergio began his task, an old, bent man who called himself Santos Yzaguirre hobbled forward and began to recite Psalms. A large cross was strapped to his chest and he clutched a battered Bible in one hand. His prayerful drone meshed rhythmically with the sound of Sergio's digging, rising and falling in a discordant chant. The agents did not interfere as he stood by the digging site; if anything, they seemed to approve of his presence.

"I am a Christian," he announced. "I came here to pray for the souls of all the people buried here."

The summery April heat had returned to Matamoros with the discovery of the mass murders. Gone was the chill, gray sky over Little Serafin's excavation party, replaced by a tropical afternoon sun that made standing near the grave site unbearable. The lunch hour had come and gone, but no one thought of food after smelling that graveyard stench.

After an hour of digging, Sergio reeled with the stink, drenched with sweat. The agents finally let him rest for five minutes, then set him back to work.

"El Padrino or Elio killed him, not me," he told a reporter during his break. "All I did was bury him."

"This man believes he is without guilt," an agent told the reporter. "He thinks burying a murdered man is like burying a rabbit."[6]

When Sergio had dug a hole four feet around and three feet deep, the grave emitted a slaughterhouse reek that sent reporters and agents nearest Sergio backpedaling in disgust. Sergio, gagging at the odor he had forced to the surface, scrambled to the far edge of the hole and begged for a face mask.

"Get back in there," an agent replied from a safe distance. "You didn't need a mask when you buried him."

But after a minute, one of the Japanese television crew members cautiously approached and slipped Sergio a surgical face mask. The police allowed it. It couldn't have helped much. The odor of death was overpowering, filling the senses—and not just smell but taste. It made you clamp your mouth shut, the bile rising in your throat.

Ten more minutes of digging exposed the naked, decomposed body of a man about thirty years old, gagged and blindfolded. A rope was looped around the body's legs and it was hauled from the grave, unrecognizable after months of decomposition, a single gold tooth glittering from the grin of its desiccated skull. The man's heart was missing, his chest was a ragged hole, cut and then pried open, ribs jutting outward like broken sticks.

Comandante Benitez watched expressionlessly, arms crossed. He surveyed the ranch and its cratered graveyard and thought, Santeria, Palo Mayombe, Satan worship—who cared what the experts wanted to call it? His only concern was ridding Matamoros of this curse. Standing there, he felt unclean, contaminated. "You can sense the evil here," he told his friend, El Lobo. "You can feel it."

How many more bodies would there be? He had to know. Yet when a reporter attending the dig asked him that same question, Benitez refused to answer. He just climbed in his car and left, steeling himself for another series of interrogations at headquarters, phone calls from Mexico City, and arguments with the local cops.

Later, in Brownsville, Oran Neck provided the quotes the press wanted, again implying that he was somehow connected with the latest discovery at the ranch, though it had been solely Benitez's work. "Now we're not even going to put out a number," the Customs chief said when asked how many bodies police expected to find. "We're going to dig until we find them all."[7]

Funeral home workers shook the latest body free of dust as best they could, then zipped it into a black body bag, the rope used to haul it from the grave still wrapped around an ankle. The body was loaded into a van and driven to a Matamoros funeral home. Once there, the autopsy doctor dutifully noted the missing heart, the throat savagely ripped open, the castration, and the now familiar tape covering the eyes. Death came from strangulation, the pathologist concluded, with most but not all of the mutilation coming after death.

When the autopsy was done, the body still could not be identified. None of the families who trooped into the funeral home looking for lost loved ones found anything familiar in the wasted face of the man Sergio Martinez had unearthed. In the end, the name funeral home workers first assigned to him would stick permanently, even after the body was placed in a pauper's grave: *Bolsa Numero Trece.* Bag Number Thirteen.

Even before Sergio broke ground at the ranch that day, Matamoros had become a magnet for every Mexican family within a hundred miles with a missing husband or son or brother. Word was out that many of the bodies had not been identified. Hundreds came.

Lines snaked outside Matamoros's two largest funeral homes, rows of old women in black shawls, weathered faces locked into expressions of mixed dread and hope. Some arrived as early as dawn, beseeching the grim proprietors with pictures of missing relatives and tearful questions. Have you seen my Jorge, señor? Is my Manuel in there? Please! Give me my son back.

A rose tattoo, a missing front tooth, a distinctive sweatshirt—these were the pitiful clues that mothers and wives and sisters looked for when they finally were admitted to the morgue. They stared down at the dirt-caked, shattered forms lined up on tables, wrapped in plastic. Each time a nameless corpse was identified, the unending, fearful uncertainty over the fate of the disappeared was transformed into the sharp but sure grief of mourning. At least we know, the families invariably said, wiping away the tears, staggering outside with unseeing eyes. He had been missing so long. Now, at least, we know.

Tomasa Garza Hernandez identified her son, Ruben Vela Garza, by his thick beard. He had been snatched from Rancho Caracol during a Constanzo dope rip-off in February.

Relatives knew Jorge Valente del Fierro Gomez from the red rose tattooed on his bloated, decaying arm. He had died when Constanzo accused him of snorting the gang's cocaine.

Stooped old Hidalgo Castillo looked in vain for his son, Moises, who had vanished from the family farm a year before. None of the bodies uncovered so far were even close to resembling his boy.

As soon as Herlinda Luna de Garcia heard the news of the killings on the ranch, she went to El Rosario funeral home. As she had two months before when she first reported her son Jose missing, she trekked the sixteen miles to Matamoros at four in the morning. Herlinda had remained certain that her little coyote had been kidnapped in February, no matter what the police said about his going across the river. She knew fourteen-year-old Jose, her pride and joy, would never have left her without a word—unless he had been given no choice.

After waiting for hours for the funeral home to open, she was admitted. Her resolution slipped and her knees weakened when she was escorted to a room filled with the vile smell of death, a smell that could not be masked no matter how many disinfectants the funeral home used. The attendant steadied Herlinda, then told her to go through a door, walk past the bodies, and note the number on her son's toe, if he was there.

Herlinda took a deep breath and walked the hardest ten steps of her life.

She emerged from the funeral home ten minutes later, sickened by the sight of those poor, dead men and the long line of family members slowly walking by them, staring from hollow, hopeless eyes, just as she had. A few had found what they feared they would—a body they knew. Most, though, left still not knowing what had happened to their missing loved ones, denied even the release of grief.

Out in the sunlight, breathing deeply, Herlinda faced her oldest daughter, Rosalita.

"He's not there," Herlinda whispered, allowing the slightest note of hope to creep into her voice as Rosalita burst into tears. "But there's one more place to go."

Clutching each other's hand, they walked to the second funeral home, El Glayoso.

"You can't see the bodies," an employee told them. "The city officials have to be present. They're all over at Rosario now."

"Please, señor," Herlinda begged. "I must know if my boy is in there. Just let us look."

"You'll have to wait," the harried worker snapped, then slammed the door. Two dozen others waited outside with them.

Four hours later, the city officials arrived. The families were told they could go in and claim their loved ones, if they could identify them. But the wait had taken its toll on Jose's mother. She could no longer face the task.

"I can't do it again, Rosa," Herlinda said. "You go. Please."

The twenty-five-year-old daughter nodded. She would do it. She was a mother herself. She understood. She left Herlinda outside, praying.

When Rosalita emerged, her face pinched and colorless, Herlinda knew without asking what her daughter had seen. Still, she had to ask.

"Is Jose there?"

Rosalita nodded. "I saw his shirt, his green and gray football shirt, Mama. It's him."

Then Rosalita's face crumpled in utter despair. "Mama," she wailed. "He had no head. It was chopped off beside him."

Mother and daughter stared at each other a moment, a second of shock and horror and unreality. For a second Herlinda thought, no, this cannot be true. It's a mistake. I still feel my son in my heart, so how can he be dead? I would have known if he were dead.

And then the second passed, and she did know. It was all true, horribly true.

The two women flung themselves together and wept in one another's arms. Next to them, three other women waiting on the funeral home's doorstep broke into tears, a chorus of strangers linked in sorrow.

The next day, across the river, two miles and a world away, a very different gathering convened in Brownsville's Saint Luke Catholic Church, the refuge where the Kilroy family had sought daily comfort during the four-week search for their missing Mark. More than one thousand people came to pray with James and Helen Kilroy one last time.

The Kilroys had flown into Brownsville from Santa Fe the day after the news broke. James Kilroy had demanded to see his son's body, but sympathetic investigators barred him from the sight. "No one should ever have to see their son like that," Sheriff's Detective Ernesto Flores told the other detectives. Now they were ready to say good-bye to their son.

"I ask you to pray for all of the young men who were found with him," Helen Kilroy told the church gathering. "And pray for the people who have done these things. Pray that they are caught and that the Lord will enter their hearts and they will know what they have done is wrong.

"Pray that they will know there is love."

She stood at the lectern, her son's picture on the altar behind her, surrounded by red, yellow, and pink blossoms, brought by the armload by mourners who had never met her or her son. Helen Kilroy was calm and poised, like her husband and younger son beside her, making her words all the more stunning to the audience. The parents said they knew their son was happy now; that, as a captive for twelve hours, he had ample opportunity to pray and to find peace with himself and his God. Many wept as they watched Helen Kilroy at the lectern, speaking of forgiveness.

If Helen Kilroy can find forgiveness in her, after seeing what happened to her son, anything is possible, Father Juan Nicolau told the congregation. Moved by the Kilroys' plea, he exhorted everyone to celebrate a resurrection, not mourn a death.

"Those criminals killed the body of Mark, but they were not able to kill his spirit and his soul," Nicolau said. "He is alive."

As the choir sang "Amazing Grace" and the service ended, hundreds of men and women formed lines in the aisles to shake the Kilroys' hands.

One other family was in mourning that day, in seclusion behind the drawn blinds of their house on the Street of the Beheaded Saints. The Aldretes were reeling in shock, unable to comprehend the accusations against their daughter, their all-American girl.

"It couldn't be our Sara that did this," Israel Aldrete kept repeating to his wife, who couldn't stop crying. "It can't be."

When the police had come two days before with a search warrant, the retired Aldrete, his salt-and-pepper hair hastily combed and slicked back, had assured them that Sara had nothing to do with murders or strange religions he'd read about in the papers. It was all a mistake. When the police trooped to the upstairs apartment, he appeared genuinely stunned to see the blood-encrusted altar his daughter had kept there.

"We knew nothing of this," Israel said, his face gone ashen. "We never came up here. We gave her her privacy."

When the police asked how his daughter afforded a new car with a phone in it, Aldrete clasped his large knuckled hands and looked at his feet. "We were afraid to ask," he whispered. "We knew it had something to do with her friends. That's all."

Later, after the police left and Israel and his wife had pulled themselves together, they found their next oldest daughter, Teresa, was missing as well. She had gone to the store just before the police arrived, then never returned. A frantic search ensued, until neighbors told Israel that the police had spotted Teresa as she walked home from the store. They grabbed her and drove her away, yelling, "We found her! We found her! We found Sara Aldrete!" The neighbors had tried to intervene, to say that Teresa merely resembled her older sister, but the police would not listen.

Israel grabbed the family photo album as evidence of Teresa's identity and rushed to police headquarters. After two hours, he managed to pry a terrified and tearful eighteen-year-old girl free from jail.

"Thank god I got you back," Israel Aldrete said, his face wet then, too. "I can't lose both of you."

"But what about Sara, Papa?" Teresa asked. "What will we do for her?"

Her father had no answer to that question. They got into his car and drove home in silence, wondering where Sara had gone. And why.[8]

23

Sara Aldrete arrived in Mexico City alone, exhausted and terrified. The trip had been harrowing. Every face she saw looked suspicious, every jostle in the crowd made her jump, as if some policeman was about to spin her around and slap on the cuffs. She had needed ten minutes to screw up enough courage to pass through the metal detector checkpoint at the airport in McAllen. When she finally did, no one gave her a second look.

Sara had packed nothing, telling her parents she was going out for the afternoon. They had no idea she was going away, but she didn't dare tell them before leaving, for fear they would try to stop her. And she didn't dare call them once she had fled. How could she possibly explain?[1]

Omar was waiting at the Mexico City airport when Sara arrived around ten in the evening on April 10. Sara thought he looked as nervous and weary as she did.

With him was Martin's pretty little sister, Teresa Quintana Rodriquez. Two months earlier, Teresa had moved into the luxurious tenth-floor condo on Calle Jalapa that Constanzo maintained but seldom used. Teresa was twenty-two and no dummy, but Sara could see she had no idea what was going on. Though she had been involved in some of the cult's more modest magical rituals, Martin steadfastly kept his sister insulated from the cult's dark and violent sides. Teresa tried to make conversation with Sara on the way back from the airport, but Sara sat silently the entire trip, brooding and staring out the window at the dark city streets.

Omar drove them to the Jalapa condo, where Adolfo, Martin,

and Duby waited. After a desultory greeting to Sara, they marched from the living room to discuss their predicament in Constanzo's bedroom, except Teresa, who was ordered to stay out. The discussion revolved around what had gone wrong—no one knew—and how important it was to lay low and out of sight for a while.

"I'll kill anyone who leaves the house without my permission," Constanzo promised flatly. "Not until we know what the police know. And who told them."

Sara said that was fine with her; she had no intention of going anywhere. She collapsed on a bed and slept fitfully until morning, not even bothering to undress.[2]

The men, meanwhile, drove to Atziapan, where they hurriedly picked up money and clothes, and removed any incriminating evidence they could find from the Calle Papagayos house. At midnight, they fled back to the city, Constanzo's home security system casting harsh spotlights on their retreating backs.

They repeated the task at the Calle Pomona apartment, removing what they could from the living quarters and the ceremonial room, jamming suitcases with a chaotic mix of clothes, money, and the tools of curses.

Papagayos and Pomona were the two addresses Elio had visited and, therefore, the two addresses the federales most likely would learn, Constanzo knew. He ordered his men never to return to them again.

The next day, Sara awoke to the sound of Constanzo cursing the morning newscast on television. He was anxious to find out what the police knew, but there was no word out of Matamoros on TV. This same day, April 11, the first twelve bodies were unearthed at Rancho Santa Elena. As Constanzo cursed, the backhoes were just getting to work, harvesting a terrible crop. But the first press conference was hours away, and news reports were further off still.

"I can't stand this waiting," Adolfo spat. "I want to know what they know."

He didn't have long to wait, though the hours ticked by unmercifully slow as the gang stayed glued to the television set. Only Teresa left the condo, at Martin's insistence. He didn't want her to see the evening news.

That night, as Constanzo flipped through channel after channel, every telecast was filled with the story of Rancho Santa Elena. Every station Constanzo tuned in started with the story of mutilation and mass murder by a devil-worshiping cult in Matamoros. "That's it," El Padrino said. "They found it."[3]

First shown were photos of the ranch, the shed, the nganga, and the graves, followed by shots of the Hernandez boys and their thugs under arrest—paraded before the cameras by a grim Comandante Benitez. Few other details were divulged, nor were there any pictures of the fugitives, although Constanzo was named as the ringleader, with Sara as his witch and second in command.

Teresa returned home from a movie a few minutes later, finding the gang sitting in silence in the living room, the television switched off. "What's the matter?" she asked.

"Nothing," Martin said after a long silence. "Go to bed."

The next day, the gang's worst fears were realized. A picture of Adolfo Constanzo appeared on the screen, with the word "Wanted" and his name. More footage of the Hernandez prisoners and the ranch followed. The Mexican newscaster branded the cult, *los narcosatanicos*—The Narcotic-Satanists.

El Padrino almost laughed. People were so ignorant. Everything magical was instantly branded satanic. The fools had no idea what real power was, he muttered. "Bastards," he said bitterly. "The boys told the cops everything."

"What will we do, Adolfo?" Sara said, overcome by a wave of nausea at the next photograph on the television. It was her own picture, snatched from a yearbook at Texas Southmost College. "We're finished."

The Mexican newscaster wound up his report by quoting a U.S. Customs official in Brownsville, who said authorities believed the fugitives were headed to Miami. Police there were on alert for the gang.

At this, Constanzo did laugh. Suddenly he seemed filled with hope again.

"Well, I'll tell you this, Sara," he said, his voice forceful, bitterness replaced by a tone of certainty. "One thing we're not going to do is go to Miami.

"But we will escape this trouble. I swear it."

They were weak," Adolfo de Jesus Constanzo pronounced. "Weak fools."

Constanzo and his gang sat staring at a televised image of Elio Hernandez. The stout trafficker stood shirtless before a mass of reporters, his sacred rayado exposed to the cameras.

"That's why they're in Matamoros, in jail, and we're here, free," El Padrino said.

The scene switched to a funeral home, where lines had formed for viewing the bodies found at Rancho Santa Elena. When the camera focused on one tearful woman asking for her son, Constanzo shut the television off with contempt.

"Weaklings," he repeated. Then he turned his attention to his bedraggled, depressed followers. "We must have a ceremony of protection. We must cleanse ourselves."

After sending Duby for supplies, Constanzo ordered his remaining followers to participate in an offering of a rooster's blood at the small marble altar he maintained at the Jalapa condo. He decapitated the fowl with relish, spilling the blood into a rancid and crusty bowl. His beads rattled as he bent to his task.

Preoccupied with worry, the others listlessly went through the motions as Constanzo directed the ritual. He seemed not to notice. Instead, as the limp, headless bird was laid before the grimacing image of Eleggua, he fell into an unaccustomed reverie, almost preaching to his small flock.

"I am the greatest palero," he said, staring out of the window of his tenth-floor condo, as he slowly paced the white plush carpeting. "My mother, my brothers, my sister—all are powerful, all are blessed. And I am the chosen one. That's why we will not be stopped."

He turned to Sara and stared at her intently, his eyes wide and glazed, directed inward. Suddenly those eyes seemed to Sara to be those of a madman. Was that something new? she wondered. Or had they always been that way, and she was only noticing now that it was too late?

"You saw the bodies on the TV, didn't you, Sara?" Constanzo asked, studying her.

Unnerved by his stare, she nodded.

"You never knew there were so many, did you?"

Sara shook her head. Perhaps she had guessed, but she hadn't known.

"Think of the power. All that blood, all those souls. They're all inside me now, Sara. I have become many men. And their spirits make my brujeria strong. They must obey me. They will crush our enemies. They are our shield."

His voice rose as he spoke, forcing the others to listen. Unconsciously, they sat a little forward on their chairs, a little less slumped, a little less hopeless.

"With the spirits' help, we will escape and go to Central America, where the religion is strong, where we can do whatever we wish."

They were all staring at Adolfo now, captivated. Duby was nodding. Constanzo's voice was hypnotic, calm, reasonable in tone if not in content.

Omar, Duby, and Martin had been jumpy, starting at every sudden sound, every passing car. They feared going near the windows, ten floors up, as if someone could see them. But now Adolfo de Jesus Constanzo, the most wanted man in Mexico and the United States, was showing no fear, only power and control. It reassured them.

He still was their leader. He would find a way around the pictures on television and in the newspaper and on the wanted posters. He would thwart the police, just as he always had.

"Even when I was a child," Constanzo said, again staring sightlessly out the window, "I had the power. My mother knew it, too. Even then we knew where it would take me."

Much later, his followers would say Constanzo seldom spoke of his past during his years as their padrino. Instead, he preferred to cultivate an aura of mystery, letting others spread the stories. But when his bloody Matamoros graveyard was thrust into the light of day, somehow the door that always sealed Constanzo off from others began to creak open, too. Starting that night in the condo, then later, cooped up for weeks with his band of fugitives in a series of dismal hideouts, the Cuban-American sorcerer began to speak of himself as never before.

He had raged at them in the past, but that was to intimidate, to dominate, to command. Now they were hearing the world through Constanzo's words, seeing it through his eyes, a universe where love was foreign, mercy a weakness, faith a fault. The padrino told his followers of a strange and depraved childhood, a succession of vile family homes filled with pain and animal sacrifice. Yet they were places he remembered not with horror, but fondness—places he had tried to recreate for his own godchildren. Somehow, when Constanzo spoke, he managed to make the abnormal seem normal, the evil seem good.

Sometimes in calm conversations, other times in machine-gun–waving monologues tinged with the delirious joy of madness, Constanzo gradually revealed his whole, sick history to Sara, Duby, and the others. Whether he was sedate or frenzied, though, never really mattered: The tale he spun during the gang's next month on the run always held his followers riveted.

They had plenty of chances to get away from this deranged subject of an international manhunt. Alone or together, they could have slipped out of that condo or the other hideouts and found refuge. But they didn't. They couldn't leave Constanzo or his strangely compelling tale. They saw no other way out.

He had always held them spellbound. He always would.[4]

We have to get out of here," Constanzo said Wednesday, April 12. A day earlier, the bodies had been uncovered and the nganga captured. "The police will find this place, too."

They had rarely left the Jalapa condo for the past two days. From the Papagayos and Pomona homes, they had snatched clothes and money, some $5,000 in dollars, pesos, and gold coins called *centenarios*. They had gathered up all the photo albums, notes, and journals they could find in the condo, taking some, burning the rest to avoid leaving clues behind for the police.

Furtively, one at a time, they each slipped out of the condo to have their hair cut short and dyed. Omar became a cheesy blonde, as did Martin, who sported a trim page-boy haircut when he returned in place of his long, shaggy mane. Sara tinted her already colored hair a dark, unnatural brown, cutting away her permed curls in the process. Duby shaved his beard and had his long hair moussed into a ridiculous pompadour, giving him an extra three inches in height. And Constanzo's long, dark locks vanished, replaced by a buzz cut, making him look like a vaguely goofy American tourist, replete with Hawaiian shirt and shorts. He dyed his hair red.

The transformation was startling. They looked nothing like the pictures in the newspaper. Only Sara, a six-foot, one-inch Mexican woman, could not be camouflaged.

For Martin's little sister, Teresa, these transformations were unsettling clues. Though Martin had kept her away from the television set when the news was on, she soon realized something was terribly wrong.

The first hint was when the police commander, Salvador, had come by the condo. He spoke in urgent whispers with Constanzo for nearly an hour, then left without a word to anyone else, not even a nod of recognition.[5] Constanzo had made Teresa hide on the balcony while he was there, but she had peeked in.

"I don't want Salvador to see you, or know that you're with us," Constanzo had said. "I'm not sure we can trust him. It will be better for you."

Later, while Constanzo and Martin were out and someone knocked on the door, Duby squealed, "Must be the police!" and refused to answer it. Teresa had to push him out of the way and turn the dead bolt herself.

It was Martin and Constanzo, returned from the hairdresser. Teresa took one look at their outrageous hairdos, and as Martin blushed furiously, she demanded they tell her what was going on.

Instead, Constanzo called her to his side. "*Niña,*" he said, using his pet name for her—little girl—"I want to tell you something. Come here."

Teresa trusted her padrino. He had always been courtly to her, deferential in a way he reserved for few others. He treated Teresa like his own sister.

Over the years, Constanzo had performed limpias on Teresa, and once, he solemnly advised her never to wear black clothes when visiting him. "They attract bad vibrations," he had warned, "and the dead could eat you." He had told her how much he loved Martin, and she accepted their homosexuality even if the rest of the Quintana family did not.

Teresa found Constanzo utterly charming, as many women did, when he wanted it that way. And he was generous with his money, which was earned, he told Teresa, from his works of witchcraft, cleansings, and card throwing, not from drugs. Martin was wealthy, too, thanks to Constanzo's generosity. He became so well off that he gave Teresa a new Chrysler New Yorker for her twenty-second birthday.[6]

When her other brother, Alfredo, had claimed Adolfo killed people in Mexico City—something Martin once confided—Teresa had refused to believe it. She said she knew Constanzo was incapable of murder. "He loves Martin. And if he did kill someone," Teresa said stubbornly, "it was probably in self-defense."

"They're drug traffickers, Teresita," Alfredo had shouted, trying to dissuade her from moving in with Martin and Adolfo.

But Teresa wouldn't listen. She had packed up from the family home in suburban Ixtapalapa and moved to the city. She planned to get her own place in the capital, but in the meantime she had accepted Constanzo's invitation to live in the Jalapa condo. Now, with so many strange and troubling things happening, she beseeched Constanzo to be truthful with her.

"Niña, I cannot tell you," he said gently. "We must go, and so must you, but not with us. Now say good-bye to your brother. It's the last time you're going to see him."[7]

Turning to Martin in a panic, Teresa asked, "What does Adolfo mean, I'll never see you again? Is it drugs? What?"

Martin looked at the others. Sara and Omar looked impatient. Duby just looked scared. "We're in trouble, Teresa," Martin said after a moment. "Don't ask me any more. It's better you don't know."

Constanzo handed Teresa a wad of bills then, about $2,000, along with the papers for Martin's Thunderbird, Constanzo's most recent birthday gift to his lover. With the money, Constanzo said, she should remove the car from a mechanic's shop, then sell it for all she could get. Later, Martin would call her so they could collect the proceeds. Constanzo also gave her two gold lockets and a Cartier watch encrusted with gems to sell.

"Take them," Martin said. "And be careful. Say nothing. I'll call you when I can."

"We're trusting you, Niña," Constanzo said. "Now let's go."

The gang members picked up their suitcases. Stunned, not sure what was happening, Teresa walked them downstairs.

"We're going to take your car, Niña," Constanzo said. "It will be safer for us. If anyone asks, tell them we had to go to Miami."

Teresa nodded. "You're going to Miami," she repeated hollowly.

"Nothing will happen to me," Martin promised. "Don't worry."

But then Martin Quintana Rodriguez, El Padrino's fearsome bodyguard, began to weep. He had become inured to killing, but it had always stayed isolated from his beloved little sister. Now that side of his life he felt was still good—his family—had been infected by El Padrino as well. He knew nothing would ever be the same. "Think of me," he said, clutching Teresa's hand, small and cold in his, tears running down both their cheeks. She asked again what was happening, but he only shook his head and cried harder.

Finally, Constanzo had to walk over and gently pry him loose from Teresa's grasp. Then he guided Martin to the car. He waved one last time to his sister. As Teresa watched, they climbed into the long, black luxury car Martin had given her and drove away.

Teresa had a feeling then, one she tried to fight off, but still couldn't dismiss: she really would never see her brother again.

When she went to her sister's house to stay the night, she watched the evening news. And then she knew for sure. Her brother was gone forever. Teresa had lived with monsters, and had never even known it.[8]

The gang's first stop was an apartment near the airport—Salvador's home. Constanzo was not sure he could still trust the possessed police comandante, but his options were few. He had to know what the police knew.

"It's bad," Chava told his godfather after peering through the blinds to make sure no one had followed the gang. "They know everything about you. The comandante in Matamoros is pumping Elio and his stupid nephew, and they're telling everything. They don't know your houses yet, but it's only a matter of time."

"I know," Constanzo said. "What can you do?"

"Do? It's too late to do anything except run," Salvador cried. "All I can do is try to stay out of it."

Salvador outweighed Constanzo by at least sixty pounds, but

when El Padrino whirled on him, face white with anger, the policeman backed up a step. "You are not 'out of it'!" Constanzo spat. "No one is out of it. If I go down, Chava, so will you. Remember that.

"Now we need a place to hide. We need money and we need to move some drugs to get it. Then we can pay off Immigration and get out of the country."

"Padrino, forgive me," Salvador said abjectly.

Constanzo dismissed the apology with a wave. "Now, I ask you again, what can you do?"

Salvador sighed. "I can go to Guadalajara."[9]

The gang had purchased and stolen cocaine in Guadalajara before, and Constanzo knew they could do it again. It was the key to their escape. Constanzo nodded his approval.

The gang members made phone calls from Salvador's apartment then, leaving a trail investigators eventually would discover: Constanzo called Miami and Monterrey,[10] while Duby called Matamoros. Constanzo wouldn't let Sara use the phone, though. La Madrina, once feared by the other members of the cult as Constanzo's right hand, was wavering in her resolve. During their last day in the condo, she had taken to asking Constanzo to let her go home. Over and over, she repeated how tired she was of running. "My parents must be worried sick," she whined.

Constanzo responded with contempt. Everything had been fine for the privileged young honor student when she felt in control of her double life, he mocked—when she was teaching her Santeria classes and directing the animal sacrifices, when she allowed the dark spirits to take hot, sweaty possession of her at the ranch and at her altar. Then she had liked the power and money and secret knowledge, the dark side of her life she hid from the college classmates and cheerleaders and teachers.

"But now that things are hard, you're ready to give up hope," Constanzo accused. "You just want to bail out. You'd betray us, your true family."

"I only want to talk to my mother," Sara pleaded.

"You're a loose cannon," Constanzo told her. "I don't want you talking to anyone. I'm not sure what you'll say."

She looked to Omar and Martin for support, but they would not meet her eyes. They had submitted again to their godfather's will, and her hopes sank further. Salvador merely eyed her coldly, as he would a chicken ready for the altar. Sara began to realize just how delicate her position in the cult was becoming.

If they escaped arrest together, she probably could resume her role as La Madrina, keeper of knowledge for the cult. Tensions and distrust would fade. Sticking it out was her best bet, Sara decided. But if things went bad, she needed a way out.

Maybe the others were ready for prison or death. But Sara vowed to herself she would not follow Constanzo down that path. Dimly, the outlines of a plan began to take shape in her mind.

After hiding all day, resting, and eating, the gang prepared to leave Salvador's home. Only Sara had refused a meal—she hadn't eaten since leaving Matamoros. She had tried, but even a few mouthfuls made her gag and run to the bathroom.

Constanzo took a government-issue Uzi machine gun, a shotgun, and two boxes of bullets from Salvador. He stuck them in a black suitcase and cautioned the police commander to remain true to the cult.[11] "Remember who controls the three spirits within you, Chava," Constanzo said. "Remember who has your soul. I can tear you apart with a word."

Salvador nodded at Constanzo's smug grin. Magical threats aside, he couldn't turn Adolfo in to the authorities, and both men knew it. How could he divulge his knowledge of their whereabouts without implicating himself? Constanzo didn't have to trust Salvador's dedication to the cult. Self-preservation would keep him loyal.

Yes, Salvador answered dutifully to Constanzo's questioning, he would go to Guadalajara soon. Yes, Constanzo could call him in a few days to check on his progress. Yes, he would find the drugs and get the money.

"Take heart, Chava," Constanzo said. "You'll go with us to Central America. We'll start over. You'll see."

Salvador said nothing. He didn't dare voice his belief that Constanzo hadn't a prayer of finding a safe haven.

From Salvador's home, the gang left for a seedy hotel a few miles away. Part of a series of barrios ringing the airport, it was rocked periodically by jetliners screaming overhead on final approach.

They checked into two rooms, holing up with a stack of newspapers and intently watching cable television news from both countries. Duby, the only one among the five whose picture had not been publicized, did the food shopping.

Watching the news over the next two nights in the motel, they saw how investigators stumbled on each of Constanzo's beautiful homes. One by one, they burst into and sacked the whitewashed home in Atziapan, the condo on Calle Jalapa, the apartment on Calle Pomona. Soon yellow tape sealed the doors to his homes and police stood guard—as if Constanzo would return there now, falling into their hands. They were so stupid, Constanzo kept saying. Did they think he wouldn't watch the news?

Sara, though, felt a noose slowly tightening around her neck. She couldn't eat, she could barely move. All she uttered, when she spoke at all, was a plea to go home. Constanzo took to slapping her face to try to rouse her or, failing that, to shut her up.[12] "I may have to kill you, Sara," he kept telling her, gun in hand. "I have to be able to depend on you."

After two days of incessantly watching television in their dingy hotel rooms, even Constanzo began showing signs of cabin fever. Mexican television, other than news shows, consists largely of soap operas, variety shows, old Mexican movies, and badly dubbed American movies. Only Duby could watch endlessly and seem to enjoy it. The others paced and quarreled and slowly lost hope.

Finally, Constanzo realized they had to move on. They couldn't wait at the hotel, he told the others. Staying in any one place too long would not only drive them crazy, it would be a tactical mistake, making them too easy to find.

He telephoned Maria del Rocio Cuevas Guerra, his santera follower in the suburb of Echegaray. "I need your help, Karla, my love," he said, watching Sara stiffen at his words, an amused smile tugging at his lips. At least La Madrina was showing some life. "We need a place to hide."

When Karla remained silent—no doubt she had seen the news, too—Constanzo rephrased his plea. "I need your help, Karla, or I'll kill you and your three lovely daughters. And then I'll make you all suffer in hell when I join you there."

Karla said she would help.

"She is my most loyal follower," Constanzo told Sara after hanging up the phone. "She'll do anything for me. If I got her pregnant, she would allow me to sacrifice our child. In fact, I'm planning to do just that."[13]

Sara moaned softly and hugged herself. She had barely slept or eaten in four days. "I just want to go home, Adolfo," she said.

Constanzo smiled at her sweetly. "Only in a box, my love," he said. "Only in a box."[14]

The next night, Saturday, April 15, Constanzo and his gang went to Karla's house. The blonde bruja watched silently as they trooped into her home, their hair cut and dyed, their posture slumped and exhausted.

"You have to find us a place to hide out, Karla," Constanzo said. "They've found all my houses."

"You can't stay here, Adolfo," she said. "Too many people know I practice witchcraft and that I am your goddaughter. What about all the clients I brought you? What if the police find out about my place?"

"There's no way for them to find out," he answered quietly. "Unless you tell them."

She looked into his gaunt face and those dark eyes, hearing the threat behind his mild words. Then she saw Martin remove the machine gun from the black suitcase and hand it to Adolfo. There was no room for argument. She knew they would stay no matter what she said.

Karla took them to a back bedroom and drew the curtains. They could stay there until she found them a safe place. With that settled, Martin left to dispose of Teresa's car.

They sat at the dining room table, surrounded by the trappings of Karla's witchcraft—black candles, bundles of herbs, ceremonial swords, dolls, statues, waxwork skulls. For a while they made small talk that seemed chillingly out of place. Karla asked how were Adolfo's mother and the rest of his family, and Constanzo told her they were well.

"Is it all true, Adolfo?" Karla finally asked. "Did you kill all those people?"

Laughing, he lied. "No. I only killed four of them. For drugs. I didn't do the other things at the ranch—that was the Hernandez family. Everything else the police made up."

This mollified Karla. To her, anything, even drug killings, was better than the horrors on television. And besides, her fascination for Constanzo still held. Her feelings for him had always been a thrilling mixture of love and fear. She would sleep with him that night if he allowed it, threats and guns and killings notwithstanding.

"It's terrible the way the government lies," she said. "We have no human rights in Mexico."

This struck Sara as particularly funny. She repeated the words, "human rights," then she began to laugh and weep at the same time. "I am an honor student," she kept saying. "This can't be happening."

At a signal from Constanzo, Martin and Duby carried her to bed. "I'm worried about her," Constanzo said soberly. "Do you know any doctors?" His concern for her well-being seemed genuine, catching Omar by surprise. He had been studying his godfather for the past several days, and was reluctantly coming to the conclusion that Constanzo was developing a split personality. He thought about confiding his concerns to Martin, then thought better of it. He'd probably tell Adolfo as soon as I left the room, Omar decided. He, too, decided just to stick things out.

The next day Sara couldn't stand up. She kept doubling over from the pain in her stomach. When Martin tried to feed her, she threw up immediately.

Karla had little sympathy for her rival, but at Constanzo's order she called a friend of hers, a twenty-nine-year-old doctor named Maria de Lourdes Bueno Lopez—Malu for short. Malu was interested in Santeria, and had met Constanzo and the others a few times. She had taken part in cleansings and other ceremonies with Karla, but she was not one of Adolfo's initiates.

"Adolfo has been in touch with me," Karla told Malu on the phone.

"Stay out of it, Karla," Malu warned. "You'll get in trouble. He kills people."

"I know," Karla replied. "But he's already here. With the others.

One of them is sick. Can you come?" Then she added, "They'll do bad things if you don't."

Malu promised to come.

Much later, U.S. authorities would marvel at Constanzo's ability to get seemingly upstanding citizens—or at least people with no criminal records—to help him. Why didn't Karla or Doctor Bueno Lopez call the police? Or Karla's new boyfriend, Enrique Calzada, a follower of Constanzo's who also showed up at the house to help the cult? It seems inconceivable to *norteamericano* sensibilities that the doctor wouldn't just pick up the phone and call the police. Let them surround Karla's house and put an end to it.

To Mexicans, though, it is not inconceivable. Ordinary citizens who call the police to report mere burglaries have their homes burglarized a second time—by the policemen who arrive to "investigate." People are pistol whipped, extorted, beaten, and shot by policemen regularly. Then, if through some miracle such offending lawmen are charged, the authorities often as not arrest the wrong people, torture a confession from them, then proclaim the case solved. If the victims say the real culprits have not been caught, the authorities will say it doesn't matter. The men in custody have confessed. The case is solved.[15]

For the doctor to have reported Constanzo to the police would have been to court disaster. She would be arrested and charged herself. The police would have said she must be guilty or she wouldn't have known where Constanzo was in the first place. Malu believed that the police might torture her until she confessed.

Constanzo knew this and depended upon it. Fear of the police, coupled with fear and devotion to Constanzo's powers, gave El Padrino a compelling means of motivating his followers to help him.

"Don't tell the police, Malu," Karla whispered over the phone, as Constanzo listened at her side.

"I won't," the doctor replied. And Constanzo knew she spoke the truth.

When Bueno Lopez arrived in Echegaray, she treated Sara for colitis and prescribed some pills. Sara began to feel better and ate some soup, keeping it down. A second prescription for tranquilizers calmed her and her constant stream of complaints and pleas ceased.

Constanzo, meanwhile, went through the doctor's purse and medical bag. Then he told her he had memorized her address and the names and addresses of her family from a notebook he had found. "If you don't help us, they will all die," he promised.[16]

The doctor nodded stiffly. She understood.

Then Constanzo asked the doctor if they could borrow her 1982 Renault. They had to leave the city for a while, and they needed a car that couldn't be traced to them. It was not really a request, but Constanzo was trying to maintain the illusion of civility. Malu said yes.

"While we're gone, I want you two to find us an apartment somewhere. And we need papers, false passports. And you, Malu, must find the name of a plastic surgeon who can operate on us. I want to change our appearances. Then we can start over."

"We'll do it, Adolfo," Karla said without hesitation.

Karla's boyfriend, Enrique, rented a car and they all drove to a place outside the city called Popo Park, a resort area near an inactive volcano, windswept and dusty. The doctor and Karla stopped at a VIPs to pick up hamburgers for the gang. Then they rented cabins in Popo Park, one for Duby and Sara, and the other for Omar, Martin, and Adolfo. Karla dealt with the desk clerk while the others settled in.

Before departing, Karla gave Constanzo $2,000, her entire savings account. "Use it to stay safe, Adolfo," she said, clasping his hands, then kissing them.

"We'll wait for you here," Constanzo said.

Karla, the doctor, and Enrique climbed in the rental car to return to Echegaray.

"Remember, I have friends with the police. I have friends everywhere," Constanzo said, leaning in the car window. "Do not betray me."

24

As the fugitives took refuge in remote cabins, they had more than just their followers' religious fervor and fear of the police working in their favor. They were also protected by the enormous enmity between the two Mexican police departments hunting them.

Like the rivalry-torn task force in the United States, the manhunt in Mexico City, which at times involved as many as three hundred officers, was stymied by lack of cooperation.

On one side were the Federal Judicial Police and the attorney general's office—counterparts to the FBI and Justice Department in the United States—which have jurisdiction over drug trafficking and crimes that cross Mexican state lines. As part of this organization, Comandante Benitez was feeding information to his comrades in Mexico City to aid them in the hunt for the fugitives.

On the other side were the judicial police and prosecutors of the Federal District of Mexico, the local authorities who have jurisdiction over most crimes committed within the capital's city limits. They, too, were searching for Constanzo and his clan, but they were not concerned with the crimes in Matamoros. They wanted to interrogate the gang about certain ritual killings in Mexico City during the past two years. The seven Calzada mutilation murders and the death of the transvestite La Claudia remained open cases. But to investigators who saw similarities between these murders and the killings at Rancho Santa Elena, they were looking more and more like cases about to be solved.

The problem was, the federal and district police departments were not speaking to one another. Feelings were running too high from the previous September, when the district police staged an armed assault on the headquarters of the Federal Judicial Police, attempting to free two colleagues charged with assault and robbery. The battle was the rough equivalent of the city police in Washington, D.C., storming Quantico, Virginia, headquarters for the FBI.

The district police felt the federales were corrupt, and vice versa. Ample precedent exists for distrust: The former head of the federales and his cousin, the former head of Interpol in Mexico before Florentino Ventura, live and work and exert great influence, even though they have been indicted in the United States for taking part in the murder of DEA Agent Kiki Camarena.[1] Meanwhile, top agents and bodyguards of Mexico's federal anti-drug czar, Javier Coehlo Trico, have been arrested for armed assault, robbery, and gang rape.[2] District police made the arrests.

It was against this backdrop that district investigators asked the federales for information on the method of killing at the Rancho Santa Elena, so they could compare autopsy reports to the Calzadas and Claudia murders. The federales said no, it was their case, not the locals'. Conversely, when Benitez's colleagues in Mexico City demanded the files on the Calzada and La Claudia cases, Federico Ponce Rojas, the U.S.–trained assistant district attorney general in charge of the two investigations, shouted into the phone, "You want us to help you, but you give us nothing. Go to hell. We'll see who gets Constanzo first."

Ponce hung up, turned to one of his top investigators, Paquito Blanchette, and shrugged. It was April 14, the fourth day since the bodies had been unearthed, and the fugitives in the biggest case in both Mexico and the United States had disappeared entirely.

"Hard to believe we're on the same side," Blanchette offered.

Ponce shook his head. "We're not."[3]

The Mexico City federales had been called earlier that same day by Comandante Benitez in Matamoros. He passed on what he had learned from Elio Hernandez about the homes on Calle Papagayos in Atziapan and Calle Pomona downtown. Until then, all the Mexico City-based federales knew about the gang's possible whereabouts began and ended at the city's airport, where Constanzo had arrived on April 10, then disappeared. More than one hundred agents had fanned out there, questioning cabbies, ticket agents, shoeshine boys, and pickpockets. But no one had seen them, or admitted it if they had.

Maybe, the federales hoped, Constanzo had just got on another plane and left. Official spokesmen for the federal police began to suggest to the press that El Padrino was no longer in Mexico City. Perhaps he had made some magical escape, they half joked.

When Benitez called, though, what had been a flailing effort to search a city of 20 million suddenly drew into sharp focus. Investigators quickly combed the two neighborhoods Elio described, and they soon came up with exact addresses: Calle Papagayos 47, where giggly neighbor girls talked longingly of a darkly handsome norteamericano from Miami; and Calle Pomona 8, apartment 3, in chic Colonia Roma, where the neighbors told a wild story about Constanzo falling from a third-floor balcony, crushing a car, then walking away unscathed.

"Maybe he did," one detective replied. "But he won't be walking away this time."

The agent's bragging turned out to be premature. Heavily armed teams of commandos arrived an hour after the investigators called in with the exact addresses. They had flak jackets, machine guns, and tear gas, ready to exterminate the dread narcosatanicos if necessary. But only one bullet was fired, and that was by accident—when a nervous young federale pressed his trigger by mistake and just missed blowing away his commander.

Constanzo was long gone. The apartment and house had been emptied and abandoned. While the police poked around looking for clues, Constanzo was already hiding in a sleazy motel near the airport, plotting his escape.

At the Calle Pomona apartment, police found Constanzo's display of life-size statues of the saints, ceramic figures lined up in the living room like grim warriors risen from the grave. Plates of fruit and candy, headless, rotting chickens, and what looked like bowls of blood lay before the eerie figures. Stumps of melted candles, cigar butts, and herbs were scattered at their feet.

The officers carefully crept though the house, searching room by room, finding no one and nothing unusual other than the ostentatious trappings of wealth Constanzo craved. Stereo equipment and color televisions were stacked in every bedroom. The rugs and furniture were from the best stores in Mexico City; the closets were jammed with fine clothes, and an army of men's shoes, polished and lined up just so, filled the closet floors.

They searched what should have been the maid's quarters last, in the back of the apartment. Beyond its closed door they found the small bedroom had been transformed into Constanzo's blood-stained room of the dead. The floor was littered with feathers, rum bottles, cigars, peppers, and other trappings of the occult, crunching like gravel beneath the agents' feet.

Had these officers been at Rancho Santa Elena when the shed was opened there, they would have recognized the smell inside this cramped and airless room. The agents backed away instinctively, then forced themselves to survey the room. Quickly.

From the smell, they had expected human corpses, but only animal remains were evident.[4] The federales noted that at the center of the altar, surrounded by bowls and plates bearing the stinking remains of chickens, goats, and turtles, there was a circular clean area on the floor. Something large and round had sat there as the filth accumulated around it, and then, recently, it had been taken away. Constanzo's Mexico City nganga, a twin to the one in Matamoros, was gone.[5]

Fifteen miles away, past the ten-foot-high wall and the five closed-circuit cameras guarding the Calle Papagayos home, police found two more altars, each made of fine imported marble. But both had been swept clean. No statues, no offerings nor blood were found in the home. Like the Calle Pomona apartment, it was obsessively immaculate. More stereos, more color televisions, more VCRs were found throughout the home, some still in the box.

When the angry federales had finished their searches, the contents of both homes lay destroyed—furniture and stereos broken, pictures smashed, papers everywhere. They made some valuable finds, though. In one of the five bedrooms of the Atziapan home, investigators found a cache of hard-core homosexual pornography in a desk drawer—the first indication police had that Constanzo and some of his followers were gay. There were also photos lying around of Constanzo, Omar, and Martin arm in arm, or lounging about in their underwear, coyly posed together on a couch or with arms linked at the beach. One black-and-white glossy showed Martin in drag.

Now, here was something the police could seize on—in their minds, a perversion that explained much. Godless, homosexual, murderous cultists were at work here—led by a pathological American, they took pains to note, not a Mexican. Finding those pictures instantly reinforced the virulent homophobia common in most Mexican men, and provided a ready excuse for the police to comb the gay bars of the Zona Rosa, brass knuckles at the ready. While agents continued to search the homes, others were sent out to roust dozens of gay men at random, questioning and in some cases, beating them. Although some admitted knowing of Constanzo or his comrades, no useful information came of this questioning.[6]

Not even the neighbors on Calles Pomona and Papagayos provided much help. No, everyone said, those people kept to themselves; they were unfriendly. They never even said hello. Only the teenage girls in the neighborhood liked Constanzo, for his looks, but they knew nothing about him.

The neighbors did provide one bit of helpful testimony. Several said they had seen the gang members packing up boxes, carrying them to a car, then leaving after midnight on April 10. This proved Constanzo had not flown from the Mexico City airport immediately after his arrival. He was—or at least had been—skulking about the nation's capital.

In their hasty attempt to remove any sign of their pasts and plans, Constanzo and his followers had left behind one more crucial piece of evidence. The police found, tucked in behind the porn in the back of the desk drawer, two small books Constanzo had discarded years before and apparently forgotten. The federales had found El Padrino's journals from his early days in Mexico City.

One was a leather-bound ledger with Constanzo's name emblazoned on the cover in gold leaf. The other was a schoolboy's composition book—the type with ruled pages and black-and-white flecked cardboard covers—incongruously crammed with the recipes of a dark and evil magic. Both books bore a strange arrow design on the inside covers: one vertical, feathered arrow intersected by three parallel horizontal shafts, pointing right, left, and right alternately. This was Constanzo's *firma,* his mystical signature, given to him long before by his own padrino. When Benitez received the notebooks in Matamoros two days later, he recognized the design immediately as a variation of the scars Constanzo had carved into Elio's shoulder.

Much of the content of the journals was indecipherable to the federales, consisting primarily of the hieroglyphics paleros use when recording tosses of the cowrie shells to divine a person's future. The long, neat rows of small symbols, repeated over dozens of pages, were mostly arrows pointing in various directions, marked by circles, Xs, and a series of half- and quarter-moons. Some of the markings featured crossed swords and vipers hissing.

Interspersed among the glyphs, in Constanzo's precise, compressed hand, were prescriptions for magical cures he had apparently designed for his clients and followers. Though these were in Spanish, they remained mysteries to the police, since they were pleas for help from African gods with names like kadiempembe and *Tiembla Tierra,* or Earth Shaker.

A page captioned at the top with the name "Salvador" contained a series of spells and prescriptions, including a command that Salvador become a palero priest, that he accept Eleggua the warrior as his guardian, and that he make daily offerings "to open the roads to illegal causes." The federales assumed this meant Salvador was a drug trafficker.

In the composition book, a page captioned "Rosa Maria" said Constanzo would grant her good luck and the "black necklace of kadiempembe" only after completion of a complex series of sacrifices called *cambio de cabeza*—change of head, a ceremony he had also performed for Karla. The journal promised this spell would chase the angry orisha who ruled Rosa Maria's life and brought her bad luck, replacing it with a friendlier spirit.

The recipe that followed differed horribly from Karla's earlier change of head spell, however, requiring the sacrifice of the soul of an innocent girl, aged one to ten. Once that was done, then Rosa Maria could assume her victim's guiding spirit and destiny, the journal promised.

Horrified investigators paged through the journals, looking for some indication of whether the spell was actually carried out. They could not tell. The change of head ceremony appeared central to Constanzo's most powerful magic—and to the terrible rumors that kept springing up about his murderous cult. The children's clothes that police found in a back room in the home on Calle Papagayos, mirroring a similar find at Sara Aldrete's Matamoros apartment, fueled the dark suggestion that the cult practiced ritual child murder, causing a widespread panic. Only later would police realize that only Palo Mayombe's most evil and deviant practitioners, like Constanzo, believe the change of head ceremony requires a human sacrifice.

The most recent entries in the journals were from 1986—obviously, the police concluded, Constanzo had finished these books and begun new ones, then forgot about them. This explained why none of the Matamoros suspects were listed.

Even these older journals indicated Constanzo had charged people hundreds, sometimes thousands, of American dollars for his magical services. These entries often included names, phone numbers, and addresses—Constanzo's clients, investigators concluded. Some, like Salvador and Rosa Maria, bore only a first name. But many others had full names, including pages devoted to the fugitives Omar Orea Ochoa and Martin Quintana, confirming their involvement in Constanzo's black-magic religion. They had already been implicated by Elio and the others back in Matamoros.

Some of the journal pages contained the names of prominent individuals in show business and government. The late Florentino Ventura, Mexico's head of Interpol, was one. There was also a flamboyant congressman and several actors and actresses. The federales removed many of these pages, then denied they ever existed. They made what was was left available to Benitez, the DEA, and selected members of the press.[7]

The federales dispatched dozens of agents to begin hunting down and questioning the people listed in Constanzo's journals. Someone among them would have to know where Constanzo and his band were hiding, investigators assumed.

The last bit of crucial evidence found on April 14 by the federales turned up at the Calle Pomona apartment downtown. It was a receipt for clothes addressed to Omar Orea Ochoa at Calle Jalapa 51. A squad of agents went to check it out, heavily armed but expecting to find the place empty like the other two.

In the center of the affluent Colonia Roma, the tall building of luxury condos, with its security guards and locked garage, looked an unlikely place for malevolent sorcery. Confirming their suspicions, a manager said the condo owners hadn't been seen in weeks. The agents reached the tenth floor, walked past the potted palms in the lobby, and approached unit 1004, as specified on Omar's receipt. They found the door unlocked.

They entered nonchalantly, some not even drawing their weapons—and found themselves staring into the bright, frightened eyes of a young woman. She had been standing by the living room couch, packing a suitcase, when the agents entered. For a moment everyone in the room was speechless.

"Who are you?" one of the policemen finally sputtered, fumbling for his pistol.

"Teresa Quintana," the girl blurted.

"Quintana?" two agents asked at once.

And little Teresa began to cry, even as the agents found themselves grinning at their good fortune.

While the federales fanned out through the Zona Rosa, following up on their discoveries by questioning gays, the district police were taking a different tack. They were rounding up witches.

A group of investigators under District Attorney Federico Ponce—dubbed "The Four Fantastiks" by their compatriots because of their many arrests—had renewed efforts to solve the Calzada and La Claudia cases. One of the investigators, Paquito Blanchette, had studied all the press accounts he could find on the Matamoros slayings, and even without access to the federales' autopsy reports, he saw obvious similarities between the condition of the Calzada bodies, the dismembered La Claudia, and the rotting corpses of Rancho Santa Elena.

"Look at this picture of the transvestite," Blanchette told Ponce. Since the district attorney had been appointed to office only a few months before, he had not seen the La Claudia file before. "They skinned the face completely off. Just left a skull.

"Now look at this newspaper," Blanchette said, handing him a full-color crime magazine crammed with lurid photos of the cult's Matamoros victims. "They did the same thing on the border."

Ponce nodded.

"Now look at the Calzada file. The inventory of the factory and the autopsies."

Ponce scanned the pages, then focused on the eggs, candles, and drawings on the wall in blood listed in the investigators' report. The bodies also had been mutilated. One man's corpse had chicken feathers stuck into the holes left behind when his fingers were cut off.

"Brujos," Ponce said. "The Calzadas were performing a ritual when they were killed, or they were killed in a ritual. And the bodies?"

"Just like Matamoros. Hearts gone. Genitals gone. Duct tape on the eyes and mouth."

The two men looked at each other.

"It could be coincidence," Ponce said slowly, rubbing his thin beard and looking at the detective's notes in the file. He pointed to one paragraph. "It could have been Colombians, like you first thought here. Or maybe copycats."

"But you don't believe that," Blanchette said.

"No. You're right."

Ponce began to pace. A thin, intense man, Ponce is a fashionable dresser with horn-rimmed glasses and a nickel-plated automatic he tucks into his pants whenever he leaves the office. Unlike their courtroom counterparts in the United States, district attorneys in Mexico must establish a reputation for machismo. They go in with the troops, guns at the ready.

At thirty-seven, Ponce presided over one of the eight judicial districts within Mexico City. His territory was called Miguel Hidalgo sector, a sprawling section of the capital containing 4 million residents, the lushness of Chapultepec Park, the president's home, and some of the most squalid barrios in the city.

A veteran prosecutor with training from the U.S. Justice Department and the DEA, Ponce speaks impeccable English and lectures periodically at symposiums in Washington, D.C. Charming at times, overbearing at others, Ponce keeps a file of press clippings on himself, framing the most impressive stories for display on his office walls, then using them as conversation openers with visitors.

Now his top investigator was handing him a chance to join what could be the case of the century. It was too good to pass up. "Okay," he said. "Let's try to go through channels first."

Ponce called the federales. They told him nothing. They said Constanzo was probably in Guadalajara or Monterrey, not Mexico City, and that Ponce should stay out of it. They never mentioned the plane tickets that proved Constanzo had come to the capital. They simply refused to share information, so Ponce did the same when the federales asked him what he knew. Ponce learned about the searches of Constanzo's homes from newspaper accounts.

The absence of cooperation especially hurt in the case of Martin Quintana's sister. In pumping her, the federales obtained a long list of cult members' names, among them a man called Jorge Montes. She described him as an accomplished witch and follower of Constanzo, but she didn't know where he lived.

Had they shared their information with Ponce—or vice versa—a connection would immediately have been drawn. The La Claudia file on Ponce's desk showed that the man who had roomed with the dead transvestite was a fashion designer who lived on Calle Londres, a man by the name of Jorge Montes. Working blind, however, Ponce and his men had no reason to suspect Montes. He had been questioned and cleared after the July 1988 killing of La Claudia. In fact, he had identified the body.

"What do you want to do first, Paquito?" Ponce asked his investigator when cooperation with the federales had been ruled out.

"Send the four of us to the Zona Rosa to talk to the witches. Somebody there knows Constanzo. And maybe they can help us find him."

Blanchette's caseload was already full, as was everyone else's at Miguel Hidalgo. No hard evidence linked Constanzo to either of the old murder cases, therefore the Four Fantastiks had no legitimate reason to turn into cult busters. And Ponce knew he would take heat from downtown if he pulled the investigators off their regular work to pursue what was clearly a federales case.

Unless, of course, he got results.

"You'd better be right about this," Ponce said after a moment.

25

They went to Miami," Comandante Benitez announced two days after Teresa Quintana's arrest.[1] "We have a suspect in custody in Mexico who says Constanzo had to get to Miami."

Teresa Quintana had been a most credible witness for the federales, speaking at length about Constanzo's black magic, his bizarre ceremonies, and his elaborate limpias performed for prominent Mexicans. She told the police of Constanzo's sudden rise from near poverty in 1983 to wealth a year later. She spoke of the boutiques Constanzo claimed to own in Brownsville and Guadalajara with Martin, though they never seemed to work there. And she told of Constanzo's fiery love triangle with Omar and her brother, Martin—their arguments, threats, and Constanzo's extravagant gifts once the fighting was done.[2]

Finally, she admitted hearing from her brother Alfredo that Constanzo was a killer, though Teresa swore she never believed any of it until she saw the awful footage on television from Rancho Santa Elena. "Then, I knew," she whispered during one of many interrogations. "Only then."[3]

Because so much of what Teresa tearfully admitted to investigators in Mexico City matched the confessions from Elio, Serafin, and the others in Matamoros, when Teresa said the gang was headed to Miami, the federales believed her.

Agents were quickly diverted from other tasks and ordered back to the airport in Mexico City to renew questioning clerks and baggage handlers. The U.S. task force was alerted, and official eyes once more turned toward the tropical streets of Miami, after giving up on looking there the week before. Constanzo never believed his ruse would stop the hunt for him in the Mexican capital—and it didn't—but resources were channeled in fruitless directions after Teresa's interrogation, just as he knew they would be.

The media reports that the cult had fled to Miami bolstered the spirits of his followers, proving once again how easily the authorities could be fooled. "They'll never take me," Constanzo swore. "Never."[4]

When the second Miami tip turned out to be wrong, investigators in both countries began to grasp at straws, repeatedly giving the fugitive cultists a source of amusement and hope.

First Sara's purse, wallet, and identification cards were found hidden at one of Constanzo's houses, leading Benitez to gleefully speculate that she must be dead, sacrificed to Constanzo's weird gods. Even the morose Sara laughed when she read her premature obituary in the Mexico City papers.

Next a map drawn years before by convicted serial killer Henry Lee Lucas turned up in Attorney General Jim Mattox's possession, in which Lucas appeared to have pinpointed Matamoros as a focal point for satanic worship and human sacrifice. Once again, confusion about satanism created hysteria in the Rio Grande Valley, though the map had been drawn in 1985, long before Constanzo came to town.

Wild rumors were a problem from the outset in the case. An alternative church was burned to the ground in Pharr, Texas, after rumors circulated that it was home to a coven of witches. Sara was "sighted" dozens of times prowling neighborhoods and schools throughout the valley. Thousands of parents began hauling their children out of school on April 13, following a radio report in Matamoros, heard up and down the border, that discussed rumors of satanic child sacrifices. The report said fugitive Sara Aldrete had called police and threatened to begin kidnapping and killing forty school children, ten for each cultist captured, unless Elio Hernandez and the others were set free. The radio station had broadcast the story even after police told reporters the call was a crank.

More than anything else, it was Sara Aldrete's girl-next-door quality that seemed to spook and fascinate people, the fact that so unlikely a suspect had turned up in the center of such monstrosities. Sara was the one everyone talked about, the one they wanted to see captured and strung up, even more than Constanzo. Of all the suspects, she was the one most often reported sighted in phone tips to the police. The tips invariably were wrong.

Then, on Sunday, April 16, reality intruded once more when two more bodies were discovered. Moises Castillo and Hector de la Fuente, the first victims on the border, were found at last.

They had almost stayed hidden forever in the quiet shadows of Ejido Morelos, amid the stunted trees and depleted soil of the cooperative's orchard. But with a father's desperate stubbornness, seventy-two-year-old Hidalgo Castillo badgered Benitez's men into searching for his son's body at the tiny grove two miles from Rancho Santa Elena. After he had failed to find his son at either of the funeral homes, the old man had spoken to some children, who told him a story of murder and secret burial in the orchard a year before. "I think he's there," the old man kept telling Benitez's agents. "Please look."

Once they finally acquiesced and began to dig, the body count rose to fifteen. The fragile skeletal remains of Moises and Hector fell apart as the bodies were lifted from the grave, crumbling like papier-mâché in a dry, rustling shower. The grave digger cursed, scrambled back into the hole, and began tossing the remnants into a bag. Hidalgo turned away.

The next day, Monday, April 17, the DEA task force had its first success after a week of internal haggling. DEA agents and Texas state policemen received a tip from an informant in Houston who knew where Serafin Hernandez Rivera—Old Serafin—was holed up with his family.

DEA Agent T. K. Solis had been drawing up a search warrant affidavit for Old Serafin's home in Brownsville when he took the call from the snitch. Sheriff's Lieutenant George Gavito and a Customs agent were with him at the time, and Solis excitedly told them of the break in the case. They had suspected Serafin was in Houston, where he had lived most of his adult life before moving to Brownsville seven years before. Now they knew.

Solis rushed out to get an arrest warrant from a federal magistrate, then FAXed it to the DEA and the state police office in Houston so they could make the bust.

Late that afternoon, a team of agents and policemen stormed a small apartment near the Houston Astrodome. They had expected a dangerous, possibly insane cult killer, but the pudgy, balding Serafin put up no struggle. He had no guns with him, no drugs, and hardly any money. It was just him, his frightened wife, and his children, cowering in a tiny, rundown apartment friends had found for him.

That same day, Solis led a group of agents on a search of Old Serafin's Brownsville home—a rundown three-bedroom bungalow with the new satellite dish and security fence encircling a weedy yard. Neighbors said the family had left in a hurry on April 10, shortly after word of the arrests of Elio and Little Serafin reached Brownsville via Ovidio Hernandez.

Four chihuahuas and two larger dogs were thirsty and emaciated after six days alone in the yard. The four parrots Old Serafin had kept on his porch were squawking hungrily at the agents, forgotten and dying. Inside the house, a half-eaten McDonald's meal sat rotting on the kitchen table, with pots still sitting on the stove, the food inside gone furry and green. But Solis found no altars to occult gods in Serafin's home, nothing like the horrors at the ranch or in Constanzo's homes in Mexico City. There were just reams of Spanish-language Christian evangelical literature belonging to Old Serafin's wife. Framed pictures of Jesus hung on every wall.

Solis also found two rifles and three shotguns, one of them sawed off to a mere thirteen inches long, a weapon with the sole purpose of killing at close range. In a closet, he found the empty case for an Uzi submachine gun, along with a cache of 9mm rounds to fit the lethal Israeli commando weapon.[5]

"Yes, I'm a drug runner. That's how we make our living," Old Serafin told Solis during the long series of interrogations that followed his arrest—part of a plea bargain that turned the old trafficker into a crucial informant. "That's how we made it to the middle class. But I never killed nobody. I didn't have anything to do with Constanzo or his sacrifices."[6]

Solis and his boss, Armando Ramirez, believed Old Serafin. They thought he probably knew about the killings from word of mouth—he admitted going to the ranch often during drug deals—but that he hadn't taken part in any rituals or human sacrifice.

"He was upset about his son. He cried like a baby when we

talked to him," Ramirez said later. "But he's a doper. He felt bad, but not like you or me—or like Sara's father. Drug families have an understanding: some people go to jail, some die, some get away. That's life."

Old Serafin was charged with drug trafficking and conspiracy charges in the United States, then offered a plea bargain in exchange for his testimony against the others, a deal he ultimately accepted—even agreeing to testify against his son, Little Serafin, if necessary.

In the meantime, Solis and Ramirez made plans to keep Old Serafin's arrest quiet for at least twenty-four hours—longer if they were lucky and no newspaper reporters were hanging around federal court when he was arraigned the next morning. The agents wanted to keep a low profile because Solis's informant not only knew where to find Old Serafin but also had two addresses in Houston being used by another fugitive cult member—Ovidio Hernandez.

Ovidio, the only Hernandez brother left free, had also fled to the familiar turf of Houston, shuttling between the homes of two old friends willing to shield him. Unlike Old Serafin, Ovidio was wanted for murder in Mexico. He was thought to be one of the more vicious members of the gang, rayado in Constanzo's murderous religion.

If Old Serafin's bust in Houston could be kept quiet, the DEA agents decided, sooner or later Ovidio would show up at one of the two houses. Around-the-clock stakeouts of the hideouts had begun even before Old Serafin was arrested. But once again, confusion, dissension, and the desire to make headlines within the task force shattered Solis's plans and provided a potential tip-off to Ovidio.

Within hours of Old Serafin's arrest, Brownsville Customs head Oran Neck and Sheriff's Lieutenant Gavito spoke with what little press corps was still assembled in Brownsville, appearing on television, radio, and in the next morning's papers. They announced Serafin's arrest, again creating the appearance that they were involved, and hinted that the entire Hernandez family would be in custody soon. "We feel pretty confident we have uncovered a large drug smuggling ring," Neck told the *Houston Post*. "This is an opportunity for us to clean up the entire clan."

The entire clan was not cleaned up. Ovidio never showed at the apartment. Informants later told the DEA that Ovidio fled Houston for good shortly after Old Serafin's arrest and the ensuing publicity.[7] Agents tracking him lost the trail when he apparently crossed back into Mexico.

A seemingly simple drug case had launched the investigation of Adolfo de Jesus Constanzo, starting with a search of a backwater ranch and the arrest of a family of contrabandista thugs. Then, with the grisly discovery inside the ranch's dusty, disused corral, the case exploded into a complex homicide investigation and international manhunt. Finally, after the last bodies were found, the case entered a third phase, as authorities began to investigate the rituals behind the crimes, hoping it might lead them to El Padrino.

So far, a mishmash of labels ranging from satanism, Santeria, voodoo, Mexican brujeria, black magic, and ancient Aztec ritual had been bandied about, with no one in law enforcement really certain what had gone on at Rancho Santa Elena. Many lawmen on the border involved in the War on Drugs had seen a rise in recent years of magical beliefs among drug traffickers, though few had thought a study of this phenomenon was necessary.[8] As the Constanzo case unfolded, they had come to believe otherwise.

It didn't take long to find out where the nation's experts on Constanzo's special brand of Cuban mysticism and black magic resided: Miami—the same place a majority of the nation's practitioners of Cuban mysticism and black magic resided. After a week of calls and negotiations, two experts were asked to come help.

Raphael Martinez, a widely respected Miami-based anthropologist of Cuban ancestry, and Candice Leek, a tall blonde law-enforcement consultant and former police chief with long experience investigating ritual crime,[9] arrived on the early flight from Miami Saturday morning, April 22, barely awake even after multiple cups of muddy airplane coffee. Two FBI agents hustled them into a car and sped off—there was no time to waste, the agents said.

This surprised the two ritual-crime consultants, since they had been ready to fly out for more than a week, when they had first been called. Their departure was delayed, though, while awaiting a final clearance from Brownsville authorities, and the bottleneck was broken only after they offered to pay their own way.

"What's the rush?" Martinez wanted to know. "The ranch isn't going anywhere."

The agent gave him a deadpan look. "In two days, the Mex feds are going to burn the place down. And all you'll have is ashes to look at. Hell, Benitez wanted to do it days ago, but we were waiting for you."

Now it was Leek's and Martinez's turn to exchange looks. Burning a crime scene? Just what were they getting into? "This should be interesting," Leek said mildly.

A few hours later, Martinez and Leek entered the little temple, their eyes adjusting to the gloom slowly, the broken glass from Eluterio's hasty cleansing ceremony crunching underfoot. Outside, Mexican agents formed a ring around the temple, guns at the ready, maintaining a safe distance. They didn't want to get too close to Constanzo's lair.

Martinez breathed through his mouth and pointed to the bottles of Aguardiente, the cigars, the peppers, clustered around the area where the nganga had sat—sure signs of the practice of Palo Mayombe. As Leek pointed a video camera at the scene, the dapper Martinez took off his coat, rolled up his sleeves, snapped on a pair of rubber surgical gloves, and plunged his hands into the nganga.

As he made room to lay out and analyze the cauldron's contents on the ground, Martinez absent-mindedly picked up the crude, five-foot-tall cross a peasant had placed in front of the building and casually tossed it aside. "No, no, no!" one of Benitez's agents yelled, running toward Martinez, his gun leveled.

For one terrifying moment, the anthropologist thought the agent was going to shoot him. Everyone froze except the charging federale, who brushed by Martinez and bent to retrieve the cross. He set it upright again, and gave Martinez a chiding, dismayed look. There was fear on the agent's face, not anger.

"Leave it here, señor," the agent reproached. "We need its blessing."

"Yes, yes, of course," Martinez said, as the agent retreated again, a safe fifteen feet away from the little temple. Martinez looked at Leek, who kept the camera rolling. "I should have known better."

As Martinez dismantled the nganga to determine if Constanzo was a genuine practitioner, they found the cauldron's contents closely matched the many other ngangas they had analyzed in South Florida. "This is a particularly evil nganga," he said, hefting a cat's skull. "This is for kadiempembe. The palero's version of the devil."

The misinformed constantly confuse such finds with satanism, a catch-all bogeyman for the likes of Oprah Winfrey, Geraldo Rivera, and the other mavens of pop culture. Just before Martinez and Leek arrived on the border, Geraldo swept into town, taping an episode called "Brownsville: A Tale of Drugs, Death and Satan." The show, broadcast two weeks later on May 2, 1989, was rife with errors—among others, leaving the false impression George Gavito led the investigation and that the crimes had occurred in Brownsville, not Matamoros. "The Brownsville horror is our focus," Rivera chimed in before and after every commercial.

Now, though, Leek and Martinez were able to give Benitez some genuine insights into Constanzo's beliefs and motivations, dispelling the hype with their thorough knowledge of Palo Mayombe and its relation to crime, especially in Miami. And they also gave him a weapon to use against Constanzo.

When they returned to the Antinarcoticos headquarters that evening, Leek and Martinez watched as Benitez drew an egg from a large carton next to his desk and began to rub its unbroken shell over his body—a Mexican curandismo ritual intended to cleanse his body and spirit of any evil he may have picked up at the ranch. The comandante performed the same ritual every time he returned from the ranch, he admitted without a trace of embarrassment.

"We hear the temple is going to be burned tomorrow, Comandante," Leek said carefully. "Is that true?"

"We will have an exorcism," he said, gauging her reaction and relieved to see no typical gringo skepticism. "But tell me. Now that you know Constanzo's religion, how can we use it against him?"

"Well, if you're going to burn the ranch and the nganga, there is one thing you can do to really get him," Martinez said. "Make sure the television networks are there. Get it on the news. Make sure Constanzo sees it—your triumph over his magic."

"Yes," Leek said, looking up from the journals. "That will drive him crazy."

26

They had developed a numbing, mechanical routine. It didn't stop them from feeling caged and miserable, nor did it end Sara's whining and vomiting and begging to go home. But Adolfo de Jesus Constanzo knew the value of an orderly regimen, and he kept his people together with it. Like the four hundred men, women, and children of the People's Temple in Guyana, who ten years before had obediently lined up to drink Jim Jones's brackish brew of Kool-Aid and cyanide, the followers of Adolfo Constanzo blindly conformed to his orders and whims, never considering any other course.

Throughout their flight from the law, he had maintained a sweaty good cheer, raving and making speeches, reminding his followers of his power. He would wave his machine gun or a knife, sometimes pressing the weapon against a follower's head, telling them he held all their lives in his palm. No bullet or blade could harm them, he would say, unless it had the power of El Padrino's magic behind it. "Remember that," he told them over and over. "They cannot kill you. But I can."

He remained their leader, control never slipping. Nothing had changed that, not even life on the run, not even the shiver of terror they felt each time a police car passed them on the road or they heard a siren in the night. They would grip their guns tightly in sweaty hands, wondering if Karla or the doctor had betrayed them, wondering if they'd be recognized. Then the police car would move on, and they would pry their fingers loose from triggers, and Duby would laugh, a nervous little bark that he had begun emitting regularly, like a tic.

The routine was simple. Every three days since leaving Karla's house, El Padrino had ordered his godchildren to pack up their clothes and their groceries and the small altar to Eleggua and Ochosi he had constructed. He would wait until darkness, then they would leave the cabins or motel rooms they had been sealed in for the past three days, and drive on to another two-bit resort.

They always stayed within a day's drive of Mexico City. Always, Sara would later recall, they kept in touch with Karla and Salvador by phone—with Constanzo asking Karla if the papers and the plastic surgeon and the hideout were ready, and asking Salvador if the manhunt was waning and the drug deal progressing. To all the questions, the answers remained no, not yet. Soon.

When they were settled in a new hideout, Constanzo would lovingly reconstruct his altar, the small pot to Ochosi the Hunter, a black bowl of blood and sticks and prayers designed to protect them from police. Then he would let the capricious spirit of Eleggua the Warrior enter him, making his body rigid, his face contorted. "The animals shall not win," Eleggua would say in Constanzo's graveyard voice, his lips pulled back, teeth bared. "We shall kill them all."

The others looked on listlessly, though, even stalwart Martin. Not only had Constanzo's states of spirit possession become commonplace to them by now, but also the magic seemed to be doing them little good. They were free, true, but they were used to living as kings, not common criminals. When would the running end?

"Where are we going to go, Adolfo?" Sara asked after one ceremony had left their cramped room reeking of chickens and blood.

"To hell, of course," Constanzo, drenched in sweat, replied maddeningly. "And only I can make sure you'll come back."

Then he slipped into one of his frequent reminiscences, tales from his Miami childhood. He would tell of his rayado, the thrill and terror he felt under his godfather's knife. Or he would recall the sweet smell of decay inside his mother's nganga room, out back in the shed—his playground of death. "I wish I could see my mother now," Constanzo said often.[1]

Duby would take care of checking in when they arrived at new lodgings, then he would do all the shopping, keeping them stocked in food and hair dye and filling Sara's prescription for her stomach. Duby remained the only one among the fugitives whose picture had not been broadcast, though Omar and Martin felt secure enough to venture out once in a while.

Only Sara and Adolfo, whose faces were known to virtually every resident of Mexico City, thanks to the media blitz on the case, kept inside at all times, wearing large hats and sunglasses when moving between the car and their rooms, even at night. Constanzo never let Sara out of his sight. He had become convinced that the arrests in Matamoros and their pursuit to Mexico City were the products of betrayal from within the group. And Sara, thanks to her constant pleas and complaints, had become his chief suspect.

"Someone has sold us out. I have seen it in the cards," Constanzo pronounced on April 18, while they were still in Popo Park. He looked steadily at Sara as he said it, and soon all eyes in the cabin were focused on her. "We were betrayed, and when I am certain who the traitors are, they will die like no one has died before."

"It wasn't me, Adolfo," Sara whispered, wincing beneath the stares of her friends. She tried not to think of the secret plan she was forming—so Constanzo wouldn't see a glimmer of hope in her eyes and grow suspicious. "I have always been true."

"Even so, Sara, you have become as I have said—a loose cannon," Constanzo replied, stroking her cheek gently, then seizing her chin roughly between his thumb and forefinger. "Can't you see, I can never let you go? You would tell everything. I can see it in your eyes."

Sara turned away. She had been his most devout believer, his proselytizer on the border. But alone among his followers, she was no criminal at heart. She was not bred to deviancy or a drug family. Sara didn't bother to object when Constanzo said she would tell the police everything if they ever captured her. There was no point in arguing: They both knew it was true.

From Popo Park, the gang took the doctor's wheezing Renault to a resort called Club Dorado in Oaxtepec, a city just a few hours from the capital. Three days later, they found a dusty, disused cabin in the town of Cuautla, then they journeyed back to Oaxtepec, to a vacation resort run by the government Social Security

Administration—a sprawling place of cabins and hot mineral baths fed by underground springs, reeking of sulfur. "This is what hell will smell like," Constanzo said. Only Duby laughed at the joke, emitting his strange little bark.

On Monday, April 23, as the gang sat silently in a small, airless room in Oaxtepec with the shades drawn, they saw the exorcism at Rancho Santa Elena.

Duby noticed first. He had been watching the television, barely paying attention, as the others read or slept or just sat and stared. Constanzo was at his altar, an indistinct figure, painted in the flickering shadows of the portable black-and-white television they had brought with them. Then the word "Matamoros" brought Duby to attention.

"They're burning the little temple!" Duby cried out. "Padrino! They're burning your nganga."

Constanzo dropped his sacrificial blade and raced to the TV. The others gathered in a circle to watch.

The temple was on fire, roaring and crackling, collapsing in a shower of sparks. In the foreground, on its side, was Constanzo's nganga, surrounded by a halo of flame.

The priest of Palo Mayombe silently watched the desecration of his object of power. Only when the camera cut back to the studio and the Mexican newscaster did he react.

A low growl rose from deep in his throat, growing in volume until he opened his mouth and the sound became a scream. The others cowered.

Constanzo began racing through the room, smashing things. He picked up his machine gun and emptied a clip of bullets into the television, sending sparks flying, plunging the room in darkness. Frightened, someone turned on an overhead light, then fled in the face of Constanzo's naked rage.

Red-faced and out of control, he kept on shrieking, blind to movement around him. He sounded like a man insane, or perhaps a man in unspeakable agony, as if the victims he had tortured and fed to that burning, despoiled cauldron in Matamoros had gathered together to scream again through their killer's mouth.

The screaming lasted nearly an hour, until Constanzo's voice grew throaty, then hoarse, then became a dry, febrile whisper—and still he screamed. Most of the others retreated from him, leaving the room for the cabin next door, waiting for the madness to pass. Sara lay huddled on a bed, curled into a fetal ball, her hands covering her ears, her eyes tightly shut. When silence finally descended, she opened her eyes and looked up. Constanzo stood alone in the center of the room, staring at the broken television set, still trying to scream—his mouth open, veins bulging in his neck and temples, the whites of his eyes showing all around, making not a sound.

In her mind, Sara could still hear the screaming.[2]

Although the Mexican television stations did not carry the report of the burning of the shed until the Monday Constanzo saw it, the ritual destruction had occurred the day before, on a Sunday. Only the Lord's day would suffice to quench the evil at Rancho Santa Elena, the curandero Eluterio had cautioned the comandante.

That Sunday, a strong coastal wind had washed the sky clean of clouds and dank humidity, leaving behind a brilliant, flawless blue and a landscape drenched in sunlight. Rafael Martinez and Candice Leek had returned to Benitez's office early that morning, slightly hung over but ready to begin analyzing Constanzo's journals—and to videotape the exorcism.

The hangovers came courtesy of some Brownsville hospitality the night before. They had stayed out until two in the morning with Lieutenant Gavito, Sheriff Perez, and the head of the local FBI office. The visitors from Miami had been treated to tablefuls of Tex-Mex food, washed down with Mexican beer. Then they shifted to tequila shooters—border tradition, Gavito told them.

As the evening wore on, the locals confided that they were concerned about the negative publicity Brownsville was receiving. Tourism and border trade might never recover, they said. Gavito kept asking Leek and Martinez if they could hold a press conference and say that there was no longer any reason to fear the cult now that the temple had been seized. Martinez said he wished they could, but that it was impossible, because it wasn't true.

"He's got other altars in Mexico. The journals make that clear, the police have found some of them," Martinez said. "Another murder to appease the spirits and keep the fugitives free is not only a possibility. It's a probability."

Shortly after the Miami experts arrived at Benitez's office in the morning, Eluterio appeared and handed the comandante a shopping list. It contained the ingredients he'd need to conduct an exorcism. Agents were sent to the grocery store to buy bags of salt, to the Catholic church to fill a bottle with holy water, and to the nearest Pemex station to fill three large jerry cans with gasoline.

In a truck outside, Eluterio's assistant, Tio, waited with a carefully covered cardboard carton, which held the most important ingredient for the ceremony about to begin. There were holes punched in the side of the box—breathing holes.

"Time to go," Benitez said simply. Leek grabbed her video camera. Martinez pocketed a notebook, and they followed him out.

By coincidence, Tony Zavaleta and a friend were exploring the ranch that same morning, shooting a video of the little shack and the objects inside. The tall and stocky Zavaleta, curly black hair flying in the wind, limped ecstatically around the ranch on a bad knee, anxious to record the scene for his anthropology class at Texas Southmost College—the same course Sara Aldrete had attended a semester before.

There were personal reasons spurring his curiosity as well. He had known and liked Sara. Before his arrest, Little Serafin had been flunking out of Zavaleta's sociology class. And his son, Tony Junior, had been a classmate of Sara's—and a spring breaker in Matamoros on the same weekend Mark Kilroy disappeared.

"Dad, if Sara had pulled up and offered me a ride that night, I would have gotten in the car," Zavaleta's shaken son had said after news of the accusations against Sara stunned the Texas Southmost campus. "That could have been me."

Zavaleta taped the deserted ranch for more than an hour, then packed up, and was driving away when Benitez's caravan roared up the ranch road past him. Stunned and intimidated, Zavaleta jammed on the brakes and gawked as the Mexican federales, armed with automatic weapons, formed a ring around the temple. Zavaleta pulled over and got out to watch.

Benitez, dressed incongruously in a beige polyester leisure suit and a black baseball cap with his department's insignia on the front, barked orders to his subordinates. With him were Sheriff Perez and George Gavito, and two other gringos Zavaleta didn't recognize—Leek and Martinez. Zavaleta faded into the background, though he was able to film much of what followed, even though Benitez had forbidden him to use his camera. Zavaleta secretly switched it on, then stuck the camera under his arm casually, aiming it by pointing his body in the right general direction.

Mouthing prayers under his breath, Eluterio the white witch grabbed a can of gasoline and rushed into the shack, splashing gas on the walls and floor, then spilling more into the nganga. He wore no ceremonial robes or special ritual gear, just a pair of white Nikes to keep him moving fast. More gasoline was dumped on the outside of the little temple by Benitez's agents.

Meanwhile, near the corral fence, Tio, the apprentice, kept watch over the cardboard box. Now and then he would lift the lid slightly and peer inside at the contents, then shut the box again before anyone else could spy what was concealed within—or before anything inside could escape.

At the curandero's signal, an agent lit a small torch and hurled it into the shack. The gasoline-drenched building burst into flame with a muffled thump. As flames quickly ran up the reddish brown tarpaper, the heat forced the onlookers back. Orange fingers of flame crawled up the beams and supports, and soon the entire temple was engulfed, crackling and creaking. Within seconds, great gouts of black smoke filled the air as the flames, whipped into an inferno by the strong winds, roared out of control, spreading to the corral and haystacks. The agents scurried for cover.

The fire billowed and cracked, and everyone stared, unmoving, as if under a spell. The moment was primeval, a gathering around the fire that is as old as man—the magic and mystery of heat and flame and smoke, whose origins are uncertain and whose power holds life, death, and future. The fire hissed a death chant.

And at the center, wreathed in flame, the nganga sat, its palos turned into flaming brands.

"You'll see, I'll bury the son of a bitch," Benitez muttered under his breath over and over. "I'll kill him. I'll kill him."

Eluterio hurled a five-pound sack of salt into the flames. It exploded in a white spray, then vanished in the conflagration. Then he threw another. Fire would cauterize the evil wound, salt would heal it.

His motion seemed to awaken the gathering, breaking the spell of the fire. People began to move and talk in whispers as Eluterio continued to throw sack after sack into the fire. A small, pot-bellied man who never stopped his string of prayers, Eluterio watched the flames with satisfaction. He grunted loudly each time he threw more salt.

The flimsy shed was consumed in minutes. The sheet-metal roof sagged, then crumpled, then finally collapsed in a shower of sparks. More gasoline was dumped on the rubble, blackening the soil and feeding the fire.

Soon the thin walls of Constanzo's temple were devoured, leaving a naked framework. Then it, too, collapsed. Finally there was only a huddled pile of smoking rubble on top of a cement slab.

Everyone joined in the ritual then. One by one, the agents, Benitez, even Sheriff Perez and Gavito filed to the shed and tossed a piece of scrap wood on the pile, feeding what was left of the fire while symbolically striking out at Constanzo.

When the flames finally died, Eluterio walked cautiously toward the nganga. Its palos were blackened and smoking, the cauldron was smudged with soot. Yet it looked strangely untouched by the destruction around it.

As the others watched, the curandero carefully crept up on the cauldron, a two-by-four in his hand. He approached the thing as if it was a wounded animal, capable of attacking anyone who entered its den. He held the piece of lumber out like a lion tamer holding a chair. Eluterio had faith in the healing power of Mexican folk magic, but he had never gone up against Cuban black magic before. He wasn't about to take any chances.

Suddenly he darted forward, rapped the cauldron smartly with his makeshift club, then fled, running fifteen feet back, his white sneakers flying.

Nothing happened. No demons rose in anger. No magical force struck him dead. He grunted with satisfaction, then repeated the rapping of the cauldron three more times, lingering a little longer each time, until he was satisfied the evil had been nearly vanquished.

The time for the final blow had come. At Eluterio's command, the cauldron was upended, emptied, and dragged to a patch of naked, cracked earth. It was filled with gasoline and some bits of wood for a final cleansing baptism of fire.

Then a mild panic rippled through the agents. No one had any matches. The curandero and the federales had used up all of theirs. They began patting their pockets frantically.

"Wait, wait, I have some," Sheriff Alex Perez said, digging into his pockets and producing a pack of matches. "Here, use these."

The next day, cooking a breakfast of eggs and beans for the entire crew at his diner in Brownsville, Sheriff Perez would emerge from the kitchen in an apron and hold the pack of matches aloft triumphantly—his most glowing contribution to the case. "Look, here they are," he would call out. "This is what did it."[3]

As the evil thing burned, Comandante Benitez, Sheriff Perez, Lieutenant Gavito, and Detective Flores posed together for a shot on Leek's video camera, smiling broadly as the flames shot skyward behind them.

Eluterio called Benitez and the Mexican agents to his side then, so they could wash their hands with holy water. After hesitating a moment, Gavito and Perez washed their hands, too. Benitez offhandedly flicked a few drops in the direction of the smoldering shack, a final gesture of contempt.

One final step remained. Eluterio went to his assistant and the carefully guarded cardboard box. He opened it up and lifted the contents above his head: a white dove.

As miners once carried canaries into the mines because of their sensitivity to poisonous gas, so did Eluterio carry the white dove, a symbol of purity, into his battleground with evil.

If the dove lived, everything was fine. Good would be victorious. If the dove died, it meant evil had won and that the exorcism had failed.

For a moment, the dove hung limply in Eluterio's hands. Then its wings fluttered and the curandero sent the bird aloft. It had lived. So would everyone at the ranch.

For the first time that day, the agents relaxed and lowered their guns.

"I'm going to bury that son of a bitch," Benitez repeated. But now he was smiling, just a little.[4]

In the end, the comandante had not taken Rafael Martinez's advice. He had not alerted the television networks—only two still photographers, one for the *Brownsville Herald* and one for *El*

Bravo, the morning paper in Matamoros. Although belief in magic and curanderos was the cultural norm for Benitez, admitting it outright on international television was not acceptable. A front of rationality and contempt for superstition had to be maintained.

"No, we did not burn the shack," Benitez would tell reporters later. "It was superstitious peasants. We would never do that."[5]

But the burning would make the television news anyway—and Benitez was secretly pleased.

As soon as he returned home, an excited Zavaleta called a Spanish-language television station in San Antonio, which eagerly bought a copy of his tape and used it as an exclusive report on its evening news show. The broadcast was distributed throughout Mexico and the United States on Monday—which is when Constanzo saw it. And the screaming began.

Constanzo didn't sleep that night. He just sat, staring. But the next day, though his voice remained a hoarse rasp, El Padrino seemed in control again. It might have been the sweaty, fevered control of a man hanging from a ledge by his fingernails, but it was control.

That morning Constanzo began carrying the Uzi submachine gun with him constantly, waving it, pointing with it, hugging it to his chest. He must have felt he needed that extra protection. All the magical power—his very essence—had been tied up in that nganga in Matamoros, in his mind at least. And now the bastard cops had destroyed it.

In exorcising his magic, they had freed all the souls he had imprisoned in the cauldron. It diminished his power proportionately. They had done what he had always thought impossible: They had bested him.

Worst of all, his followers had seen him vanquished. Constanzo knew then what would happen. Things would fall apart, and they would all have to die. Sooner or later, it would come to that.

His opinion was confirmed the next day when he called Salvador to check on the drug deal in Guadalajara, their best hope of financing an escape to Central America.

"No, I haven't done it," Salvador replied tersely. "And I am not going to do it."

"What?" Constanzo exclaimed angrily.

"I saw the television. I saw how your magic was destroyed. My advice to you is to turn yourselves in. I shall not help you."[6]

Constanzo was speechless. He slammed down the phone. "You'll die for that," he cried, talking to the phone as if it could hear. "Over and over, you'll die."

Then, waving his gun at his remaining followers, Constanzo said he would kill them all on the spot unless they immediately agreed to a suicide pact.[7] "If they come for us, if we are about to be arrested, then we will all die," Constanzo said. "Omar, you will take the machine gun and kill Martin and I and then the others, and then you will kill yourself."

They all stared at him. "I can't do that," Omar said. He appeared on the verge of tears.

"Don't you understand? They will torture you. They will try to kill you, but they won't be able to. You will live on in horrible pain, because with the protection of the nkisi we have, only my bullets and my gun can kill us. And if we die, then can we live again. Don't you see? We'll all come back. I will lead us back from hell."[8]

"Maybe it won't come to that, Adolfo," Martin said.

"But if it does?"

"Then," Martin said, loyal to the last, "we will do it."

Constanzo clasped Martin's shoulder. Then he stared the others down until all had nodded their assent, Sara last.

"Good. Otherwise, I would kill you all now," he said. "Now get packed. We're going back to Mexico City.

"I'm through running."

27

The weather in Mexico City was abysmal by late April, when the filth and squalor of 20 million people swirled about the valley in a murky brown haze trapped by the mountains ringing the sprawling capital. Tons of dried sewage particles whirled up from a vast, caked, windswept plain outside the city, where wastewater is treated through evaporation. It combined with the emissions from leaded fuel spewing from 10 million trucks and cars. An inversion layer pressed down on the city from above, keeping the noxious mixture from dissipating, at times making the sun look as dim and distant as the moon.

Springtime in Mexico City: skies the color of sand.

To combat the toxic air, all drivers were issued a sticker in 1989, barring them from motoring one day a week. This was supposed to cut the five million tons of pollution pumped every year into the air, a world's record.[1] Driving, in effect, was rationed. And there had been an improvement: The atmosphere above the national capital was toxic only eighty-five percent of the time, thanks to the new pollution controls.

Constanzo had to delay his return to Mexico City a day because of the sticker on the doctor's Renault. They could not risk even the slightest chance that they would be stopped. As a result, Constanzo's uncanny luck held once again. The pollution regulations inadvertently protected him from capture when the police arrested one of his oldest and most loyal followers.

The arrest came because Assistant District Attorney General Federico Ponce and his investigators had persisted for the past ten days, questioning witches and card readers and psychics. They hit the card parlors of the Zona Rosa and walked the cramped, exotic aisles of the Mercado Sonora—the witches' market—where investigators were amazed to find many of the same implements on display that Constanzo had used at his altar. Elegguas, Ochosis, and pictures of the saints bearing Santeria names were all over—an influx of foreign magic unheard of in Mexico City just five years before.[2] The black arts Constanzo used were more widespread in Mexico than anyone had imagined.

Questioning the secretive, difficult denizens of the city's occult underworld was no easy task. They lied as a matter of course, and professed knowledge they could not possibly have. Those initiated in the same religions maintained their tradition of secrecy. All denied knowing Constanzo personally; they had only heard of him. Yet everyone had an opinion as to where to find El Padrino.

"Constanzo is dead—I have seen it," one psychic after another told the investigators, until it finally became a joke among half the men in the office. The other half grew more uneasy, since they already were convinced they were pursuing an evil spirit, not a man.

On April 24, however, a card reader in the Zona Rosa gave Detective Paquito Blanchette information he really could use. The witch said he not only knew of Constanzo from the bars and cafes in the zone, but he also knew a card reader named Doctor Hindu who was a devout follower of Constanzo's. "I still see him around," the witch said. "He's not in hiding or anything. He lives around here and throws the cards. You should talk to him."

Blanchette handed the man a wad of pesos and said, "And where can I find this Hindu doctor?"

"He lives on Calle Londres," the witch said, pocketing the bills.

Alarm bells began sounding in Blanchette's head then. Calle Londres was where the murdered transvestite La Claudia had lived. "What's his real name?" Blanchette asked, grabbing the little witch and shaking him. "What is this doctor's real name?"

"Montes," the man said, uncertain at what caused the detective's outburst. "His real name is Jorge Montes."

Blanchette let the man go and raced back to his office. "I think we've got him," he told Ponce breathlessly.

For the past year, police had thought Montes was a fashion

designer, not a *cartomatico*. To the police, Montes was simply the roommate of the unfortunate Ramon Paz Esquivel, alias La Claudia, the transvestite who was chopped into thirteen pieces and dumped on a street corner inside several Hefty bags in 1988. Montes had been taken in for questioning after the murder as a matter of routine, but he had never been a suspect. After all, he had reported La Claudia missing, and he had identified what was left of the body.

But suddenly the circumstantial evidence was overwhelmingly against Montes.

"One, he's a follower of Constanzo," Blanchette said, ticking off the facts on his fingers. "Two, his roommate was ritually killed and dismembered. Three, he's a witch.

"And four, one year before, just three blocks from Montes's house on Calle Londres, an entire family of drug traffickers, the Calzadas, gets dismembered and dumped in the river. I think Montes is the key," Blanchette told his boss.

"Bring him in," Ponce said. "The federales will eat their hearts out over this one."

Later, Ponce would learn the federales already had known the name of Jorge Montes from Teresa Quintana, though they did not realize his significance or where to find him. Their jealous guarding of information and unwillingness to cooperate with Ponce's men had delayed Montes's arrest—and kept Constanzo free.

"A week ago," Montes said after his arrest, "I could have told you where to find him—in Popo Park. But now I don't know where he is."

Still, the arrest was a major breakthrough in the case—the first arrest of a suspect since Elio had been taken down on the border.[3] It didn't take long for Montes to break. He was already panicky even before the police had arrived at his flat, then hauled him to the basement of the Miguel Hidalgo District offices.

Old and frail, fearful for his life, Montes had seen the burning of the nganga on television and decided everything and everyone that had been touched by Constanzo was doomed. He accepted his arrest with resignation, speaking willingly and at length to the police. He delivered a long-winded but expert lecture on Santeria and Palo Mayombe to the fascinated and appalled investigators.

"But I killed no one," the fifty-four-year-old card reader told

Ponce during his first interrogation. "It was El Padrino, not me. I am innocent. Only Salvador, Martin, and Omar could assist Constanzo in the sacrifices. They are the bosses. I am only a follower."[4]

Montes said he knew nothing of the Calzada deaths, and though he was present at the killing of La Claudia, he denied taking part in the murder and dismemberment. "It was Constanzo. I swear."

However, he did implicate Martin, Omar, and another follower of Constanzo's, Juan Carlos Fragosa, as accomplices. Ponce's men arrested Fragosa that same day, charging him in the murder of La Claudia.

Fragosa talked long and hard, too. He promptly implicated Constanzo, Martin, Sara, Omar, and a federale named Salvador Vidal in conducting rites using human blood. All of them, including Salvador, had received payment in the form of cars and expensive jewelry from the godfather, as well as his magical blessings, Fragosa said, eager to please his interrogators.[5]

"A federale?" Detective Blanchette said, pulling Ponce over to confer. "What do you think?"

"Montes mentioned this Salvador, too," Ponce reminded him. "I think Constanzo had federales on the payroll."

"We have to check it out," Blanchette said.

"Yes, but quietly. Very quietly."

A district police allegation that a federal sub-comandante was involved could start another war, Ponce and Blanchette agreed. They would make some discreet inquiries, but they would keep their suspicions quiet for a time. Until Constanzo had been brought down.

"You can make it easier on yourself," Ponce told Montes in relentless questioning. "Tell us where to find Constanzo. We want him much more than we want your sorry bones."

But though Montes briefed the police on Constanzo's beliefs, customers, and associates, he could not help Ponce find El Padrino. He really did not know.

The air-pollution sticker on the borrowed Renault had saved Constanzo, though he never knew it—in fact, he had cursed the delay it caused him. But if he and the other fugitives had been able to travel a day earlier, they would have arrived before Montes's arrest. They would have contacted him, perhaps even have been on hand when the police arrived to arrest Doctor Hindu.

Instead, Jorge Montes was in jail when Constanzo arrived back in Mexico City on Tuesday, April 25, unaware that his godfather was looking to his followers for help. He called Jorge's house and got no answer.

Once again, through the magic of luck and coincidence and the failings of police bureaucracy, Adolfo Constanzo and his gang remained free. And the police remained frustrated.

Constanzo and his gang spent the next two days holed up at Karla's walled suburban home. Expecting the police to arrive at any moment, a nervous and increasingly irrational Constanzo paced and fretted, waiting for Karla to find them a safer hideout.[6] The machine gun never left his hands, even when traveling. He just shoved the stubby black weapon into an athletic bag and toted it with him. He even slept with it during the fitful few hours he allowed himself to lie down each night.

Martin, Omar, and Duby moved like concentration-camp prisoners, barely animated, speaking in monosyllables, and following Constanzo's commands to the letter. They ate when he said, showered at times he designated, slept when told.

Only Sara remained the wild card, her nerves destroyed, her appetite gone—and her loyalties in question. Constanzo had begun to deal with her bouts of hysteria and crying by speaking kindly to her while kicking and punching her. "That's it, my love," he would say sweetly, punctuating each word with a slap to Sara's face. "Shut up now, or I'll kill you."

Karla's boyfriend, Enrique Calzada, cared for the gang during this period, shopping for food and bringing them the occasional live chicken to sacrifice in rituals of protection.[7] Meanwhile, the faithful Karla and her friend Bueno Lopez combed the city for an apartment where the gang could hide out and the landlord asked few questions.

They found it at 19 Rio Sena, a sooty, pinkish apartment building in a decaying area downtown called Colonia Cuauhtemoc, named for an ancient Aztec god. Catty-corner from a neighborhood market called Superama, it had rusting rain gutters running down the walls and the windows were narrow and smeary, framed in brown metal. Trash was piled high outside, and the dark and uninviting lobby was filled with the smell of urine only partially masked by cheap, nose-burning disinfectant. The gated entrance was guarded by a hunched and unpleasant old woman who brooked no intruders, her gnarled shadow appearing monstrous and huge beneath the one naked light bulb illuminating the lobby.

In a word, 19 Rio Sena was perfect.

Inside, the two-bedroom apartment for rent, number fourteen, was furnished with tables, a sagging floral couch and chair, whitewashed walls, and a chipped brown linoleum floor.

Until that month, the owner of the apartment, Rosa Eugenio Gamas, had made her home there. When she decided to rent it, the one million peso deposit and the one million peso monthly rent Karla waved in front of her face (totaling about eight hundred dollars at the then-current exchange rate) was enough to convince Rosa that she didn't have to meet her new tenants. "They're good people. They'll make no trouble," Karla and the doctor assured the landlord. "They just need a place in a hurry."

"That's fine," Rosa said, handing them a rental agreement to sign. "I can tell just by looking at you ladies that's true."[8]

When the apartment hunters returned home, Constanzo didn't even thank them. He merely announced they would leave for their new hideout as soon as night fell. He paid the doctor about four hundred dollars for use of the Renault and for some damage it had suffered during their travels. He urged Karla to contact a forger to get them all fake papers, which she promised again to do. And he reminded them both that the price of betrayal would be death.[9]

On the night of April 27, the doctor drove Constanzo, Omar, Martin, Duby, and Sara to their final hideout. She left them there with some bags of groceries and some clean clothes. They didn't even have the materials to build an altar.

For three days and three nights they stayed inside, unwilling to venture out. Constanzo screeched at anyone who went near a window, even though the curtains remained drawn at all times. The television constantly played, but the cult's story had faded from the news—a good sign, Constanzo suggested. The police had not made public the arrest of Jorge Montes and Juan Carlos Fragosa, and with no new developments in the case, the headlines turned elsewhere.

"Soon they'll forget all about us," Constanzo cackled. "Then we can leave."

"They'll never forget us," Sara murmured, prompting more slaps—hard enough to sting but not bruise.

Constanzo counseled her and the others to have faith. "Otherwise, none of you will ever leave here alive," he prophesied.

The day after they moved in, the gang had a minor scare when the landlady came by to pick up a television set she had left behind. At first, when she knocked on the door, no one answered. But when she started to insert her key in the door, it opened a crack and a red-rimmed eye stared out at her.

"What do you want?" Duby asked. Next to him, out of sight, Constanzo stood with his machine gun cocked, while Martin stood behind the door with Salvador's shotgun. Sara and Omar hid in the closet in one of the bedrooms.

"I'm the owner," Rosa said. "I came for my television. Didn't Karla tell you?"

Duby asked her to wait a moment, then closed and bolted the door. A few moments later, he emerged from the apartment and handed her the television. She tried to step inside, but he refused to allow Rosa even a glimpse of the apartment.

"Is there something wrong?" she asked, noticing the perspiration on Duby's face, craning her neck to see into the living room.

"No, no, I just don't want to wake my roommate. Good-bye."

Duby scuttled back into the apartment and shut the door. Rosa shrugged and left. Eight hundred dollars was eight hundred dollars. She never knew how close she came to dying.

The gang was spared further visitors, which almost surely prevented another murder. Anyone else who tried to enter, Constanzo said, had to die. But no one came.

Still, the tension climbed each day. The bedrooms were small and cramped, and the shabby apartment soon became oppressive. They were forbidden to use the phone, severing ties to the outside world. Plans for such mundane tasks as going to the store began to assume spectacular importance, for they represented everything the fugitives had lost when their cult was discovered. Omar joined Sara in a constant stream of complaints.

On the third day in the apartment, Duby traveled across the street to do some shopping. He was inordinately excited about it—

and the other followers were jealous of his opportunity to get some fresh air. But then, after filling his cart with groceries, he stupidly tried to pay with a U.S. $100 bill. The store clerks refused to accept it, assuming the bill was counterfeit, and even if it wasn't, they could not possibly make change for such a large amount. It would empty their tills.

Embarrassed and fearful of being identified, Duby had to slink off to one of the many money exchanges that dot Mexico City. He had forgotten Constanzo's instructions to do that before going to the store. Now he had drawn attention to himself.

He compounded the problem by going back to the same Superama for the groceries, instead of going somewhere else, where he would have remained anonymous. Everyone in the store eyed him as he stiffly picked up his bags and walked out. He darted around the corner and entered the apartment building through the side street, Rio Balsas, so the people in the store would not see where he had gone.

He had been almost comically suspicious. But no one recognized him or guessed his identity. Constanzo beat Duby until he cried once he returned and admitted what had happened. "Fool!" he raged, throwing furniture, losing control. Everyone turned away.

Trying to maintain his grip on the group, Constanzo imposed another rigid routine on his followers, making them clean the apartment, stack the groceries, and scrub the bathroom on a strict schedule. The busywork did not stop tempers from flaring, though. Omar and Martin bickered constantly. Sara was in a foul mood, too, insisting she needed some fresh air and some time away from the gang, or she would go insane.

Then she began to claim she was pregnant in order to garner sympathy from Constanzo.[10] "That's why I'm so upset," she declared.

Also at this time, she apparently penned her unsigned love note to Constanzo, in English—which meant only he could read it. Among the flowery sentiments, she included a phrase she knew would please her godfather: "If for just one brief moment I can feel your lips against mine, I would die a happy women [*sic*]." Constanzo apparently was moved by her pleas and avowals of love—just as she had hoped. He finally relented and agreed to send her on a mission outside the apartment.

Doctor Lourdes had come up with a name of a plastic surgeon. They were supposed to call and offer him a large fee to alter their faces. Karla, meanwhile, had lined up a forger who was preparing documents for their new identities. Then, one by one, with their faces in bandages from the surgery, they would travel to Central America and hide out until they had healed. With new faces and identities, they could return and start fresh.

"We will build a new nganga," Constanzo promised as he explained his plan. "We will be stronger than ever. We will avenge ourselves and send our enemies to hell."

Then he turned to Sara. "It will be up to you to meet the surgeon and deliver a down payment," Constanzo said. "I will trust you because you are La Madrina—and because your family will die if you betray me."

Unspoken was another reason for choosing Sara: Omar, Martin, and Constanzo might be recognized too easily from pictures in the newspaper. And though Duby's appearance was not widely known, Constanzo believed the assignment was beyond his limited abilities, especially after the Superama fiasco. But Sara, despite her distinctive height, no longer looked anything like the Sara Aldrete whose picture was in the newspapers. That Sara wore fashionable dresses and makeup, with her hair stylishly curled, sometimes in a bouffant. She had bright eyes and a large smile and the erect bearing of an athlete. No more.

Fugitive Sara was twenty pounds lighter, gaunt and pale, and slumped, with purplish circles under her eyes. The loss of fullness in her face made her look older. Her hair hung limply and straight, and her eyes had a vacant, wandering aspect, as if she were focusing on memories rather than the sights before her. She wore a bulky, oversized bomber jacket and pants, large clothes she seemed lost in, that downplayed her height. A chronic slouch made her shorter still.

Only her family and closest friends might recognize her, Constanzo decided. No one else could.

For her part, Sara eagerly accepted the mission—but not too eagerly, for fear of making Constanzo suspicious. "I'll do exactly what you tell me, Adolfo," she promised.

Sara thought the plastic surgery plan ridiculous, but she knew Constanzo would not be dissuaded. He had fixated on it as their only hope. Martin, Omar, and Duby fell in step, brainwashed to the end, offering no argument. And Sara was in no position to argue about anything, for Constanzo was still threatening to kill her daily.

But on the afternoon of May 2, he allowed her to leave the apartment. Her instructions were precise: She was to walk several blocks, then take a taxi to another neighborhood, near the surgeon's office. Then she would telephone him from a phone booth, since Constanzo would not use the apartment phone for fear of having the call traced. If the surgeon agreed to their proposal, Constanzo said, Sara was to meet him, make a partial payment, and arrange to schedule the surgery, at night, as soon as possible.

"Be careful," Constanzo told her as she left. "Talk to no one."

Sara walked out into the sunlight for the first time in almost three weeks. She turned her face upward to the sun and brown sky, savoring the warm feel of it. Then she heard someone walking down to the lobby behind her and she began hurrying away. Adolfo probably sent Martin to check up on me, she thought. She turned the corner and kept walking for several blocks, then took a cab.

She continued to carefully follow her instructions, telephoning the plastic surgeon from one of the city's free phone booths. Ever since the 1985 earthquake rattled the phone company's underground circuits, the public phones in Mexico City have refused to accept coins. They operate free of charge. Leaving them that way is cheaper than fixing them.

Sara waited interminably for the surgeon to come to the phone after she had identified herself as Sara, a friend of Doctor Lourdes. She was certain that the police would arrive any moment to seize her. She was almost looking forward to it, she realized as she craned her neck, looking for police cars, listening for sirens.

But none appeared. Finally the doctor came on the line, uttering only one word. "Yes?"

"My name is Sara . . ."

"I know who you are," the surgeon said, cutting her off. "I was told you would call. And the answer is no. I cannot take the job. It is too dangerous. Do not call again."

The phone clicked. Sara stood a moment, holding the receiver, wondering what to do next. People walked by on the street, paying her no notice at all. No police arrived to slap handcuffs on her. No one pointed a finger and said, "There she is!" No one came to relieve her of having to decide her next step.

So she began to walk aimlessly, hands thrust deeply into her jacket pockets, barely looking where she was going. After a few minutes she found herself at a street corner, waiting to cross with a group of pedestrians. In the center of the intersection, a traffic cop was waving and whistling, his white glove standing out in the sooty air. When he motioned for the pedestrians to cross, Sara strode up to him.

"Can you help me, sir?" she asked. "I need directions."

The policeman looked at her hard. Here it comes, she thought. He knows me.

"I'm sorry, señorita, but I'm busy now," he said. "Go ask someone else."

He turned back to his traffic. He had not recognized Sara.

Sara asked another policeman she found walking on the next street. He spent five minutes giving her directions to places she had no intention of visiting, smiling pleasantly and giving no indication that her face was the least bit familiar.

Twice she walked into stores and a restaurant where she saw police eating, where she made a pretense of buying small things, or asking for assistance. No one recognized her, as she secretly hoped.

Still, she never identified herself, unwilling to take responsibility for turning herself in. If she was discovered by accident, she reasoned, then Constanzo wouldn't exact revenge on her family. If she turned herself in, something terrible would happen. She stuck with that peculiar logic.

Finally, Sara stopped at a phone booth and called a neighbor in Matamoros to see how her family was. She didn't call them directly, not wanting to incriminate them in any way.

"Everything is fine with me," Sara said. "Tell my parents I love them and that I will come to Matamoros to explain what happened and to turn myself in. I was kidnapped, I am being held against my will. But I will get away from them."[11]

This was the plan Sara had hatched: to portray herself as a prisoner of the cult, not a willing member. The phone call was her first step in realizing it.

Not knowing what else to do, she called the apartment next.

Constanzo answered on the first ring. "Where have you been?" he shouted. "It's been hours. If you've betrayed us . . ."

"The surgeon turned us down," she interrupted, then decided to lie. "Now I think I'm being followed."

"Don't come back until you ditch them," Constanzo hissed. "Take a cab across town, walk around for a while until you lose whoever is following you, then take a cab back here. Now go!"

Sara had hoped he might tell her not to come back at all, but she followed his instructions. After wandering about for another hour, she took a cab back to the apartment and trudged up to the fourth-floor flat. She told them she must have been mistaken about being followed.

Constanzo was furious. "The only reason I don't kill you now is because I wouldn't want the body stinking up the place, and I wouldn't want to risk going out to get rid of it," he said. "Out of my sight."

Karla, who had stopped by to deliver some food and to check on the gang, also berated Sara, accusing her of betrayal. She gave Constanzo some tranquilizers and he made Sara take several, then locked her in a bedroom. Karla left to talk to her friend the doctor about finding another plastic surgeon.

"What are we going to do now?" Omar asked. "What if we can't find someone to operate on us?"

But Constanzo had no answers. He just paced the flat like a caged animal, saying nothing. From behind the closed bedroom door, they could hear Sara weeping.

By Saturday, May 6, after nine days in the cramped Rio Sena apartment, Constanzo announced they would have to try leaving the country without the benefit of plastic surgery. Now that their story had been off the television and out of the newspapers for two weeks running, perhaps hair dye and phony documents would be enough, he said.

"No one recognized Sara when she went out," he said. "We can do the same if we're careful."

Constanzo had stopped speaking to Sara since her return from the plastic surgery mission. He pointedly looked only at Omar, Duby, and Martin when addressing the group.

After a few days of this treatment, Sara had become convinced that Constanzo planned to kill her before leaving the apartment.

Martin and Omar kept trying to tell her it wasn't so, but she had decided Constanzo was insane and irrational. When he excluded her from discussion of their impending departure to Central America, she was certain she would die.

"He's not the man I used to know," she whispered to Martin. "He used to be a gentleman. He used to treat me well. Now he looks at me like I'm already dead."

With similar thoughts running through her mind, Sara had used her time alone on May 2 in the locked bedroom—a rare moment of privacy, away from Constanzo's prying eyes—to scrawl a small note. She had kept it in her pocket at all times since, her tiny safety valve. In Spanish, it said:

"Please call the judicial police and tell them that in this building are those that they are seeking. Give them the address, fourth floor. Tell them that a woman is being held hostage. I beg for this, because what I want most is to talk—or they're going to kill the girl."

Then, as if in an afterthought, Sara decided she would get one last shot in at her nemesis, Maria del Rocio Cuevas Guerra, whom she had decided long ago deserved to be punished: "A woman named Karla who lives in Echegaray helped them." She did not sign the scrap of paper, but she knew her handwriting could be identified.

On Saturday afternoon, when Adolfo seemed to be excluding her from the gang's escape plans, she decided it was time to use the note. From one of the bedrooms, she peeped out the window and saw two young men on the street, moving furniture onto the bed of a pickup truck. She opened the window and waited for one of the men to look up. She waved at him, caught his attention, and threw the note down to him. Then she quickly walked away from the window.

The act of opening the window, waving, and throwing had taken barely five seconds. No one, not even the watchful and paranoid Constanzo, had noticed.

That note would become a major point of controversy in the days to come. Sara would say that it proved she was being held captive, that she was trying to escape, and that she had nothing to hide.

The police would say it proved nothing of the kind. They would say it was all part of a carefully laid plan. "The note was just an alibi," Federico Ponce would say. "Just like the phone call to Matamoros. If she wanted to escape, she could have—because she was never a prisoner, except of her own crimes.

"Sara wants to have it all ways. On the one hand, she says she was too afraid to escape or contact us, because Constanzo would kill her family. On the other hand, she claims she threw this note, which surely would have triggered Constanzo's threat to kill her father and mother and sisters. We don't believe either story. We believe she threw the note after she saw a police officer outside the building, and she assumed their arrest was imminent. That way, she could set up an alibi."

In any case, the controversial note ended up playing no role in the strange events of May 6. The man who caught it eventually did turn it over to the police, but only much later, long after the gang's hideout was empty—and after new headlines about Constanzo's murderous cult screamed from the newsstands.

Only then did the man realize that the silly scrap of paper the skinny woman in the apartment building had thrown to him was no joke, as he had first thought. But by then it was too late.

That same morning, several of District Attorney Ponce's men were investigating the disappearance of a fifteen-year-old girl in a case entirely unrelated to Constanzo. The detectives merely were questioning people where the girl had last been seen—in Colonia Cuauhtemoc. As a matter of routine, though, while asking about the girl's whereabouts, the detectives also asked if any of the cult members had been sighted. All of Ponce's men had done this for weeks, regardless of what case they were working on. So far the questions led nowhere. Until that afternoon.

"Well, I did see a strange-looking woman," said a street vendor whose cart was a few blocks from 19 Rio Sena. "She didn't look like the picture in the newspapers I saw, but she was very, very tall."

By itself that tip would have been far too vague to warrant any significance. But that same team of detectives, not twenty minutes later, heard from a clerk at a Superama market about a young guy with a dyed punk hairdo who had tried to buy groceries with a hundred dollar bill.

"He was very strange," the clerk said. "He wasn't one of the cult members we saw in the paper, but he was definitely from the border. He had that accent. He lives around here somewhere."

Sensing a possible break in the cult case, the detectives reported back to the chief of police for the Miguel Hidalgo District, Rodrigo Martinez. Martinez went to his boss, Ponce, and asked that they put the area around the market under surveillance.

To his immense discomfort, Chief Martinez was nicknamed Superman because he was a dead ringer for the comic book character Clark Kent—broad shoulders, square jaw, heavy glasses, even that impossible blue-black hair.

"That area is not in Miguel Hidalgo District," Ponce pointed out. "In fact, Colonia Cuauhtemoc is miles outside our jurisdiction."

"It's still our case," Martinez said. "If the murder is in our district, then we can pursue the suspect anywhere."

"Okay, Superman," Ponce said, making his chief wince. "We'll do it. And screw anyone who doesn't like it."

An hour later, two teams of plainclothes detectives arrived in two drab Plymouths, prepared to set up a stakeout near the Superama market. Everyone considered it to be a long shot, but the tips had to be checked out. Both teams parked in front of the market.

One of the detectives, Carlos Padilla Torres, got out to check an old, apparently abandoned car parked near the store. This was police routine, checking out everything and hoping something useful turns up, even if it hardly ever does. The car was no exception.

But it just happened to be parked directly across the street from the fourth-floor living room window of 19 Rio Sena, apartment 14. Sara saw them first and quickly walked away from the window.[12] But Adolfo de Jesus Constanzo also just happened to be pulling back the curtain at that moment to survey the street scene, something he did every few minutes with monotonous regularity.

There's a strange thing about unmarked Mexican police cars. They aren't really unmarked. Many of them have a serial number in black stenciled on their doors—not huge, not visible through a suspect's rearview mirror, but a dead giveaway when you look at the car from the side. Every crook in Mexico City knows what that string of numbers and letters on some nondescript car's door means.

"They're here!" Constanzo screeched, bringing his followers to their feet. "They've come for us. This is it!"

As Martin ran for the shotgun, Constanzo flung the window open. The unsuspecting detective was still peering in the abandoned car's window. Constanzo took aim at him with his lethal Uzi submachine gun. With his teeth gritted, he whispered, "Mother, this is it."[13]

Then he squeezed the trigger.

28

At five minutes after two in the afternoon on May 6, Detective Padilla Torres's reflection in an abandoned car's window vanished in a sudden explosion of glass.

The young policeman stepped back in a moment of bewilderment, not sure what had just happened. In the next split second it occurred to him that the group of boys he had seen playing nearby must have thrown a rock at him, and he began to turn around to admonish the little punks. Then a split second later, a sharp burning tore into his side and he instinctively dove to the ground, knowing that something other than a stone had just pelted him. Only then did the sound of gunshots register in his consciousness.

"Help, I've been hit," he cried out, watching blood ooze from a flesh wound just below his left nipple, a graze that missed his heart by about four inches. He crawled toward his companions.

The other detectives scrambled for cover behind parked cars, where they were immediately pinned down by wild sprays of bullets from somewhere above. They heard a man yelling from the same direction, and they frantically tried to spot their assailant as Constanzo's gun continued its ugly burping. Finally they saw the flashes of gunfire erupting from the fourth-floor window across the street.

The police tried to return fire, but their handguns were no match for the 9mm slugs streaming from Constanzo's Uzi. They were caught unprepared and vulnerable.

Men and women on the street fled screaming as Constanzo's

submachine gun chewed into the sidewalk, then splintered a food vendor's cart. A display window in the Superama burst inward in a shower of fragments, leaving patrons inside the crowded store crouched in the aisles. The distant sound of a crying baby in some other apartment filled the silences between the bursts of gunfire, drifting eerily out an open window like a plea for mercy.

Throughout this sudden midday Armageddon, an elderly woman at a pay phone in front of the supermarket stood her ground, looking confused but continuing to shout into the phone, doggedly trying to finish her conversation. Finally, one of the policemen dashed over and dragged her to cover, leaving the receiver dangling by its cord and a tinny voice crying out, "Mama! Mama, are you there?"

"But I wasn't through," the old woman yelped.

Chief Martinez—Superman—had pulled up just as the shooting began. He had come only to supervise the surveillance, but he ended up in the midst of a firefight. Bullets smacked the side of his car and he ducked out the passenger side, crouching low.

Martinez had a machine gun with him. He reached into the car for it, then took aim at the screaming man in the white shirt firing from the apartment. The gun jammed. Superman couldn't fire a shot.

In the apartment building across the street, the dark-haired gunman was leaning out a window, raking the street and sidewalk, sending bits of concrete flying with each burst. Then he shouted a stream of obscenities and threats, and dashed to a different window, where he resumed shooting from his new vantage point. The tactic was effective. The policemen remained pinned down and helpless.

"You'll all die! You bastards can't get me," the shooter cried. "I'll see you all in hell!"

Martinez squinted, trying to make out the man's features, but he was too far away. There was no way to tell who it was. But who else could it be?

Still crouching behind his car, Martinez reached inside for his radio microphone, then punched in a code that activated a police emergency frequency. "Suspects are firing on police units from a building at the corner of Rio Sena and Rio Balsas in Colonia Cuauhtemoc. Need assistance," he shouted in classic, clipped cop talk. Then he added the words that would send 180 policemen and federal agents scrambling to his aid. "Suspects believed to be the narcosatanicos."

District Attorney Ponce was driving to his favorite restaurant when he heard the call come over the radio at ten minutes after two (the lunch hour traditionally begins late in Mexico City, then lasts several hours). He flipped on his siren and sped to the scene to take command—and to keep the federales, who surely had heard the call as well, from taking over. He was determined this would be his case, not theirs.

Ten minutes later he was crouching next to Superman. "I've got a new name for my gun," Ponce joked grimly, brandishing his nickel-plated Smith and Wesson automatic. "This is the Satanico Buster."

"We'll see," Martinez replied. "Wait until we bust someone."[1]

Inside the gang's apartment, chaos reigned. Sara and Omar were wailing that they didn't want to die, that they had to get out of the apartment. They wanted to flee before it was too late.

Duby obediently stumbled from room to room, pulling fresh magazines out of suitcases for his padrino, then loading empty ones with more bullets. His hands shook, sending bullets skittering across the carpet.

Martin kept firing shotgun blasts from the window, a useless gesture at that range. Most of the pellets rained down harmlessly, though the noise was terrifying. He quickly exhausted the shotgun shells.

Constanzo shouted at Omar and Sara, who were cowering in the living room. Several shots from the streets had already pocked the apartment's windows with holes, and one slammed into the far wall. Omar covered his ears.

"Don't hide," Constanzo shouted. "We'll kill them all."

Constanzo handed Martin the machine gun and ran into the bedroom where the suitcase of money was hidden. He threw it down on the floor in the living room, snatched two bundles of bills, then ran to the window. He ripped the rubber bands off the money bundles and threw wads of U.S. twenties and fifties out the window. The bills fluttered majestically to the street, drifting like confetti.

He followed up with handfuls of gold centenarios, which fell to the ground with a ringing clatter, rolling across the pavement and street. "This is for you, poor animals!" he shouted. "Take it!"

Pandemonium erupted on the street. Over the shouted protests of the police, people began running into the street to gather the cash, heedless of police warnings and Constanzo's bullets. Some of the officers moved to pick up the money as well, abandoning their positions for the wealth tumbling out of the sky.

Grinning viciously, Constanzo fired several more blasts at the street, wounding one of the cash-hungry spectators in the arm. Then he ran to a side window, facing a building across Rio Balsas. On a second-floor landing opposite the apartment, he had spotted a large propane tank. He began directing his machine-gun fire at it. "When the tank explodes, we'll run for it," he shouted, laughing madly. "They'll be too busy picking up money and running from the fire to even see us."

But though he emptied three clips from the machine gun at the tank, he could not cause it to explode. He implored Ochosi and Eleggua to intervene and tried a fourth magazine. The squat tank remained impervious. His gods had abandoned him.

Constanzo began screaming incoherently as their chance to escape faded. The street below filled with police cars, one after another. Blue-suited men wearing flak jackets and toting rifles took positions across the street and set up police barricades. Pedestrians, store customers, and clerks were cleared out and safely ensconced behind a roadblock down the street.

The money was scooped up. The brief period of confusion had passed. They were surrounded.

"We're trapped, Adolfo," Martin said sadly. "What will we do now?"

"No one will have my money if I can't," Constanzo shouted. He shoved the suitcase with the remains of the five thousand dollars toward Omar. "Burn it."

"What?" Omar asked, his small face wet with tears.

Constanzo pointed the machine gun at Omar and screamed, "Burn the money. Burn it! Do as I say or I'll kill you right now!"

Omar quickly scooped up the suitcase and ran to the oven in the tiny kitchen. He lit a burner and began feeding cash to the blue flame.

Satisfied, Constanzo directed his fire back at the police. Bullets peppered the street, pinging into parked cars. In response, heavy police fire began to pock the building's grimy granite walls.

"More bullets," Constanzo yelled when his machine gun clicked dryly, its magazine empty once again. "Now. Hurry!"

Reluctantly, Duby walked to Constanzo holding a magazine of bullets in each hand. "This is it, Padrino," he said timidly, fearful of bringing ill tidings to his crazed leader. "These are the last bullets."

"Then there's no hope," Constanzo announced. "We've got to use them to die."

Suddenly he seemed calm, almost relieved. An odd look of hope passed over his face, and he stopped yelling and stalking from window to window with his gun. He calmly took Martin's hand in his. There was a furious burst of gunfire from the street, then silence.

"Remember our pact. We'll die now, but we'll come back. We will be born again."

Then he called Omar to him. "It's time, Omar," he said, offering his little mayordomo the machine gun. Then he wrapped an arm around Martin's shoulder. "Shoot us, then the others, then yourself. They think they have us, but we'll still escape them. We'll escape them in death."

"No, no! I don't want to die," Omar screeched. He flung the gun down as if it had burned his flesh, then ran into the front bedroom.

"Omar, do as I tell you," Constanzo implored. "We'll be together. I told you, I've been reincarnated three times already, and each time I move higher, I become more powerful. In the next life I'll be even more powerful. So will you."

"No, I want to live," Omar cried, his voice muffled. He had crawled under the bed.[2]

"I'll die with you, Adolfo," Martin said, kissing his padrino's cheek. "As long as we're together."

Duby stood there, staring dumbly, paralyzed. "Alvaro," Constanzo said. "Pick up the gun. You do it."

"No, Padrino, I don't want to kill you," Duby replied, backing up a step.

Constanzo picked up the gun and growled, "Do as I say."

Duby shook his head. Constanzo reached out and slapped him twice. "Do it or I'll make things tough on you in Hell."

"I don't want to, Padrino. I don't want to kill you."

Constanzo thrust the gun out to him. With shaking hands, Duby took it. He held the machine gun awkwardly, out from his body, like a man who picks up a baby for the first time.

Everyone in the apartment fell silent for a moment. Shots continued to pelt the building sporadically. Another one smacked a wall, making Duby jump.

"Don't worry," Constanzo said, almost kindly. "I'll be back."

Sara, who had been weeping into her hands, suddenly looked up and yelled, "If you're going to do it, do it already. Do it now. Now, now!"[3]

She watched as Constanzo nodded his approval at her and smiled. In the end, La Madrina had reemerged in the nick of time, he seemed to be saying. Then he led Martin into the back bedroom. They walked into a closet, out of Sara's sight. Duby followed them.

From her spot on the living room floor, Sara heard a door open a moment later. At first she wondered if they might be sneaking out somehow. Then she heard Constanzo say in an almost dreamy voice, "Now. Do it."

"Obey him, Duby," Sara called out. "Do it now!"

Seconds ticked by, long and unbearable. Then Sara was jerked erect by the sudden sound of the machine gun spitting bullets in a long, sustained burst as Duby held the trigger, emptying a full magazine. Sara winced. A flood of emotions gripped her unexpectedly—relief, sadness, love, hate—at what she assumed was her beloved Adolfo's death.

"Adolfo!" she cried out, and she began to weep again.

Her mind continued churning, though, even through the grief. Funny, she thought, she had heard no cry of pain when the shots sounded, no sound at all, really, except for the sharp, staccato pops from the gun. Suddenly, she realized something wasn't right. Why did he go into a closet to die, out of sight? It didn't make sense. Maybe he was tricking her, escaping. Perhaps she should go see what had happened. . . .

Her resolve vanished quickly, though, replaced by stark fear when the machine gun fell silent. She remembered their mass-suicide pact. She heard the sound of Duby slapping the last magazine into the machine gun and she ran into the other bedroom, where Omar was hiding, wondering if Duby would come for them next. Then she heard Duby speak.

"Padrino?" he said in a small voice. "Now what do we do? Please, Padrino, you shouldn't have left us. Tell me what to do."

But El Padrino didn't answer.

Duby did come for Sara then, but she had crawled under the bed with Omar. He was supposed to kill them, then himself, Duby knew, but somehow the suicide pact didn't seem to matter anymore. Instead, he went to the window and angrily fired the last magazine of bullets out the window, hitting only pavement.

"That's it, no more bullets," he said, throwing the gun down and slumping to the floor. "We're through. We're all dead. Let them come and take us."

Sara crawled out from under the bed, took one look at Duby, then flung open the apartment door, knowing what she had to do next. She shambled down the hall, then careened down the stairs, yelling, "Don't shoot, don't shoot. I'm coming out. I've escaped."

She reached the lobby and dashed outside to the street, still yelling for them not to shoot, saying again and again that she had escaped and wanted help. "Please, help me," she cried. "Don't shoot."

The police stopped firing as she burst outside, though their guns stayed trained on her long, thin form. Sara kept running blindly forward, arms pumping, chest heaving—right into the arms of Superman. He grabbed her and pinned her wrists behind her. "I've got you," he grunted, surprised at the strength in this tall, thin woman.

"Thank God," Sara said. "I'm saved."

Ponce and Superman stared at her in surprise, then exchanged curious looks. They had expected crazed cultists, not grateful ones. "Are you Sara?" Ponce asked, not sure if this was the woman whose pictures he had seen.

She nodded, then seemed to swoon. Ponce and Superman were relieved: Until that moment, they had not known for sure who they were battling in that fourth-floor apartment. Conceivably, it could have been some other insane gunman.

Now they knew for sure. They had cornered the narcosatanicos.

Less than a minute later, Duby came tumbling down the stairs, barefoot and disheveled, his dirty white shirt untucked and flapping. Three agents descended on him and he took a vicious clout to the side of the face with the flat of an automatic pistol. A towering agent grimly wrapped his arm around Duby's neck, put a pistol to his head, then dragged him across the street. The other agents crouched, ready to return fire at the apartment if necessary. Their eyes were as wide with fear as Duby's.

"What about the others?" Ponce asked Sara.

Sara didn't seem to hear the question. She stared up at the apartment window with eyes wet but serene. A deathly silence had fallen on the street.

"I've been through hell since they kidnapped me. I thought I'd never get away," Sara said at last. Then she burst into tears. "I'm so glad you came."

Ponce found himself trying to comfort her, surprising even himself. She did seem more victim than criminal, though. Perhaps she really was just a bystander, held prisoner by a madman.

"What about the others?" Superman demanded harshly. He remained skeptical, though even he found Sara's demeanor convincing. She looked like a prison-camp survivor, skinny and pale, possessed of that terrible, thousand-yard stare.

"Omar's under the bed," she said. "And Adolfo and Martin committed suicide."

"Are you sure?" Ponce cried. "You saw them?"

Sara shook her head. "But I heard it happen. I heard Alvaro shoot them."

"Where are the bodies?" he yelled. But Sara shrugged. She didn't know. She hadn't seen them.

Ponce was suddenly gripped by a terrible fear. What if Sara and Duby had been sent down as a diversion while Constanzo crept away? Sure, the building was surrounded, but a lot of attention had been drawn away by Sara's exit. Everyone had wanted to see La Madrina.

Not only that, but the federales he had shouted down when he arrived and assumed control of the operation had started bickering and jostling with his district police. And investigators from the central district attorney's office, another competitor of Ponce's, had arrived and were trying to assert themselves as well. Suddenly everything was confused and undisciplined—and dangerous.

If someone were to make a break for it, he couldn't have chosen a better time.

"Get up there," Ponce yelled suddenly to one of his lieutenants. "Go, go. I want that apartment secured!"

Orders were shouted down the line and a heavily armed team of agents in blue jumpsuits and flak jackets pounded up the four flights of stairs. They burst into the apartment, Ponce and Martinez on their heels.

Omar was, indeed, cowering under a bed in the front bedroom as Sara had said. They dragged him out by his heels, set him upright, and led him downstairs at gunpoint.

A quick search of the rest of the apartment led them to the other bedroom. And its closet.

"Is that him?" an agent asked. "Is that the bastard Constanzo?"

Ponce and Martinez peered inside. There were two bodies slumped on the floor of the closet. The walls were sprayed lightly with their dried blood. To the right lay a Mexican man, olive-skinned, with short hair dyed reddish, wearing blue jeans, white moccasins, and a mink-trimmed jacket. He had several visible bullet wounds, including one in the eye.

"Martin?" Martinez asked. Ponce shrugged.

The body was slumped against a taller dead man, whose hairy legs were thrust straight out in front of him. He wore blue and white shorts, a white shirt stained red with blood, and blue moccasins. He had a trim mustache and very short, very American-looking dark reddish hair, nothing like the shiny mane Constanzo had always sported. He was light-skinned and almost classically clean cut—except for the bullet holes in the bridge of his nose and left cheek. Ponce would later observe that he looked less like a mad killer and more like a character from *Leave It to Beaver*.

"He doesn't look much like the pictures we have," Martinez said uneasily. "Do you think it's really Constanzo?"

Ponce stared hard at the corpses. Neither one looked familiar.

A sick dread gripped his stomach. Was this a setup? Phony bodies while the real padrino slipped away?

"I don't know, Rodrigo," he said finally. "We'll have to get some fingerprints. All I can say is, it better be him.

"It just better be."[4]

29

After the shootout at Rio Sena, Sara, Omar, and Duby were whisked off to the basement of the Miguel Hidalgo District offices for questioning. Ponce and his men stayed up all night with them, determined to put to rest any question about the identity of the bodies in the closet.

Omar and Duby were thrown into separate cells, dark and rank, so they could stew alone and fearful for a few hours. But Sara was escorted to a side office. Ponce was thinking she probably had been kidnapped, that she would end up being a key witness, not a defendant in the mass-murder case. He ordered Cokes and hamburgers for her, and coaxed her to talk—unprecedented, gentle treatment in a system known for its rough justice.

For a while, Sara maintained the appearance of victim, sipping her Coke and nibbling at her sandwich, telling her tale of kidnapping and imprisonment by a man she once revered. She was forced to go along with the gang, but she had never been part of it, she said. She had been a captive.

"I never knew when they were going to kill me. I thought I'd never get away."

In the end, though, Sara's obsession with being at the center of every story—even a story of murder and human sacrifice—took hold and betrayed her. Just as she had portrayed herself as the romantic center of Constanzo's life when she had spoken to her girlfriends in school, so she had to show Ponce how involved she was with Constanzo's life and his confidences, even when it came to murder. Instead of keeping quiet, she told Ponce how much she knew. And she knew far too much.

First there were the drug deals, meetings with gangsters, and police payoffs, which she recounted in great detail, especially the part where all the mobsters toasted her beauty. Next she spoke at length about Constanzo's religion, describing in detail the rituals of Santeria and Palo Mayombe, though later she would claim she knew nothing of the evil black magic of Palo. Then, most damning of all, she described all the murders she claimed to have had nothing to do with—the killing of her boyfriend Gilberto Sosa, fellow cult-member Valente del Fierro, Salvador's two partners, and the torture and murder of the man who had pursued Duby, Victor Saul Sauceda. She knew how they had been cut, what organs were taken, and why.

"Before sacrificing these people, Adolfo would remain by himself in the room of the dead with them, so he could have sex with them just before the sacrifice," Sara said wisely. She took a bite of hamburger, then dabbed neatly at her lips with a napkin. "It satisfied him."

Ponce and Paquito Blanchette stared at Sara, horrified at what she was telling them—and the calm manner in which she spoke. She might as well have been describing a trip to the market. She smiled, she gestured vigorously. She peppered her tale of murder by telling them how she had traveled alone to Mexico City, thinking they were going to Acapulco, not even realizing they were fugitives. Adolfo took her on many vacations, she said, as she recounted how much Constanzo loved her, how obsessed he was with her.

"But aren't Omar and Martin his lovers?" Blanchette asked, confused. "Aren't they—I mean, weren't they—homosexuals?"

Sara's expression clouded for a second. Then she brightened. She would not be swayed from her version of reality. "Yes, but he was still obsessed with me."

"And if you weren't involved in the cult's crimes, how do you know so much about the drug deals?" Ponce asked coldly, sweeping away the Cokes and the burgers. "And the murders?"

"Adolfo told me everything," she said patiently. "As I said."

"Yes, you said that," Ponce snapped. "You also said you were kidnapped. And then you said you came here alone from McAllen, thinking you were on vacation."

"Well I did," Sara said defensively. "They only kidnapped me after I found out about the murders on television."

"Then why didn't you tell your parents? You left without telling them anything. You didn't pack a bag. We know that, Sara. Vacationers don't do that. Fugitives do."

Sara fell silent, trapped in a lie.

"You know what I think, Sara?"

She shook her head.

"I think it's going to be a long night."

While Sara had talked incessantly with little prodding, Omar and Duby were another matter.

"We had to do some work on them," Ponce admitted candidly. "After a few hours, a glass of water or a little rest can become very powerful inducements. We had to apply the moral pressure."

With Omar, that meant first pumping him for information about the cult, the followers, the clients, and the drug deals. Omar tearfully insisted he had nothing to do with any murders. He just kept house and slept with Adolfo and helped with animal sacrifices when the famous people came to visit. He attended ceremonies only in Mexico City, not Matamoros.

After all of Omar's willing statements had been taken down, Ponce stationed policemen in shifts in his cell, spelling each other every few hours, each of them asking him a single question, over and over: "Who killed the queer? Who killed the queer?"

Ponce knew, from Jorge Montes and Juan Carlos Fragosa, that Omar was present at the killing of La Claudia. He was determined to get a confession to bolster his case.

For four hours, Omar kept saying, "I don't know what you're talking about. I don't know what you mean. I don't know. I don't know."

He asked for water, he asked for food, he asked to go to the bathroom. The police didn't even say no. They just kept asking the same question. After three shifts with different interrogators, Ponce entered the cell.

He nodded at the investigator, who turned and left. Then Ponce leaned next to Omar's ear and whispered. "Who killed the queer, Omar?"

"I didn't do it," Omar blurted. "It was Adolfo."

"Bingo," Ponce said.[1]

Duby was a different story. He had no fear, just like the boys in Matamoros had been. Once the terror of the shootout had faded, the horror of Constanzo's threat about Hell passed, and he remembered everything else El Padrino had taught him.

The magic would protect them, Duby said. The police were powerless against the magic.

"Constanzo will be back," Duby told Ponce, a gleam in his eye. His right cheek was swollen and bruised, closing one eye to a slit. Later, the police who had struck him would say he fell down the stairs at Rio Sena—a story he was forced to repeat in ensuing press conferences. "You'll see. The godfather will not be dead for long."

Duby freely admitted killing Constanzo and Martin at his leader's orders. Duby described how he had closed his eyes tightly, screamed, and pressed the trigger, holding it until the magazine was empty and the gun had stopped jumping in his hands. When he opened his eyes, Martin and Constanzo lay slumped and lifeless on the closet floor, bleeding from wounds in the head, chest, legs, and arms.[2] The interrogators accused him of lying, of covering up for Constanzo's escape, but he stuck to his story. He seemed proud of what he had done.

"So they were dead when you left them?" Ponce asked. "And it was definitely Constanzo in the closet?"

Duby looked at Ponce contemptuously, and said, "Of course. Who do you think it is?"

Ponce nodded. "I want you to tell me about all the other murders."

Duby jutted out his jaw. "Why should I tell you anything?"

"Because all the pretty things Constanzo did to people, we can do to you if we want."

Duby shook his head.

"You'll see," the young thug spat. "Constanzo will be back. He'll be born again. He'll come for us. And you. You see, I know I'm going to Hell. But I also know he'll bring me back. You'll just burn." Then he laughed. He refused to speak further.[3]

Ponce was disturbed. He considered Duby to be "brainwashed,

like someone who followed Hitler." He decided on a novel approach to make Duby more pliant, to convince him that Constanzo wouldn't be helping anyone anymore. He brought Duby to the morgue.

Ponce, Blanchette, Duby, and an escort of uniformed officers arrived at the district morgue after midnight. Inside the aging building, at the end of a long hall, lay the autopsy laboratory, with its antiseptic tile and sweetish odor of death. The empty room was lit by the harsh, buzzing glare of fluorescent bulbs suspended over a series of stainless-steel tables. Two bodies lay there partially covered.

Without hesitating, Ponce dragged the handcuffed Duby to the table on which the tall, light-skinned, Leave It to Beaver corpse lay. The autopsy was finished. The chest had been opened and the organs removed. The top of his head had been lopped off for examination of the brain, a hideous surgical parody of El Padrino's own mutilations and human sacrifices.

Duby tried to recoil, gagging in horror, but Ponce pushed his head down toward the bodies.

"There, there's your godfather," he yelled. "You think that is going to get up and save you?"

Duby began to shake and cry. Defiance evaporated. "Padrino!" Duby wailed, racked with sobs. "Save us!"

"Get him out of here," Ponce said with disgust. The uniformed cops hauled Duby out, still keening with grief and fear. At first weepy and despondent, then merely resigned to his fate, Duby would confess to everything in the next few hours—from chopping off Mark Kilroy's legs to hacking Victor Saul Sauceda to death.

"I can tell you what those fingerprints will show us when they come in, Paquito," Ponce said as they stood alone in the morgue, Duby's cries still retreating down the hallway, echoing in the cold, reeking room. "Either that bastard on the table is Constanzo, or we just saw the best damn acting job in the world."

"That was no act," Blanchette said simply. "That's him." Fingerprint comparisons would confirm their conclusion within a day. Constanzo's only escape had been through death.

As they were about to leave the laboratory, Ponce paused at the door and looked back at the ravaged body on the table. For a long time afterwards, he would vividly recall the strange feeling that swept over him—a feeling that still haunts him now and then, late at night, when he's alone working and the night noises creak and rattle his office building.

"I don't believe in magic. I'm not superstitious. The only spirit that possesses me is my job," Ponce explained. "But when I saw Constanzo lying there down at the morgue, I felt something."

Ponce gropes for words when he tries to describe this moment, but finally, he has to settle on a word he is loath to use, finding no other term that will do: evil.

"I felt a force, an evil force," Ponce said. "I don't believe in such things, really, and it only lasted a moment, but in those seconds I felt it, an evilness inside that sonavabitch, still there, waiting and hating.

"I didn't know the true meaning of that word, 'evil,' until then."

In the morgue that night, Ponce sighed and turned his back on the corpse. He walked out of the lab, switching off the light with a flip of his right hand, leaving El Padrino in darkness.

EPILOGUE

OCUKWA ARO

(Moon of Death)

When we remember that we are all mad, the mysteries disappear and life stands explained.

—Mark Twain, *Notebook*

30

Sara, Omar, and Duby were placed in solitary confinement in a maximum-security prison, freed only to be trotted out for two mammoth and chaotic press conferences in the aftermath of the shootout and the exhausting interrogations.

Duby, sullen and unrepentant, repeated his confessions and boasted of the fingers and toes he had sliced from bodies. Omar delivered to the international press corps an oddly singsong lecture on the fine points of Santeria and Palo Mayombe. Sara, as pale and remote as a Madonna freshly stepped from a Renaissance painting, seemed to stare past the reporters when it was her turn to speak, proclaiming at various times conflicting accounts of her innocence, her intimate knowledge of the murders, and her willingness to follow Constanzo anywhere.

Shortly after the shootout, Karla, her boyfriend, and the doctor also were rounded up and charged with *encubrimiento*—cover-up—for aiding the fugitives. A few days later, after yet another confrontation between federal and district authorities, Salvador Vidal was arrested as well, though he was charged only with drug trafficking, not murder. Federal authorities would not accept as credible testimony from the other suspects that he participated in the Calzada killings or that he supplied the weapon that killed Constanzo, which under Mexican law could make him an accomplice to murder.

Back in Matamoros, meanwhile, Elio and the others had hired expensive lawyers who put a stop to the interrogations. Suddenly, Little Serafin and the others were protesting their innocence and blaming everything on their dead padrino. At the same time, they used a portion of the $300,000 left from their last drug deal to bribe their way into luxurious accommodations at the city jail, where they obtained fine clothes, new boots, and restaurant-prepared food. Each of them opened a small business in the jail—a woodworking shop for Elio and Little Serafin, a seafood restaurant for David and Sergio. Prisoners vied with one another to become their well-paid lackeys as their drug money, funneled in by other family members, ensured a comfortable stay while they awaited trial.[1]

Soon they began bragging to other inmates and officials that they would buy their way out of prison within the year.[2] In court, they attempted to withdraw their confessions, alleging torture.

"We'll be out of here soon, you'll see," Little Serafin said, only this time he was referring to the magic of money rather than his departed padrino. They really had learned a lot from Constanzo.

Sara, Omar, and Duby—lacking the bribe money to live so comfortably—made the same allegations of torture in the Mexico City courts, a standard tactic, since the justice system in Mexico is designed to extract confessions from every defendant. Confessions are considered a legal necessity, since police have little interest or training in gathering physical evidence of crimes. This philosophy is based on Mexico's Napoleonic Code of justice, where every defendant is presumed guilty unless proven innocent—the opposite of the U.S. system, which Mexican legal experts consider chaotic and incomprehensible. As such, treating defendants badly is considered acceptable, since they are regarded as guilty anyway.

After their arrests, each of the defendants spent the next year attending a series of hearings at which they attempted to prove they were tortured into confessing their guilt. Because torture alone is insufficient to free them in Mexico (the theory being that "moral pressure" only forces individuals to tell the truth), they also labored to prove the confessions were untrue. At each hearing, the defendants issued a seemingly endless series of denials as each of their voluminous confessions were read into the court record.

The setting for these less-than-dramatic encounters had little in common with their U.S. counterparts—trials south of the border have none of the trappings Americans know and expect. There is no jury of peers to hear and weigh the evidence, no witness stand to freeze men and women with oaths of truthfulness and the spotlight of scrutiny. There is no stately, berobed judge ensconced behind his raised bench, and no courthouse filled with walls and furniture of deep, dark woods, familiar symbols of the solidity and roots of the law. In Mexico City, the courts are spartan and plain, located inside the *reclusorios*—the prisons—foreboding concrete edifices surrounded by parapets, spiked with barbed wire and surveyed from guard towers bristling with machine-gun mounts.

Reclusorio Oriente—Eastern Prison—was chosen for the cult members because of its high security and towering double walls. It lies on the far edge of the capital, straddling the border between Mexico City and the suburb of Ixtapalapa, surrounded by a maze of crooked streets and neighborhoods shown on no maps and marked by no signs, the product of the capital's explosive and haphazard growth. Cows graze on weedy lots and men break horses in a small corral next to one side of the prison, while on the other, a busy boulevard is filled with bus traffic and street vendors.

The courtrooms inside are open-air offices with linoleum floors and chipped plastic tabletops. Past a front counter, where secretaries accept legal papers in a constant, noisy series of transactions, a long table lies. This is where defense lawyers and prosecutors cram together for hearings.

The judge does not bother to attend—his assistant presides. The assistant controls the course of every case and, as such, he is the most powerful person in the Mexican justice system, since the judge will base his verdict on the transcripts the secretary prepares after each hearing.

The table abuts a black metal grille set in the wall. This is about the size of an average storefront window, anchored in concrete, made of flat bars about an inch thick. Beyond this grille is a small room where defendants are brought through tunnels from the prison grounds, minimizing the risk of escape. The defendants are never allowed in the courtroom itself; they must press their ears against the grille to hear proceedings against them, then shout answers to questions. Lawyers must whisper loudly through the grille to confer with their clients. The disembodied words that drift in through the grille have given rise to a unique convention in Mexican justice: in transcripts, the defendant is always referred to as *La Voz*—the voice.

"I can't say anything about what happened here in Mexico City. I can't say anything about what happened at Rancho Santa Elena," Sara testified time and again at her hearings, reciting the testimony by rote. "My previous declarations were taken under force, under psychological pressure, under moral pressure. They took my clothes off, they tied me. I was choked, they put a plastic bag on my face, they pulled my hair, they hit me in the stomach. They wanted me to tell people's names, but I didn't know any."

Omar and Duby followed in her footsteps, making similar declarations of torture and innocence, sharply disputed by police witnesses to their previous confessions. Then another witness would enter the room, and the process would begin anew.

Between breaks in hearings, Sara and Omar would chat behind the metal grille, giggling occasionally at whispered jokes. They wore street clothes and seemed well treated. After a few months in custody, they had been released from the mush diet and psychological isolation of solitary confinement. Sara had gained her weight back and more, to the point of looking chunky. Omar, however, looked frail and ill after a few months in custody. His face was covered with brown spots and he had been through three hospitalizations for mysterious fainting spells and weight loss. His sisters, small and pixieish like Omar, petitioned the court to release him for health reasons, but the judge refused because of the gravity of the charges against him.

Sara's father, Israel Aldrete, also attended often, sitting quietly in the back of the courtroom for most of Sara's hearings, then timidly approaching the grille during a break so he could whisper words of encouragement to his daughter, or thrust a pack of Lifesavers through the metal slats. In the first months after Sara's arrest, Aldrete came to the capital every weekend to see her. By July, he had moved in with friends so he could stay with her constantly.

"I have to pay the guards," he confided. "You have to pay for everything here if you want someone treated right."

In his own quiet way, the gray and weathered father of Sara Aldrete maintained a solemn dignity and a profound faith in God throughout his family's ordeal—reminiscent of the grace shown by another tragedy-torn family, the Kilroys. "We were relieved when we heard she was arrested, because the police had told us when they found her purse that she had been sacrificed," Israel Aldrete explained during one hearing in August 1989. "We were in despair when they told us that. Still, in some ways, being here in prison is worse than dying."

Later, the elder Aldrete spoke quietly with his daughter, touching her hand gently, almost shyly, through the slot in the metal grille. His workshirt was carefully pressed that day, and his battered black shoes bore a new shine. He seemed a simple man, a good man, caught up in something he could not understand. He has mortgaged the house and offered his life savings to lawyers in hopes of freeing Sara.

"We believe in Sara. We know she is innocent," Israel insists. "She is our daughter. What else can we believe?"

When the hearing ended and Sara was led back to the tunnel, Señor Aldrete turned to leave. He was greeted warmly by Detective Carlos Padilla Torres—the investigator wounded in the shootout, long since recovered. They shook hands.

"He's a good man," Sara's father said with a tired smile. "I have no hard feelings. He was just doing his job."

Padilla patted Aldrete's shoulder. "I would be here too, certain of my child's innocence, if my daughter were on trial," the detective told him. Then he added hastily, "May God forbid."

"Yes," the father of La Madrina said sadly. "God forbid."

Once all the investigations in Mexico were completed, Sara Maria Aldrete Villareal, Omar Orea Ochoa, and Alvaro de Leon Valdez (El Duby) stood charged with two counts of murder in the deaths of Constanzo and Martin. They also were charged with thirteen counts of murder for the deaths at Rancho Santa Elena, and an array of drug-trafficking, criminal association, and cover-up charges.

Omar, with Jorge Montes and Juan Carlos Fragosa, was also charged with the murder of Ramon Paz Esquivel, alias La Claudia, in July 1988.

Elio Hernandez Rivera, Serafin Hernandez Garcia, David Serna

Valdez, and Sergio Martinez Salinas were charged with fifteen counts of murder, various narcotics and weapons violations, cover-up, and burial law violations—for the graveyard at Rancho Santa Elena.

Maria del Rocio Cuevas Guerra (Karla), Enrique Calzada, and Doctor Maria de Lourdes Bueno Lopez were charged with encubrimiento (cover-up) for helping the cult members as fugitives, and for concealing knowledge of murders. Domingo Reyes Bustamante, the caretaker at Rancho Santa Elena, was also charged with cover-up.

Salvador Vidal Garcia Alarcon was charged with cocaine possession and sale.

No charges were filed in the eight deaths of the Calzada drug family, though the case officially is considered solved and closed.

In August 1990, Duby was convicted of the murder of Constanzo and Martin and sentenced to thirty years in prison. Jorge Montes and Juan Carlos Fragosa were convicted of the murder of La Claudia. Each received prison terms of thirty-five years.

Sara Aldrete's trial in Mexico City ended with a judge acquitting her of participating in the murder of Constanzo. But he disbelieved her tale of being kidnapped and convicted her of criminal association for staying with and helping the fugitive gang. She received the maximum sentence for that crime under Mexican law—six years.

As of fall 1990, the other charges in Mexico City, and all of the murder cases in Matamoros, were still pending.

Only Omar Orea Ochoa escaped sentencing. His lawyer had commissioned psychiatric reports in hopes of proving Constanzo had so dominated Omar's thoughts, beliefs, and actions that the young man should not be held responsible for his crimes. Constanzo was Svengali whom Omar loved and obeyed unquestioningly, to the point of insanity, the lawyer argued.

The judge never had to weigh this argument. At age twenty-four, Omar died of a heart attack related to AIDS on February 7, 1990, after twenty days in a prison hospital. The spots that covered his face had been telltale signs of his immune system breaking down, raising the fear that the entire gang might be infected with the deadly virus. However, no tests of the other suspects were ordered.

As for the survivors of the cult of Adolfo de Jesus Constanzo, should Sara, Duby, Elio, Little Serafin, Sergio, or David ever be released from Mexican prisons for some reason, U.S. authorities stand poised to act. Grand jury indictments and arrest warrants issued in April 1989, alleging possession, importation, and conspiracy to import marijuana and cocaine, remain in effect.

The DEA's investigation in the United States, crippled by rivalries while Constanzo was alive, finally accomplished something after he was dead. Information gained from El Gancho and Old Serafin Hernandez led to U.S. indictments of El Gancho's boss, his drug suppliers, and several major traffickers in Matamoros. A widening investigation that linked Constanzo's drugs to mob bosses in Chicago is still underway.[3]

In exchange for his cooperation, Old Serafin pleaded guilty to trafficking charges. He was sentenced to eighteen months in prison and was freed in June 1990. He returned to his home in Brownsville.

Relations between the DEA and Customs remained strained in Brownsville, where relief over the death of Constanzo was palpable, but where bitterness over the back-stabbing in the cult case stayed sharp.

Despite their minor—and perhaps detrimental—role in the conclusion of the cult investigation, Customs head Oran Neck and Sheriff's Lieutenant George Gavito received several civic awards for "solving" the case. Later, charges of corruption and other problems with both their offices were leveled, though investigations ended with inconclusive results. At the same time, Justice Department memos called the credibility and integrity of Customs agents in Brownsville into question, noting, among other problems, that the local federal magistrate would not sign warrants for Customs agents because of their lack of credibility.[4] Late in 1989, an involuntary transfer was ordered for Neck, only to be rescinded later. Eventually, he left Brownsville for a post in Hermosillo, Mexico. Gavito, meanwhile, left the sheriff's office, taking an investigator's job at the Cameron County District Attorney's Office. Both men spoke of collaborating on a book or movie about the case.

"Who's in a better position to know what really happened?" Neck commented.

DEA Agents Armando Ramirez and T. K. Solis, meanwhile, continued the search for the remaining fugitives in the case. Charged in both countries, Ovidio Hernandez, leader of the Hernandez drug operation once Elio was imprisoned, remains free, assisted by a network of contrabandistas and concunios. He had been seen in Chicago in early 1990, but eluded arrest. His father, Brigido Hernandez, wanted on drug and weapons charges, and the former ranch foreman, Aurelio Chavez, also are fugitives.

Most bitter for the U.S. investigators has been Malio Fabio Ponce Torres's elusiveness. The alleged kidnapper of Mark Kilroy, released by mistake by the Cameron County Sheriff's Department, remained free, even though informants twice led DEA agents to him in Monterrey, Mexico, and later in the Yucatan Peninsula. Each time, El Gato managed to elude capture. Well-versed in the religion of Adolfo de Jesus Constanzo, Mexican investigators believe he retrieved the nganga found to be missing from the room of the dead in Mexico City, then put it to use as a means of magically preserving his freedom.

One final chapter remained for authorities to deal with in the saga of Adolfo de Jesus Constanzo: the fate of his mother, Delia Aurora Gonzalez del Valle. On Monday, May 8, 1989, two days after her son died in Mexico City, Delia appeared in Dade County Circuit Court in Miami, where she faced sentencing for trashing yet another home and stealing from yet another landlord, then violating her probation by moving, changing her name, and starting the cycle once again.

The petty crimes she was accused of normally would never have attracted the attention of the news media. But the fact that her son was one of the most wanted men in the hemisphere until two days before the hearing brought reporters flocking to the courtroom of Judge Ellen Morphonius.

Delia told the gathering that she had raised Constanzo and all her children in a "good Catholic home," and that her Adolfo was incapable of the crimes police accused him of committing. Not one of her children was into Santeria or Palo Mayombe, she avowed. And she spoke of how her son reached her from Mexico to proclaim his innocence in a last, desperate phone call. "There was so much fear in his voice," Delia recalled. "He told me he had to run very fast and hide because he was so afraid of the Mexican police. Then he said, 'I have to run, Mom,' and I asked why. He said, 'Because I have to. I am innocent, but I have to hide.' "[5]

When Delia finally had been tracked down after despoiling a series of homes, police found her in a new rental house already filthy after a mere two weeks of occupancy, with an altar in the kitchen and a stinking nganga nestled in a utility room out back.[6] Still, she denied any participation in black magic.

Judge Morphonius sentenced Delia to two years in prison.[7] But even then, the old Delia luck persisted to the end. Morphonius agreed to release her while her lawyer, Ed Salnik, appealed the case. The judge apparently felt sorry for the grieving mother, who at the time was trying to claim her son's body from the Mexicans.

The next day, though, when Salnik tried to talk to Delia about her legal bills, the grieving mom launched into a bitter tirade against him, then fired him. "She basically told me to go to hell. She has an accent, you know—in her words, I was a 'piece of chit.' "

No new lawyer was hired to replace Salnik on the case and no appeal was ever filed. With no appeal, there was no legitimate reason for her to remain free—Delia should have been placed in custody immediately to serve her two years in prison. But the overburdened court system in Miami, bogged down with far too many murders, rapes, and robberies to be overly concerned with Delia's crimes, didn't take notice. She remained free, back in hiding, having beaten the system once again, as if by magic.

On May 20, 1989, Constanzo's body arrived in Miami from Mexico. Rafael Martinez had a chance to examine it at the Medical Examiner's Office, where he found and photographed the tattoos and scars of Palo Mayombe on Constanzo's shoulders, thighs, and forearms.

Two days later, Delia and her son Fausto Rodriguez claimed the body, which they insisted bore no mystical marks. Later, they said the body was cremated in a private ceremony, with only family and a few close friends in attendance. "We don't want anyone there that doesn't belong here to curse the funeral," Fausto said.

Months later, attempts to arrange an interview with Fausto and Delia for this book failed when Fausto insisted that they be paid for their time. "We want a percentage, too," he said. "Our story's worth money."

Subsequent attempts to reach the family in Miami failed. Their phone was disconnected. Delia had moved again.

31

Rancho Santa Elena stood abandoned a year after the murders, the fields choked with weeds, dry and untended. The animals were gone, except for one starving pig. Field mice scurry for cover in the abandoned caretaker's house, a tiny rattle of footsteps. The hot wind still moves through the fields with its dry, husky hiss, a whispering of secrets buried and lost.

The Mexican government owns the ranch now, its warehouse and its fields and its gray, cratered graveyard. The government took possession of everything, even the charred, glass-strewn slab where the little temple once stood. Amid the debris, small pots, beads, railroad spikes, and the wire used to hang victims from the ceiling still lay scattered about, untouched after many months.

The government tried to hire workers to harvest the corn and the sorghum at Rancho Santa Elena, but no one wanted to work those fields. The crops withered and rotted where they stood. Perhaps next year the memories might fade, a caretaker who visits the ranch every few days suggested. Or maybe the year after.

Spring break continued unabated in Matamoros in 1990. Fear gave way to relief, then forgetfulness. Hotel bookings were down a bit on South Padre Island in the year after the killings—the beaches didn't seem to be as crowded, and at night the streets and saloons didn't seem as choked with revelers as in years past. But nearly two hundred thousand visitors still came, and the city elders pronounced the season an unexpected success. Few spring breakers remembered or spoke of Kilroy or the cult as they partied.

Months after the case was closed, new holes were dug at the

ranch, a futile unofficial search for more bodies. By day, families did the digging, seeking lost loved ones the police might have missed. By night, though, a more covert scratching at the ranch's poisoned soil came from brujos looking for a last snatch of Constanzo's magic. What they found, no one can say.

A vague panic ensued when this unauthorized digging was made public in early 1990, showing how, despite the arrests and the death of Constanzo, the same fears and questions remained. Why did it happen, and how? What made our neighbors become monsters?

The Kilroy family proposed an answer, channeling their grief into a campaign. They met with George Bush, they drummed up articles in the papers. They knew what killed Mark: It was drugs, they said, over and over. Drugs did it, pure and simple. If we could wipe out narcotics abuse, such things never again would happen, they said, devoting their lives and their memories of Mark to an anti-drug campaign.

And there certainly was a measure of truth to that point of view. Drugs drove the machine that was Constanzo's organization, and drug deals provided the motive for the selection of many of the cult's victims. But in the end, the Kilroys' answer does not satisfy.

During the manhunt, police and public alike had expected eventually to find that the cult had been a group of drug-crazed maniacs, with Constanzo the most debauched of all. It would all come clear when they were arrested, and it would explain so much, it would provide a framework to slip the horror into. Wasn't Hitler a hype? Charlie Manson a junkie? Anyone could understand that. Drugs made you crazy.

Except, Adolfo de Jesus Constanzo wasn't an abuser of drugs. Neither were his followers. So rigid was Constanzo on this point that he killed one of his loyal minions for snorting a few lines of cocaine. Once they were arrested, neither Sara, nor Duby, nor any of the other suspects showed the slightest medical or psychological evidence of drug abuse or addiction. There were no needle marks on Constanzo's cadaver, no ravages of addiction on Martin's body. They killed sober and fully aware of what they were doing. And Constanzo and Martin died the same way—eyes open and unflinching, a bullet piercing Martin's left eye, but not his eyelid.

No, drugs weren't the answer behind Constanzo's special brand of terror and belief.

But when you can't answer the question of why or how your neighbor turned into a monster, then you wind up like the people on the Street of the Beheaded Saints in Matamoros. This is the street where Sara once lived, where Sara's family still strives to survive their grief, and where Sara's neighbors still have questions.

Will it happen again? they ask, whispering from behind barely open doors. Don't use my name, but tell me: Are there more of them out there? This is our home and we've got to know. Is it still happening, the killing, the sacrifices? The horror?

The answers are not reassuring.

The first hint that the cult might not have died with Constanzo came from Martin Quintana's sister, Teresa, as she babbled to the Mexican police three weeks before the shootout.

She told them that Mara, Constanzo's first madrina, was not dead after all, but had moved to Guadalajara. Martin had said Mara ran boutiques for Constanzo there, but Mara confided to Teresa that she really was a witch, in the same religion as Constanzo.[1]

According to Teresa Quintana, Mara originally came from Veracruz, Mexico's center for witchcraft, with magical roots as deep as those in Salem, Massachusetts. Every year, a witch convention is held in Veracruz, where spells are traded and magic is compared in dark and private ceremonies. "She is dedicated to Constanzo's religion," Teresa said. "She practices the same magic."[2]

Mara is not accused of any crimes, but police wanted to question her. They could not find her. Nor could police locate Damian the transvestite or Francisco the real estate speculator.

Weeks later, when Omar was arrested, he too would speak of others who practiced black magic and sacrifice—sister groups of Constanzo's. He knew no details, though. Then Sara said something very similar at one of the big press conferences. "I don't think that the religion will end with us, because it has a lot of people in it," she said. "They have found a temple in Monterrey that isn't even related to us. It will continue."

The authorities in Mexico City already knew that. In the previous two years, there had been sixty ritual killings of adults in Mexico City. Two of them occurred after Constanzo was killed. Fourteen babies were found sacrificed during the same period.

At first, Constanzo's gang was the principal suspect in all of those killings, as well as several other unsolved ritual homicides in Veracruz. But as investigators looked at different methods in some of the murders—which suggested different belief systems might be at work—as well as the timing of some of the crimes, it became painfully apparent that more than one group of ritual murderers was at work in Mexico City.

"We would like to say, yes, Constanzo did them all, and poof, all those cases are solved," said Guillermo Ibarra, a prosecutor with the district attorney general's special investigations division, assigned to report on ritual crime in the capital. "And the fact is, we believe he was responsible for some of them, though we'll never prove it now. But he didn't commit all of those murders. Which means someone else did.

"Someone who is still out there."

For many in U.S. law enforcement, the Matamoros case demonstrated the need for more police expertise and training in the investigation of ritual crimes—an area in which U.S. police departments are dangerously inept. Authorities in Texas (as well as in Mexico) had no idea what they were looking at or who they were dealing with when they viewed the awful mutilations, cauldrons, and notebooks of Adolfo de Jesus Constanzo. This impeded their investigation and, arguably, allowed the gang to roam free longer than they might have.

Uninformed speculation by some lawmen that satanic worship and witchcraft had been employed at Rancho Santa Elena only confused the issue—and offended those who practice such religions in a legitimate and law-abiding way. As repugnant as the worship of Satan may be, the Constitution guarantees freedom of worship to satanists along with every other religious movement, so long as the religion hurts no one. And the satanists took a bum rap in the Matamoros case. Palo Mayombe is not satanism.

The dangers of such confusion are twofold. First, because of rampant and exaggerated publicity about the dangers of satanism, panic erupts when news of ritual crime breaks. In the Matamoros case, such fears led thousands of parents to keep children out of school, and may have led to the deliberate burning of a New Age church accused falsely of supporting satanism. Tabloid television shows like "Geraldo" and the so-called experts who appear on them irresponsibly spread this confusion, feeding off the panic.

At the same time, these "experts" attempt to fill the void in police training in ritual crime, spreading the disinformation further. As Kenneth Lanning, supervisor of the FBI's Behavioral Science Instruction and Research Unit, pointed out in a controversial post-Matamoros article, such experts have created "a growth industry," charging exorbitant speaking fees, then distributing to police grossly inaccurate books and manuals that misrepresent the facts of ritual crimes while making ludicrous assertions. These manuals declare, among other things, that rock music "is a carefully masterminded plan by none other than Satan himself."[3] Such is the state of much police training in the investigation of ritual crimes.

The second serious problem brought on by confusion about ritual crime is more insidious: lumping the evil magic Constanzo pursued with hysterical rantings about witchcraft, Satan worship, and rock music masks the real dangers posed by Constanzo's religion.

Palo Mayombe and deviant forms of Santeria are strange and alien to Anglo-Americans and, as such, they are easily dismissed. But an explosion of crimes involving these religions—drug dealing, grave robbing, extortion, and murder—has been reported nationwide. Following the Matamoros case, ngangas were found at crimes scenes from Florida to Philadelphia to Kentucky to Sacramento—confusing police and frightening the public.

National figures on the number of such crimes are unavailable; no one keeps track. News reports from 1989 alone reveal more than fifty such finds at crime scenes, mostly involving narcotics. A study by the Texas Department of Public Safety revealed that, from 1985 through April 1989, 226 cases of ritual crime were reported, mostly in South Texas near the border. Again, most of the crimes involved drugs, and most were related to Afro-Caribbean black magic, not satanism.

Even before Constanzo burst on the scene, the tide of violence attached to his religion had been on the rise. In early 1989, a month before the bodies turned up in Matamoros, two rival Miami drug gangs fought it out with both Palo Mayombe and bullets—until one was killed.

Juan Vera, a twenty-two-year-old Miami cocaine dealer, rip-off artist, and crack addict, was found shot to death on March 7, 1989, his bloated body stuffed into the trunk of an abandoned Cadillac. Vera had been no choirboy—a few weeks before his death, he had kidnapped a rival drug dealer, then burned him alive in order to steal four kilograms of coke from him.

The brutal murder led to a war between Vera and the victim's gang. Each side hired a palero to work magic against the other, leading to a mystical standoff of sorts. Finally, a shootout was needed to see whose magic was greater—who would be bulletproof, and who wouldn't be.

In the end, Vera may have been betrayed—his sorcerer, a brujo named Inelio, was a best friend and a follower of his rival's palero, El Pisa. In any case, Vera was not protected from his enemies' bullets. Nine of them found their mark—head, heart, and spine all were pierced, killing him quite thoroughly.

When Detective Mike Fisten searched Vera's home, he found an altar to Palo Mayombe in the laundry room, along with a statue of the trickster god Eleggua made from a coconut—a combination of Santeria and Palo Mayombe much like Constanzo's household altars.

Inside the coconut was a scorpion, dried blood, and a piece of stained paper with six names on it—a list of enemies Vera was dooming with a curse. This is a common means of asking an orisha to strike out at an enemy.

The men on the list, of course, were Vera's enemies—his killers. So in a way, Fisten said, Vera's magic actually worked. The dead drug dealer was able to reach out from the grave and lead police to his murderers with a curse. Some have been arrested and charged with murder; the others remain fugitives.

In this case, there had been no human sacrifice to the religion, but murder had been committed in response to a magical attack. As in the Matamoros case, magic and murder were directly linked.

"We see this kind of thing every day now," Fisten's boss, Sergeant Ken Singleton, said. "We have murder cases pending all the time in which black magic plays a role."

If the physical act of slaying an animal in order to curse and magically kill a human is acceptable, it is only one step removed from sacrificing a human directly, Singleton says. And the line, more and more, is being crossed.

Other cases abound. In 1986, a baby in Miami was found murdered, its tongue and eyelids cut off and offered to various orishas in what was clearly a warped Santeria or Palo Mayombe ceremony.

A year later, three people were found dead in the Miami River, tied and shot in the head, with a ritually sacrificed goat floating with them—"payment" to the orishas for the sacrifice of the human lives. Again, the crime bore the trademark of Afro-Caribbean worship.

The same year, in Fort Myers, Florida, a search of a drug-dealer's home and shrimp boat turned up an nganga with two human black male skulls that were not medical specimens and still had flesh attached, as well as human organs that had not been embalmed—suggesting they were not obtained through grave robbing, but through murder. Homicide could not be proven conclusively, however.

In 1988, a child pornography case investigated by the Port Authority in New Jersey uncovered an altar to Santeria to protect the illegal enterprise—along with a large container filled with human blood. Investigators suspected but could not prove that the blood came from one of the children in the porno movies, who disappeared shortly after appearing in the film. If so, it would have been a fatal draining of the child's blood. He was never found.

General Manuel Noriega of Panama relied upon Afro-Caribbean magic and curses to stay in power and to fuel his drug-trafficking exploits. He kept several witches on his payroll and one of his homes in Panama City was filled with altars and magical bundles. In fact, army investigators unfamiliar with the trappings of Candomble, Santeria, and Palo Mayombe mistakenly assumed they had found wrapped packages of cocaine when they stumbled on a series of magical bundles Noriega used to curse Presidents Reagan and Bush, as well as other enemies.

The basic tenets of Palo Mayombe in its most deviant form include a tradition of human sacrifice—Constanzo was not making it up as he went along. Modern-day human sacrifice by a palero was recorded as early as 1903, when a young girl was murdered in Palo Mayombe rites in Cuba.[4]

And now comes Rancho Santa Elena—the event Candice Leek and Rafael Martinez had been dreading for years. The two consultants on the Matamoros case, instructors for a nationally recognized ritual-crime training program at the University of North Florida's Institute for Police Technology and Management, came back from the ranch certain that Constanzo represented the wave of the future.

As Latin American immigration continues in the United States, the practice of these religions will grow, they say. Most of the new believers will be devout, law-abiding citizens. But the unique black-magic, amoral aspects of Palo Mayombe and Santeria will continue to attract criminals. The bizarre finds—and the links to drugs and violence—inevitably will rise.

"The question that consumes us now is, how many other paleros would take this step?" Martinez said. "How many already *have* taken this step?"

"There was always talk of Palo and Santeria being related to numerous murders, but I was always skeptical," Leek said. "I always said, 'If it's true, where's the bodies?' That's why we don't buy all these reports of satanic covens killing babies that you hear about on television. If you're a cop, you want hard evidence. You say, okay, where's the bodies?

"Well, now we have the bodies, fifteen of them, killed for Palo Mayombe. If it could happen near Brownsville, where no one has even heard of Palo Mayombe, it can happen anywhere."

Just as the memories of Rancho Santa Elena began to fade, just when the notion that ritual crime was banished from the border, FBI agents on a drug case in Brownsville made a strange discovery. While serving a search warrant on a suspected drug dealer's house in October 1989, they found a back room painted crimson red. Walls and ceiling were all the same blood-red color.

At one end of the room, a stinking refrigerator stood, filled with strange vials of blood and noxious fluids, each with a tiny piece of paper inside with names scrawled on them—curses and spells of control, cast on the people whose names were written. (These are common to Santeria and similar to items found in Noriega's home during the U.S. invasion in December 1989.)

At the other end of the room was an altar. On it were three stick figures, painted black, made from twigs, with pins sticking in them. Next to them were three blue, glass-encased votive candles with the words "Law Be Gone" written on each.

And at the center of the altar lay a black-and-white newspaper photograph of Comandante Juan Benitez Ayala of the Mexican federal Antinarcoticos, the man who broke Constanzo's gang. Through the center of the picture, someone had thrust a large hatpin, pinning it to the rough wooden altar. The suspects had fled and eluded arrest. The unnerved agents who found the altar left perplexed and worried, suddenly certain that the horror born at Rancho Santa Elena would never leave the border.

When Armando Ramirez at the DEA passed on the information about the altar to Benitez a few days later, the comandante laughed. But when he hung up the phone, Benitez called his curandero Eluterio to the office, and ordered him to perform a cleansing ceremony.

Just to be sure.

NOTES

CHAPTER 1

1. In the last three fiscal years, about 40 percent of all U.S. drug seizures near the southwest border occurred in South Texas, in the Rio Grande Valley—even though the valley contains less than a tenth of the 2,010 miles separating Mexico and the United States. To put this in perspective, in fiscal years 1986–88, 385 tons of marijuana, 30 tons of cocaine, and 338 pounds of heroin were seized along the entire southwest border. Seized tractor-trailer loads of marijuana and thousand-pound lots of cocaine have become commonplace in the Lower Rio Grande Valley, and because the amount seized is only a small fraction of the total amount smuggled, these seizures are an indicator of massive quantities of drugs moving through the area. Source: "Report to the Attorney General on Narcotics Trafficking, Southern District of Texas, July 1989." The report is contained in the four-volume *President's Report on Drug Trafficking*, released by the U.S. Justice Department, August 3, 1989.

2. This account is contained in affidavits filed with Mexican Judge Francisco Salvador Perez of Matamoros by the Mexican Federal Judicial Police. Mexican and DEA officials confirmed the account in interviews and provided additional details. Most press accounts of the incident misidentified the driver as Serafin's uncle, Elio Hernandez, or put the date at April 9, incorrectly suggesting Serafin's blunder led to the immediate discovery of bodies at the ranch that same day.

3. A note on Mexican names: Most last names are made up of the father's surname—Benitez—followed by the mother's maiden name—Ayala. This is the reversal of the (sometimes) Anglo tradition of using the mother's maiden name as a middle name. Thus, Comandante Juan Benitez Ayala

is referred to by his men as Comandante Benitez, not Comandante Ayala. (In fact, using the mother's maiden name in that fashion would constitute an insult, suggesting illegitimacy.)

4. Source: U.S. Drug Enforcement Administration, Brownsville, Texas.

5. State narcotics trafficking charges filed in Grimes County, Texas. Charges eventually were resolved through a plea agreement.

CHAPTER 2

1. Throughout this book, references to the Hernandez family are intended only to describe those directly involved with drug trafficking or Constanzo's religion: Serafin Senior and Junior, Elio, Ovidio, Saul, and Brigido. But there are two other Hernandez brothers who were never involved in the family's drug business or the cult, and therefore are not part of this story.

2. This account is drawn from a summary of the case filed in federal district court in Matamoros and from an interview with Comandante Benitez.

3. Benitez recounted tapping the Hernandez cellular phones in an interview. The Mexican court files, however, are silent on this point.

4. Numerous prisoners of Mexican custody have described this method of torture as a matter of routine, including U.S. DEA Agent Victor Cortez, who was arrested by Jalisco state police in Guadalajara, Mexico, in August 1986. A formal protest was filed with the Mexican government by the U.S. State Department in that case. Comandante Benitez, however, in an interview denied that his prisoners were abused in any way.

CHAPTER 3

1. Serafin's original confession is contained in the court file in Matamoros. He has since recanted it, claiming he was forced by torture into speaking against his will. There appears to be little doubt that he and other gang members were abused by police; several U.S. and Mexican officials have confirmed it. But at subsequent press conferences, Serafin confessed without any apparent coercion before more than one hundred U.S. journalists assembled at Benitez's offices. On April 14, he again repeated his story for a DEA videotape, also without apparent coercion. In any case, the information Serafin provided in the confessions proved to be accurate in terms of the members of the cult and the location, description, and cause of death of the cult's victims.

2. The account of the April 11 search of the ranch is drawn from a videotape of the event shot by Mexican federal agents, supplemented by the recollections of Sheriff's Detective Ernesto Flores, Comandante Juan Benitez Ayala, and U.S. Customs Resident Agent in Charge Oran Neck, and an untitled memo by Customs Agent Robert Gracia. In reporting these events, the author has sought to present the most accurate scenario drawn from these various sources. While most accounts are consistent, several key points have varied. Many press accounts incorrectly reported that all the arrested gang members were brought to the ranch to assist in the search. Further, in a press conference and in subsequent interviews, Customs RAC Oran Neck said he was present during the interrogation of Serafin Hernandez, that he personally broke the case by showing a photo of Mark Kilroy to the caretaker Domingo, and that he was present during all events at the ranch on April 11. These claims are contradicted by all other accounts.

3. According to Sheriff's Detective Ernesto Flores, and to prosecutors in Mexico City familiar with the tape. Comandante Benitez, however, denied physically abusing any of the cult suspects, although he admitted employing "moral pressure."

4. Sara denies having such a necklace. She said she had only a necklace of beads common in the practice of Santeria that Constanzo had given her.

CHAPTER 4

1. This account was provided by Maria del Rocio Cuevas Guerra, a longtime friend of the Constanzo family and a follower and former lover of Adolfo Constanzo. Constanzo's mother and brother, however, deny that they or Adolfo were involved with Santeria or Palo Mayombe. This assertion is undercut by all of Constanzo's followers, as well as former neighbors and the Miami police, who have evidence of the family's involvement in magical religions, including the discovery of an nganga in the home of Constanzo's mother.

2. From *Santeria: The Religion*, by Migene Gonzalez-Wippler (New York: Harmony Books, 1989).

3. Estimate provided by Rafael Martinez, anthropologist and law-enforcement consultant. Ernesto Pichardo, santero priest, estimates that there are 20,000 active priests of Santeria and about 2,000 priests of Palo Mayombe in Miami to cater to believers.

4. Gonzalez-Wippler, *Santeria: The Religion.*

5. The process of cultural adaptation that allows religions to survive by combining with others is called syncretism by sociologists. The phenomenon is common throughout history and is not limited to Afro-Caribbean religions. A similar process led imperial Rome to assimilate Greek religious beliefs (a largely identical pantheon of deities was shared by both cultures). Likewise, many European pagan rituals have survived in a guise of Christianity, notably the celebration of Christmas during the winter solstice and the character of Saint Nicholas, a Christian incarnation of an elfin nature spirit.

6. Information provided by Rafael Martinez.

7. "Brujeria: Manifestations of Palo Mayombe in South Florida," by Charles V. Wetli, M.D., and Rafael Martinez, M.A., *Journal of the Honda Medical Association,* August 1983. "Indeed, many santeros claim they have also been 'Rayado en Palo.' "

8. Account provided by Maria del Rocio Cuevas Guerra.

9. Ibid.

10. According to Comandante Juan Benitez Ayala, members of the Hernandez family, and Sara Aldrete. All sources agree that Constanzo was fanatical in his opposition to drug use by followers.

11. "River of Chickens: A Day with Metro's Santeria Patrol," *New Times* (Miami), March 7, 1990.

12. From "*Palo Mayombe,*" a September 1989 report of the Florida Department of Law Enforcement. "In Miami, where the probability of such [grave robbing] activity is higher, caretakers of cemeteries do not report such incidents for fear of adverse publicity. When the incident is not reported, the origin of the human bones and skull [used in Palo Mayombe] cannot be determined. There are also incidents other than grave desecrations which can be attributed to Palo Mayombe, such as late-night intruders and items being buried at or removed from a grave site."

13. Wetli and Martinez, "Brujeria."

14. Anecdote related by DEA Agent T. K. Solis and Rafael Martinez.

15. Figures provided by the Institute for Police Technology and Management, University of North Florida, Jacksonville; and Rafael Martinez. Although the Mariel boatlift refugees of 1980 have been branded as mostly criminals, only a minority were from Cuban prisons. Their immediate entry into criminal lives in the U.S. garnered massive publicity, overshadowing the fact that the vast majority of Marielitos have led law-

abiding, productive lives since emigrating—as have most of the 812,000 Cuban immigrants who came to the U.S. between 1959–1980.

16. Gonzalez-Wippler, *Santeria: The Religion.*

CHAPTER 5

1. Sara Aldrete recalled in an interview that Constanzo told her he learned to sacrifice animals as a child. Maria del Rocio Cuevas Guerra confirmed this, as did Mexican authorities investigating Constanzo's background. Finally, neighbors who knew Constanzo as a boy described the family's devotion to black magic, animal sacrifice, and living in filth.

2. According to Sara Aldrete. Constanzo's mother refused repeated requests for an interview, as did his brother, Fausto Rodriguez, who demanded unspecified cash payment before he would agree to speak at length.

3. Information supplied by Ernesto Pichardo, priest of Santeria in Miami; a former landlord of the family, Marisa Cobian; and in published interviews with numerous neighbors, among them, "Suspected Leader of Drug Cult Grew Up in a Santeria Family," Associated Press, April 12, 1989 (published in the *Brownsville Herald* on April 13, 1989).

4. Confirmation of this was provided by police and court files in Mexico City. While holed up in Mexico City, Constanzo told several of his followers that he had been schooled in magic in Puerto Rico, Haiti, and Miami.

5. The family may have practiced Catholicism, but this does not disprove its involvement with Santeria and Palo Mayombe. Many santeros and paleros are also practicing Christians—sometimes as a cover, sometimes through genuine belief. The two religions are not mutually exclusive in the minds of devotees, because one of the fundamental principles of Santeria is that all religions have power and worth.

6. This information was provided by Constanzo's mother, Delia Aurora Gonzalez del Valle, and Constanzo's brother, Fausto Rodriguez, in their only previously published interview, contained in a copyrighted report by Melinda Henneberger in the *Dallas Morning News,* May 14, 1989.

7. From the *Dallas Morning News* article, and confirmed in interviews by the author with Fausto Rodriguez. Court records show, however, that it was Delia's third husband, Joaquin de Posada, who filed for divorce in 1975, not Delia.

8. According to Maria del Rocio Cuevas Guerra. Police found an nganga at one of Delia's homes while she still occupied it.

9. According to Dade County Circuit Court and County Court records, criminal and civil. Among numerous cases, Dade County Circuit Court Criminal Case 89-3332 contains a fairly comprehensive criminal history; Cases 86-816, 85-4445, and 78-13614 fill in the gaps. Charges include shoplifting, armed assault, hot-check writing, vandalism, child abuse, and grand theft.

10. The above-cited cases often fail to take note of one another, with one charging Aurora del Valle with a crime, another charging Delia Aurora de Posada, and so on, treating the same person as an entirely new defendant—a first-time offender.

11. See Dade County Circuit Court Civil Case No. 86-41905, Dade County Civil Court Case No. 88-1347-CC-05, and Dade County Circuit Court Criminal Case No. 88-8043 for three examples.

12. Dade County Court Criminal Case No. 87-62193 and Metro Dade Police Department report 168903-4, April 18, 1987, by Officer Maria Elena Pla.

CHAPTER 6

1. The description of Constanzo's initiation into Palo Mayombe and his thoughts during the ceremony are based on statements by Sara Aldrete and Omar Orea Ochoa, and an interview with Maria del Rocio Cuevas Guerra, all of whom were initiated by Adolfo in ceremonies he said mirrored his own initiation. Details of the ceremony are inevitably speculative, owing to the absence of living witnesses, though they match witness descriptions of initiations Constanzo conducted for others, as well as scholarly descriptions of actual ceremonies. See Gonzalez-Wippler, *Santeria: The Religion* (New York: Harmony Books, 1989) for details.

2. *Dallas Morning News,* May 14, 1989.

3. From the statements to police of Sara Aldrete and Omar Orea Ochoa.

CHAPTER 7

1. From Omar Orea Ochoa's declarations in Mexican court and from his school notebooks, seized by police.

2. From a longtime building resident who, because of fears about her personal safety, asked to be identified only as Señora Sara. Much of her

information was corroborated by another building resident and Montes's former roommate, Victor Vizuett.

3. Omar's declarations in court give a brief account of how he met Constanzo. Sara Aldrete and the Mexican attorney general's office provided the details.

4. From the sworn declaration of Omar Francisco Orea Ochoa, filed in Mexican federal court in Mexico City.

5. From the declaration of Alfredo Quintana Rodriguez, Martin Quintana's younger brother.

6. From the notebook of Omar Francisco Orea Ochoa.

CHAPTER 8

1. According to Sara Aldrete, Omar Francisco Orea Ochoa, and Serafin Hernandez Garcia, as well as the families of Martin and Omar. Photographs of Omar, Martin, and Constanzo together in affectionate, sometimes sexually suggestive poses provide additional evidence of Constanzo's sexual orientation. His mother and brother, however, vehemently deny that Constanzo had any homosexual relations.

2. This account is drawn from statements by Omar and Sara Aldrete filed in Mexican federal court. Constanzo's sexual proclivities are as mysterious as everything else about the man. His family denies he was a homosexual, saying he impregnated a young girl when he was fourteen, and another woman when he was twenty—though the children that resulted from these unions and the women who bore them have never come forward to attest to this dubious honor. Constanzo's brother, Fausto, says he knew Omar and Martin well, and that neither was gay. But Omar and Sara both insist that Constanzo was bisexual, with a preference for men. Reams of gay pornography, much of it depicting violent, sadomasochistic sex between men, were found when Mexican police searched several of Constanzo's homes.

3. From court declarations of Alfredo Quintana Rodriguez, brother of Martin.

4. Ibid.

5. From the declarations of Omar Francisco Orea Ochoa, Sara Aldrete, and Teresa Quintana.

6. *Dallas Morning News*, May 14, 1989.

7. From court declarations of Omar Orea Ochoa, Sara Maria Aldrete Villareal, and filings by Mexican prosecutors. Constanzo's journals have entries referring to a client named simply as "Francisco." He was considered a Constanzo follower—primarily because he paid handsomely—but Francisco was never involved in any of the cult's crimes.

8. According to Maria del Rocio Cuevas Guerra.

9. This account was provided by Maria del Rocio Cuevas Guerra, a follower and former lover of Constanzo, charged with the Mexican crime of *encubrimiento*—coverup—in connection with Constanzo's murders. The story was corroborated by another follower of Constanzo's, Enrique Calzada, also charged with encubrimiento.

10. According to Maria del Rocio Cuevas Guerra and Sara Aldrete.

11. This is a standard practice in Palo Mayombe.

12. The authenticity of the initiations and other rites Constanzo performed in Mexico City and Matamoros is questionable—part of a continuing controversy over whether he was a genuine palero devoted to that religion's most evil side or a psychopathic charlatan who created his own religion, à la Jim Jones or Charles Manson. Many aspects of the ceremonial initiations he performed were exactly as prescribed by the religion. Yet even for a prodigy of magic, Constanzo was most likely too young and inexperienced to be a master of palo, capable of singlehandedly initiating new paleros, according to Ernesto Pichardo, priest of a Santeria church in Hialeah, Florida. Though his journals show Constanzo was very knowledgeable of his religion, it also seems clear he was ad-libbing many of his ceremonies—though this could have been out of showmanship or a lack of the proper implements rather than ignorance. The final argument used to brand Constanzo a fake is that mainstream Palo Mayombe does not involve human sacrifice, only the use of human remains obtained legally or, at worst, through grave robbing. However, there have been documented cases of murder for the purpose of obtaining a skull for an nganga—the death of a young girl in 1903 in Cuba being the most recent. The original religion practiced in Africa also endorsed human sacrifice. More recently, in the United States, numerous cases of killers using a combination of similar magic and gunplay to commit murder have cropped up in Miami, according to police.

CHAPTER 9

1. Some investigators have discounted the murder theory because of Constanzo's clear preference for male victims. Also, there was testimony

from some of the cult members that a witch named Mara, affiliated with Constanzo, had relocated to Guadalajara, though police efforts to locate her there have failed.

2. This ceremony took place in mid- to late 1984. Only minimal information is available on the conduct of the ceremonies to build Constanzo's first nganga, and the preceding paragraphs are speculative as to the details. The recreation is based in part on information from court statements by Omar, Jorge, and Sara, combined with the procedure most often used by paleros to create an nganga, as described in *Santeria: The Religion*, by Migene Gonzalez-Wippler (New York: Harmony Books, 1989).

3. For this same reason, paleros and santeros prefer Jewish to Christian cemeteries for working curses, believing the powers there to be greater.

4. Sara Aldrete, for example, says Constanzo first broached the subject of his witchcraft with her by claiming to be a "Santero Christiano."

5. Kadiempembe is an African figure of evil, and has no relationship to the Christian vision of Lucifer. Devotion to kadiempembe cannot be equated with satanism.

6. References by suspects to the nganga "drinking" blood and "eating" various body parts were strictly metaphorical, but they may have led to an initial misimpression that Constanzo and his followers committed acts of cannibalism. In fact, many paleros refuse to give their ngangas human blood for fear that the spirits inside will become vampires, sucking the life from all humans in the vicinity.

7. From the sworn testimony of Oscar Eduardo Athie in Mexican court.

8. From the court declaration, testimony, and an interview with Oscar Athie.

9. Oscar Athie testified in Mexican court that Constanzo was in the business of selling black-market foreign goods. Though his testimony remains uncontradicted, Athie is the only witness to make this statement. Police believe Constanzo was at most a dabbler in the black market, making most of his money from magic and drugs, not foreign goods. However, smuggling stereos and other appliances into the country, avoiding the heavy tariffs the Mexican government imposes on imported goods, is a multimillion-dollar industry, and if Constanzo was involved, the potential profits were enormous. Police never located the Satilite apartment Athie described.

10. In some interviews, including a May 10, 1989, Mexican television broadcast, Athie contradicted his sworn testimony in court by saying his only contact with Constanzo came in the form of being harassed and threatened for failing to take part in ceremonies. Yet his sworn statements in court clearly say he took part in harmless rituals.

11. Serrano and Palacios, like Athie, were named in court declarations by Constanzo's followers, who said the celebrities were clients only, and did not take part in any human sacrifices or other crimes. Serrano and Palacios were interrogated by Mexican police and denied any involvement.

12. More than twenty pages of Constanzo's journals were ripped out by Mexican authorities before the documents were photocopied and turned over to the DEA, which supplied copies to the author. Presumedly, the pages contained additional names of clients and followers deemed too sensitive to make public.

13. Omar Orea Ochoa, Sara Aldrete, and Constanzo's brother, Fausto Rodriguez, all have named Ventura as a client of Constanzo's. Assistant Attorney General Federico Ponce Rojas of the Federal District of Mexico said circumstantial evidence suggests this relationship was two-way, with Ventura providing information to his padrino. However, DEA agents stationed in Mexico who worked closely with Ventura for years find the allegations difficult to believe, though they have no way to disprove them.

14. According to DEA investigators.

15. This account of Montes's meeting with Salvador Vidal Garcia was provided by Federico Ponce Rojas and Guillermo Ibarra R., prosecutors with the *Procuraduria General de Justicia* (Attorney General) for the Federal District of Mexico, Mexico City, who interrogated and arrested Salvador Vidal Garcia.

16. Copies of the notebook, seized by police, document Constanzo's sessions with Salvador.

17. This account of Constanzo's performance for Salvador was provided by Assistant District Attorney Generals Ponce and Ibarra.

18. Constanzo's journals provide few clues to the identities of alleged traffickers, using only first names: Jose, Rafael, Francisco. Spells meant to protect these and other individuals from jail and the police are recorded in the books, however, offering a clue to the business of the clients. Based on his interrogations of Constanzo's followers, Assistant District Attorney General Federico Ponce estimated Constanzo had six to eight traffickers

as clients for his magic, possibly more (not counting the Hernandez family).

CHAPTER 10

1. From court records and interviews with Assistant District Attorney Generals Federico Ponce and Abraham Polo Uscanga for the Federal District of Mexico.

2. These are U.S. Drug Enforcement Administration estimates, though their value is suspect. According to the General Accounting Office, such estimates are impossible to make accurately, because the actual quantity of cocaine entering the country is not known—only the amount seized is. The DEA has arbitrarily decided that the amount of cocaine entering the country is ten times the amount seized by lawmen, but there are no data to back this assertion, according to GAO.

3. According to Assistant District Attorney Generals Federico Ponce and Guillermo Ibarra.

4. Constanzo's ambivalence about his youth was related in interviews with Sara Aldrete and Maria del Rocio Cuevas Guerra.

5. The details of this encounter with Calzada were provided by Mexican prosecutors.

6. From an interview with Sara Aldrete.

7. From court declarations of Omar Orea Ochoa, Sara Aldrete, and Maria del Rocio Cuevas Guerra.

8. From court declarations of Sara Aldrete.

9. From Ponce and Ibarra.

10. From court declarations of Sara Aldrete, Omar Orea Ochoa, and case reports filed by Mexican prosecutors. The allegedly corrupt comandante in Monterrey was identified by both Sara and Omar, but Mexican prosecutors discounted the allegations for lack of supporting evidence. The charges have not hurt the man's career. In October 1989, he was promoted and transferred to Mexico City.

11. From the court declarations of Omar Orea Ochoa, Sara Aldrete, and Teresa Quintana and Mexican police who interrogated Sara. The followers' statements regarding Constanzo's decision to commit his first murders are based on conversations they had with Constanzo and Martin regarding the Calzada incident.

12. According to Sara and Omar, the second follower was allegedly Salvador Vidal Garcia. However, he has denied being present and has never been charged in any cult murder—just drug trafficking.

13. This account is drawn from court declarations by Sara Aldrete and Omar Orea Ochoa, from files provided by Assistant Attorney General Abraham Polo Uscanga of the Federal District of Mexico, and from interviews with the attorney general's spokesman, Octavio Campos, and the federal comandante in Matamoros, Juan Benitez Ayala. These sources implicate Constanzo, Martin, and Salvador Vidal in the Calzada killings. Criminal charges in the case have not been filed and, according to officials, probably never will be because of insufficient evidence. In particular, Salvador has not been charged with any violent crimes, only drug trafficking. Police, however, consider the Calzada case solved. According to Benitez, as many as six other federal agents—comrades and subordinates of Salvador's—were suspected of taking part in the case as well, either through bribery to keep silent or in a more active role in the murders. Again, evidence was too scant to prosecute.

14. From Omar Orea Ochoa's court declarations.

CHAPTER 11

1. Perez's record and affiliation with Matamoros mob figures are discussed at length in United States of America v. 235 Haggar Street, Case b89-257M, Southern District of Texas, Brownsville Division.

2. This account, including dialogue, was provided by Sara Aldrete in an interview.

3. This account was provided by Sara Aldrete.

4. This is a genuine tenet of the religion.

5. Account provided by Sara Aldrete.

6. Ibid.

7. Ibid.

8. According to Mexican federal district prosecutors, based on interrogations of suspects and witnesses. In an interview, Sara corroborated some of this chicanery, though she still maintained that Constanzo possessed magical or psychic powers.

NOTES

CHAPTER 12

1. Preceding paragraphs are drawn from interviews with Jim Lemons and Anthony Zavaleta, teachers at Texas Southmost; Patty Galvan, friend and fellow office worker of Sara's; and other students at the college.

2. In an August 7, 1989, interview in Mexico City.

3. The letter is included in Sara's court files in Mexico City, seized with Constanzo's journals and other papers. Sara denies writing it.

4. From Sara's teacher and employer in the athletic department, Coach Jim Lemons.

5. Sara and Delia, in the latter's interview with the *Dallas Morning News*, shared similar recollections of this conversation.

6. From an interview with Sara Aldrete.

7. Sara's confessions recount many of Constanzo's drug deals and meetings with Matamoros mob figures.

8. Though in initial confessions to Mexican police Sara said she was Adolfo's lover, she later denied ever having sex with Constanzo, though all the other followers of El Padrino, as well as the police of both nations, say otherwise. Sara has maintained throughout that Constanzo was merely using their relationship for his own ends, and that his professed ardor for her probably was insincere.

9. Only Sara says Adolfo's business was unknown to her. Other cult members, U.S. and Mexican police, and Sara herself—in her original confession—maintain that she had knowledge of Constanzo's border drug dealings and at least some of the killings from the beginning. Sara later repudiated her confession, alleging it was obtained under torture. However, in those confessions, she described in detail several drug deals that were independently corroborated by investigators. She also recalled that the "business dinners" she attended with Constanzo were with Matamoros gangsters, and that the dinner conversation consisted largely of drug negotiations.

10. Constanzo's familiarity with the gay community of Brownsville was disclosed by a member of that community, who spoke on condition he remain anonymous. Sara confirmed in police statements and in an interview that Constanzo frequented gay haunts there.

11. From an August 1989 interview with Sara Aldrete.

CHAPTER 13

1. As alleged in affidavits filed in U.S. District Court in Brownsville by the Drug Enforcement Administration in USA v. 235 Haggar Street, Case No. B89-257M, U.S. District Court, Southern District of Texas, Brownsville Division. The affidavits link the Juan Garcia Abrego organization to extensive drug trafficking and several murders.

2. The affidavits filed in B89-257M say, in part, that "the five million dollars [found in Perez's desk] is but a minor amount compared to the quantities of marijuana and cocaine seized and sold by ex-Comandante Perez in Matamoros during his eight-month assignment."

3. This information was supplied by DEA Agent T. K. Solis, based on his interrogations of Serafin Hernandez Rivera and Serafin Hernandez Garcia, as well as the in-law of the Hernandez family known as El Gancho. In a separate interview, El Gancho confirmed portions of this account.

4. This information was supplied by DEA Agent T. K. Solis, Cameron County Sheriff's Detective Ernesto Flores, and Comandante Juan Benitez, and confirmed by sworn statements by Sara Aldrete and, in part, Salvador Vidal Garcia. However, none of the reputed Matamoros crime figures has been charged with any crimes directly tied to Constanzo or his gang.

5. Some accounts of the shooting say the gunfire came from inside Piedras Negras, based on the spray of window glass on the sidewalk, as if it had been shot out from inside. Either way, Saul is still believed to be an unintended victim. The specific motive for the shooting of Morlet, and the identity of the shooter, has never been established with certainty. DEA officials believe Morlet was moving drugs through the area without permission from established crime figures. The meeting at Piedras Negras may have been set up to resolve that issue; the shooting suggests Morlet failed to appease his enemies.

6. According to Sara Aldrete, Comandante Juan Benitez Ayala, and DEA Agent T. K. Solis. Perez, a fugitive, has not spoken to this issue.

7. In her original court declarations, Sara Aldrete named Juan Ñ. Guerra and Juan Garcia Abrego, the alleged mob bosses of Matamoros, as having dealings with Salvador Vidal Garcia and, by extension, Constanzo. DEA investigators T. K. Solis and Armando Ramirez have asserted that Constanzo was brought into Matamoros, or at least tolerated, in order to weed out upstart traffickers.

8. Sara, Omar, and Elio, in their original statements to police, provided similar accounts of the events leading up to Sara's initiation (the details in the preceding passage were based primarily on an interview with Sara). However, in later statements in court and in interviews, Sara has contradicted herself, maintaining that she refused to renounce Catholicism and Constanzo therefore refused to initiate her into Palo. Instead, she claims, he performed only a cleansing of her to protect her from malevolent spirits during Elio's subsequent initiation. She claims she pretended to be a palera and a madrina in order to sway Elio and to provide a good show. Still, Sara's description of this supposed cleansing actually adheres more closely to the ritual of rayado—initiation in Palo Mayombe.

9. The account of Sara's rayado is drawn from sworn statements by Omar, Elio, Sara, and Salvador, as well as an interview with Sara Aldrete. See previous note.

CHAPTER 14

1. Elio's initiation is based primarily on statements by Sara Aldrete. Elio's court statements provided only basics on the ceremony—day, place, a few details. What little he did describe matches Sara's more vivid recollections.

2. This account of Constanzo's means of attracting followers was pieced together from statements by Sara Aldrete, Alvaro de Leon, Elio and Serafin Hernandez, Omar Orea Ochoa, and from information supplied by the Mexican attorney general's office for the Federal District of Mexico.

3. From Sara Aldrete's original Mexican court declaration.

4. Ibid.

5. According to Comandante Juan Benitez Ayala.

6. Account provided by the attorney general's office for the Federal District of Mexico.

7. From confession of Elio Hernandez and statements by Sara Aldrete.

8. Although DEA and Mexican federal investigators have concluded Castillo and de la Fuente were involved in a low-level drug deal when they encountered Constanzo, there have been conflicting statements. Early in the case, Mexican Comandante Juan Benitez Ayala theorized that Castillo may have been targeted by the cult simply because he accidentally witnessed a drug transaction, then had to be silenced. Castillo's

family has denied he was involved with drug traffickers. He has no prior criminal record.

CHAPTER 15

1. From Serafin Hernandez Garcia's videotaped confession to the DEA.

2. As related by DEA Agent T. K. Solis, who interrogated Old Serafin.

3. U.S. law-enforcement officials estimated that the gang, at its zenith, was moving up to a ton of marijuana a week.

4. Alvaro de Leon confessed to this killing, according to documents filed in court in Mexico City. He has not, however, been officially charged in the killing.

5. Information provided by the Drug Enforcement Administration.

6. From the sworn declarations of Sara Aldrete.

7. According to documents filed in court in Mexico City by the Mexican attorney general for the federal district.

8. According to their confessions to police and sworn declarations in court, Omar and Jorge were not aware of Constanzo's plans for Ramon Paz Esquivel when they set out that night.

9. As recounted by Sara Aldrete and Omar Orea Ochoa in police confessions. Sara claims to have stayed behind that night. She is charged only with covering up the crime, not with participating.

10. According to Mexican prosecutors.

11. According to statements by Omar, Sara, and charges filed by Mexican prosecutors.

12. In her statements to police, Teresa Quintana described her brother Martin's nonviolent nature, but his willingness to behave counter to it to please Constanzo.

13. From the sworn statements of Omar, Sara, and from police investigators. Fragosa denied complicity in the killings, though, according to Mexican authorities, he admitted his presence during the murder of La Claudia as Constanzo's assistant.

14. As described in sworn declarations of Omar, Juan Carlos, and Sara Aldrete.

15. According to Carlos Padilla Torres, one of the investigators on the case.

NOTES

CHAPTER 16

1. Accounts of this random choice of victims were provided in the videotaped confession of Little Serafin and in sworn declarations by all of the gang members captured in Matamoros.

2. From the sworn statements of Sara Aldrete, filed in federal court in Mexico City.

3. El Gancho is now a cooperating witness for the U.S. Drug Enforcement Administration in numerous criminal cases. He was interviewed by the author. Because his life has been threatened, his location has been kept secret and he is living under an alias. His true name is being withheld here for his protection, at his and DEA's request.

4. From prosecution summaries and the sworn statements of Omar Francisco Orea Ochoa and Alvaro de Leon, alias El Duby, filed in federal court in Mexico City.

5. As recounted by El Duby, El Gancho, and DEA.

6. According to DEA Agent T. K. Solis and El Gancho.

7. The plan was conceived when the exchange rate hovered around 170 pesos to the dollar. As of summer 1989, the exchange rate was 2,500 pesos to the dollar and climbing. The collapse of world oil prices and the drastic devaluations of the peso that followed in the 1980s shattered the Mexican—and border—economy. Amigoland became an unsupportable luxury in an economy struggling to survive.

8. Account provided by the DEA and through an interview with El Gancho.

9. Albert Caesar Tocco was arrested in January 1989 by the FBI on a 48-count federal racketeering indictment.

10. Charges filed in U.S. District Court in McAllen, Texas, and detailed in "Jaramillo thought to be linked with Chicago mob boss," a copyrighted story by Lisa Baker of the *Brownsville Herald*, July 18, 1989.

11. As recounted by El Gancho in an interview, confirmed by DEA Agent T. K. Solis.

12. Investigators pieced together an account of the kidnapping and those involved over the course of a year, eventually naming El Gancho, McCoy, and Habiniak as the kidnappers while in the employ of Manuel Jaramillo, according to testimony in U.S. District Court in Corpus Christi (U.S. v.

Habiniak, Cases C-88-313, C-88-257, and C-88-239-m); and the Brownsville Police Department.

13. From transcripts of cellular-phone conversations monitored by police, filed in Cameron County District Court Case 88-09-48-16-c, an action by prosecutors to seize Ovidio's pickup truck as the profit of illegal drug sales.

14. This account is contained in sworn affidavits filed in court by Old Serafin and Elio Hernandez. Later, according to police, the pair admitted that the kidnapping was the result of a botched drug deal, and the two men allegedly implicated El Gancho, McCoy, and Jaramillo.

15. According to DEA accounts of the kidnapping.

16. Ibid.

17. From the confession of Elio Hernandez, filed in Mexican federal court in Matamoros.

18. According to Sara's statement to the Mexican police, Constanzo sodomized most of his victims just before killing them.

19. From Serafin Hernandez Garcia's videotaped confession to the DEA, and Alvaro (El Duby) de Leon Valdez's confessions to Mexican police.

20. According to Elio and Sara, Constanzo always asked for guidance from the devil figure of Palo Mayombe before a human sacrifice.

21. This version of events is according to the Brownsville Police Department and Sheriff's Lieutenant George Gavito. Elio and Serafin, however, filed in court sworn affidavits claiming they made no such admissions. Elio also swore that the city policeman who interrogated him, Lt. Victor Rodriguez, threatened and hit him softly with a rubber hose, attempting to intimidate him into admitting he was a drug dealer. Elio took pains, however, to say Gavito did not take part in this alleged abuse.

CHAPTER 17

1. According to Perez's successor, Comandante Juan Benitez Ayala.

2. As described in autopsy reports.

3. According to Sara Aldrete, Joaquin Manzo was an *ahijado*—a godson—of Constanzo.

4. According to Sara Aldrete, Salvador sent his assistants to be killed. Salvador denies involvement in the killings. He has not been charged with any murder.

5. A preferred method of sacrifice, according to Sara Aldrete.

6. According to Cameron County Sheriff's Detective Ernesto Flores, based on statements by informants.

7. Because Jose fears retaliation from fugitive cult members or their relatives, he asked to remain anonymous.

8. According to statements to police by Sara, Elio, and Little Serafin. However, in subsequent interviews, Sara denied ever sleeping with Elio.

9. From an interview with Maria del Rocio Cuevas Guerra, aka Karla.

10. Both Sara and Maria del Rocio attested to their enmity in separate interviews, each blaming the other for the onset of ill feelings.

11. According to Sara Aldrete, Ovidio's ceremony occurred in the Calle Pomona condo in October 1988; other gang members say December.

12. He was, in fact, successful at this. Neither of their immediate families was implicated in any wrongdoing in either Mexico or the United States.

13. From the confession of Elio Hernandez, filed in Mexican federal court in Matamoros.

14. Ibid.

15. From the confessions of Elio and Little Serafin Hernandez.

16. The account of Elio and Ovidio's meeting with El Chequel and the subsequent kidnappings was assembled from statements to police by Elio and Little Serafin Hernandez, filings in Mexican federal court, information provided by Comandante Juan Benitez Ayala, and accounts of the actual abduction at Rancho Caracol provided by police, relatives, and witnesses.

17. From statements of Elio, Little Serafin, Comandante Benitez, and autopsy reports filed in Mexican federal court in Matamoros.

18. From the confession of Little Serafin and court statements of various gang members.

19. The account of the slaying of Jose Luis Garcia Luna is drawn from statements by Elio Hernandez, Little Serafin Hernandez, Alvaro de Leon, and Sara Aldrete, combined with information supplied by Comandante Juan Benitez Ayala.

20. From an interview with Herlinda Luna de Garcia.

NOTES

CHAPTER 18

1. From the confession of Serafin Hernandez Garcia.

2. According to DEA investigators.

3. This insight into Constanzo's motivations is based on the observations of Sara Aldrete and on a psychological assessment of Constanzo by U.S. authorities. It is, of course, speculative. However, it fits observed patterns in other cases of serial and ritual violent crime.

4. According to Sara Aldrete, Constanzo's predilection for violence, rape, and murder grew to an obsession toward the end of his days in Matamoros, finally raging out of control. According to her sworn statements filed in court in Mexico City, "Adolfo was violent, bloodthirsty, impulsive, schizophrenic, epileptic, and enjoyed the suffering of others." Her reference to epilepsy is metaphorical, a comment on his convulsive rages.

5. This account was provided in the confessions of Elio and Little Serafin.

6. According to gang members, they were out trolling the bars for potential victims that night.

7. Little Serafin, in his videotaped confession, recalled informing Sara of the kidnapping. He also indicated she had knowledge of most of the group's activities and several of the murders. Sara denied knowing anything about Mark Kilroy or the other kidnappings and murders.

8. From the statements of Alvaro de Leon at a Mexico City press conference.

CHAPTER 19

1. Sara Aldrete claims she helped post fliers after Kilroy disappeared because she felt sympathy for his parents. She contends this proves she had nothing to do with the killing. Other members of the cult, however, said she knew about the Kilroy kidnapping, though they agreed she was not present when he was killed.

2. According to Sara Aldrete.

CHAPTER 20

1. This account is drawn from statements by Elio and Little Serafin Hernandez, and the Mexican authorities. Sara, however, denies knowing what would happen to Gilberto, claiming she did not participate in his

kidnapping or go to the ranch for his murder. She said that Gilberto was headed for her house, but never showed up. Only later did she learn that cult members had snatched him at Constanzo's orders, Sara said.

2. From Serafin Hernandez Garcia's sworn statement to police, and videotaped interview with DEA Agent T. K. Solis.

3. According to Comandante Juan Benitez Ayala.

4. According to Cameron County Sheriff's Detective Ernesto Flores, confirmed by the DEA.

5. From the statements of Little Serafin and Alvaro de Leon Valdez. Alvaro further speculated that Victor may have been motivated less by vengeance and more by profit; he suggested Victor had been hired to kill him. Mexican authorities have not determined if Victor was paid or not.

6. According to the sworn statements of Little Serafin and El Duby.

7. This account of the abduction of Victor Saul Sauceda is contained in a videotaped confession by Serafin Hernandez Garcia, recorded by DEA Agent T. K. Solis. It is corroborated by several other gang members in their sworn statements.

8. According to Serafin Hernandez Garcia's account, Sara Aldrete, the cult's alleged godmother, was present at the killing of Victor Saul Sauceda and had knowledge of other sacrifices as well. But Serafin and other gang members also testified that Sara never actually committed any acts of violence, though she allegedly lured one or more victims into the gang's clutches. Sara has consistently denied taking part in or being present at any killings, claiming she first heard about them through news reports on television.

9. From the videotaped confession of Serafin Hernandez Garcia, and statements to Mexican authorities by Alvaro de Leon, alias El Duby.

10. From Sara Aldrete's sworn statements to police.

11. Ibid.

12. Information provided by DEA Agent Armando Ramirez.

13. From the *Houston Post*, May 10, 1989, quoting Delia Aurora del Valle.

14. Sara did travel to Mexico City alone, seemingly contradicting her contention that she was brought from Matamoros against her will and held captive there.

NOTES

CHAPTER 21

1. Federal studies have pinpointed drug trafficking, as opposed to legitimate capital flight from Mexico, as a principal source of this cash surplus. According to the "Report to the Attorney General on Narcotics Trafficking, Southern District of Texas, July 1989": "Federal Reserve analysis indicates a 1.6 billion dollar cash surplus in the banks serviced by the San Antonio District of the Federal Reserve. Eighty-eight percent of this surplus is in banks within fifteen miles of the Mexican border in the Rio Grande Valley. . . . This is particularly interesting in view of the rural nature of this area and the depressed state of its economy. . . . Cases initiated in this District have identified extensive use of financial institutions to launder and invest drug trafficking proceeds." The report is contained in the four-volume *President's Report on Drug Trafficking*, released by the U.S. Justice Department, August 3, 1989.

2. Poor relations between DEA and Customs in Brownsville were exacerbated by the cult case, but the rivalry existed long before. In some cases, cooperation is unavoidable. When Customs agents arrest traffickers in the act of crossing the border with drugs—Customs' primary "interdiction" mission—the case often is handed over to DEA so the suspects' activities in the United States can be probed. But in most Brownsville narcotics investigations, Customs works with the sheriff's department, while DEA works with every other agency except the sheriff and Customs. This split alliance has created its own institutional absurdities: The largest law-enforcement agency in town—the Cameron County Sheriff's Department—has not joined the Cameron County Drug Enforcement Task Force, a DEA-sponsored effort to unite local police departments in the War on Drugs. And Customs, a federal agency, obtains many of its search-and-arrest warrants from Cameron County courts rather than U.S. District Court, where relations with prosecutors also are poor.

3. Internal U.S. Justice Department memoranda identify the Cameron County Sheriff's Department and U.S. Customs Service officials in Brownsville as targets of several investigations. From an April 29, 1989, memo to Henry K. Oncken, then U.S. Attorney for the Southern District of Texas from Assistant U.S. Attorney John Crews: "The Brownsville area of Customs . . . both the office of enforcement [where Neck works] and Inspections [the bridge people] have been well compromised. Both are the targets of several different investigations. Neither are trusted with sensitive information. There is information to suggest that evidence in a major [racketeering] case being run by Customs Corpus Christi agents Louis Smit and John Graham and which is related to the killings in

Mexico was destroyed or rendered useless by Customs Enforcement Office in Brownsville. . . . The FBI is preparing to launch an extremely important operation including a wiretap and has made it plain that the operation will be run in McAllen. The reason is to insure that *no one* in [Brownsville] Customs has *any* access to the information. That is the reputation that office enjoys in the valley federal law enforcement community." In an interview, Neck dismissed the memo as a lie, and Crews as a vindictive prosecutor who harbored a grudge against him.

The memo went on to criticize the Cameron County Sheriff's Office and Customs in Brownsville of endangering the cult investigation with premature press releases.

Suspicions were further stoked during the cult case when Sheriff Alex Perez and his lieutenant, George Gavito, took the curious position of publicly defending reputed Matamoros mobsters. They were responding to a San Antonio newspaper's claims (*San Antonio Light*, April 15, 1989) of a possible link between the son of alleged kingpin Juan Ñ. Guerra and the ranch used by Adolfo Constanzo's cult. The sheriff was quoted in the newspaper as saying Guerra's son, Juanito, had telephoned him angrily to complain about the article and to deny any connection to the cult or its ranch. Then, offering some good-character testimony, the sheriff of Cameron County revealed that he had telephoned Guerra a month earlier to ask him for help in the search for Mark Kilroy.

"Juan Ñ. Guerra cooperated in the investigation more than some of the police officers," Gavito confirmed in the article. "In fact, he assisted us in the search for Mark Kilroy and had people working."

The claims of the connection to the ranch were untrue. The son, Juanito Guerra, filed a libel suit against the newspaper, and the paper settled the suit for $20,000. No charges were ever filed in Mexico linking either of the Guerras to Constanzo or the ranch.

4. This is according to Assistant U.S. Attorney John Crews and DEA Agent Armando Ramirez. Customs officials have also attested to the bad feelings generated by DEA's dominance of the task force. Neck was quoted in a November 12, 1989, news article by *San Antonio Light* reporter Lisa Baker as saying, "DEA just took it [the cult case] and ran with it. . . . I was not totally satisfied, but those decisions were above me." Neck's friend and colleague, Marvin Milner, Resident Agent in Charge of the Corpus Christ Customs office, was quoted by Baker as saying, "For DEA to come in johnny-come-lately—a lot of people are upset about that." Neck confirmed in an interview that he was upset by the decision, but said he was trying to forget it in the interest of good relations with DEA.

5. As recounted by both Comandante Benitez and Armando Ramirez.

6. Oran Neck was quoted by Knight-Ridder Newspapers on April 14, 1989, from an April 13 interview: "We're looking in Texas and in the Miami, Florida, area." Television news reports carried the same information. In an interview, however, Neck denied that investigators ever really believed that the gang was headed to Miami. Therefore, he argued, his statements to the press were harmless.

7. According to DEA's Brownsville Resident Agent in Charge Armando Ramirez, and statements by Sara Aldrete and other witnesses in Mexico City, Constanzo apparently avoided a DEA trap by listening to news reports quoting Neck and Gavito as sources.

8. According to Comandante Juan Benitez Ayala, DEA Agent Armando Ramirez, and Assistant U.S. Attorney John Crews.

9. From an April 27, 1989, DEA memorandum to Marion Hambrick, DEA Special Agent in Charge-Houston, and Ken Miley, DEA Resident Agent in Charge-McAllen, from Armando Ramirez, DEA Brownsville.

10. This account is drawn from Ramirez's April 27 memo to his superiors, and an independent account provided by Assistant U.S. Attorney John Crews, who had general supervision of the entire task force. However, their account is disputed by Customs. An undated, untitled memo from Brownsville Customs Agent Robert Gracia, outlining the cult case, says that the questioning of El Gancho was done with Ramirez's permission.

11. The April 27, 1989, memo. The memo goes on to accuse Customs agents in Brownsville of impeding the cult investigation by lying, hiding informants, and speaking to the press against DEA orders. Oran Neck denied the allegations in an interview, calling the El Gancho incident a misunderstanding.

12. According to Armando Ramirez and John Crews.

13. Account provided by T. K. Solis and Armando Ramirez, and detailed in Ramirez's April 27 memo to superiors.

14. According to Ramirez, Solis, and Crews, and confirmed by a series of memoranda between the DEA and Customs. Oran Neck later claimed he was forced off the case by Ramirez and Crews, and that he would have continued cooperating as long as he was welcome. He said DEA made it clear his assistance was not welcome—something Ramirez disputes. Neck also criticized DEA for pressuring to take over the case, then failing to avidly pursue the fugitives.

CHAPTER 22

1. According to DEA and Cameron County Sheriff's Department officials, local authorities in Matamoros may have withheld evidence regarding Duby's shootout at Los Sombreros and covered up evidence of Constanzo's and the Hernandez family's connections to Matamoros narcotics traffickers. Comandante Benitez, however, noted that these allegations were mere suspicions that have never been the subject of formal criminal charges. Representatives of the local and state police in Matamoros denied impeding any aspect of the cult investigation.

2. This account was pieced together from separate descriptions of the incident by Comandante Juan Benitez Ayala, DEA Agent T. K. Solis, and several other law-enforcement sources.

3. No human infant remains related to the cult were ever uncovered, nor did any cult member admit to such a killing. Authorities have no explanation for the children's shoes at the ranch, or the clothing and pictures at Sara's house. Sara denied putting them in her apartment, suggesting instead that the police planted them there to stoke public sentiment against her.

4. According to Sheriff's Detective Ernesto Flores and cult experts Candice Leek and Rafael Martinez, who consulted on the case. Gang members denied killing any children other than Jose Luis Garcia Luna, though Little Serafin spoke of another sixteen-year-old murdered by the gang. No bodies of sixteen-year-olds were found.

5. From the statements to police in Matamoros by Elio and Little Serafin Hernandez, and in Mexico City by Sara Aldrete.

6. "Suspect Leads Police to 13th Body," by the Associated Press, April 14, 1989, *Orange County Register* and elsewhere.

7. "Greed, Not Cultism, Blamed in Killings," by Knight-Ridder Newspapers, April 14, 1989, *Orange County Register* and elsewhere.

8. From an interview with Israel and Teresa Aldrete.

CHAPTER 23

1. According to Sara's family and Sara's original statements to police. Later, however, Sara claimed that she thought she was taking a vacation in Acapulco with her friends when she flew from McAllen, unaware that they were fugitives. Sara's later statements are contradicted not only by her parents and original statements to police but by other cult members

and the fact that she packed no bags for this alleged vacation. The discrepancy is crucial because Sara's defense against criminal charges is based largely on her claim that Adolfo and the others kidnapped her, forcing her to stay in Mexico City against her will once she had learned from television news reports that they all were fugitives.

2. From the sworn statements of Sara Aldrete and Teresa Quintana Rodriguez.

3. According to Sara, this is the moment she first learned of the cult killings. In her version of events—markedly different from other gang members—Constanzo then gave her a detailed account of the gang's murders and drug trafficking.

4. From the statements of Sara Aldrete, Alvaro de Leon, Omar Orea Ochoa, Maria del Rocio Cuevas Guerra, and court files.

5. From the sworn statement of Teresa Quintana Rodriguez. Salvador has denied this meeting took place.

6. Ibid.

7. Ibid.

8. This account is drawn largely from statements by Teresa Quintana. She had denied any knowledge of the cult's criminal activity, though initially, Comandante Benitez accused her of heavy involvement. Later, authorities backed down from those statements, saying they believed her innocent. She was never charged with any crimes in Mexico or the United States.

9. In court declarations, Salvador denied aiding Constanzo, although he admitted meeting with him in April, without specifying the date. He admitted going to Guadalajara, where he was arrested. Sara and Omar swore they went to Salvador's apartment after leaving the Jalapa condo.

10. Sara claims Constanzo has a grandmother in Monterrey, but this could not be corroborated.

11. Salvador told police he did not know how Constanzo obtained his firearms.

12. From sworn statements of Sara Maria Aldrete Villareal.

13. From the declarations of Maria de Lourdes Bueno Lopez.

14. From an interview with Sara Aldrete.

15. Just such a case was widely reported in the Mexican media in January 1990. Five drunken policemen tried to extort a group of Mexican jour-

nalists. When the reporters refused, they began to pistol whip one of the men. As they struck him with the butt of a handgun, it went off, killing a woman reporter in the group, Elvira Marcelo Esquivel. Three men eventually were arrested and confessed to the crime. The surviving victims said none of the men was involved, but the authorities accepted the convictions. This case—and another involving the Mexican drug czar's bodyguards—both surfaced in early 1990, at a time when the government of Mexico was complaining about a television series called "Drug Wars," based on the Camarena case. Mexican officials complained that the series falsely accused the Mexican police of widespread corruption. Yet a poll by the newspaper *El Nacional* of Mexico City found 76 percent of the capital's residents had no confidence in the 25,000-man police force.

16. From the sworn statement of Maria de Lourdes Bueno Lopez.

CHAPTER 24

1. "2 Ex-Officials in Mexico Indicted in Camarena Murder," by Henry Weinstein, *Los Angeles Times*, February 1, 1990.

2. "Rape Case in Mexico Fuels Outrage at Police," by Larry Rohter, *New York Times* (national edition), January 1, 1990.

3. From an interview with Deputy District Attorney Federico Ponce Rojas of the Procuraduria General of the Federal District of Mexico.

4. No human remains were found during the searches of Constanzo's Mexico City abodes.

5. From Rafael Martinez, law-enforcement consultant to the DEA task force and expert in Afro-Caribbean religions. Constanzo did not take the nganga with him; its whereabouts are unknown.

6. Information provided by District Attorney Federico Ponce and Mexican press accounts. Federal authorities in Mexico City confirmed their search of the Zona Rosa, but denied abusing any suspects or witnesses.

7. Copies of the two books were obtained by the DEA from Benitez and provided to the author. A copy of the journals also was examined by Rafael Martinez, a law-enforcement consultant in Miami who specializes in the criminal aspects of Afro-Caribbean religions. He was sought out by Benitez and the DEA task force to interpret the journals, and his conclusions about the meaning of certain entries have been used here. Furthermore, both DEA agents and Martinez said they were told by Mexican sources that the federal authorities in Mexico City removed some pages of the journals to avoid compromising prominent individuals. In

the end, many of these people were identified anyway, in court statements by cult members.

CHAPTER 25

1. "Mexican Authorities Believe Drug Cult Leader Fled to Miami," by R. A. Dyer and Cindy Rugeley, *Houston Chronicle,* April 18, 1989.

2. From the sworn statement of Teresa Quintana and court summaries, filed in Mexican federal district court in the Reclusorio Oriente, Mexico City.

3. As recounted by Comandante Juan Benitez Ayala in Matamoros and Octavio Campos, spokesman for the attorney general's office for the Federal District of Mexico.

4. From the sworn statements of Alvaro de Leon Valdez, Omar Francisco Orea Ochoa, and Sara Aldrete.

5. From Case B-89-171, U.S. District Court, Southern District of Texas, Brownsville Division, and Case Cr-H-389M, U.S. District Court, Southern District of Texas, Houston Division.

6. From DEA Special Agent T. K. Solis.

7. From Armando Ramirez. Oran Neck, however, disputed this criticism: "There was nothing to indicate Ovidio was in Houston," he said. "This is basically a non-issue." He also suggested that the press in Houston had aggressively pursued the story and already knew of Old Serafin's arrest when he announced it.

8. Press accounts of the cult murders reflected this confusion, employing all these terms and more to explain the rituals Constanzo conducted at Rancho Santa Elena. Even those newspapers that found experts who correctly identified their religion as Palo Mayombe continued to use the terms devil worship and satanism in their stories when referring to Constanzo's cult, though the two religions have nothing in common. Satanism idolizes the Christian concept of Lucifer and all things un-Christian, and has nothing to do with the culture and traditions that spawned Palo. But satanism has become a source of hysteria for the public and a favorite topic of tabloid TV, where it has been linked to a variety of murders, kidnappings, and molestations with little credible evidence. The distinction is important, though. Lumping Constanzo's beliefs with easily debunked claims about satanism tends to mask the real and growing dangers posed by criminal gangs like Constanzo's, devoted to Palo Mayombe and its malevolent offshoots. While police experts and religious

scholars agree that the satanism threat has been vastly overstated (see "Satanism: Scholars Find No Evidence of Spreading Occult Cults," by John Dart, *Los Angeles Times,* October 29, 1989) the number of violent crimes related to Santeria and Palo Mayombe continues to rise.

9. Rafael Martinez is a consultant on Afro-Caribbean religions and crime for the Dade County Coroner's Office, the FBI, the DEA, and other law-enforcement agencies. Candice Leek, a veteran police investigator, is an instructor at the University of North Florida's Institute for Police Technology and Management, one of the nation's foremost training centers for investigating ritual crime.

CHAPTER 26

1. From an interview with Sara Aldrete.

2. From court statements of Sara Aldrete, Alvaro de Leon, and Omar Francisco Orea Ochoa.

3. As told by Candice Leek and Rafael Martinez.

4. This account of the exorcism and burning of the shack was drawn from two videotapes of the event—Tony Zavaleta's and Rafael Martinez's—as well as the recollections of Candice Leek, Ernesto Flores, Martinez, and Zavaleta.

5. Despite the comandante's denials, videotapes of the burning, along with unanimous testimony from eyewitnesses (other than his agents) clearly show the exorcism was at his direction.

6. From the statement of Sara Aldrete and from an interview with Octavio Campos, spokesman for the attorney general for the Federal District of Mexico.

7. According to Sara and the others, Constanzo became irrational, threatening, and violent toward them after he saw the nganga burn.

8. From the statements of Sara and Alvaro de Leon.

CHAPTER 27

1. Pollution figures provided by the Mexican federal government.

2. From interviews with shopkeepers in the market and research by Anthony Zavaleta, who studied the items on display in the Sonora Market for use in his anthropology class. Just as Afro-Caribbean magic had been carried to Miami by immigrants, so had it been brought to Mexico City

by a similar, though smaller, wave of immigration to a city where an affinity for the supernatural already existed.

3. Teresa Quintana and Martin's other relatives were classified as witnesses, not suspects; they had been released by the federales on April 19 after four days in jail, with no evidence that they participated in any cult crimes.

4. From the sworn declaration of Jorge Montes, and allegations filed by the attorney general's office for the Federal District of Mexico.

5. From the declaration of Juan Carlos Fragosa.

6. Constanzo's fears were justified. Karla was heavily involved in the cult, and a santera priestess in her own right who performed works of magic for profit. She was an obvious suspect, and the Federal Judicial Police knew of Karla from interrogating Teresa Quintana as early as April 15. Yet no investigators appeared at her door until much later. Officials explained that they had not known the depth of Karla's involvement at first, mistakenly believing her to be just one of many clients, not a follower.

7. From an interview with Enrique Calzada and Maria del Rocio Cuevas Guerra.

8. From an interview with landlord Rosa Eugenio Gamas and the sworn statements filed in court by Doctor Maria de Lourdes Bueno Lopez.

9. The doctor also said in her sworn statements to police that she continued to help Constanzo because Karla and Karla's children were being threatened by Constanzo.

10. Sara mentions being pregnant in her sworn declarations, though it remains unclear if she was claiming to bear Constanzo's child, Elio's, or someone else's. In any case, there was no pregnancy, and Sara later claimed never to have made the statement.

11. This account is exclusively Sara's, though some aspects have been corroborated by Mexican police. It has been proven that Sara did leave the apartment on May 2, did contact the plastic surgeon, and did call neighbors in Matamoros. However, her wanderings and halfhearted attempts at getting caught cannot be verified, and police believe it was part of her attempt at constructing an alibi, along with her claim to her Matamoros neighbor that she was kidnapped. Sara cannot adequately explain why she didn't turn herself in on May 2, nor how she could take Constanzo's threat to kill her parents seriously—since the threat could have been eliminated if she went to the police and led them to the hideout.

12. According to Sara Aldrete's account. Ponce alleges that it was at this point that she threw the note out the window; Sara says it was an hour earlier.

13. As recounted by both Sara and Duby.

CHAPTER 28

1. The description of events leading up to the shootout at Rio Sena is based on interviews and court testimony of Assistant Attorney General Federico Ponce, Miguel Hidalgo Police Chief Rodrigo Martinez, and Detective Carlos Padilla Torres.

2. The description of events and dialogue in the apartment during the shootout are based on sworn statements and press conferences by Sara Aldrete, Omar Francisco Orea Ochoa, and Alvaro de Leon Valdez, supplemented by an interview with Sara and Federico Ponce Rojas. The dialogue and sequence of events were described in markedly similar ways by the three cult members, although each paraphrased Constanzo in slightly different ways.

3. Sara recounted making this statement in her sworn declarations to police. Duby recalled her making it as well. Later, she recanted, claiming she was tortured into saying it, as well as signing the confession. Instead, she claimed she actually told Duby to "Stop it. Now, now, now!" The dispute is crucial, since the evidence for charging Sara with the murders of Constanzo and Martin is slight, consisting solely of the allegation that she ordered Duby to shoot.

4. This account of Constanzo's death, pieced together from the statements of police and suspects, remains the Mexican government's official version of events. There have been contradictions, however. Initial police press releases on the day of the shootout stated that Constanzo and Martin were fatally shot by police during exchanges of gun fire. Photographs of an allegedly blood-stained living-room wall and couch in the apartment—not the bedroom closet—were shown in early Mexican news reports portraying the death scene. The next day, the new version of events was revealed: Photos of the bodies in the closet were released by police and, in an internationally televised press conference, Duby admitted killing Constanzo and Martin, while Sara confirmed this confession. Months later, they both recanted. Duby said police shot Constanzo, then beat Duby until he agreed to confess. In recanting her statements, Sara said she did not know who killed Constanzo, but that police threatened her with death if she did not accuse Duby. She continued to confirm that

there had been a suicide pact. As for physical evidence, the number of bullet wounds in the corpses—fourteen entry and exit wounds in Constanzo, nineteen in Martin—seemed high for one shooter to have inflicted without reloading. Mexican officials, however, insisted the number of actual bullets recovered from the bodies matched the number in a full magazine, with each bullet having inflicted two or more wounds. This question remained clouded because the Uzi submachine gun used in the killings—a police weapon allegedly supplied by Salvador Vidal Garcia—mysteriously vanished from an evidence locker within a few days, before ballistics tests could be performed. District prosecutors put this off to an inside attempt by federal police to save Salvador from being charged as an accessory to murder; defense attorneys suggested a more insidious cover-up. In subsequent hearings in Mexico City, Judge Bernardo Tirado found sufficient evidence for charging Duby with killing Constanzo and Martin and, under Mexican law, presumed Duby to be guilty of the offense. Much later, the dispute over the actual location of the shooting—living room versus closet—was resolved by the owner of the apartment, Rosa Eugenio Gamas. She said that when she cleaned up the mess on the couch, she found the red substance to be ketchup, not blood, which she presumed was either spilled accidentally or placed there by an unscrupulous news photographer eager to stage a dramatically gory photograph.

CHAPTER 29

1. Recounted by Federico Ponce. Omar, who confessed to being present at the killing of La Claudia without taking part, later said he had been tortured with beatings and electric shocks into confessing (although there was no visible evidence of abuse the next day when he was trotted out before the media at a massive press conference). Despite the allegations of torture, he did not recant the confession.

2. Duby admitted shooting Constanzo and Martin in his sworn confessions and in subsequent interviews with the press. Later, he recanted and claimed the police killed Constanzo. Omar and Sara, however, continued to state that Duby killed Constanzo and Martin.

3. Related by Federico Ponce. Statements attributed to him by Ponce jibe with similar comments he made in sworn testimony and at press conferences.

CHAPTER 30

1. The luxury accorded jailed Matamoros defendants was ascertained through interviews with numerous Mexican and U.S. inmates at the Matamoros jail. Sergio Martinez was seen wearing a trustee's cap, with free run of the yard, while prison officials maintained that all the cult defendants were in high-security confinement. Little Serafin bragged in an interview that he never had to eat jail food. Furthermore, DEA officials and the U.S. Attorney's Office in Brownsville confirmed the defendants' favored status in the jail, and expressed fears that they might be allowed to escape at some time in the future. The treatment the Hernandez gang members received in jail has ample precedent. The Mexican prison system (like the U.S. prison system) operates on a system of mordida. Food, clothes, books, visits from prostitutes—everything is for sale, and only the poorest inmates suffer deprivations. The drug lord Rafael Caro Quintero, convicted in Mexico for the slaying of DEA Agent Enrique Camarena, was able to purchase cocaine, a VCR, and catered meals while in Mexico City's Reclusorio Norte prison, where Sara Aldrete and other cult members were imprisoned part of the time. The Mexican government was so embarrassed by the incident, they adopted new regulations that can require jail administrators to serve the terms of prisoners they allow to escape. Citing this law, Matamoros jail officials said there was no chance of the Hernandez gang members escaping.

2. As told by DEA Agent T. K. Solis, confirmed by jail officials and Richard Hoffman, attorney for Old Serafin. A visit to the jail confirmed the gang member's luxurious accommodations.

3. From DEA Agents Armando Ramirez and T. K. Solis.

4. Memorandum to Henry K. Oncken, U.S. Attorney, Southern District of Texas, from Assistant U.S. Attorney John Grasty Crews III, dated April 29, 1989. See previous reference in Chapter 21 for details.

5. "Cult leader's mom says he insisted he was not guilty," by the Associated Press, May 10, 1989, reprinted in the *Houston Post*.

6. From an interview with Metro-Dade Detective Henry Choren.

7. Dade County Circuit Court Criminal Case 89-3332.

CHAPTER 31

1. From the sworn statement of Teresa Quintana, filed in Mexican federal district court.

2. Ibid.

3. "Satanic, Occult, Ritualistic Crime: A Law Enforcement Perspective," by Kenneth V. Lanning, in *The Police Chief,* October 1989.

4. F. Ortiz, "Los Negros Brujos," Ediciones Universal, Miami, 1973.

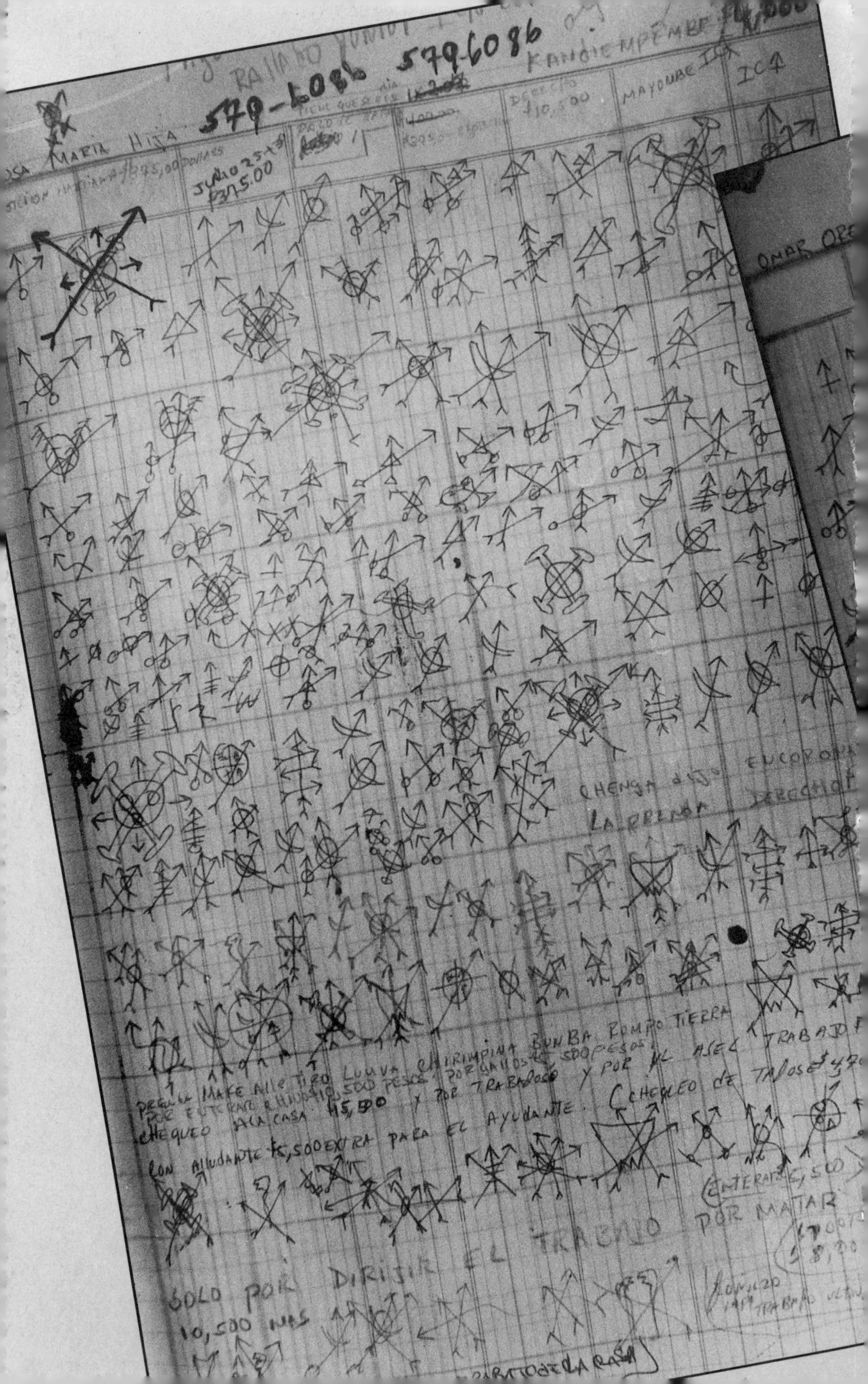

579-6086
579-6086
MARIA HIJA
MAYONBE
CHENGA DIJO
LA PRENDA
CHEQUEO ACA CASA
PARA EL AYUDANTE
POR MATAR
SOLO POR DIRIJIR EL TRABAJO
10,500 MAS